Of Modern Dragons
and other essays on Genre Fiction

John Lennard

Tirril: Humanities-Ebooks, 2007

First published in 2007 by Humanities-Ebooks LLP.
Tirril Hall, Tirril, Penrith CA10 2JE

Published in paperback by Troubador.co.uk in 2008

ISBN 978-1-84760-038-7 EBOOK
ISBN 978-1-84760-069-1 PAPERBACK

For

Reginald Hill

a criminally great novelist

with admiring thanks for Mid-Yorks.,
the Unholy Trinity,
serendipitous Joe Sixsmith,
an unswerving civility and kindness,
and very many happy hours of reading.

For Hea'en and Hill begin wi ane letter,
And if Hea'en's good, yon Hill is aye better.

Contents

List of Illustrations

Acknowledgements

Photograph of Reginald Hill © 2007 Reginald Hill

The cover illustration is of Fáfnir, by Arthur Rackham, from Richard Wagner's *The Ring of the Nibelung ... Translated into English by Margaret Armour with Illustrations by Arthur Rackham* (London: William Heinemann, & New York: Doubleday, Page & Co., 1910).

Thanks also to Francis Ingledew, Claire Kilroy, Rosemary Daley, Gregorio Stephens, James Robertson, and Julian Lobban for readings and suggestions.

Many years ago my brother David Lennard told me to start reading Reginald Hill, while Roger Luckhurst (now of Birkbeck College) told me to start reading Octavia Butler—recommendations for which I remain deeply grateful. Most of the other writers discussed here I discovered for myself, but for some of the older ones, and for my habits of reading in general, I am, always, fundamentally indebted to my father, Michael Lennard, *sine qua non*.

Foreword

As the first more-or-less explains, these essays are the product of trying to think professionally about more than 30 years of reading genre and series fictions. Neither my subjects nor the tones and movements of prose that have seemed right for them are always in the Academy's current *Manual of Lit. Crit.*, and as I imagine myself writing as much for fellow readers as for a narrower academic audience, I let them stand. That does not mean scholarship or rigour are disregarded, and footnotes appear informatively or discursively as they ought. It does mean, however, that (for example) details of fictions merely cited appear only in the Bibliography, and cultural events etc. are assumed as common territory between writer and reader. Alternatively, a ▣ Web-link may be provided, for those who wish to use it. It also means that even with novels considered at length I have tried not to give away needless spoilers, that those who like the sound of one can read with full pleasure.

I long thought that essays on different genres (Crime, SF, Children's Lit., Romance) needed to be separate, or at least sectioned-off, but those gathered here coalesced as a sequence. The subjects have in common their serial forms and my extended attention, but range as widely as authors' interests. Reginald Hill and 'J. D. Robb' (in that identity) are primarily crime writers; Octavia Butler, Ian McDonald, & the dragon-folk are SF writers; and Tamora Pierce is a children's writer. Then again, I'm damned if 'Robb' isn't also an SF *and* a Romance writer; Pierce similarly mocks generic distinctions; and Hill, Butler, & McDonald are all absurdly denied proper recognition *precisely because* they embrace genre and write in series. So my essays are what they are, and if that is unconventional, so much the better.

This collection also launches Humanities-E-Books' *Genre Fiction Monographs*, and in some measure therefore serves as model and manifesto. The series is avowedly open to *any* relevant proposal, because we don't yet know what proper attention to genre fiction should look like, but my willingness here to move between genres, concentrate strongly on the experience of reading, and go where that has taken me, are certainly meant as markers of intent. Very many people spend a good deal of time and money as serial readers, and the absence of serious thinking about the practice is as odd as it is improper, so please think of this e-book, and the series it launches, as seeking to redress a gross imbalance.

John Lennard
Gordon Town, St Andrew, Jamaica
February 2007

1. Of Serial Readers

Living with Genre Fiction

I read for pleasure, for information, and for a living. My work as a teacher and professor of literature requires me to read new poetry and fiction, and bookish surprises are an invigorating part of my life. Books are therefore given and bought in such numbers that even the worthiest inevitably pile up awaiting attention, but each year among those I read most promptly are a dozen or so hardback instalments of series fictions, revisiting established protagonists, locales, and supporting casts for a further round of adventures.

This serial reading is a habit of long standing. The genres involved have ranged over more than 30 years through thrillers, science fiction of many kinds, and Napoleonic naval novels to children's literature (where Harry Potter provides the most obvious current example of mass serial reading), but crime writing has come to dominate. For more than twenty years I have had an annual meeting with Robert B. Parker's Spenser, a Boston PI with entertaining friends and superior dialogue, who in that time (however formulaic he may sometimes be) has confronted contemporary evils while evolving emotionally in ways I find compelling. For nearly ten I have had biannual dates with J. D. Robb's Eve Dallas, a New York cop in the late 2050s who as a romance heroine in an unreal world ought in many ways to be negligible, but isn't, because her childhood abuse and continuing struggle to be healed of its consequence provide a ballast that allows Robb to make of her populist and otherwise critically sinful books a vehicle for serious thought. My current crime list also features Reginald Hill, James Lee Burke, Lawrence Block, John Harvey, Ian Rankin, Bill James, Peter Robinson, Walter Mosley, Michael Connelly, Nevada Barr, Deborah Crombie,and Stephen Booth—some (like Hill, Burke, & James) companions for a decade or more, others (like Crombie & Booth) pushing their way in. Newcomers may expand the list, but time is limited, and old friends sometimes have to make way, falling back with consecutive disappointments from automatic hardback to occasional paperback purchase.

I usually read (and re-read) these books fast. Daily schedules may preclude it, but I have read many literally 'at a sitting', which for a fiction of 80–100,000 words lasts three to six hours. In a positive sense most genre novels are 'page-turners', generating that intense involvement in a fictive world that is one great joy of reading, but such reading is often (and not only by professional critics) supposed 'shallow', as opposed to a 'deep' mode associated with 'literature'—hence the persistent characterisation of genre fiction as 'airport' or 'railway' books, fit for journeys, not studies, and discardable without loss. Even without the curious but characteristic British denigration of 'genre fiction' as intrinsically *déclassé*,[1] readers who prefer 'literature' often suppose from the speed of writing implicit in series publication that quality of the kind they seek and praise cannot possibly be found in such books, and in parallel suppose from the speed of reading implicit in page-turning that such rapid consumption cannot reward serious attention. Literature, that is, should have been agonised over by its authors, as by its readers, while the generic should take as little effort to write as is invested in reading it.

The academic corollary of this speciousness includes a widespread Anglophone (especially British) prejudice, that while paid professors of literature are entitled (or even expected) to read some mass-market fictions 'as a hobby', and conversationally to grade the bestseller lists, they are not supposed to spill serious ink on the matter. W. H. Auden in his critical and poetic prime knew better (as poets often do), but the intensity and sacramental conservatism of his confessions about reading Golden-Age whodunits in 'The Guilty Vicarage' (1948) represent a very particular sensibility, and have obscured the nature and challenges of serial reading.[2] Auden's comparison of Golden-Age whodunits with the great classical tragedies of pollution and ritual cleansing attracts critical citation precisely because it counters the imputation to crime writing (and reading) of unliterary shallowness, but it is clear that Auden's critical response was *not* associated with deep and scholarly ponderings of one text, but rather with habitual and rapid reading that rejoiced in long series, narrative formulae, artful variations, and iterated structure.

In one sense the paradigm for most judgements of literary merit is a class system, leisured 'literature' being the nobility, and hasty generic scurriers through the

---

1   The real point often seems to be the reverse formulation, that 'literature' is somehow not 'generic'. Thus Reginald Hill, despite his very varied output, is a 'crime writer' but the rather more limited Martin Amis, say, is a '*novelist*' who can cleverly deploy crime topoi when he judges that right.

2   In *The Dyer's Hand and other essays* (1963; London: Faber & Faber, 1975), pp. 146–58. Auden admits, for example, that he cannot re-read a whodunit, saying that he sometime started one only to realise "after a few pages" that he had read it already (p. 146).

market-place the proletariat or *petit bourgeoisie*—and class-privileges are always fiercely defended. In interesting parallel, European metaphors and etymologies point clearly to the literary (and political) use of validating *depth*: we get to the bottom of things and the heart of the matter, strive to be profound and deal with the basics and fundamentals, so value comes with age and the overwritten surface. But US politicians and some critics instead 'go the extra mile', finding sincerity in extent, and the US mass-markets in newspaper features, genre paperbacks, and TV drama have been the great engines of serial writing and reading in the late century. Conversely, British critics in particular, beholden to literary snobbery reflecting class mores and blind to sincerity in instalments, have been uninterested in genre writing and the worlds of reading it generates. Yet it seems widely known, for example, often by people who have read none of them, that Julian Barnes and Ian McEwan write 'literature', while Ian Rankin and Peter Robinson do not; that attention to J. K. Rowling is (despite her extraordinary achievement in becoming the first authorial billionaire) at best a clever and well-executed jape; and that Salman Rushdie is intrinsically a more responsible and thoughtful writer than Reginald Hill.

Prizes are a prime arena for showing such prejudice. One of the more telling indicators of the true nature of the Booker Prize (founded in 1969) is that in nearly 40 years not one book usually regarded as 'crime writing' or 'SF' has been short- or even long-listed, let alone won.[1] During the decades since 1970 crime writing has undergone an astonishing efflorescence and (as the ever-growing crime sections of every highstreet bookshop demonstrate) been a mainstay of the fiction market. The intense absurdity of the British situation is limned in the fact that Dame P. D. James chaired the panel of Booker judges in 1987, but could never herself as a committed and serious crime writer have made even the shortlist, despite producing in *Innocent Blood* (1980) and *A Taste for Death* (1986) eligible novels that go far beyond any simple generic model, and were certainly among the most discussed and widely reviewed UK publications of their respective years. To say either 'should' have won the Booker Prize would be silly, but they were just as stupidly excluded from consideration on generic grounds, and continue to be vapidly supposed unfit for study or inappropriate to teach. As much might be said of SF, for despite its evident British strengths since the 1980s not one such book has troubled the Booker judges for even

1   Complete lists of winning and short-listed books from 1969, and long-lists from 2001, are available at ▣ http://www.themanbookerprize.com/about/previous.php. Arguably, only one acknowledged 'genre fiction' appears on any of them, Philip Pullman's *The Amber Spyglass*, long-listed in 2001. The fullest published analysis of the Booker is Richard Todd, *Consuming Fictions: The Booker Prize and Fiction in Britain Today* (1996).

a moment. There may be fair questions about how genre fictions are best read, taught, and contextualised, but there are also false assumptions underlying this unhappy bias that must be foregone.

Fast as many readings may be, crime writing is a time-consuming and expensive study to maintain seriously, and ever more so as the field remorselessly expands in all directions. Whatever my feelings about a given novel, series or freestanding, I don't discard it when I'm done but shelve it—my crime-library now runs to over 200 feet—so that particular series and a general sampling of the field accumulate. For series on my active list this also means periodic re-reading, rarely *in toto* (especially once they grow to 10 or more books) but in smaller runs—typically anticipating a new arrival by going back a few instalments to refresh my sense of people, places, and what was left unresolved. The chance to write an article, or a particularly good instalment, especially an unpredictable success or breakthrough, sends me back to the beginning even of the longest series, but any instalment may direct renewed attention to any precursor. Contrary to the 'airport book' paradigm, details and narrative textures are often at a premium, and to the serial reader with proper lengthwise bearings apparently casual fragments of dialogue or narration may catch most interesting light—first time round if you're good and lucky, but more probably with hindsight.

Some of what is intellectually and emotionally at stake here is suggested by the lack of any established vocabulary for the common readerly states and actions I am describing. Scholarship has begun to remember the serial publication of Augustan, Romantic, and Victorian novels, and Penguin editions of Dickens, for example, have always marked where the original weekly parts ended—but they were parts of a singular whole, and the divisions are often clearly signalled within the narrative by a cliff-hanging chapter-ending. While there is a proper connection with modern TV soap-opera and drama series, experience as a modern serial reader is different.

There are of course novels that actually end with a cliff-hanger (as the original version of *The Italian Job* famously and literally does on film), either leaving it tantalisingly at that or obliging readers to wait a year or so to know if (typically) *x* has survived. The vast majority of these, however, have single sequels or are first and second novels of trilogies (where publication of vols 2–3 may be deliberately delayed); none to my knowledge are true series fictions. The closest example is probably Patrick O'Brian's *The Thirteen-Gun Salute* (1989), *The Nutmeg of Consolation* (1991), *Clarissa Oakes* (1992), and *The Wine-Dark Sea* (1993), vols 13–16 of 20 chronicling naval service and political culture during the Napoleonic and Revolutionary Wars of 1793–1815, which send heroes Aubrey & Maturin on a single circum-navigation through four books. No formal ending for the first three is provided: one simply comes to the last page of the volume in hand, and (now) may turn directly to the next for full continuation of the narrative. Anthony Powell's 12-volume *A Dance to the Music of Time* (1951–75) is in some ways similar, as much a *roman fleuve* in equal parts as a series of individual novels, while crime writer 'Bill James' (A. J. Tucker)—a published critic of Powell[1]—habitually leaves a great deal unresolved in closing each of his Harpur-&-Iles novels. He may or may not later supply some frag-ment of explanation, and his serial readers have by definition accepted this; only a (lazy) newcomer to his work could wait for the next instalment in expectation of any 'proper' continuation or resolution.

Stylistically and structurally, James's terminal irresolutions are products of frag-mentation, alienation, and dandified irony, not devices to keep readers waiting in suspense. In general, even series writers with a high degree of complex continuity between instalments, like James and Reginald Hill, show no interest in ending indi-vidual books with anything that might seriously be thought a 'cliff-hanger'. It seems as much a commercial as a craft-based distinction: cliff-hanging works well but in-tensely, and is best kept to a fixed duration, but a good series of genre fictions may be written and read over 30 or more years. Its pleasures are subtler than the agonies and rampant marketing of not knowing for six months if J. R. Ewing survived the shots that felled him, who among President Bartlet's staff had taken a bullet, or whatever the hook might be. If a print-series character has truly seized the public mind, some looming possibility may become a prolonged issue in conversation: the putative death of Harry Potter in J. K. Rowling's final volume is a current example, and may prove the most traumatic fictional death since Dickens hardened himself against Little Nell in 1841—but it also shows how rare this phenomenon is in print compared to the an-nual series finales of TV dramas like *Dallas* and *The West Wing*.

Just how a writer manages the commercially requisite balance between the epi-sodic, satisfactorily concluding within the volume, and the ongoing drive of a series in exploring the continuing lives of people and place, is a primary interest of serial reading. The proliferation of series in crime fiction is probably explained principally by the ease with which successive, intrinsically distinct criminal cases map onto a book-by-book structure, providing consecutive volumes with individual casts and plots whereby all necessary page-turning tensions may be generated, while allowing the personal, emotional, and usually family life of the protagonist to flow through all

---

1 See James Tucker, *The Novels of Anthony Powell* (1976).

and yet (if an author wishes) provide terminal irresolutions or dissonance to haunt any neatness of episodic closure. There is a close equivalent that serial fictioneers of the Georgian Royal Navy learned from C. S. Forester's Hornblower novels (which in 1937–8 & 1945–66 occasioned mass serial reading)—that a one-voyage-per-volume formula does very nicely, while too much jumping-about inhibits sales. Dudley Pope's Ramage (18 novels, 1965–89), Alexander Kent's Bolitho (26 novels since 1968), C. Northcote Parkinson's Delancey (6 novels, 1973–82), and Richard Woodman's Drinkwater (14 novels, 1981–98) have all sailed on that basis, while the most important current Georgian fighting hero, Bernard Cornwell's Sharpe (22 novels since 1981), develops a military variant of the formula, one major battle or campaign per volume.[1] O'Brian's departure from it in four of his 'Aubreiad' volumes is thus odd even by its own lights: they may be brilliant (devotees differ on the merit of those volumes); they are exceptions.

What matters to the serial reader is that with deferred expectations of returning with avowed interest to a given world and people, but without tensed expectation and irresolution, one is released to consider differently the emotions and behaviours of protagonists whose lives one is choosing to share. If a series is discovered when already complete there is a marvellous moment when the endless craving for new fiction is sated in anticipation, but not the experience of reading a life as one's own is lived, *in extenso*, and so inevitably muddled up with, in, and over other reading and experience. Crime writing in particular dwells closer to daily news than most fiction, and the reaction of a familiar protagonist to a real event, incorporated mimetically into a known fictional world but first experienced by author and reader in their own lives, is like the reactions both of a friend and of a respected public figure—testimony to ponder, a prod to recall one's own reactions. Series characters may thus become, perhaps more widely than canonical literary figures, referents and agents of conversation, symbols of known values and probable reaction, while also being, in the few days before and after reading a new chapter in their lives, powerfully open within imagination. How will they grow, cope or fail to cope, or be diminished in this instalment? and the next?—for which one is, in the nature of the beast, always waiting, save only in those few hours while a new book is first read.

A profound challenge to a protagonist, such as displacement from a usual setting to some alien ground, typically arouses as much anxiety and condemnation among devotees as it does pleasure at an unfamiliar prospect, but few serial readers of crime want the stereotypically formulaic repetition to which Agatha Christie came close,

---

1   These Napoleonic series are not (save for Forester & O"Brian) listed in the bibliography.

and Barbara Cartland closer. Demand for variation, pressure of some kind to think and cope anew, informs reception of successive instalments—for serial readers, strung over time with their protagonists, will like their protagonists' creators face such pressures themselves. In this at least the relationship of reader to protagonist is one of identification—the protagonist as fantasy avatar, an idea informing conversational dismissal of 'escapist fictions' in (supposed) opposition to a 'literature' that bears down on fantasy. Crime writing, though, is interestingly awkward for such talkers, for (if they bother with it at all) they must defuse its evident topicality, and accept that the practices of reading and living (not to mention writing) have more complex modes than escape or fantasy, not even but especially in series fictions. Readers may gawp, tut at alarmist headlines and tabloid salacities, or like their sex scenes nicely anatomical, but when public concerns over crime and security express themselves over decades in extensive, often highly discriminating reading of crime novels, one has to do with a mode of engagement, not of escape.

Series writers, in particular, ask readers to lend a good deal of themselves to a character, not only by intellectually organising facts and impressions, but by sharing over decades in emotions and difficulties. One part of the payoff may surely be some form of vicarious satisfaction in particular aspects or actions, but there is more, and readers do not so lend for free, or without condition. Even in the post-war thrillers of Alistair Maclean, Hammond Innes, and Desmond Bagley, close cousins of the true series and more obviously escapist than much contemporary crime writing, there are unbreakable readerly contracts—most importantly, that while convenience and (if properly flagged) new technologies are allowed, absurdity, impossibility, and *dei ex machinae* are not; just as stated facts must indeed be facts, as incorrigible for the protagonist as for the readers imagining themselves in that same situation. What happens depends on the quality of the facts from which the author has constructed the difficulty, and it is a basic strength of the contemporary crime novel that its facts are as often social, moral, economic, journalistic, or political as forensic and topographical. A series may in this way become part, not of any escapist or prurient satisfaction, but precisely of ongoing thought about structural or otherwise recurrent social problems—so much so that some contemporary crime writing is probably the most overtly *engagé* genre of English prose fiction there is. Conversely, new fiction dubbed as 'literature' is far too often self-protectively uninterested in anything resembling political or practical engagement with quotidian contemporary concerns.

My own serial reading suggests the best series writers respond positively to the sense of a stringent contract with their (paying) readers, often through conscious engagement with it and with shared current events. Reginald Hill, particularly, has persistently experimented with series-novel form while keeping the beadiest of eyes of the doings of the Thatcher, Major, and Blair governments, trusting in the basic affection he and his readers share for detectives Dalziel & Pascoe to give him sufficient rope. Knowledge (through advance publicity) that the next instalment will face us with a case involving child abuse, serial killing, animal rights, or (as now, awaiting *The Death of Dalziel*) either a series Götterdämmerung or a terrible tease, becomes an intriguing proposition. Novel by novel Hill delivers fictional essays on matters that are often on my mind when his fictions are certainly not; meaning that when they are, as I lend pleasurable sense to Dalziel's tragicomic *force majeure* and Pascoe's flattering literariness, I also bring to bear, novel by novel, not innocent consumption of fantasy but informed questing for intelligent observation or analysis—and find it. In retrospect, my literary and civil judgements of individual novels (repeatedly re-read in their growing series context) naturally become more critical, but identification of specific failure is informative. Hill has, for example, had recurrent difficulty with serial killers—a difficulty I share in a general way, having lived through the days of the Yorkshire Ripper in 1978–81, and read ever since of other such days elsewhere—and this difficulty is intriguing, because it offers a context to consider one of the great themes of the late century.

Now we are in the 2000s, should conversation turn to serial killers (when yet another has made the news) we have words and ideas to offer one another. Knowledge of many cases is commonplace, and the FBI's distinction of 'organised' and 'disorganised' types, with other analyses developed by their special behavioural units and programmes at Quantico, are as disseminated in popular culture as any comparable scientific paradigm. Some understanding of the supposed role of childhood abuse in making a serial killer is also common (if often tangled with emotional responses to reported paedophilia), and may recognise an implicitly Freudian mechanism, though none is needed for the perception that a recurrent need to kill is probably linked somehow to the constant renewal of human sexual desire. Bizarre and horrifying as the Sutcliffes, Bundies, and Dahmers may be, the interested or concerned can now easily find reasonably thoughtful analytical paradigms that offer rational explanations for an observed behaviour—a recurrent need to kill strangers, selected on the basis of broad somatypical resemblance to one another and a model from the killer's childhood whom s/he repeatedly re-embodies and slays. And so many of these strange people have been revealed in the last thirty or so years that we can no longer comfortingly think them inhuman or otherwise deny their bloody place among our ranks.

In my carefully correct "s/he", acknowledging that women too may be serial killers, lies a whole other story. Only after the 1992 convictions in Florida of Aileen Wuornos did the FBI's ingrained assumption that serial killing was an exclusively male phenomenon give way, obligating them to re-examine all open cases in which a putative female suspect had been automatically ruled out. In retrospect the FBI look foolishly sexist, and made a costly mistake whose price may well have been more than money and justice can measure. More strikingly, they were also well behind the novelists, notably David Lindley, whose *Mercy* (1990) plausibly applied the paradigmatic psychology of serial killing to a woman and turns precisely on the unwillingness of investigative authorities to consider a female suspect. But retrospect equally shows that our present advanced understanding has made indecent haste to forget how recent it is, and how shallow its foundations.

For me, as for many Britons (Jack-the-Ripperiana and 'Midnight Rambler' notwithstanding), the idea of serial killing became real only in 1978–81 with experience of the 'Yorkshire Ripper'. The killer is now known to be Peter Sutcliffe, but then, as the awfulness and fear grew through months of waiting helplessly for the body-count yet again to rise, 'he' was unimaginable; the infernal among us, or conversely, as Blake Morrison later put it in *The Ballad of the Yorkshire Ripper*:

> ... Ripper's not a psychopath
> but any man in pants.
> All you blokes would kill like 'im
> given half a chance.[1]

It was not just the epistemology of unknown identity, for almost every crime offers that; it was ontology—never mind whodunit, *what*-dunit? How could tried and tested motivations for murder *and* the whole investigators' triad of 'means, motive, opportunity' be rendered seemingly worse than useless by a human murderer? With each tabloid splash and twist of events—a false Geordie-growling confession someone sent in; new victims; the Elland Road crowds who chanted 'Ripper Twelve, Police Nil' at Leeds FC games—pub and workplace conversations returned again and again to

---

1   The poem was published in the *London Review of Books* in 1985, and collected in Morrison's *The Ballad of the Yorkshire Ripper and other poems* (London: Chatto, 1987); I quote from p. 30. See also Gordon Burn, *'...somebody's husband, somebody's son': The Story of Peter Sutcliffe* (1985).

what or who and dear God why. But throughout that whole dismal time I don't recall hearing much common sense, let alone any uncommon, and my dominant memory is of endless, febrile and fearful threats of what should be done when 'they' caught 'him'.

Only after Sutcliffe's arrest, trial, conviction, and injury in prison[1]—that is, in 1985–6—did anything that made helpful sense begin to emerge, some from journalism (Morrison is also a newspaperman), some from US psycho-social and law-enforcement understandings, much with Gordon Burn's study of Sutcliffe; but progress was slow. Even if connections were made with, say, Hitchcock's *Psycho* (1960) or Tobe Hooper's *The Texas Chainsaw Massacre* (1974), understandings were stymied, because (for example) both films, each based in substantial part on grave-robber and serial killer Ed Gein (arrested in Wisconsin in 1957 and suspected of 15+ murders), necessarily play on the geographical isolation of the murderer's den as a metaphor for psychic isolation and as a means of rendering their extreme plots at once more plausible and safely distant from the screening cinema. But the problem was precisely that Sutcliffe (as elsewhere Bundy) had been among us, hideously blending in to troll 'our' streets. The queasy politeness of Anthony Perkins as Norman Bates came closest (and *Psycho* was a mainstream hit, which *Chainsaw Massacre* for all its cult success has never been), but his mad eyes and desert motel were disabling departures from Sutcliffe's Yorkshire reality. Nor, in the 1980s, was it easy to get through the fictions to the Gein case, and if one did there was then much less literature on it, nor of course any friendly, well-publicised FBI website to satisfy public enquiries.

What intervenes between then and now is not only (from 1991) the Web, and a great burgeoning in public interest, such that a serial-killer plot is now Hollywood cliché, but *the* book on serial killing—not a breakthrough psychological or criminological essay, but a crime novel and rapidly an award-winning film, Thomas Harris's *The Silence of the Lambs* (1988, filmed 1990). As most now know, infamous anti-hero Dr Hannibal 'the cannibal' Lecter had been created in *Red Dragon* (1981, filmed as *Manhunter* 1986), and there is in these two novels an object lesson, for their plots, structures, and imports are closely identical. After this staggered pair, Harris provided in a third Lecter novel, *Hannibal* (1999, filmed 2001), a sequel to *Silence of the Lambs*, and in a fourth, *Hannibal Rising* (2006), a prequel, making a 'Lecter series' that is one of the slowest and oddest on record.

The lesson of *Manhunter* and *The Silence of the Lambs* arises because their simi-

---

1   He was 'bottled' in the face by a fellow inmate for repeated tearing the page with a picture of a woman's breasts out of a communal tabloid newspaper, the *Daily Star*.

larity in plot is so close as to suggest careful, studied tweaks to a formula as tautly calculated as one in chemistry or physics. In both an FBI investigator is stymied and endangered by an active serial killer, and seeks help from imprisoned serial killer and über-psychiatrist Lecter. Drawn into a Faustian bargain by a need to engage with and reward Lecter, the investigator feeds him psychically with personal data in return for insights into the present prey, who is eventually caught and so stopped from killing. The active serial killers offer complex models of psychic and other disturbance which readers, like the investigators lead by Lecter, come to 'understand'—but that induced illusion is slyly offset against Lecter, to whom no Freudian or FBI paradigms seem to have the slightest application. The only substantive differences are that (i) the rôle of active investigating detective, in *Red Dragon* given to weary expert male Will Douglas, is in *The Silence of the Lambs* given to fresh but haunted trainee female Clarice Starling; and (ii) in *Red Dragon* Lecter stays in prison, while in *The Silence of the Lambs* he stages an escape.

In one sense Harris's repeated plot-strategy is amusingly clear in Michael Crichton's *Jurassic Park* (1990, filmed 1993), where everything (including their own presumptions) primed readers to expect an enormously terrifying but singular *Tyrannosaurus rex*, only for the main threat to prove (with satisfying shock) the smaller and smarter velociraptors, who also pose a far greater threat of escaping the park and eating pretty much anything they fancy. This narrative coup has serious bearing on a common misconception of carnivorous dinosaurs as solo monsters like *T. rex* rather than intelligent, co-operative hunters like velociraptors, sufficiently so that one could reasonably argue the film, despite fantastical premises and absurd action, successfully communicated to an enormous public a significant revision in scientific understanding. In a similar way, Harris has twice played off public preference for a serial killer assumed to be knowable, serving up the pathologies of Francis Dolarhyde and Jame Gumb (the latter yet again based on Ed Gein) in juicy helpings to fuel the illusion that in understanding these men sufficiently to catch them one somehow understands their breed. And tskt-t-t-t, there is Lecter looking out of the shadows with a forkful of human sweetbreads in one hand, asking if we're sure we understand him now. The velociraptors can easily seem kinder.

The two principal differences between *Red Dragon* and *The Silence of the Lambs* are related, for it is Lecter's sexual dynamic with Starling as a woman that allows him to leverage his escape by playing her off against Senator Martin. A central male–female rather than male–male pairing activated a distinct set of models, and Harris made sublime use of Lecter as a Svengalian beast to Starling's beauty,[1] but also freed that beast, and in *Hannibal* drew a necessary conclusion by bringing Lecter and Starling together and reversing the serial killer's preference for death over sex. Clarice, that is, can finally catch Hannibal only in the romantic sense, and in doing so controls his murderous and gluttonous desires by evacuating them as lust. The set-up for the ending, too much of a spoiler to be revealed, proved so disturbing to most readers that *Hannibal* has never had the same attention as *The Silence of the Lambs*, and the film-makers burked it altogether, offering two alternative, infinitely clichéd and pointless endings of their own. Quite a few people do recall, mostly from the film, that Lecter's originary trauma turned out to have been a childhood experience of wartime cannibalism in the Ukraine, but the point of Harris's (and Lecter's) continuing analysis of serial killing has not been absorbed.

That is, I think, genuinely a shame, for the transformation in public knowledge and understanding that *The Silence of the Lambs* achieved is remarkable, though it did not, of course, have to work alone. By 1989 many fictions had confronted the problem; *Red Dragon* itself had been on shelves for eight years, and *Manhunter* on screens for three. But by putting an erotic relationship at the centre of investigation, and an act of fabrication at the heart of the crime/s—Jame Gumb tailoring himself a woman-skin (as Gein did) to remake himself as he wishes—*The Silence of the Lambs* made the theorised dynamics of sex and death patent to all. The idea of self-development is just as central in *Red Dragon*, but however memorable Dolarhyde's obsession with William Blake's painting *The Woman Clothed With The Sun, Moon And Stars And The Great Red Dragon* (which he eventually *eats*, for Heaven's sake), it did not carry the charge *The Silence of the Lambs* delivered with Jame Gumb's breeding of Death's-Head Moths. The explicit imagery of insect metamorphoses (cocooned pupae, voracious caterpillars, and what entomology happily calls imáginés[2]) interpreted the iteration of serial killing as (for the killer) a process of *becoming*. In parallel, Gumb's desperately insane tailoring fused the detestability of merciless and insensible killing with the logic and pitiable desires of his hellish life. And where in *Red Dragon* erotics came only incidentally from Dolarhyde's kindness to blind Reba McClane, in *The Silence of the Lambs* they come centrally from Starling and Lecter, leaving Catherine Martin's naked ordeal as a captive of Gumb's free to be seen as the murderous, wholly self-serving exercise in power that it is. This more than anything enabled director Jonathan Demme to show on screen Harris's understanding that for

1   See Harriet Hawkins, 'Thank you, Dr Lecter', in *The Modern Review* (Autumn 1991), pp. 30–1.
2   A plural of 'imago', the fully adult insect.

serial killers control and murder are not adjuncts of sex, but substitutes for it.

There is a more polysyllabic Freudian version of this working theory, involving the erotic and thanatic (or sex and death) drives and the powerful notion that the primary emotional effect of childhood abuse is to arrest particular aspects of mental growth, leaving a stunted set of pathways within the maturing adult. *The Silence of the Lambs* made the populist case, and Harris's work has ever since been rehashed and formulaised by Hollywood and TV networks, one cause of the relative failure of *Hannibal*. Lecter and Starling, however, are something else. In the narrowest possible view (and leaving *Hannibal Rising* out of account), their dance of dynamics enacts the investigative inversion of what remains our primary psychopathological model of serial killing. In any wider view, they became to the 1990s what Holmes and Watson were to the 1890s, odd-couple heroes on the criminal frontier, with that added modern frisson of sexuality and (for the interested) the full expression at decade's end in *Hannibal* of what could justly be called a fucking cure for evil.

Back in (Mid-)Yorks., where Reginald Hill was living and working, the obligation of a crime novelist to deal with the kinds of crime that happen in his own town was proving awkward.[1] The archetypal Yorkshire riding and modern administrative county that Hill had since 1970 created around Dalziel & Pascoe hosted action that was fundamentally *comedic*—as series rather have to be, granted the survival of their protagonists—but also increasingly *comic*. There were, for example, finely timed conversations, sly allusions, and rich Wodehousian or Rabelaisian metaphors for Dalziel's gargantuanism and the matching ugliness of his highly efficient CID organiser, DS Wield. With these structural and modal qualities, Mid-Yorks. was throughout the 1970s a superbly flexible setting for five Dalziel-&-Pascoe novels, *ab initio* accommodating tragic farce in *A Clubbable Woman* (1970), and by *A Pinch of Snuff* (1978) able intelligently to manage the peculiarly vile reality of snuff movies amid a more basic local porn industry. Hill is sometimes thought too cosy a crime writer, and certainly plays (often brilliantly) on the Golden-Age legacy, but in Mayhem Parva (as Colin Watson dubbed the eternal cosy-crime village[2]) there could never have been a place for snuff movies, nor the mindset their consumption implies. Whatever southern shire Mayhem Parva may be in, Mid-Yorks. was by 1978 a very different county.

---

1 A different summary of some of this argument appears in my long essay on Hill for the Scribner's *British Writers Supplements* series. See also 'Of Yorkshire and Purgatory' in this e-book.

2 See *Snobbery with Violence: Crime Stories and Their Audience* (1971). 'Parva' means 'small' or 'lesser', and there is implicitly a nearby Mayhem Magna.

From 1978–81, however, still teaching in Doncaster, Hill lived the intense local and national bewilderment of the Ripper years. If he and Yorkshire were in that acid reality, so was Mid-Yorks., and *A Killing Kindness* (1980) tried honourably to raise its body-count. Without giving away either the plot or a blazing narrative coup with a clue, Hill's problem was that killing many people and serial killing are not the same, legally, psychologically, or literarily. If deaths become truly excessive, as in Dashiell Hammett's notorious *Red Harvest* (1929), readers may suspect a pathology at work, probably the author's, but the whole point about serial killing (manifest in talk of the Ripper) was the sheer incomprehensibility of iterative murder-mutilation. Even such ideas as *lustmord*, familiar to cinema buffs since Fritz Lang's superlative *M* (1931), didn't seem to leave one any the wiser in 1978, and if Hill was clueless, so must Dalziel & Pascoe be. But having set about depopulating Mid-Yorks. with a serial strangler who dominates local and national journalism, just as Sutcliffe did in Yorkshire reality, Hill needed his coppers to catch someone and couldn't wait on the real police. He had to invent, and not knowing himself what made such a killer tick went with what he knew. The result is a satisfying and highly literary multiple murderer, but not the serial killer whom the plot began by supposing at work; nor in 1980 could Hill risk any recuperative satire of mistaken hysteria, for the Ripper was still ripping and hysterics all too real.

That Hill finished the novel at all is commendable; that composition and publication came *before* Sutcliffe was caught is sharply germane, and in so far as *A Killing Kindness* attempted in fiction to confront a reality the Ripper imposed on Yorkshire, it failed. Though an admirable attempt, measured against the following year's best serial-killer novel, *Red Dragon*, Hill's analysis fell short—hardly surprisingly, given the proliferation of US serial killers and Harris's knowledge of Quantico, but illuminating a previously invisible limit to Mid-Yorks.

There is also a surprising dénouement in *A Killing Kindness* that should not be revealed but can be described as supernatural vengeance compensating for a failure of human justice. Hill is a long-standing master of the ghost-story—try the dazzling *There are No Ghosts in the Soviet Union and other stories* (1987) or *The Stranger House* (2005)—and had in 1980 just daringly juggled the explosively antithetical genres of crime and ghost fiction[1] in 'Pascoe's Ghost' and 'Dalziel's Ghost', both

---

1   The second of Mgr Ronald Knox's famous 'Decalogue' of detective-story commandments (in his introduction to *Best Detective Stories of the Year 1928*) forbids "All supernatural or preternatural agencies [...] as a matter of course". Given my argument 'Of Purgatory and Yorkshire', it is interesting that one of the few other writers to manage a supernatural touch is Sayers, in *Busman's Honeymoon* (Epithalamion, part 3).

collected in *Pascoe's Ghost and other Brief Chronicles of Crime* (1979). But in Sutcliffe's shadow the villain's escape in *A Killing Kindness* from human but not paranormal justice looks like an authorial fantasy responding to the unknown Ripper's continuing freedom, and in its closing juxtaposition of incongruent genres a wry acknowledgement of the larger failure I outline.

British graphic novelist Alan Moore, who also lived through the Sutcliffe years (though not in Yorkshire), channelled his experience into a *Jack* the Ripper tale, *From Hell* (1991–8, filmed 2001), and in the film-version Jack memorably says in November 1888, after butchering Mary Jane Kelley, "I have given birth to the twentieth century".[1] This Jack has a complex, Masonic theory as well as insane delusions of grandeur and duty backing his claim, but neither is needed to understand it. Never before that London autumn had the British public had to confront the phenomenon of serial killing, and while Jack's lesson had faded in Britain before Sutcliffe refurbished it 90 years on, his infamy lived at all levels of culture. The most serious accounts of literary and social modernity do not ignore the thread that runs from those Whitechapel dismemberments of fellow humans to the pulverised flesh of the WW1 trenches, Munich *lustmord* in the 1920s, and even Auschwitz, nor the tide Jack emblematises that has seen over a century the alienated killer-of-strangers evolve into a commonplace of plots and prisons alike.[2]

Serial killers are accommodated in fiction as they are apprehended in reality, through a new kind of mass-scale police work. Almost every major serial-killer novel (including *From Hell*, Lindley's *Mercy*, the Lecter series, and David Peace's nightmarish *Red Riding Quartet*, based on Sutcliffe[3]) is at least in part a detailed police procedural strongly rooted in a real and predominantly urban geography. But Mid-Yorks., though verisimilar and well-populated, is importantly *un*real, an archetype not a mimesis, which is perhaps why it could accommodate supernatural revenge but did not possess a sufficiently massive, unseen 'real' population to sustain the practice or capture of a killer like Sutcliffe. For Hill to make plots live and work in Mid-Yorks.

1   In the novel he says "It is beginning, Netley. Only just beginning. For better or worse, the twentieth century. I have delivered it." : Alan Moore & Eddie Campbell, *From Hell, being a melodrama in sixteen parts* (Paddington, Aus.: Eddie Campbell Comics, 1999), ch. 10, p. 33, top central panel.

2   For the best recent fictions deploying the same awareness see Rennie Airth, *River of Darkness* (1999), in which an Inspector with trench traumata of his own must hunt a serial killer of families whose pathology stems from wartime experience; Faye Kellerman, *Straight into Darkness* (2005), confronting the confluence of serial killing with the NSDAP in Munich in 1929; and Pavel Kohout, *Hvězdná hodina vrahů* (1995, as *The Widow Killer*, 1998), set in occupied Prague during WW2.

3   David Peace, *Nineteen Seventy Four* (1999), *Nineteen Seventy Seven* (2000), *Nineteen Eighty* (2001), and *Nineteen Eighty Three* (2002).

he must find or make connections to acquire meaning and accumulate clarity, but a serial killer does neither, and in one sense Sutcliffe escaped Hill's Mid-Yorks. Force in 1979–80 just as he escaped the Yorkshire police and everyone else until 1981.

In its serial nature, however, the proper context of *A Killing Kindness* has grown with its movement from 'new D.-&-P # 6' to '# 6 of 20', and the problem and interest have triangulated nicely. Hill's immediate response in D.-&-P # 7, the magnificent *Deadheads* (1983), was to rework the problem in a form Mid-Yorks. could accommodate whole. Patrick Aldermann, a charming, soft-spoken man whose wife knows Ellie Pascoe, finds life a bed of roses because all who stand in his way (grandmother, rival, boss ...) fall victim to unfortunate and invariably fatal accidents. Aldermann may have killed half-a-dozen human beings without breaking sweat, or quite possibly no-one; in the end, as at the beginning, irresolution rules. In the clear self-interest and asexuality of his supposed murders there is no trace of the core problem with Sutcliffe's kind of killing, but severe contrast of Aldermann's pleasant courtesy with the ruthless inhumanity of his putative deeds confronts readers constantly with an uncomfortable problem—and as it lines us up with the detectives' problem (being *in its own terms* both epistemological—how may we know?—and ontological—if we are right, what is he?), it can adequately stand for the problem Sutcliffe posed in reality. The crucial structural difference is that with a suspect always in open view the problem isn't 'Who is serial killing?', but 'Is this man Aldermann a ('serial') killer?', and the definition of serial killing is thereby included throughout in the problems to be considered, rather than being (as in Yorkshire reality and *A Killing Kindness*) predetermined by a string of butchered or strangled corpses and a media moniker. Lacking a safely anonymous monster to name and vilify, the national media are also excluded from *Deadheads*, giving Dalziel and especially Pascoe (drawn in personally through Ellie) much more space to ponder the problem and the nature of its irresolution.

Even for a novelist of manners as skilled and witty as Hill such space might spell danger. Unless devotees of the cosy and complacent, modern serial readers of crime are likely to prefer something at least slightly hard-boiled, and can have damagingly little tolerance for extended conversation,[1] particularly when it takes a philosophical turn. Dorothy L. Sayers, for example, who in *Gaudy Night* (1935) and *Busman's Honeymoon* (1937) bought the crime novel of manners to something very like per-

---

1   Hardened and vulgarised as commercial rule-of-thumb, this becomes the story that Jonathan Demme had trouble financing *Silence of the Lambs* because prospective producers balked at the first, eight-and-a-half minute conversation between Lecter & Starling. Because they cannot move, 'action', it seems, must unacceptably stop.

fection, is far less honoured than she should be, in large part because her tremendous conversations—whether a set-piece at an Oxford high table or literary by-play with a local copper—go not only unappreciated in our action-packed world but often to shallow damnation as dull and snobbish wordage. And if a good deal more generous with dead bodies (albeit mostly in retrospect), Hill was, like Sayers in *Gaudy Night*, attempting a novel low on obvious villainy and high on the daily business of living with a stubbornly inchoate problem. Although he denies conscious influence, it is thus notable that *Deadheads* also adopted in very striking form a practice on which Sayers depended in *Gaudy Night & Busman's Honeymoon*, and that might be called 'structural epigraphy'.

Hill had used linked novel-and chapter-epigraphs before in both series and non-series work. *An Advancement of Learning* (1971, D.-&-P # 2) takes them with great profit from its eponymous work by Bacon, and *An April Shroud* (1975, # 4) has very funny (if un-Keatsian) chapter-titles, but *Deadheads* went a long step further. As the title suggests, roses (whose fading blooms must be lopped to encourage new ones) and their breeding are central to the plot, and novel-epigraphs from Defoe and Swinburne ("*I shall never be friends again with roses.*") are backed by glittering part-epigraphs from canonical luminaries including Pope ("*Or, quick effluvia darting through the brain, / Die of a rose in aromatic pain.*") and Lewis Carroll ("*'It's my opinion you never think at all,' the Rose said in a rather severe tone.*"). What really punches, though, are the unified chapter-titles and -epigraphs, the names and (parenthetically) the catalogue descriptions of well-bred roses:

YESTERDAY

(Floribunda. Multitudinous tiny lilac-pink flowers with an olde-worlde fairy-tale air.)

RIPPLES

(Floribunda. Free-flowering, lilac-mauve blooms, rippled petals, abundant foliage, susceptible to mildew in the fall.)[1]

A rich sense of the possible applications to each small unit of narrative, and hence (with plainly consistent epigraphs) of unity in all, is balanced by the resistance of quotations that are stubbornly themselves, and import their own worlds to jostle for

---

1   Reginald Hill, *Deadheads* (London: Collins, 1983), pp. 33, 52 ; previous quotations, pp. [5], [7], [147].

an enriching place in Hill's unfolding scheme.

In just that manner Sayers gave to the chapters of *Gaudy Night* epigraphs revealing a depth and breadth of Renaissance scholarship, raiding the Bodleian Library's Jacobethan collections for a chorus of antique English voices who (with the stone force and undergraduate populations of the 'Dreaming Spires') crucially help to make real, by grounding them in articulate history, the landed and ideological inheritances of both her aristocratic sleuth, Lord Peter Wimsey, *and* simultaneously of his rural–Bloomsbury middle-class *objet d'amour*, Harriet Vane. Miss Vane, like Miss Sayers, had the chance to learn of such Renaissance authors while reading English at Oxford as a very early female student, and the resonating, memorable epigraphs (in that Elizabethan prose that is at once sonorous and tack-sharp in its unfamiliar patterns of thought) do far more than decorate the narrative. As each is highly individual, summary is hard, but beyond summoning a range of very real and opinionated minds whose judgements sit uncomfortably amid the daily shocks and compromises of modernity, they also (because known to Peter and Harriet) mediate in the romance plot—and it was a large part of Sayers's genius to force that mediation (though that is another story[1]). Hill's rose-catalogue quotations seem very different, and sometimes reek ("*an olde-worlde ... air*") of exactly that debased modernity that Sayers's epigraphs rebuke, but they do very much the same kind of job in mediating between the strands of Hill's plot, and through their sustained focus on the titular metaphor keep the novel, for all its conversations, grippingly taut.

After two novels wrestling with their horrors Hill reasonably backed away from serial killers, who are, after all and despite everything, fortunately rare in every county. In January 1981 Sutcliffe had finally been caught, so urgency receded, and if the arrest in London in February 1983 of Dennis Nilsen (who admitted 15 murders of young *men* and was later convicted of six) fixed the phenomenon much more widely in British reality, it also made for a still more complex problem than Sutcliffe had posed. Thereafter Yorkshire politics stumbled into the bitter violence of the Miners' Strike of 1984–5 and its long aftermath, about which Hill (who had been thinking of the mining communities Mid-Yorks. must have when the Strike began) would produce his best work to date in *Under World* (1988, # 10). And after all that, once Mrs Thatcher had fallen in 1990 there came the long and unlovely pseudo-transition to Blairism, a recurrent motif in Hill's work throughout the 1990s–2000s.

Yet further responses to Sutcliffe's butcheries were neither burked nor forgotten, but rather displaced into a notable new motif in Hill's non-series writing. Settings in

1   See 'Of Purgatory and Yorkshire'.

the 1914–18 trenches inform several stories and a remarkable novel, *No Man's Land* (1985), based on tales of an international band of deserters living in a shell-bastardised wilderness behind British lines near the Somme. Of particular concern is the official British butchery of their own private soldiers and NCOs for cowardice, insubordination, and suchlike military offences with which Other Ranks were charged, so *No Man's Land* crackles with injustice. The same indignant rage is evident in an irruption of this material into *The Wood Beyond* (1996, # 14), when Pascoe discovers his great-grandfather (also Peter) to have been so executed, after a travesty of a court martial. A case simultaneously takes him to a once-stately home where some relentless Yorkshire rain and a *cordon sanitaire* created by the pharmaceuticals firm now controversially using it for vivisection have made of a woodland garden a sucking mire bad enough to summon the murderous bogs and shell-craters of Passchendaele that the older Pascoe knew. Fascinatingly, Mid-Yorks. has no problem absorbing this fragment of the European front lines, for in its creation the county's own native flora and fauna have alike been anonymously dismembered, and remain in memory to haunt and curse the scene. *Under World* had gifted Mid-Yorks. with a Hell, and *Pictures of Perfection* (1994, # 13) had in marvellous fashion managed a spree killer of sorts, but this discovery of the older Pascoe's antique loyalty, service, and casual betrayal to official murder after surviving a futile slaughterhouse in battle abruptly extended verisimilar historical depth, and created space for a different order of experience.

The Wood Beyond thus gave advance notice of Hill's formal return as a crime writer to the unhappy matter of serial killing, in the diptych of *Dialogues of the Dead* (2002, # 17) and *Death's Jest-Book* (2003, # 18). But comedy will out, and they are perhaps the strangest of all his books, defying analysis except at very considerable length. This is partly because they deploy a great deal of material deriving from canonical subluminaries George Lyttelton (1709–73) and Thomas Lovell Beddoes (1803–49), who respectively supply the novels' titles, and partly by introducing a blindingly whimsical means whereby an ill, troubled, and wretchedly *sympathetic* serial killer selects victims. A flavour of events is offered by the full title of the first novel, *Dialogues of the Dead : or Paronomania!* ~~an aged worm for wept royals a warm doge for top lawyers~~ *a word game for two players*, and the ethical challenge of a serial-killer comedy is confronted throughout the diptych, sometimes straying perilously close to open disrespect for victims. More than 20 years after Sutcliffe's capture and permanent imprisonment, with far greater public awareness and considerably less tender Yorkshire sensibilities, there was a sufficiently clear need for debunking obsession with serial killing to allow satire, congenial to Hill, while a larger, more visible population (generated by various devices, including a bustling workplace setting) allowed a greater anonymity of successive victims, lessening any *frisson* at brisk narrative disrespect for their lives. Perhaps the only obvious weakness one might identify is that the psychopathology of the killer, logical in its own terms and appealing purely as a puzzle, is not in persuasive relation to the likes of Dolarhyde and Gumb, nor yet Sutcliffe and Nilsen. If anyone, Lecter might be summoned, for sheer idiosyncrasy of motive and politeness of speech, but, truth to tell, Hill's double narrative has more to do with older ideas of death and revenance as they inform modern ideas of predation than with particular problems Peter Sutcliffe once posed a place where Hill then lived.

It would be nice to report Hill's triumphant return as a serial writer to a fence he found he had balked, but neither serial writing nor serial reading can often work thus, for both writers and readers move on. With Clarice Starling we have all found ways enough to make those lambs keep schtumm, or pass them by; and the British serial killers caught since Sutcliffe, Nilsen and the Gloucester tag-team of Fred & Rosemary West, were unknown before a 'house of horror' was dug up, so there has never again been the kind of pressure Sutcliffe exerted to understand a serial killer at work. After the West case in 1994–5 Hill might have opted for the retrospective scenario, as Peter Robinson brilliantly did in *Aftermath* (2001), and still might—but the percentages are falling and the subjects to which he has, stunningly, turned his archetypal county down the years command their own abiding respect.

In another way Hill has in any case done the diviner thing, for the complex oddity of his return to serial killing in the diptych shows a Lecter smile, velociraptor intelligence pushing aside all the rapidly formulaised sub-generic conventions of explanatory abuse and abducted torture with a renewed search and fresh questions. Not being God, even in Mid-Yorks. and despite creating Dalziel, Hill cannot grant understanding of the moral nullity represented by Sutcliffe's infamous remark to his brother, "I were just cleaning up streets, our kid. Just cleaning up the streets", nor better knowledge of the Sutcliffes still among us.[1] But he can and does provide rich ways of living with and thinking about our knowledge of their existence.

Just how civil an experience reading Hill is should not be underestimated. Very few novelists can hope to impose corrections of general understanding within their

---

1   Sutcliffe is quoted in Burn, *"... somebody's husband ..."*, p. 355, and thence as one of Morrison's epigraphs to *The Ballad of the Yorkshire Ripper*.

lifetime, and in measuring him against the extraordinary (and far less literary) work Harris achieved with *The Silence of the Lambs* aesthetic comparison is unfairly disabled. Hill's particular gifts as a novelist do not well suit the territories of serial killing, and he knows as well as any the deep shadow Harris casts, yet he managed in his mid-sixties a lengthy double work that for all its whimsies bites any number of bullets. Perhaps his best single novel, *On Beulah Height* (1998, # 15), also tackled the problem with equally stern (but not grim) determination in making an uncaught but inactive serial killer part of the backstory to a search for a missing child that turns astonishingly on Mahler's *Kindertotenlieder* and becomes a requiem for all lost children. All in all, in keeping with his plainly civil and civic practice throughout his (writing) life, Hill has kept his and readers' noses to the grindstone, cheerfully insisting on attention, thought, and good humour while we notice what as citizens we must. One of his heroes is Dickens, for crusading journalism alongside and within the novels as well as that stylistic genius that Ruskin diagnosed:

> Allowing for his manner of telling them, the things he tells us are always true [...] But let us not lose the use of Dickens's wit and insight, because he chooses to speak in a circle of stage fire. He is entirely right in his main drift and purpose in every book he has written; and all of them, but especially *Hard Times*, should be studied with close and earnest care by persons interested in social questions.[1]

The same is true of Hill, substituting *Under World* or *On Beulah Height* for *Hard Times*, and if Dickens saw the worst of Victorian exploitation and indifference, Hill has had his own neo-Victorianism to beard in its latter-day dens. Just as Dickens did (and Addison or Steele, come to that), Hill understands what he does as both joyful privilege and ethical arena, and just as for all those literary luminaries, that means for him *serial* writing and engagement with readers.

As a new generation have very audibly been discovering through the arts of J. K. Rowling, serial reading can sometimes be a white-knuckle ride. The mistake made by those exasperated with Potteriana and prone to dismiss attempts at analysis as intrinsically risible, is to think that it is merely Harry himself, or the pleasing details and inventiveness of the plots, that are being supposed important. What actually matters, of course, and the reason Rowling is of entirely serious critical and scholarly interest, is that her series—and it could only be what it is as a series, in and over time—has become a vehicle for its readers' thinking. The argument is complete in every publi-

---

1   John Ruskin, *Unto this Last* (1862), XVII, 31.

cation-day image of an eight-year-old at 1 a.m. happily lost to the world in a Rowling tome much fatter than his or her head, and the sustenance of children's mass attention as they and the series have grown has seen her pull together a very substantial cohort as the Potter generation. The first novel appeared in 1997 and was filmed in 2001; the seventh and last will be published in 2007; the sixth film is scheduled for release in 2008, and the seventh will presumably follow in 2009, so the *primary* span will be a long decade 1997–2009; and the six novels to date have sold more than 300 million copies, many of which have been re/read by multiple readers. Put another way, most 'First World' and many other children born since 1983 (i.e. those under 14 when *Philosopher's Stone* came out) either already or soon will have experience as serial readers, and when talking heads celebrate the gift of reading Rowling has given so many children, her serial qualities should not be thought sugar for the medicine, nor a merely commercial phenomenon, but an intrinsic feature of what she has wrought. Her model clearly lies in old school stories, probably via the Mallory Towers series by Enid Blyton, and she takes from them with boarding-school conventions the critical one-school-year-per-novel form—without which Harry could never have developed as he has.

Moreover, Rowling evidently understands an ethics in her profession of series fiction for children.[1] Media discussions have oddly avoided the matter, even with the word *Half-Blood* in her sixth title, but the fundamental concerns of Rowling's world with racism have been plain since Malfoy, Crabb, and Goyle first snarled 'Filthy mudblood!' at a magically talented child of one or more untalented 'muggle' parents. Way back in *Harry Potter and the Philosopher's Stone* Dumbledore's collectable Chocolate-Frog-card, described during Harry's first train-journey to Hogwarts and later crucially recalled for its information about Nicolas Flamel, says directly that Dumbledore's greatest achievement was his "defeat of the dark wizard Grindelwald in 1945".[2] Grindelwald would anglicise as 'Grendelwood', a name that potentially means something quite other, but Germanic form in conjunction with the date 1945 leaves no possible doubt that association with Nazism (and perhaps Hitler's paranormal interests) is deliberate, and the issue thereby invoked can only be ideologies of race. Quite what form Rowling's massively extended parable about racism and growing up will take in completion with *Harry Potter and the Deathly Hallows* re-

1   For a range of more and less persuasive views see Lana A. Whited, ed., *The Ivory Tower and Harry Potter: Perspectives on a Literary Phenomenon* (2002; rev, 2004), and John Granger, ed., *Who Killed Albus Dumbledore: What Really Happened in Harry Potter and the Half-Blood Prince? Six expert Harry Potter detectives examine the evidence* (2006).

2   J. K. Rowling, *Harry Potter and the Philosopher's Stone* (London: Bloomsbury, 1997), p. 77.

mains to be seen (though Rowling has now made it clear that two more characters will die), but the qualities she has shown so far, including resistance to tremendous pressure from publishers and the mass-media, relaxed control over the fundamental faithfulness of the film-scripts, and the clear novel-by-novel escalation of action into more adult territory, give real confidence. Being of Rowling's generation I see in her the legacies of Rock against Racism, Two-Tone music, and the great cause of anti-*Apartheid*, but anyone acknowledging the reading-life of a nation as a sphere of civil action must also acknowledge the ethics of her writing practice—and so potentially at least of the serial reading practices it induces, merchandised Potter pencil-cases or no.

Not every reader is a serial reader, but many are, and with good reason. Much, alas, as Sutcliffe forced a nation to understand the meaning of waiting and increments, so Rowling as a commanding serial writer at patient work has forcibly reminded us that the running narratives we devour in the broadcast media originated in print, and have pleasures to offer that no airwave or celluloid can capture. They can be experienced only by living with books through time, and the charge of escapism so often levelled at genre fiction is almost as often pure foolishness or bad irony. The work of Harris is enough to bring anyone up short, and the far more literary Hill has been deprived through what must now be the great bulk of his writing life of the plaudits and na-tional admiration he merits both as a fine and as an outstandingly civil novelist. His (and my) comfort must be that what the critics have steadfastly ignored legions of readers have not, and the home Hill has found at HarperCollins (whose Crime List has been superb under editor Julia Wisdom) has enabled continuous development in craft and art to his present age of 70, and there is every reason to hope well beyond. By the time literary criticism catches up with him I imagine I shall be long gone my-self, so I'm happy to enjoy the real thing first-hand, in the world of serial living where responsibilities come with the job.

2. Of Purgatory and Yorkshire

Dorothy L. Sayers and Reginald Hill's Divine Comedy

The curious career of Dorothy L. Sayers (1893–1957), deeply beloved of some as the Golden-Age 'Queen of Crime' responsible for Lord Peter Wimsey, and cordially despised by others on the same grounds, tends to be cast in disparate halves. Both in her biography of Sayers and her five-volume edition of the *Letters* Barbara Reynolds divides matters on the cusp of 1936–7, just before the publication (in February 1937) of *Busman's Honeymoon* as both a novel dedicated to, and a play co-written with, Sayers's Oxford friend Muriel St Clare Byrne.[1] In October 1936 Sayers was already sketching out *Thrones, Dominations*, the next Wimsey novel,[2] when she received an invitation from Margaret Babington to write a play for performance in Canterbury Cathedral.[3] Over some months Christianity and the stage-success of *Busman's Honeymoon* displaced new detection, setting Sayers on a course that led her to abandon crime fiction for sacred plays (including *The Man Born to be King*) and 15 years translating Dante's *Commedia*. The resulting *Hell* (1949) and *Purgatory* (1955) appeared before her early death, *Paradise* (1962) was posthumously completed by Reynolds, and the whole verse-translation (a Penguin Classic) became for some decades the standard English text.

Reynolds, a professional Italianist, has written of their collaboration in *The Passionate Intellect: Dorothy L. Sayers' Encounter with Dante* (1989). Unsurprisingly, like all work on Sayers, this too tends to divide her life and thought between criminal

---

1 See Barbara Reynolds, *Dorothy L. Sayers: Her Life and Soul* (1993), and *The Letters of Dorothy L. Sayers, Vol. 1: 1899–1936: The Making of a Detective Novelist* (1996) & ... *2: 1937–1943: From Novelist to Playwright* (1998). The other volumes are *1944–1950: A Noble Daring* (2000), *1951–1957: In the Midst of Life* (2002), and *Child and Woman of her Time* (2002); see also: ▣ http://www.sayers.org.uk/publications.html.

2 Eventually completed by Jill Paton Walsh and published in 1998; a final Wimsey novel, *A Presumption of Death*, based on sketchy notes by Sayers and credited jointly to her and Paton Walsh, appeared in 2002.

3 Reynolds, *Letters, Vol. 2*, p. 401 ff.. Eliot's *Murder in the Cathedral* was similarly commissioned.

& Christian or English & Italian periods, and given Reynolds's profession a general sense in which 'Dante, Alighieri', figures far more prominently in her indices than 'Wimsey, Lord Peter D. B.' can hardly be grumbled at. There is an oddity nonetheless, for the *Letters* especially are closely connected with the Dorothy L. Sayers Society, of which Reynolds is the long-serving president—and the DLSS, of course, is considerably more concerned with Wimsey than with anything Italian.[1] It has, however, greatly appreciated Reynolds's work and patronage, and in 1994 did her the honour of producing *Studies in Sayers: Essays presented to Dr Barbara Reynolds on her 80th birthday*. To the best of my knowledge none of Reynolds's more conventionally academic colleagues produced any *festschriften* for her, and in consulting *Studies in Sayers*, which honourably looks beyond Wimsey but has a heart much closer to detection than Dante, I often wonder with what wryness of appreciation it must have been received.

It would seemingly take an unliterary heart to regret Sayers's turn to Dante, and for Wimsey's haters she simply came to her senses, but for his friends and admirers life is harder. About the first four Wimsey novels and first collection of stories—*Whose Body?* (1923), *Clouds of Witness* (1926), *Unnatural Death* (1927), *The Unpleasantness at the Bellona Club* (1928), and *Lord Peter Views the Body* (1928)—disagreement is of little consequence. Yes, the plots are clever, the writing good, Wimsey something of an ass, and other characters generally no rounder than immediate context requires: that some appreciate the mix while others don't is entirely unremarkable. With *Strong Poison* (1930), however, Sayers introduced Wimsey and her readers to Harriet Vane, and a long struggle to humanise him began.[2] Harriet does not appear in *The Five Red Herrings* (1931), nor in the four Wimsey stories collected in *Hangman's Holiday* (1933), but she stubbornly refuses Peter's repeated proposals of marriage in *Have His Carcass* (1932), and lurks offstage in *Murder Must Advertise* (1933) and *The Nine Tailors* (1934). With these two novels the stakes begin to rise, for both show extremely interesting development in presenting (respectively) a genuine, highly commercial workplace and the carefully expounded subtleties of campanology as a means of Anglican devotion. Harriet may herself be missing, but it would be hard to argue that the higher quality and greater density of prose (by com-

---

1   Besides sponsorship of the *Letters*, the Society's most impressive publication is Stephan P. Clarke's *The Lord Peter Wimsey Companion* (1985; 2nd ed. 2002), which runs to 9,819 entries & 11,853 cross-references—evidence not (as sometimes supposed) of obsession with Sayers, but of the dense social historicity of Sayers's fiction, creating the sharply observed culture and mores amid which Wimsey deals, and her many allusions to English, French, and classical literature.

2   The fullest recent account is Robert Kuhn McGregor, *Conundrums for the Long Week-End* (2000).

parison with Sayers's work in the 1920s) are unrelated to her.[1] Dislike them as one may, these novels begin to distinguish Sayers from almost all other Golden-Age writers, and make Wimsey a very different figure from Agatha Christie's Poirot and Miss Marple (a confirmed bachelor and spinster). Even Margery Allingham's Campion, another aristocratic sleuth whom his creator sought during the 1930s to humanise through prolonged engagement to a woman of high intelligence but troubled mind, fades in comparison, and Allingham's great later works, notably *The Tiger in the Smoke* (1952), did not develop with or through Campion, but by relegating him to background passivity and observations.

Peter's long courtship finally concluded (sending the stakes through the roof) in a diptych—*Gaudy Night* (1935), at the end of which he and Harriet become passionately engaged in New College Lane, and *Busman's Honeymoon: A Love Story with Detective Interruptions* (1937), which comprehends their nuptials and an unwelcome corpse. For confirmed loathers of Wimsey's aristocracy, reserve, and intellectual chatter, Harriet's mature love for him is a self-dismissal, 'revealing' her as just another dupe of the class-war, from her origins as a death-row prisoner whom Peter saves, to full embodiment as a crime writer, and post-series future bearing his children in a few short stories. Far from 'humanising' or 'deepening' Wimsey, they say, she simply joins him in Sayers's hierarchised, clichéd world, unsurprisingly (in this view) because Oxford-educated Harriet is an avatar of Oxford-educated Dorothy and Sayers was in love with both Wimsey and the class-ridden world he and Oxford represent. Honourable proponents of this dismissal may feel obliged to deal with Wimsey's trench-service in 1914–18 and neurasthenic dreams, or his remark in *Gaudy Night* that "our kind of show is dead and done for. What the hell good does it do anybody these days?",[2] but most (if they read them at all) simply ignore the complexities of the later novels. In the opposite view, though, it isn't just that Harriet *does* humanise Wimsey, movingly and memorably, but that in having her do so Sayers developed the detective novel in an extremely influential manner.

How she managed to do so can be variously described. Looking to character and plot, one could say that in the closed worlds of most Golden-Age fiction (including her own early novels) what matters is a limited pool of suspects who may be paraded as red herrings; but in *Gaudy Night*, as a straightforward consequence of the colle-

---

1   See vol. 5 of the *Letters*, which presents the unpublished drafts of two non-Wimsey novels, clearly drawing on autobiography, that were re-used in *The Nine Tailors* and *Gaudy Night*. See also Carolyn G. Heilbrun, "Sayers, Lord Peter, and Harriet Vane at Oxford' (1986), Nicolas Freeling, 'Dorothy L. Sayers' (1992), & H. R. F. Keating, 'Dorothy L. Sayers' (1996).

2   Dorothy L. Sayers, *Gaudy Night* (London: Gollancz, 1935), p. 299.

giate setting, all students of the university and inhabitants of the town are candidates as the poison pen troubling Harriet's fictional *alma mater*, Shrewsbury College. This problem is precisely why Harriet is called in as an outsider, and the consequences of its intractability occupy most of the lengthy text, so that everything *hermetic* in the Golden-Age paradigm becomes *hermeneutic*, throwing the lazily conventional parade of suspects back on itself (and charting those consequences too). Alternatively, thinking of territory and topography, one could take Mayhem Parva, Colin Watson's archetypal Golden-Age village where dastardly murder always strikes, and say that Sayers understood that to escape its clichés one cannot dilute but must concentrate the problem. The cloisters and dreaming spires of Oxford, rooted in old isolations of the sacred and intellectual life but subject to the reluctant modernity that had made Sayers a graduate, offered a real city and set of institutional topoi onto which elements and conventions of Mayhem Parva could be closely mapped, transforming the unreal village into an infinitely more responsive and talismanic locale. The pressure on Harriet's investigation from would-be hermetics, Fellows closeting themselves with their work or desiring to protect the college's name, in tandem with the mechanics of living within walls and portered gates, subject the impossibility and misguided ethics of such self-isolation (in fiction or life) to relentless examination—a process itself summoning one major purpose of the university. In Shrewsbury's old rooms and quadrangles one might still be in the manor house of Mayhem Parva, but the city outside the walls knows otherwise, and at every turn what some hope to seal off gives way to consequences and vistas of the world. And the romance element, that might be mere distraction, is no such thing, for Harriet, after five years of denying (though in differing ways) her own and Peter's feelings, and amid her last attempt to withdraw from a world so full of demanding otherness, must unveil her eyes and future by raising them to see Peter truly and consider her own changed perspectives.

In addition, the structural epigraphy Sayers developed from her wide knowledge of Renaissance writers powerfully modulates literary self-reference (hermetics) into outward enquiry (hermeneutics). The novel's general epigraph, setting-up the setting, is from Donne's court sermon of 4 March 1624/5, published as # 17 of his *LXXX Sermons* (1640) :

> The University is a Paradise, Rivers of Knowledge are there, Arts and Sciences flow from thence. Counsell Tables are *Horti conclusi*, (as it is said in the Canticles) *Gardens that are walled in*, and they are *Fontes signati*, *Wells that are sealed up* ; bottomless depth of unsearchable Counsels there.

Nearly 500 pages later, the last of 23 chapter-epigraphs is from Burton's compendious *Anatomy of Melancholy* (1621), Partition 3, Section 2, Member 5, Subsection 5:

> The last refuge and surest remedy, to be put in practice in the utmost place, when no other means will take effect, is, to let them go together and enjoy one another; *potissima cura est ut heros amasia sua potitur*, saith *Guianerius* .... *Æsculapius* himself, to this malady, cannot invent a better remedy, *quam ut amanti cedat amatum* ... than that a Lover have his desire.[1]

These and all epigraphs are sufficiently literary to demand readers' joy in language as well as dappling light across the novel's action, but Sayers's own prose, the romance story, and especially the formal, funny, and sensitive dialogue in any case require readers of *Gaudy Night* to enjoy a leisurely pace and considerable depth of narrative focus. Thus framed and framing, the choric Renaissance voices echo in the actions they preface like Oxford's bells in its narrow streets, tracing within both city and novel a web of history and learned opinion. Mayhem Parva may be discussed here, but it has no power and effects no limitations.

Having understood that with the right tools much can be mobilised, Sayers and Muriel Byrne (in drama), or Sayers alone (in prose), took the next great and logical step. The premise of *Busman's Honeymoon* is strikingly modern, in that invasive 'press hounds' force Peter and Harriet into a reclusive holiday, but in choosing Paggleham, a village of Harriet's rural childhood with its "quaint old farmhouse called Talboys"[2] and a corpse in the cellar, events may seem to revert to Mayhem Parva. As most readers who admire Peter and Harriet understand, this is (like much of the novel) a very intelligent tease, for what *Busman's Honeymoon: A Love Story with Detective Interruptions* truly manages, and its subtitle proclaims, is the transfer of the territory of investigation from *where* Peter and Harriet as sleuths happen to be during a given book, to *how* events affect them as partners, leaving *who* (as ever) *dunit* to detonate at the end. The chapter-epigraphs, still largely Renaissance but predominantly from dramatic comedy, point the way to the three-part prose 'Epithalamion' (or wedding-song) that Sayers furnished as an epilogue, and used to fuse the consequences of *who*, followed through trial to the gallows, into the emotional lives and civil conversations at her novel's heart. The glimpses of Peter and Harriet with children in the few later stories Sayers wrote (and even the recent continuations by Jill Paton Walsh) are not

---

1   Sayers, *Gaudy Night*, pp. [3], 475.
2   Dorothy L. Sayers, *Busman's Honeymoon* (London: Gollancz, 1937), p. 32.

simply welcome to devotees as new cases and investigations, but precisely because the continuous, paired movements of *Gaudy Night* and *Busman's Honeymoon* mean the world becomes larger where the Wimseys together turn their minds to seeing it—and that is *not* the effect of Poirot, Miss Marple or Campion, who like the young and silly-ass-about-town Wimsey reduce their surroundings to a stage for their own dandyism or mock-humility.

In Sayers's superbly successful attempt to write herself out of her genre's pressing Golden-Age constraints lies the exemplum of the post-1945 crime series. Raymond Chandler's related Californian work was distinct, tracking Marlowe's inner life through sequential novels but (in keeping with the eternal PI of Chandler's imagination and criticism) keeping him until the very end a loner whose rejections of male and female blandishments alike are vital. Chandler began a bit later than Sayers and wrote of Marlowe into the late 1950s, but not until Ross MacDonald began to steer Lew Archer through the Californian 1960s was the historicity of late Sayers (anchored in Wimsey's occasional diplomatic work and the oppressive international atmosphere of the 1930s) matched, and then in a very different manner. Within the English tradition Wimsey's social and Sayers's literary class blinded some to her achievement, but (barring the nostalgics of Mayhem Parva) every series writer since, of PI novels or police procedurals, has known that individual cases, however gruesome or cleverly concocted, can never on their own be enough, nor compensate for an inner life not otherwise given to its investigators. It is understandable to be annoyed (even furious) that it should have been a once languid aristocrat and a confirmed *bourgeoise* who showed the forward way, but that cannot make it less true.

The career that Christ and Dante abruptly ended was thus not simply of a silly sleuth, and neither sacred drama nor an impressive (if now dated) translation of the *Commedia* are unquestionably adequate compensation. Something was abandoned at birth, and the Wimsey novels Sayers might have written between 1937 (when she was 44) and her death in 1957 would have been the work of her and most novelists' prime. The Wimseys in wartime London or confronting post-war austerity and transformed European politics are not negligible losses. For British readers of crime (and readers at large) it is also unfortunate that Sayers's life should offer so apparent and handy a divide between genre fiction and 'literary' work, playing explicitly and pervasively into the crippling British snobbery about genre, and reinforcing an orchost of false distinctions and ugly generalisations. Julian Symons's open distaste for Sayers in his seminal (and seriously misleading) history *Bloody Murder: From the Detective Story to the Crime Novel* (1972; Penguin, 1974) severely compounded the problem, and its unhappy legacy remains horribly visible in (for example) the rigidly *kleinbürgerlich* events in Ruth Rendell's Kingsmarkham and the class-caricatures of the Inspector Lindley novels by Elizabeth George. But one of Sayers's legatees, committed to crime writing as one aspect of all literatures, has done his considerable best to see things whole, and bring us, as Sayers brought Peter and Harriet, through the 'dark wood' to a new upland.

In interview, Reginald Hill denies any particular liking for or well-timed reading of Sayers, but as he once said he had no particular memory of Thomas Browne, and I later discovered an early novel of his called *Urn Burial* with chapter-epigraphs from the remarkable book of the same name by ... Thomas Browne, I take a liberty of scepticism.[1] He certainly knows her translation of Dante's *Hell*, or at least cantos 1 & 4 of it, for they provide the general and section-epigraphs in *Under World* (1988), his tenth novel chronicling the archetypal modern administrative county of 'Mid-Yorks.' and featuring policemen Andy Dalziel & Peter Pascoe. As it is set against the aftermath of the Miners' Strike of 1984–5 and deeply concerned with murders in mines, whether the continuing hell of an active pit like Burrthorpe Main or dangerous shafts and galleries in abandoned workings, an epigraphic inferno is appropriate:

> Hear truth : I stood on the steep brink whereunder
> Runs down the dolorous chasm of the Pit,
> Ringing with infinite groans like gathered thunder.
>
> Deep, dense, and by no faintest glimmer lit
> It lay, and though I strained my sight to find
> Bottom, not one thing could I see in it.
>
> Down must we go, to that dark world and blind.[2]

---

1   I interviewed him in 1994 when reviewing *Pictures of Perfection* for the *London Review of Books*, and asked about a misquotation of Browne in the text (identified on sight by the late Jeremy Maule). (Browne: "Ready to be any thing, in the extasie of being ever"; Hill: "Enscombe is a living organism, make no mistake about that, and an incredibly adaptable one too, androgynously apotropaic, ready to be anything in the expectation of being ever, an Artful Dodger of a village making one demand only of its inhabitants, which is unquestioning love."). Hill blandly evaded the question and I was silly enough to forget that writers are among the most fictive people on earth.

2   Hill, *Under World* (London: Collins, 1988), p. [5], quoting *The Comedy of Dante Alighieri the Florentine: Cantica 1: Hell* (1949; as *Dante: Hell*, Harmondsworth: Penguin, 2001), IV.7–13 (p. 21).

The last line ought to have inverted commas, for it is spoken to the narrator by his guide, Virgil (whose *Aeneid* insistently turns up in two later Dalziel-&-Pascoe novels[1]), but Hill has excised and adapted to precise purpose. In Yorkshire parlance a pit is a working mine, as well as a fate or categorisation ('going down t'pit'), so Virgil's resolution to Dante becomes Hill's to self and readers, who know pits to be hell but ignore them; out of sight, out of mind—until the Strike. The novel's opening line on the next page gives pause—"'Another fine mess you've got me into,' said Detective Superintendent Andrew Dalziel."—but Laurel-&-Hardy relief lasts barely another sentence, most of the novel is in flashback, and knowledge of foregone calamity gives events (especially for serial readers previously fond of the protagonists) an oppressive, louring feel.

So far, so good, but the three section-epigraphs all come from canto I of *Hell*, lines 31–52, and present a very different set of connections:

> And see! not far from where the mountain-side
> First rose, a Leopard, nimble and light and fleet,
> Clothed in a fine furred pelt all dapple-dyed,
>
> Came gambolling out, and skipped before my feet.
>
>   * * *
>   ... I fell to quaking
> At a fresh sight—a Lion in the way.
>
> I saw him coming, swift and savage, making
> For me, head high, with ravenous hunger raving
> So that for dread the very air seemed shaking.
>
>   * * *
> And next, a wolf, gaunt with famished craving
> Lodged ever in her horrible lean flank,
> The ancient cause of many man's enslaving;—
>
> She was the worst ...[2]

According to Sayers's notes at canto's end these beasts "may be identified with Lust, Pride, and Avarice [...]. The gay *Leopard* is the image of the self-indulgent sins— *Incontinence* ; the fierce *Lion*, of the violent sins—*Bestiality* ; the *She-Wolf* of the

---

1   *On Beulah Height* (1998, # 15), and *Arms and the Women: An Elliad* (2000, # 16).

2   Hill, *Under World*, pp. [11], [87], [219], quoting *Dante: Hell* I.31–4, 44–8, 49–52 (p. 2).

malicious sins, which involve *Fraud*'.[1] Hill's readers might not use the same words but surely get the point, and after that pithy pun in the general epigraph need lit-tle encouragement to identify leopard, lion, and wolf among the novel's cast. The identity of the lion is disputable (both investigators and suspects being defensible candidates), while that of the wolf is a spoiler and shouldn't be revealed. The leopard, however (whom Sayers memorably illustrated in a linocut reproduced by Reynolds in *The Passionate Intellect*), is beyond doubt a young miner called Colin Farr, whom DI Pascoe's wife Ellie is teaching Industrial Sociology on a union-sponsored day-re-lease course (the sort of thing promoted in the aftermath of the Strike), and for whom she comes very close to wrecking her marriage.

Her only moment of physical intimacy with Farr is involuntary, a shocking assault in which he thrusts a hand up her skirt, not exactly to grope but to rest still fingers against her, and withdraws it as soon as she slaps him. But she does not stop seeing him, and her long-swallowed rage at the use Mrs Thatcher's government made of the police to protect strike-breakers has brought her affection (rather than her love) for her husband into sustained doubt. An affair and sequent divorce could not in first reading *Under World* be ruled out (the TV Dalziel-&-Pascoe adaptations of the 2000s did separate Peter & Ellie, and real policemen have high divorce rates), and as Ellie's rage and Peter's case, with the leopardly and lustful Farr, all centre on the miners of Burrthorpe, the territories of marriage and investigation are (as in Sayers) deeply fused. The public weal necessarily takes precedence—Peter & Ellie can no more ignore his duty than Peter & Harriet could have gone back to their honeymoon bed ignoring the corpse in their cellar—but the dual connection of case *and* marital crisis with the Strike *and* the use of a Crown service against it, both profoundly public matters, makes for a true fusion. Mining community and investigative or sympathetic outsiders alike must draw deep on themselves, facing memories and present realities with intelligence and care if the case is to be resolved, and the marriage and com-munity survive untainted.

This was not in itself a new departure for Hill, nor the Pascoes. Having dated at university, they met again in *An Advancement of Learning* (1971, # 2)—a novel in evident relation with *Gaudy Night* that consciously moves the academic crime-scene from Oxford to a modern Northern college. In *Ruling Passion* (1973, # 3) a mutually exploratory weekend-visit to friends found the friends murdered and Peter well off his own patch, nominally suspect and utterly without investigative authority, but led to Ellie proposing and Peter accepting. Their marriage, the gestation and birth of their

---

1   *Dante: Hell*, p. 5.

only child Rosie, Peter's promotion to DI, and Ellie's evolutions in politics and ambition variously occur in #s 4–6, while the trope of Ellie's friendship with a suspect first became centrally important in *Deadheads* (1983, #7). Strains within the marriage began to show in *Exit Lines* (1984, # 8) and the very clever, very funny *Child's Play* (1987, # 9), but the precipitation of crisis in *Under World* and its thrilling resonance with public issues of topical importance was an enormous development, and for Hill a breakthrough. He had started *Under World* as # 9, in 1983–4, but it had been forced on hold by the Strike (explaining the three-year gap before *Child's Play*, the actual # 9); maturing on hold, and brought forward again as # 10 as soon as events allowed, *Under World* delivered magnificently on the special investigative *and* marital promise of *An Advancement of Learning*, and renewed Hill's vision of Mid-Yorks..

Perhaps in consequence, the series-novels that followed—*Bones and Silence* (1990, # 11), *Recalled to Life* (1992, # 12), & *Pictures of Perfection* (1994, # 13)— wittingly or otherwise form with *Under World* a remarkable sequence. To single out a run from a series as a sub-series is a common epiphenomenon of serial reading, and perceptions are, to say the least, malleable, so unless there is a clear narrative criterion—a major change in a protagonist's personal life, say, or a master-villain it takes multiple instalments to catch—such singling-out probably tells one more about the reader than the series; and I cannot claim any such singular criterion here. Yet *Pictures of Perfection* not only profoundly fuses territories of investigation and marriage, and invents with a village called Enscombe the funniest, most suasively delightful remaking of Mayhem Parva since *Gaudy Night*, but raises the soiled dead to heavenly union—for all its epigraphs from Austen rather than Dante, a *Paradise* to the *Hell* epigraphised in *Under World*. And looking at them thus, the two intervening novels step smartly into place as Siamese (or Laurel-&-Hardy) purgatories, *Bones and Silence* for Pascoe and *Recalled to Life* for Dalziel, each mediated through a very particular form of doubt acutely attending an individual who matters to their respective well-beings. Peter's purgatory is also Ellie's, *Bones and Silence* seamlessly resuming the fused marital-and-investigative territory of *Under World*, so it too follows where Sayers led. *Recalled to Life* in no sense ignores marriage, but given Dalziel's pre-series divorce and lack (at that stage) of any constant partner, Hill had to substitute his *de facto* marriage to his job as a policeman. The powerful air of Austenite romance invigorating Enscombe and the glorious, *case-solving* marriage with which *Pictures of Perfection* ends thus bind it strongly into a series constant that had reached a new level in *Under World*, and the most sceptical must agree the course of novels # 10–13 is from damnation to redemption.

There is, moreover, a happy bonus for friends of both in taking seriously the cue Hill provided in choosing Sayers's *Hell* as a source of structural epigraphy. Beyond the means of approach it provides to these (and later) novels in a crime series of real merit via the thickened and relit details of Hill's individual books and their sequent modulations of atmosphere, understanding a Dantean sequence to organise novels profoundly engaged with a territorial fusion the Wimseys pioneered goes far to heal the unhappy rift in perception of Sayers's work. Far from respecting the assumed boundaries of detection and Dante, Hill happily lined them up, effectively extending a career that for Sayers was precluded by Dante through a judicious application of Dante himself. It would be silly to think these Dalziel-&-Pascoe books anything like those Sayers might have but didn't write—Hill is himself, and Paton Walsh has taken the 'lost' novels as far (and as well) as they can ever go—but it is not silly to think Hill, like many, indebted to Sayers for a centrally animating series-pulse; nor to contend that Hill uniquely has repaid the debt in extraordinary measure. Through his fierce intertextuality and intensive use of structural epigraphy, Woolf, the anonymous authors of Northern English Mystery cycles, Dickens, and Austen were roped in as needed, and the desire of even serial readers for good mystery and resolution, case by case, was never forgotten; but the path up from the pit, if narrow and twisty, is clear enough to follow, and may be mapped in three steps.

Hill courteously and implacably resists in interview almost any critical enquiry beyond matters of fact, explaining that while he is well aware Parnassian springs *can* be excavated, he would rather not risk turning his own into a muddy pool while he still plans to drink from it. He also says that after more than 20 years of teaching he is happy to pass the baton, and the buck, if one is so oddly disposed as to think such a thing involved. But the evident civility and social responsibility of his self-conception as a novelist, of which his rapid (and shamefully rare) literary response to the Miners' Strike in *Under World* is emblematic, necessarily extends to his reception, and the entrenched British class-hierarchisation of 'literature' over 'genre fiction' is therefore a trouble and annoyance. As a friend of the late Julian Symons, Hill has neither any wish nor the heart to castigate the views expressed in *Bloody Murder*, but his essays reveal complete opposition to the interpretative paradigms Symons imposed.

The problem with that wretchedly influential Penguin is flatly declared in its double subtitle, *From the Detective Story to the Crime Novel: A History*. Like Auden in his famous essay about reading crime writing, 'The Guilty Vicarage' (1948), Symons posits a fundamental difference between the 'detective story', hermetic but English and specifically Golden Age from Victorian sources, and the 'crime novel', supposedly not only hermeneutic but 'American', distinctly post-Golden, and *sui generis*. While I too have no wish to dishonour Symons, whose fictions are very enjoyable, few other writers have in this field so clearly shown what is critically pernicious about any concept of the Golden Age: that what follows must be Fallen. Symons (in a nutshell) allowed strong personal distastes to colour exposition, particularly where his powerful dislike of Sayers and admiration for Christie were concerned,[1] and gave too free a rein to crusty anti-Americanism. He also disdained engagement with literary Modernism as a relevant phenomenon, despite (for example) mentioning Eliot and Faulkner, and the result is a book as skewed as it has been seminal. Relatively uninformed readers in particular tend (justly) to be left with a strong impression of the 'English Golden Ages' of 1890–1914 and 1918–39 as possessed of antique perfections now sadly decayed, and for all Symons's attention to structural differences between 'detective stories' and 'crime novels' he conveys no real sense of how stunningly complex and ethically subtle the evolution thereby summarised has been, and still is.

Most gravely, despite his strong beliefs in the historical specificity of 'detective stories', Symons's failure to confront the interaction of crime writing with Modernism was only part of a wide refusal of context. *Bloody Murder* is also the major source of a common, potted archaeology of crime writing that can be summarised as 'Vidocq, Godwin, Poe, Dickens'. Unless one believes with Symons that 'detective stories' (i) define good crime writing, and (ii) popped out of the later nineteenth century like gods from Titan's ear, there can be no sense in a history that ignores everything from Oedipus to *Jane Eyre* while asserting it has found the headwaters of the Nile in Eugène Vidocq—yet it is the true blight of *Bloody Murder* that it has normalised as 'historical facts' what are actually little more than silly propositions. One can readily grant that a particular form of crime writing featuring an habitual and later professional 'detective' as protagonist grew (from various proximate roots) in the later nineteenth century, shortly after the emergence of detection as a profession, without thereby agreeing that all previous literary crime and criminals are wholly irrelevant. Auden had done so, expressing his strong personal preference for Christie over Chandler but still bringing Attic tragedy into the case. Symons, however, seems on every re-reading more rigidly uninterested in any view wider than his own, and excludes even as passing comparisons pretty much everything history offers that

---

1   See (in whatever edition of *Bloody Murder*, or in the U.S. *Mortal Consequences*) Ch. 9, § (ii), "Van Dyne, Sayers, Christie: two stories end".

preceded his own designated origin. Without rehashing a wearily self-evident case, wishing cannot make it so, and in any scholarly view Symons's refusal to consider Modernism sensibly, not only where Chandler and Faulkner are concerned but with all post-1918 writers and even a figure like Himes,[1] makes his a house built on sand.

Hill, contrariwise, understands his art and craft as literary perennials. In the decade around his decision to become a full-time writer in 1981, while teaching was a habitual response and he remained willing to spend time writing things other than fiction, he produced a number of essays that tell the story, typically for guides of one or another kind to crime as a genre.[2] On the back of *An Advancement of Learning* he was commissioned to produce for Dilys Winn's *Murder Ink: The Mystery Reader's Companion* (1977) a short piece on educational crime, 'The Educator: *The Case of the Screaming Spires*', that omits *Gaudy Night* but conjoins Austen with Christie and was illustrated with a photograph of Oxford graduates at *Encaenia*. For the first edition of the monumental *St James Guide to Crime and Mystery Writers* (1978) he wrote entries on post-war thriller writer Desmond Bagley and crime writers Michael Kenyon & H. R. F. Keating.[3] For two volumes edited by Keating—*Crime Writers* (1978, accompanying a BBC series) and *Whodunit? A Guide to Crime, Suspense & Spy Fiction* (1982)—he wrote pieces on Sherlock Holmes and (tellingly) 'A Pre-History: Crime Fiction Before the 19th Century'. Hill is also credited as one of three collaborators with Keating in producing the major reference section of *Whodunit?*, 'Writers and their Books: A Consumer's Guide', occupying 140 pages and considering some 500 writers across all three titular genres. Later pieces have been more scattered—three for a Boston journal called *The Writer* in 1985, 1988, & 1995, a couple of introductions to reprints of classic works by Kenyon and Hillary Waugh in 1996 & 1999, and a few later morsels—but before relinquishing the *rhetor*'s pointing-stick Hill did make one plain and personal statement of what he thought, in response to an unusual invitation.

Professional crime-reviewer and Yale Professor of History Robin Winks, an annual reader (he says) of some 200 crime novels, wrote in 1985 to his "fifteen favourite living authors" to ask for explanations of "themselves, their work habits, and the words they use as authors".[4] Hill was among 11 respondents whose offerings were

---

1 Chester B. Himes is widely known as African-American, but less widely to have written the Harlem Cycle (1958–69) for Gallimard while living in Paris.

2 All details are in the Bibliography.

3 All survived into the 3rd edition (1991), but that on Keating was dropped from the 4th (1996).

4 Robin Winks, ed., *Colloquium on Crime* (New York: Charles Scribner's Sons, 1986), p. 1.

collected in *Colloquium on Crime* (1986), and his essay 'Looking for a Programme' lays it on the line from the first:

> Chandler is arguably a fine serious novelist; Christie clearly isn't; but in the Pantheon they stand on level plinths. The trouble stems in part from the fundamentalist approach adopted by most historians of the genre. They all set out looking for a common father, a universal Adam who started it all. Godwin's *Caleb Williams* wins the popular vote, though you could with equal justice hop back to Defoe's *Roxana* or Nashe's *The Unfortunate Traveller*, or even *The Canterbury Tales* or *The Odyssey*, in the search for criminality made literary for the reader's delectation. The truth is there is no more a single starting point for modern crime fiction than there is for modern society. Rather, in both cases, for they are curiously interdependent, there is a gradual shift, with the occasional sudden lurch, from one set of attitudes which may be categorized as superstitious, aristocratic, and pastoral, to another which may be categorized as scientific, bourgeois, and urban. In the first condition, society's rules are essentially religious; man defects: God detects. In the second, the rules are secular, and divine detection and retribution, though perhaps still atavistically valued as fail-safes, are by themselves no longer enough. [...]
>
> [...] I still recall with delight as a teen-ager making the earth-shaking discovery that many of the great "serious novelists," classical and modern, were as entertaining and interesting as the crime-writers I already loved. But it took another decade of maturation to reverse the equation and understand that many of the crime writers I had decided to grow out of were still as interesting and entertaining as the "serious novelists" I now revered.
>
> It was this hard-won conclusion that finally released me creatively.[1]

An additional "decade of maturation" after being a teenager gives us Hill perhaps *aetat*. 25–9 in 1962–6, five to nine years after completing National Service and two to six after taking his Oxford degree in English, more-or-less the years in which he started writing. His first novels, completed by the late 1960s, were published in 1970–1, and their bold invocation of canonical texts via titles, epigraphs, and allusions confirms that Hill did indeed then take his own literary potential seriously, as he says.[2] It is also interesting that this essay, written in 1985–6, must date from late in the composition of *Child's Play* (1987) or the interval before resuming work on

---

1 Winks, *Colloquium on Crime*, pp. 150–1,

2 Considering only titles, one can find among Hill's early novels *An Advancement of Learning, A Fairly Dangerous Thing* (1972), *Urn Burial, A Very Good Hater* (1974), & *Another Death in Venice* (1976). Bacon, Pope, Browne, Dr Johnson, & Thomas Mann are not casual sparring-partners.

Under World, and its diction may in its sacred register ("man defects: God detects ... secular ... divine ... revered") already reflect Sayers's *Hell*.

Hill's 'Programme' underwrites his structural epigraphy and allusions in general, insisting on his own behalf as a writer, and in the name of his readers, that Defoe, Nashe, Chaucer, and Homer (not to mention Browne, Dickens, Bacon, Pope, and more or less anyone else, not necessarily in any order) are quite as relevant to the writing *and comprehensible in the reading* of crime writing as they might be to Northrop Frye or Lord David Cecil doing what they did with 'literature'. In the case of *Under World* Virgil's loss of inverted commas is diagnostic, for Hill's simple refusal to recognise any barrier between Mid-Yorks.'s public & criminal or the Pascoes' would-be private & marital travails, and Dante's struggle to survive 'the Pit' with hope and wisdom, honourably makes coextensive the eternal and the contemporary. It needn't—pretentious epigraphy or undue self-esteem are painfully exposed in all genres of fiction—but it does, and the principal reason, crucially, is not due reverence for Dante's ancient greatness but the demanding gravity of the mess in which British miners and police had by an irresponsible and dogmatic government been left to stew. If Dante has nothing to say of this, so much the worse for him: but of course he does, and so did Hill. Something as Bernard Shaw reviewing productions of Shakespeare happily supposed Will and himself on a level footing as playwrights, so Hill more politely introduces himself fictionally to the canonical greats by talking to them as fellow-citizens of another republic than Plato's, and leaves it to his detractors, usually citizens of neither, to explain (if they can) why on earth he should do otherwise.

Grounds are thus laid, especially with the cue to think of Sayers as a Dantean, for refusing to disconnect either canonical and genre fictions, or writing and life. Following the faint hope Hill allowed Peter and Ellie at the end of *Under World* (reminiscent in its desperate truth of Peter Wimsey at the end of *Busman's Honeymoon* burying his head in Harriet's arms as the church clock tolls the time of execution for the man he put in the dock), the next move for serial readers was the title *Bones and Silence*, arrestingly explained on first opening that novel by an epigraph from Virginia Woolf's *The Waves*:

> We insist, it seems, on living. Then again, indifference descends. The roar of the traffic, the passage of undifferentiated faces, this way and that way, drugs me into dreams; rubs features from faces. People might walk through me ... We are only

lightly covered with buttoned cloth; and beneath these pavements are shells, bones and silence.[1]

The cramped imposition of this on the title-page was explained by a lengthy section-epigraph on its own page, God on high proclaiming the badness of humanity and His repentance "That ever I made either man or wife" from 'The Building of the Ark' in the mediaeval York Mysteries. The regional Middle English diction fitted well with Hill's established uses of Yorkshire dialect and colloquialisms in dialogue, and 'Fat Andy' Dalziel has always been easily mistaken for a deity by objects of his wrath. Later section-epigraphs raid other Cycles and this intertext seems the more important, especially when the action gloriously promises, then delivers on, the prospect of Dalziel truly playing God in a town-processional performance of those very Mysteries. One Philip Swain, a suspiciously smooth talker just contracted to resurface the car-park at Police HQ and perhaps responsible for a string of deaths and disappearances, is promptly cast as Lucifer, York Minster sets the stage, and all is enlivened by the Master of Ceremonies, Eileen Chung, an exotic incomer to Mid-Yorks. as Artistic Director of the local playhouse, after whose nubile thespian energy a performative Dalziel, convalescent Pascoe, and even a tolerant, guilt-stricken Ellie, happily lust.

But Virginia Woolf and the suicide that her haunting passage from *The Waves* anticipates were established first, and immediately following the first of the seven section-epigraphs from the Mysteries comes an anonymous letter dated January 1st from a woman announcing her decision to kill herself. Addressed (it turns out) to Dalziel, it shortly lands as make-work in Pascoe's lap, and further letters open each section after its mediaeval epigraph, so the absurd, irresolvable conundrum is never forgotten even as the battle of God and Lucifer is literalised by Dalziel and Swain, who would have us believe him no more than his pastoral name suggests. For Pascoe, unable to help Dalziel as he would, the threatened suicide becomes a haunting agony of self-mistrust—if he cannot even solve this, what can he do?—that Ellie senses without really understanding. So things draw out to their ends, with a stunning resolution in the main case that miraculously allows both God and Lucifer to play their parts; but behind it, mid-performance, the other shoe drops, shifting all to shattered tragedy. Identity would be a spoiler, but the datum explaining the lacerating *anagnorisis* for both Peter and Ellie is friendship with the suicide, and the failure of both to recognise *extremis*.

So it often is, with suicide, for those left to mourn the waste, but Peter and Ellie do

---

1 Reginald Hill, *Bones and Silence* (London: HarperCollins, 1990), t.-p. (p. [3]), quoting Virginia Woolf, *The Waves* (1931; Harmondsworth: Penguin, 1964), pp. 96–7; Bernard is speaking.

have one another; if mutual guilt is devastating it is also mutually apparent. Neither is left as Leonard Woolf was in 1941, strangely alone after all had passed, yet the shades of Virginia Woolf's fictitious but convincingly blind couples are a comfort, an acknowledgement of human limitations and inscrutabilities beyond that runs seditiously counter to the divine omniscience and decisive actions of God and Andrew Dalziel. He too after his triumph over crime and Lucifer must learn some limitations from old bones beneath today's pavement. Long divorced and childless, Dalziel's affections are reserved (after god-daughter Rosie Pascoe's share) for the police service to which he has given his adult life and seen change past recognition. His old mentor Wally Tallantyre, with whom he first worked a major case, the 'Mickledore Hall Murder' of 1963, has pride of place in his pantheon—but now (in *Recalled to Life*) one convicted killer, American nanny Cissy Kohler, has been released after a TV documentary and campaign, and the late Tallantyre is set to be a scapegoat for the Inquiry, his widow's plight and Dalziel's rage notwithstanding.

The complex details of what truly happened and was thought to have happened at Mickledore Hall are unimportant here, save that while the Inquiry is thoroughly contemporary, invoking a sequence of real Inquiries into IRA convictions that began in the 1980s, the crime inquired into epitomises isolated stately-home murder and is detailed in 'Part the First: Golden Age'. Later parts head in other directions, bearing the names 'Golden Bough', 'Golden Apple', 'Golden Grove', & 'Golden Boy', but the critical reference of 'Golden Age' explicitly signals many overlapping evolutions from 'detective stories' to 'crime novels'. After Dalziel's performance as God in *Bones and Silence* Hill also needed to shift towards the secular, and as well as linking the Mickledore Hall Murder to the Profumo Scandal (with which it coincided) his title and epigraphs invoke neither heaven nor hell, but Dickens:

> *'You had abandoned all hope of being dug out?'*
> *'Long ago.'*
> *'You know that you are recalled to life?'*
> *'They tell me so.'*
> *'I hope you care to live?'*
> *'I can't say.'*[1]

This general epigraph is once again fitted unconventionally into a title-page, in a curious centred & italicised form with the following page given over to a two-line 'Author's Note' identifying the epigraphic source, which suggests an authorial con-

---

1   Hill, *Recalled to Life* (London: HarperCollins, 1992), t.-p. (p. [3]), quoting Charles Dickens, *A Tale of Two Cities* (1859; New York: Signet Classics, 1960), p. 18 (Book I, Ch. 3 [The Night Shadows]).

cern to oblige readers' attentions to the intertext. Those who obey are immediately rewarded, for the novel begins with a thumping thematic pun—"*It was the best of crimes, it was the worst of crimes*"[1]—and (allowing New York to stand in for Paris) delivers on it with a story best negotiated through clear memory of both Dr Manette's long experience of wrongful imprisonment and Sidney Carton's self-sacrifice with its probable explanation. The allusive structure also brings with it some airs of Revolutionary Paris (taken by Dickens from Carlyle) that transfer nicely to Dalziel's maverick rampage off-patch in the US. In the end, as befits the Dickensian, there is more resolution than revolution, and Dalziel is better able than Pascoe to save his friend, but if the moral of *Bones and Silence* is that evil may be damned but you cannot always redeem the good, the moral of *Recalled to Life* is that you may redeem the good but cannot always secure the damnation of evil.

Larger arguments aside, the tenor of both novels can properly be called purgatorial in the secularised sense, places of trial and suffering that one must hope have some purpose, and seek to endure. The overt cosmography of the Mysteries and the stress on revival and rebirth in Hill's Dickensian choices keep a sacred awareness alive throughout, but in *Recalled to Life* negations of the post-Golden as fallen or devolved also begin to revision the ascent from pit to perfection as chronological and relative rather than moral or absolute. The Christian extremes, that is, acquire less dizzying perspectives as part of a modernisation that subsumes and qualifies their absoluteness without dismissing their values, a trick Hill manages partly through multiple narrative framing. The times/crimes pun, for example, is not ostensibly his, but quotes a 'published history' of the Mickledore sensation by a witness who later appears in person for re-interview. *Bones and Silence* similarly offers a staggered opening with double epigraphs and will-be suicide's letter, and both summon the famous barrage of letters and diary-entries opening *Busman's Honeymoon*, where the trope was, if not invented, enormously popularised. In their iterative fragmentation such beginnings (as much as the famous multiple ending of Melville's *Moby Dick*) signal a Modernist enterprise: the trope wasn't new, but its proliferation after *c.*1900 across the literary genres (a process leading eventually to Beckett's astonishing dramaturgy) is distinctive. Its primary function of course is to posit other, anomalous voices and registers within a narrative, and to mimic the documentary shuffle whereby modern humans generally make sense of their own lives, but its inherent capacity to register doubts, hesitations, rewrites, and ambiguities receives in crime writing a special *frisson*.

---

1   Hill, *Recalled to Life*, p. [9], modulating the opening sentence of *A Tale of Two Cities*, "It was the best of times ..." &c..

Sayers's assemblage in *Busman's Honeymoon* is chronological and primarily narrative, however allusive to the eighteenth-century epistolary novel. Hill's, however, explicitly dips back into history (the book about the Mickledore case was published between ancient crime and present Inquiry) and so requires a different kind of triangulation. How good a writer was this witness? and what axes had he to grind? Implicitly, also, one might ask about Dickens's agendas, or Hill's—and amid the literariness and affectionate respect for Dalziel in purgatory there are blazes of satire about the British propensity to whitewash whitewash as all quite right too. Within this particular Dantean sub-sequence the widening flurry of perspectives both echoes Sayers's movement through structural epigraphy and *Busman's Honeymoon* to break out of her Golden-Age Handcuffs, and extends further than Sayers (or Wimsey) was willing to allow a relativity of judgement. Absolutes and absolution are no longer affordable save as luxuries, and even then remain millstones, in keeping with the shift of background intertext from Dantean or mediaeval visions of truth to Victorian and Modernist apprehensions of contingency. In other hands such painful progress has too often granted moral licence, but Hill knew precisely what he could now achieve both with license and with a happy dose of whimsy.

During the early afternoon of 19th August 1987 an unemployed labourer called Michael Ryan walked through the town of Hungerford in Berkshire with (among other weapons) an AK-47 Assault Rifle and a Beretta pistol, killing 16 and wounding 15 before shooting himself. It was Britain's introduction to 'spree killing' or 'going postal', but stunning as the massacre was, the revenge psychology of such singular self-/destruction was far less disturbing than the serial killing with which Hill (like many crime writers) had struggled since the late 1970s.[1] Even the giggling amorality of the berserker state in its chance targeting was already familiar through video-gaming and the curious paramilitary 'paint-balling' weekends that had become a feature of Yuppie R. & R. in the 1980s. Only Hill, however, would have noticed that Hungerford stood on the borders of Austenite Hampshire, home of all those "Country Village[s]" with "Three or four Families" that are "the very thing to work on"—a famous quotation from Austen's letters he used in 'The Educator'—and then had the glorious temerity to connect this coincidence with the recurrent need to do something serious about the continuing, supposed attractions of Mayhem Parva. The result was an exceptional, additional dale, the valley of the River Een, burgeoning in Mid-Yorks., as that county itself had bloomed within the real ridings of Yorkshire; and in

1   See 'Of Serial Readers'.

Eendale lies the distinctly fairy-tale village of Enscombe.1 Its utter improbability in Yorkshire is indicated by the mild consideration that its pub, the Morris Men's Rest, features a sign showing not the folksy dancers of pastoral imaginings after a hard day working the tourist trade but pre-Raphaelite craftsman William Morris, still famous for his fabric- and paper-prints and of much proto-Modernist interest besides.

Under World having been an inferno for everybody, and the Siamese purgatorios having applied to Dalziel and the Pascoes, attention had also to turn to the third in Hill's Unholy Trinity of detectives, DS Edgar Wield. Introduced in *A Pinch of Snuff* (1978, # 5) as a necessary underling following Pascoe's marriage and promotion to DI, Wield's major claim to fame had been his rugosity of feature, an ugliness sufficient even in the face of Dalziel's gargantuan proportions to justify their joint comparison to Godzilla and King Kong. Just as entertainingly and considerably more subtly, Wield had always used his savage appearance to hide the dangerous fact that he is gay, and after some close-run things following a 'don't ask, don't tell' policy at work, necessity caught up with him in *Child's Play* (1987, # 9) :

> Dalziel's face across the table looked about as sympathetic as a prison wall. But it was not sympathy he wanted, Wield reminded himself. It was the right to be himself. He thought of the effect saying this was likely to produce on Dalziel and felt his courage ebb. He had to admit it—the man terrified him! Here before him in awful visible form, was embodied all the mockery, scorn, and scatological abuse which he had always feared from the police hierarchy. At least, to start with Dalziel was to start with the worst.
>
> He drew a deep breath and said, 'I want to tell you. I'm a homosexual.'
>
> 'Oh aye,' said Dalziel, 'You've not just found out, have you?'
>
> 'No,' said Wield, taken aback. 'I've always known.'
>
> 'That's all right, then,' said Dalziel equably. 'I'd have been worried else that I'd not mentioned it to you.'2

Wield's drop-jawed doubletake was and is, much to Hill's credit, echoed by most readers, Dalziel the Tolerant being a little too close, every which way, to the bone. But the point of course is only partly the tolerance; it is also that Dalziel "like power

1   The etymology of this improbable Yorskhire name may be from *Enna's Combe*, "suggesting a connection with the Sicilian vale where Prosperpine, gathering flowers, herself a fairer flower, by gloomy Dis was gathered", or from OE *entisc cuma*, 'the monstrous visitor'. See Hill, *Pictures of Perfection* (London: HarperCollins, 1994), p. 271.

2   Reginald Hill, *Child's Play* (London: Collins, 1987), p. 259).

divine / hath look'd upon [Wield's] passes",[1] and cared not a jot so long as they do not interfere with his sergeant's righteous efficiency as a policeman. Law for Dalziel comes a long way before prejudice, and he knows well enough to distinguish the two without ever being unrealistic—hence his long complicity in Wield's mask of silence.

Once out to his superiors (and the revelation to Peter, but not Ellie, Pascoe is a gem of characterisation), Wield was released in the sequent *Inferno* and *Purgatorios* (#s 10–12) to grow into genuine friendship with both Pascoes and even to some extent Dalziel, now politically respectable to Wield in a surprising new way. His romantic status thus moved up a necessary series agenda, for otherwise the flow of comic metaphor about his landslide of a face would threaten imbalance of humanity (or 'roundedness') too close to the heart of the procedural action each case must generate, and each novel acknowledge. Quite how Hill, musing on Austen and the late Michael Ryan, managed to fuse all this together into a *Paradiso* remains a miracle of art, and *Pictures of Perfection* has a serious claim to be the finest post-Modern crime novel yet written—a spangled farrago of disparate material from every part of several canons that, ludicrously, joyously, coheres with shocking density around a terminal marriage. To reveal almost anything about the house-of-cards Hill somehow casts in best modern bronze is a spoiler, for each seemingly random airborne trajectory of a card, and its subsequent bronzing into perfect place, is a narrative delight. But I have already implicitly blown one gaff and must stay that course, for the "Oh, Mr. D'Arcy!" (or even "Oh, Beatrice!") engagement with which the novel ends—unbelievably and with brazen, creative cheek resolving at least three plots that have cheerfully imbrangled themselves during the hours of Wield's investigations in Enscombe—is Wield's, to Edwin Digweed, sometime solicitor and antiquarian bookseller of that parish.

Trying to describe a novel that begins with what appears to be Hungerford-goes-Mid-Yorkshire and triumphantly ends with a gay betrothal at the squire's annual ceremony for receiving rents is (as Francis Thompson once said of imitating Coleridge) like trying to pack jellyfish in hampers. Fortunately, all that truly matters here are the facts that within the conjoined territories of detection and marriage Hill manages a memorable (and laugh-out-loud) eucatastrophe, and that in doing so he capped a potent movement within his primary series away from an explicit *Hell* to a very peculiar but indubitable paradise:

---

1 Shakespeare, *Measure for Measure* 5.1.369–70.

The Bishop sipped his Screwdriver and said, 'Old Charley used to claim, when the port had been round a few times, that after the Fall God decided to have a second shot, learning from the failure of the first. This time He created a man who was hard of head, blunt of speech, knew which side his bread was buttered on, and above all took no notice of women. Then God sent him forth to multiply in York-shire. But after a while he got to worrying he'd left something out—imagination, invention, fancy, call it what you will. So he grabbed a nice handful of this, intend-ing to scatter it thinly over the county. Only it was a batch He'd just made and it was still damp, so instead of scattering, it all landed in a single lump, and that was where they built Enscombe!'[1]

So is paradise regained, not as another Mayhem Parva, but rather, like Paggleham (if more magical, and always willing to stand in for Brigadoon), a real village with some unusual but not incredible, exaggerated but not unrecognisable, and singularly amusing inhabitants who are sufficiently part of Mid-Yorkshire's reality to have lives and concerns that matter. Archetype within archetype and inwoven meta-argument coalesce, the permissive Enscombe fusing with both a wilful transcending of Gold-en-Age values lost to modernity, and a celebration of partnership as the necessary balance for detection. Wield could no more give up his police career for Digweed than Digweed could honourably or lovingly ask him to do so, and the echo of their mutuality with Peter Wimsey's determination that marriage to him should not stop Harriet Vane writing crime fiction is a true multiple resonance.

Enscombe and Wield, unlike Paggleham and the Wimseys, survived their encoun-ter with Dante, and in the nature of a series still going strong the perfections of Enscombe have had to face challenges from which Paradise has always been supposed free. For all its glory and licence, both abattoirs and the consequences of Thatcherism and the CAP for rural life have been of its Mid-Yorks. substance from the first, and Wield's life there has no more been all poppies and lilies than any surviving sexual and life-partnership of professionals. Much delightful detail in marital conversations also suggests that if Hill is not a closet fan of the Wimseys, or at least Sayers, he has put his own exactly equal status as an Oxford graduate to close pursuit of very similar wisdoms. Had Sayers lived in Mid-Yorks. in Hill's post-war century she might not have felt that translating Dante and pursuing her respectful creation of the Wimseys were such disparate endeavours.

---

1   Reginald Hill, *Pictures of Perfection* (London: HarperCollins, 1994), p. 33.

3. Of Pseudonyms and Sentiment

Nora Roberts, J. D. Robb, and the Imperative Mood

What should one make of Lieutenant Eve Dallas, Homicide shift commander for the New York Police & Security Department in the late 2050s, in (to date) 23 ½ novels and three novellas by J. D. Robb?[1] As unbeatable top cop, hard-case scourge of murderers, gruffly kind senior partner of soft-focus sidekick Delia Peabody, and unconventional wife of ludicrously handsome ex-criminal billionaire industrialist Roarke, one might think Eve only a mildly diverting collage of demi-feminised clichés. Such unkind judgement might also note that 'J. D. Robb' is a pseudonym of Nora Roberts, by most measures the world's best-selling novelist since *c*.2000, with more than 300 million copies of some 160 novels, overwhelmingly Romance fiction, in print—the implicit relevance being that in Romance (more than most genres) formula rules supreme and clichés are only to be expected. One should thus (such judgement continues) make little of Eve, save perhaps to note as no mean authorial feat that she successfully fuses Romance with Crime *and* SF, selling to fans of all three.

That feat should be admitted. Modern prose Romance has a fearsome reputation, supposed by almost all to be written and read exclusively by women. That was never true of the older, protean genre fused with epic from Homer to Milton, and with the novel as soon as it came hot from the press, but Modern Mills & Boon or Silhouette titles, where Roberts began, really do seem mostly female productions for female consumption. And even if they have more male readers (and perhaps writers) than admit to it, gendered perceptions mean that in developing a Crime career Roberts could not rely on cross-genre appeal. Successful in Romance as she was by 1994–5,[2] she needed to adopt a pseudonym for the Eve Dallas series,[3] and usually that would be

1 The half is *Remember When* (2003) by 'Nora Roberts & J. D. Robb'; Eve appears only in part 2.

2 Roberts had by 1994 won at least 11 Romance Writers of America Golden Medallions (later RITA awards), and in 1988 became the founding inductee of the RWA Hall of Fame.

3 According to *The Official Nora Roberts Companion*, p. 286, Roberts "resisted getting a pseudonym for years"; her change of heart was linked to her move from the Berkley to Putnam colophons, and hardcover issues.

that—'two' authors marketed separately, to stand or fall with readers as they may.

But Robb and Roberts have become a striking instance of an always interesting phenomenon, a successful pseudonym of a successful author. Eve's adventures now appear as by 'Nora Roberts *writing as* J. D. Robb',[1] and the time may come when her publishers (without whose help one does not sell 300m copies of anything) decide 'Robb' is no longer necessary, absorbing her back into 'Nora Roberts'. But the book market, always an economic oddity,[2] is changing fast, and commercial use of pseudonyms for brand-protection (mocked by Iain Banks in his SF *alter ego* Iain M. Banks) may change too. 'Nora Roberts' has become a global brand with its own 'NR' colophon indicating a genuine work, and her effect on the market is strikingly indicated by the hardback issue since *c.*1998 of earlier Roberts paperback originals, and the introduction from 2004 of hardback first editions of Robb.[3] Such tranching is normal in some genres with new fiction, but has always been very limited in Romance while few books of *any* kind appear in hardback a decade after a paperback first edition. Nor is this simply ultra-efficient commercial exploitation, for Roberts has won sales by transforming herself from a good writer of Romances into something more—and Robb has been central to that process.

For one thing, Robb is a serial writer, which Roberts despite a fondness for trying them cannot be.[4] Romance novels are in their generic nature incapable of forming true series (with a running cast and constant locale), for each plot must drive to the protagonist's tall, dark, & handsome union, after which new lovers-to-be are needed. Even generational sagas like *Poldark* or *The Mallen Streak* that repeatedly deploy Romance plots and dialogue originated as mere print tetralogy and trilogy (by Winston Graham[5] and Catherine Cookson respectively) before becoming extended TV series, closer to soap opera than Romance. Yet well before beginning, as Robb, her distinct serial development in Crime, where sequent investigations offer an ideal

1   There is now a standard abbreviation, 'w/a', based on the retail formula 'trading as' (Joe Bloggs t/a 'Joe's Juices').

2   Although books are bought in the same way as food, they are not commodities and are not consumed. In many ways it makes more sense to see the purchase of a book as renting the text, but the resaleability of books is then anomalous. See William St Clair, *The Reading Nation in the Romantic Age* (Cambridge: Cambridge University Press, 2004), Chs 1–4.

3   Roberts first went hardback in 1992 with *Honest Illusions*.

4   Roberts has written many trilogies and several 'series', typically dealing with siblings—'The Stanislaskis' & "The Calhoun Women' have 5 books each, 'The MacGregors' has 9—but these remain more like extended 'Aga sagas' than true series.

5   Graham's tetralogy was published 1945–53; after Poldark's TV success he wrote a further eight, published 1973–2002.

series structure, Roberts had been showing how the single Romance novel can be stretched into a kind of Bildungsroman (or 'novel of education') following a protagonist through mistaken liaisons to a 'true' match, or a closet 'Aga Saga', sequencing generational episodes through successive women ruling a family hearth. Improving on her Crime–Romance mix of the 1980s, represented in its Silhouette phase by *Storm Warning* (1984) & *Risky Business* (1986), and in its early Bantam phase by *Sacred Sins* (1987) & *Brazen Virtue* (1988), later Bantam novels like *Sweet Revenge* (1989) and *Public Secrets* (1990) trace women from compromised birth and early victimisation or abuse to psychologically complex and haunted adulthood; a mature sexual relationship brings relief only after psychic combat with memory and conflict with some remnant or revenant of the childhood wound. In these classy polygeneric fusions, the original crime suffered by the protagonist, its damaging recurrence, and her romantic liberation with a proper lover are seamlessly and intelligently merged in plots that if never marketed as Crime surely qualify as both Crime and Romance. Risking narrative complexity, Roberts also developed Bildungsromance dimensions by insetting systematic flashbacks or other tessellations generated by the plot. In *Genuine Lies* (1991) the trigger is the protagonist's profession as a celebrity biographer, and in both *Divine Evil* (1992) and *Carnal Innocence* (1992) a lurking menace (satanism, a serial killer) in the hometown to which professional and personal crisis brings an artist (sculptor, violinist) of genuine talent. All these novels vary in location, some jet-setting, some settling to one US state, and Roberts's talent for evoking place is important, as it would prove (true to Crime writing's obsessions) in the oppressively urban New York of Eve Dallas.

Once Eve was underway crime also moved to the fore of Roberts's Romances. In *Montana Sky* (1996, filmed 2007), one of her first mass-market cross-over breakthroughs, three daughters running a cattle-ranch face stalking by one's abusive ex-husband *and* an emergent serial killer.[1] Nor can Romance and Crime sensibly be separated in *Sanctuary* (1997), *Blue Smoke* (2005, filmed 2007), or *Angels Fall* (2006, filmed 2007),[2] in which a lunatic stalker, a peculiarly unpleasant arsonist, and a self-protecting villain-in-authority do their damnedest, like Frankenstein's monster, to usurp with vengeful death the bed where children may be made. Some Roberts sits slightly oddly with the Robbs on my Crime shelves, but these novels can take places there without deferring to any purists of the genre. The historicist tendencies of both

---

1   *Montana Sky* may also owe something to Jane Smiley's celebrated redaction of *King Lear*, *A Thousand Acres* (1991, filmed 1997).

2   The films were all made by the Lifetime Movie Channel and first screened in Jan.–Feb. 2007.

Crime and Romance also happily fuse with the ghost story in *Midnight Bayou* (2001), where the only serious crime is a century old but vividly present, and the Romance plot encompasses the male lead's haunted, preternaturally real dreams of pregnancy and childbirth—given the New Orleans setting, a riff on Caribbean practices of *couvade* as well as a very funny take on feminist slogans.[1]

Roberts, that is, might be said to have achieved her commercial eminence not only through a clear increase in the quality and range of her craft, but by developing branded identities in two major genres and working against strongly entrenched market perceptions to conjoin readerships. Breaking out of the (supposedly) sharply circumscribed Romance market to sit, with Robb, front-and-centre on bookshop and airport-kiosk racks of new bestsellers, Roberts has in some ways done for Romance what the hypercelebrity of Harry Potter has done for Children's Literature, making it acceptable fare for reading adults in general. On-line reviews at Amazon.com and other commercial websites suggest a growing number of male readers, and by definition more who are willing to acknowledge it, insisting on Roberts as an enjoyable, often thought-provoking novelist without reference to genre. All this is well and good—the habitual contempt of men and literati for the readership of Mills & Boon or Silhouette has never been attractive—but intriguing questions arise, about Roberts's need to create Eve Dallas, and about Robb's narrative territory, a sustained marriage of professionals whose work occasions emotional friction and ethical conflict. This is historically where some of the best crime writing prowls, not at all where romance saunters—and for the same structural reasons that preclude Romance series—but it is where Robb/erts has taken Romance, with rather more than entertaining and commercially fabulous results.

Romance is a confusing word. The adjectival sense 'derived from Roman Latin' is clear ('Romance languages'), and lax application to film, distinguishing love stories from action adventures, is merely commercial convenience, but between Rome and the cinema lies a bewildering historical jumble. In older literary criticism and many dictionary definitions 'romance' is specified as a later mediaeval genre, long narratives of chivalric adventure emerging with the astonishing body of Arthurian materials generated in the wake of Geoffrey of Monmouth's *History of the Kings of Britain* (written in the 1130s). These were 'romances' partly because they were written in Romance languages, the vernaculars we now call French and Spanish, not

---

1   *Couvade* is a cultural practice in which a husband takes to his bed during his wife's accouchement and sympathetically mimics the behaviours and pains of childbirth.

in the official, pre-eminent Latin of history and theology. The presence of love and sexual desire in tales of Tristan and Isolde, Guinevere and Lancelot, Sir Gawain and the lady who so insistently offers him her girdle, gives the term its modern generic 'definition', but in all these stories love is set against a history (and therefore politics) that modern readers usually fail to recognise; there are also connections with classical epic, especially the tale of Aeneas and Dido in Virgil's *Aeneid*, that should not be ignored. More recent scholars, notably Colin Burrow in *Epic Romance: Homer to Milton* (1993) and Francis Ingledew in *'Sir Gawain and the Green Knight' and the Order of the Garter* (2006), have opened the door to a much more integrated view, both insisting (though in very different ways) that what has been dismissed as 'romance' (fictions of love) needs to be understood as intrinsically historical and political (fictions of state). The love stories, that is, do not function as escapism either for protagonists or readers, but confront both with choices and consequences that ramify directly from the personal to the civil and national.

In this light the epic course of imperial history, from Troy to Rome and Britain, is recorded in literature as tragic romance. Cuckolded Menelaus launched a thousand ships after Helen, Aeneas abandoned Dido to suicide and founded what became Rome, Lucrece gave her chastity and life to make the republic, and King Arthur (according to Geoffrey a direct descendant of Trojans) had to deal in various versions of many tales with Morgan, mother of his patricidal nephew or incestuous son Mordred, and/or the adulterous Guinevere, in the end coming through them to the ruination of self and kingdom. Virgil and Shakespeare between them suggest much of what matters in the pattern, Virgil (translated by Dryden) just after the moment of Dido's stormy surrender to lust:

> The queen, whom sense of honor could not move,
> No longer made a secret of her love,
> But call'd it marriage, by that specious name
> To veil the crime and sanctify the shame.[1]

and Shakespeare in the last couplet of *Lucrece*:

> The Romans plausibly did give consent
> To Tarquin's everlasting banishment.[2]

In both highly mythologised historical episodes, proto-imperial change rides on the

---

1   *Virgil's Aeneid* (1697), IV.247–50, at:▣ http://darkwing.uoregon.edu/~rbear/dryden/book4.html
2   William Shakespeare, *Lucrece* (1594), ll. 1854–5; see also the introduction and notes in Colin Burrow's excellent *Complete Sonnets and Poems* (Oxford: OUP, 2002).

suicide of a 'fallen' woman. Dido willingly lay with Aeneas, Lucrece was raped by Tarquin, but both responded to male post-coital abandonment with anguished suicide intended as self-restoration of integrity, and provoked political fate. Moving forwards with Rome's star in his eyes, choosing imperial epic over domestic romance, Aeneas left behind a queenless Carthage that became Rome's greatest enemy, and took with him a bad conscience (the juxtaposition here of 'marriage' and 'crime' begging the nasty question). Tarquin took Lucrece, choosing the imperative over the interrogative mood, and his disregard for her consent threw his family out of power when the Romans, considering his violence and her suicide, "plausibly did give consent" to banish all royal Tarquins and become a republic instead. Despite their modulated differences, in both episodes (as in Arthur's and Lancelot's various sexual encounters) romance and epic are opposed and romance loses, leaving true love as the price of regnal destiny or rule as the cost of false love.

In Virgil, writing to glorify the nascent imperium of Augustus Caesar, the political equations were and still are writ large, but the equivalent epic and political signs in the Arthurian 'romances' are now lost on most readers. Despite Arthur's still potent status as a British national hero, erasure from all but scholarly knowledge of the political structures and realities in which these 'epic romances' functioned leaves their chivalric love stories as only that, lacking even the civic resonance of *Romeo and Juliet*. And the later one looks, the blurrier things get, in Ariosto, Tasso, Spenser, and even Milton, where the state-changing fallen woman of romance takes her Christian place as Eve, apple-core to hand, headed for the Gates of Eden. But proper as it is for Adam to be with her, in so far as *Paradise Lost* is (however sacred) also an epic and a romance, sustained and fruitful union is the topos of Aeneas and Lavinia (his eventual wife), not Aeneas and Dido, and like Rome happens only implicitly, after the end of the poet's tale. Dressed for tragedy but balanced within and pivotal to the overall epic narratives, romance had played a critical part in the highest forms of cultural and political self-explanation, but with the Renaissance birth of the nation-state and precipitation of individual citizenship the formula catastrophically lost cohesion.

This clarifies the fallen state of modern Romance novels, which in pure form do not even flirt with tragedy, let alone desire political change. Cut free from all but personal meaning, and laden with rhetorics of romantic destiny as sugary as they are thin, the genre at its worst trades remorselessly on the tug-of-opposites transforming Tall, Dark, & Handsome-But-Trustless into Mr Right. If Rome had depended on a Barbara Cartland man, Dido would have died a grandmother with Aeneas doting by her side; the only empires in modern Romance are period frames or commercial, and a happy ending is an iron guarantee—good for tired readers wanting only a fix, but no condition of art. That in turn clarifies Roberts's strategy, both as herself and as Robb. Even she could not simply abandon the happy ending without alienating very many readers, but she could modulate it, and by introducing contextual patterns of criminal loss and murderous violence set it as an intaglio design against a far darker background. A series, moreover, requires thoughtful and systematic modulation of endings far more than a sequence of single novels, and in an odd, interesting way the very scale of the clichés packed into the Eve Dallas series, above all killer-handsome and industrially baronial Roarke, bring a much larger civil, and sometimes national or global world into play, as do the best of Eve's cases, jointly restoring something of the political.

It is tempting, given Roarke's gargantuan industrial and real-estate empire, to claim it as a coextensive imperial restoration, but there is a better candidate, as evident in Roberts as Robb. Given the fate of women in classical and mediaeval romance, it isn't surprising most modern female writers of Romance are happy to let Rome go hang and bother the imperial—but the imperative mood of male command and pro-hibition has gone nowhere, and their women, feisty or delicate, are still persistently on the wrong end of it. Rutting machismo and female coquettishness, it seems, yet require that women be literally swept off their feet, overpowered and denied voli-tion—a scenario rescued (after a fashion) by the woman's implicit or retrospective consent, but uncomfortably close to the typical self-justification of rapists and persist-ently valorising physical arousal over mental hesitation or refusal, which side-steps 'informed' consent. These male imperialisms are (with commercial formulaism) the great reason for the low modern status of Romance, understandably drawing feminist ire and putting off most reconstructed male readers who sample the genre.

Setting aside for a moment my disinclination to give away spoilers, the potential severity of this problem with imperative moods can be brought into sharp focus. Roberts's *Sanctuary* (1997, filmed 2001[1]) dates from early in the Robb series, and at 500 pages seems another solid increment in grounding and rounding the genre. The title names a barrier island off the Georgian coast, where the surviving Hathaways run a hotel: father Sam, son Brian, and daughters Jo Ellen and Alexa (Lexy). Twenty years ago, with the children aged 10, 8, and 4, mother Annabelle vanished without trace. Annabelle's cousin Kate moved in to raise them and has stayed, holding all together, but the four Hathaways believe Annabelle deserted them and remain deeply traumatised. Sam has been stone-absent ever since, walking the beautiful woods and

---

1   The film was a CBS TV movie first broadcast on 28 February 2001.

coves of the island in grief and utterly neglecting his children. Brian too runs on autopilot, using the kitchen where he lovingly and skilfully cooks much as his father uses the island. Jo Ellen (the protagonist) left to establish herself as a photographer, and succeeded, but has returned after a breakdown to seek sanctuary. Alexa always secretly blamed herself, thinking a third child had driven her mother away, and compulsively acts out her self-loathing; she too left, to act in New York, but found the going too hard and returned to Sanctuary some while before to wait tables and sulk. The necessary cast is rounded out by local handyman Giff Verdon, new island doctor Kirby Fitzsimmons, and Nathan Delaney (the antagonist), a tourist's-child playmate of the Hathaways in the summer Annabelle disappeared, who has returned to visit following the accidental deaths of his parents and brother.

The Romance half of the plot is easily dealt with: Brian gets Kirby, Alexa gets Giff, Jo Ellen gets Nathan, and Sam and Kate might make it sometime after the last page should either come into a lick of sense. Nor is there any problem with most of the craft in the novel—description is strong, especially of cove, forest, and swamp, all well-wrapped in Southern heat, while individually the Hathaways, Giff, and Kirby are perfectly interesting and workable. But Nathan and the Crime plot are another story altogether. He discovered, among his father's papers, a journal and photographs making it clear that daddy David Delaney was the cold-blooded, wholly amoral abductor, rapist, and murderer of Annabelle, and it is this that brings Nathan back to Sanctuary with some notion of making amends. Most of this data is withheld until late on, and its ethics suspended—necessarily so, for after Nathan found the evidence he allowed his brother Kyle angrily to talk him out of reporting it to the police, then to steal it. Now presuming it all destroyed by Kyle, who drowned while drunk, and making no mention of this recent family revelation and fight to anyone as relevant to his brother's death, he continues schtumm. But as it happens Kyle faked his death, and aims to emulate his dad. He began stalking Jo Ellen (who strongly resembles her mother), sending her candids of herself and planting a paternal study of her mother's nude corpse where she will stumble on it. During her brief hospitalisation for a consequent hysterical breakdown he retrieved the print, so she is left uncertain of its reality and her own sanity. Disguised as a summer visitor among the Sanctuary tourists, he invisibly stalks the island, abducting, raping, and killing two women—a friend of the Hathaways and a tourist. The friend he disposes of successfully, as his father did Annabelle, via the alligators in the island's swamp, so that everyone again, despite their misgivings (and presumable knowledge of alligators), concludes she has flitted off. The tourist's corpse, however, is washed out by heavy rain with clear marks of strangulation, and found by Jo Ellen and Nathan.

Playing hardball as a reader, Nathan is not simply in trouble, but morally null. Legally speaking, one might push not only for accessory after the fact in Annabelle's murder but accessory, however unwitting, before the fact in the present murders. Humanely speaking, he has over several weeks, while keeping Jo Ellen in ignorance and watching her and everyone's continuing suffering, nevertheless encouraged her to fall for him, and repeatedly had sex with her both for the personal release and as insurance against the hatreds and convulsions he knows confession will induce. Knowing her to have been stalked by a photographer, he nevertheless thinks it funny to 'rile' her (that is, scare, insult, outrage, and humiliate) by taking a photo of her sprawled post-coitally, and fancies it extremely clever of himself to use a roll of her film with work already on it, so that she cannot recontrol her image and dignity by exposing the undeveloped roll except at professional and emotional cost. Confronted with the tourist's corpse, he decides he must be responsible for the murders himself, and runs away for more than a week to have medical tests, leaving and sending Jo Ellen no word. Cleared by the neurologists he returns, screwing up 'courage' (if one is willing to call it that) finally to tell the Hathaways what he knows, goes to the house, and finds not surprisingly that he gets Jo Ellen's cold shoulder—which as she is working in her darkroom is delivered *pro tem* via Lexy. Does he stop to think? Does he hell.

> When [Jo Ellen] heard the footsteps, she turned toward the door, prepared to hear Lexy's report. When Nathan filled the doorway, his temper shot straight into hers.
>
> "I need you to come with me." His voice was clipped and anything but apologetic.
>
> "I believe you were informed I'm busy. And you haven't been invited into this room."
>
> "Save it, Scarlett." He grabbed her hand and pulled. When her free one reared back, whipped forward, and cracked hard across his face , he narrowed his eyes and nodded. "Fine, we do it the hard way."
>
> The room turned upside down so rapidly she didn't even get out the curse burning on her tongue. He was halfway out of the room with her slung over his shoulder before she got past the shock enough to fight.
>
> "Get your godamn belly-crawling Yankee bastard hands off me." She punched at his back, furious that she couldn't manage a full swing.
>
> "You think you can send your sister to brush me off? In a pig's eye." He shoved open the door with his shoulder and started down the narrow stairway. "I've been

travelling the whole fucking day to get here, and you'll have the courtesy to listen to what I need to say."

"Courtesy? Courtesy? What does a snake oil New York hotshot know about courtesy?" In the confines of the stairway, her struggles only resulted in her rapping her head against the wall. "I hate you." Her ears rang from both the blow and the humiliation.

"I've prepared myself for that." Grim and determined, he hauled her into the kitchen. Both Lexy and Brian froze and gaped. "Excuse me," he said shortly, and carried her outside while she left a trail of threats and curses behind them.

"Oh." Lexy sighed, long and deep, holding a hand to her heart. "Wasn't that the most romantic thing you've ever seen in all your life?"[1]

It doesn't take Lexy's immediate and salacious bet with Brian—"Twenty dollars says he's got her in bed, fully willing, within an hour."—to know that she is about as wrong as she can be, and the timeworn shades of Scarlett and Rhett from *Gone With the Wind* can save nothing with their humour because they arrive only via Nathan's impatient dismissal of Jo Ellen's right to control her own life. The grotesque paradox of Nathan demanding courtesy while he commits an assault and the sheer inanity of Lexy's remark are (I imagine) intended to work comically in a melodramatically heightened scene, and if sexual romance were all that were at stake they might—but it isn't, for the knowledge that drives Nathan, and his protracted failure to be honest, still make his actions both repugnant and criminal. He has neither right nor privilege of anything resembling this behaviour, and adds assault and kidnap to his own legal sheet (with accessory charges to Brian's and Lexy's) while grossly extending a complete moral blankness and emotional insensitivity by once again deliberately provoking, insulting, assaulting, and humiliating the woman he claims to care for.

This being Romance, Lexy makes Brian pay up despite losing her bet: it's nightfall before Jo Ellen, having learned the truth of her mother's murder and begun to suspect what is happening in the present, gives Nathan unconditional forgiveness for everything and respreads her heart. Roberts lets her get in some good blows and a volitional departure and return, while he offers a brief apology or two, but if one has bothered to take the characters and crime as more than empty formulae, moral realities intrude. To be worth caring about Jo Ellen must realise what evil Nathan has done—""You took me to bed knowing." Nausea made her dizzy as she surged to her feet. [...] "I let you inside me. [...] Do you know how that makes me feel?""[2]—but for

1   Nora Roberts, *Sanctuary* (1997; New York: Jove, 1998), pp. 412–13.
2   Roberts, *Sanctuary*, p. 419

the novel to conclude he must be briskly forgiven without legal question, so the issue evaporates in a little pink heart. As news spreads to the family Kate and Lexy chip in to muddy the waters, Kate telling Sam that he was "no more at fault for believing what [he] did about Belle than Nathan was for believing in his father", and Lexy declaring to Giff that blaming Nathan for anything at all would be "like blaming that bastard Sherman's great-grandchildren for burning Atlanta".[1] Both comparisons are irrelevant, and Kate's (wilfully equating a ten-year-old child and a married father-of-three) is the blandly self-serving lie Sam will have to tell himself hereafter, because he lacked the faith to believe that his loving wife and children's mother vanished involuntarily. The issue with Nathan is not that he didn't suspect his father before finding the dead man's photos and journal, but what he has (not) done since, and if Roberts had let the police in these questions would have had to resurface. Instead a handy hurricane and the rather *Key Largo* emergence of murderous Kyle from the storm, badly injuring Brian for Dr Kirby to save and imperilling Jo Ellen for Nathan to save, wraps all up in departing sirens and a shower of confetti.

In wreaking this dismal eucatastrophe the imperative mood finds rich echoes for Nathan's offensive absurdity. Cousin Kate seems to know no other grammar, delivering at least two-thirds of her 'loving' words as snippy commands to eat, sleep, or behave, and with the escalating coercions of photography, sibling pressure, stalking, induced psychosis, murder, and nature red in tooth and claw, there are the materials for what might have been an impressive novel. But for once the generic elements are not fused, and the imperative runs unorchestrated and inharmonious riot throughout, leaving Nathan's perfunctory shooting of Kyle perhaps the lamest fratricide I know. Roberts, I imagine, felt by then as well shot of him as the poor Hathaways, but what makes *Sanctuary* of substantive interest all the same is that while its degree of failure is very unusual (and at surprising odds with the brisk and impressive plotting of the contemporaneous early Robbs), it is an exemplary nadir. Two other Roberts novels touched with Southern Gothic, written nearly a decade apart but neatly bracketing *Sanctuary*, show that she had before and would again challenge her genre's reliance on presenting untempered male imperative modality as sexually attractive and emotionally mature.

In *Carnal Innocence* (1992) Caroline Waverley returns to her dead grand-mother's house in Innocence, Miss., a very small town in the lee of a plantation and Great House. In its scion, Tucker Longstreet, she faces an easygoing man of real arrogance, grounded (to be fair) in natal rank and inherited wealth but deeply unattractive. His

---

1   Roberts, *Sanctuary*, pp. 466, 476

string of prior women is unproblematic, but adolescent machismo in a red Porsche, at speeds relying on personal skill and sustained good luck to avoid killing something, like his uncaring, careless habit of riling women for fun, point to immaturity and recklessness. Having scared Caroline badly with his driving he sees only an opportunity for titillation—"He'd always figured if you couldn't avoid a woman's temper, you might as well enjoy it."[1]—and for much of the novel, despite (i) their mutual physical attraction, (ii) Caroline's belief in him while he is suspect in a vile series of local killings, and (iii) his knowledge of the psychic maternal assaults that drove her (suspending her career) back to Innocence, Tucker can deploy only command and seizure. Sometimes on nominal grounds of care, always as a matter of habit, he simply knows he must as a man be entitled, and the liberties he takes, unearned and ungranted, are always Caroline's. The clear and present danger presented by the local killer/s, to which involvement with Tucker exposes her, once provides (as bullets fly) the only valid excuse for taking any liberties at all, but it is later Caroline alone whom one killer assaults, and Caroline alone who puts several .45 slugs straight into him:

> Tucker found her in the parlor, sitting in the rocker with the dazed dog across her lap.
> "Honey." He crouched down beside her, stroking her face, her hair. "Honey, did he hurt you?"
> "He was going to kill me." She kept rocking, afraid if she stopped she'd go mad. "With the knife. He could have shot me, but he had to do it with the knife. Like Edda Lou, he said." The dog began to stir and whine in her lap. Caroline lifted him up against her breast like a baby. "It's all right now. It's all right."
> "Caroline, Caroline, look at me, honey." He waited until she turned her head. Her pupils were so dilated, the irises were hardly more than a green aura around them. "I'm going to take you upstairs. Come on now, I'll carry you up and call the doctor."
> "No." She let out a long breath as Useless licked her chin. "I'm not going to be hysterical. I'm not going to fall apart. I fell apart in Toronto. All kinds of pieces. Not again." She swallowed, pressing her cheek against the dog's fur. "I was making corn bread. I've never made corn bread before. Happy gave me her recipe, and I was going to take it over to Susie's. It feels so good being a part of this place." Useless licked away a tear that trickled down her cheek. "You see, I thought I was coming here just to be alone, but I didn't know how much I needed to be a part of something."
> "It's going to be all right," he said helplessly. "I promise it's going to be all right."

1   Nora Roberts, *Carnal Innocence* (1992; New York: Bantam, 2000), p. 34.

"I was making corn bread in my grandmother's oven. And I shot Austin Hatinger with my grandfather's gun. Do you think that's strange?"

"Caroline." He cupped her face. She could see the streaks of violence and fury in his eyes that he so carefully filtered out of his voice. "I'm just going to hold you for a while, is that all right?"

"All right."[1]

Men trying to coerce women into accepting medical care is a recurrent topos in Roberts and Robb. Sometimes the men genuinely care in love or friendship, and are trying to override refusals of urgently needed help; sometimes they are trying with despicable calculation to use medication to disempower. The surprise here is Tucker's reactions to Caroline's refusal: pushed by circumstance and (belated) guilt at having endangered her, he modulates his habitual imperatives first into the future determinative ("I'll carry you ..."), and (*mirabile dictu*) after she speaks, despite invasively 'cupping' her face, the interrogative mood at long last—"is that all right?" The novel has another 200 pages to go, and before the end Tucker will have to endure a sickening revelation that frames his understanding of female consent in an unexpected manner and completes his development, but from this turn to the very last (his acceptance that he must travel with Caroline to support her musical career) he is in business as a self-reconstructing man.

In *Midnight Bayou* (2001), however, Declan Fitzgerald is more than that from the beginning. Conveniently wealthy (if less so than Roarke), he has fled a broken engagement, stifling legal career, and family criticism in Boston to buy and restore a Great House near New Orleans that he saw and fell for as a student. His female interest, Lena Simone, is a law-school friend's cousin who owns and runs a bar in the French Quarter, and has a wonderful grandmother (figures at whom Roberts is very good) as well as serious emotional trauma from a runagate, drug-addict mother. Quietly going about restoration of his house and determinedly courteous, uninvasive courtship of Lena, Declan becomes a medium for the violently angry and pitifully lost ghosts whose reality explains the mansion's dereliction. A century before, as the roaring but still nineteenth-century nineties ran their course, a cross-class tragedy played out there, a bayou woman married to the plantation-heir being secretly raped, murdered, and erased from record by the wastrel brother and bitter matriarch. Now ghosts of victim, killer, and colluders possess living inhabitants of the house through their care for it, in sleep or moments of inattention, and the necessary discovery of

1   Roberts, *Carnal Innocence*, pp. 306–07.

the past by its victims in the present maps historical and present romance onto one another. The excellent central twist is Declan's female and Lena's male identities in the past, and the whole problem of imperative moods is shifted to the bitter class-imperatives of the historical crime and the gross imposition of its devalued priorities on the present, leaving both present lovers free to be reasonable, independent modern people of complementary genders. Beautifully plotted, with sidelights from Declan's and Lena's personal battles against family embarrassments and mistrust, *Midnight Bayou* is a reconstructed treat for those who believe, with Peter Wimsey and Shake-speare but unlike anyone in *Sanctuary*, that true lovers, married or otherwise, can never "possess one another" but only "give and hazard all we have".[1]

No writers could be less like Dorothy Sayers in style or sensibility than Roberts and Robb, but the Wimsey connection matters in reading Eve Dallas, and implicitly (if without series force) rebukes the spineless surrenders to male command to which even Roberts's toughest heroines are prone. When Sayers managed in *Gaudy Night* (1935) and *Busman's Honeymoon* (1937) to transform the territory of Crime from a given locale to the emotions of paired investigators,[2] she insisted on equality within their relationship. Jill Paton Walsh, introducing her completion of the unfinished Wimsey novel *Thrones, Dominations* (1998), says it clearly:

> As one might expect of a person born in 1890 [Wimsey] has some old-fashioned mannerisms; but his undying charm arises from a characteristic which he shares with Ralph Touchett (in *Portrait of a Lady*); Benedick (in *Much Ado About Nothing*) and even somewhat with Mr Rochester in *Jane Eyre*, but with none too many others in literature or in life: that is, that he requires as his consort a spirited woman who is his intellectual equal.[3]

Loving intellectual equals don't have much call for the imperative mood, even if they marry and the woman says 'obey' in the old *Book of Common Prayer* style, and Sayers made the issue central to the Wimsey–Vane novels. It is built into Harriet Vane's reactions to Wimsey throughout *Strong Poison* (1930) and *Have His Carcass* (1932), and comes explicitly to a head near the end of *Gaudy Night*.

With the case solved at personal cost to Wimsey, the relieved but not self-excusing don who inadvertently triggered the trouble takes Harriet to romantic task:

---

1   Sayers, *Busman's Honeymoon*, p. 361 (Ch. XVIII), quoting *The Merchant of Venice*, 2.7.16.
2   See 'Of Purgatory and Yorkshire'.
3   Dorothy L. Sayers & Jill Paton Walsh, *Thrones, Dominations* (London: Hodder & Stoughton, 1998), p. [v].

"[...] I really don't think you can go on like this. You won't break [Wimsey's] patience or his control or his spirit ; but you may break his health. He looks like a person pushed to the last verge of endurance."

"He's been rushing about and working very hard," said Harriet, defensively. "I shouldn't be at all a comfortable person for him to live with. I've got a devilish temper."

"Well, that's his risk, if he likes to take it. He doesn't seem to lack courage."

"I should only make his life a misery."

"Very well. If you are determined that you're not fit to black his boots, tell him so and send him away."

"I've been trying to send Peter away for five years. It doesn't have that effect on him."

"If you had really tried, you could have sent him away in five minutes. . . . Forgive me. I don't suppose you've had a very easy time with yourself. But it can't have been easy for him, either—looking on at it, and quite powerless to interfere."

"Yes. I almost wish he had interfered, instead of being so horribly intelligent. It would be quite a relief to be ridden over rough-shod for a change."

"He will never do that. That's *his* weakness. He'll never make up your mind for you. You'll have to make your own decisions. You needn't be afraid of losing your independence ; he will always force it back on you. If you ever find any kind of repose with him, it can only be the repose of very delicate balance."[1]

The delicate repose to which Peter & Harriet eventually win through is what most modern Romance heroines (brains permitting) are seeking, mutually fulfilling, intensely passionate *and* respectful love—but Peter & Harriet win through precisely because Peter would no more back a woman against her kitchen-counter to force an uninvited kiss, throw one over his shoulder because of his own fouled conscience, or sleep with one knowing her ignorance of his father's guilt for her mother's murder, than he would strike a servant or commit rape. Harriet's academic interlocutor is rightly impatient with the blindness of Romance, for it is precisely Peter's 'powerlessness' to interfere or ride rough-shod over—not from lack of money or strength, but in self-disciplined respect for equality—that even Roberts's Romance male leads, otherwise well-rounded and interesting, so persistently and grievously lack. The balance of love with respect *is* "very delicate", its nuances central to *Busman's Honeymoon* as pressures of violence and processes of investigation breach confidence and impose their own imperatives, but it holds. "What kind of life could we have if I

---

1   Sayers, *Gaudy Night*, pp. 473–4 (Ch. XXII).

knew that you had become less than yourself by marrying me?"[1] asks Harriet in the gravest crisis, and Reginald Hill became Sayers's greatest direct successor by making that the truth to which Ellie Pascoe clings when her husband's policemanship most oppresses.

It is also the truth fatal to Dido that Romance cannot seem to stomach, for Aeneas will not often give up Rome.[2] Build up her heroine's careers and self-confident passions as Roberts may, Declan Fitzgerald remains, like Wimsey, a striking rarity. Even in a recent and otherwise rather good novel like *Angels Fall* (2006), ruggedly caring writer Jamison Brody (fully aware of heroine Reese Gilmour's gunshot injury, fragility, obsessive-compulsive disorder, and malevolent victimisation) remains a man with an eye for kitchen counters and a disagreeable lack of courtesy, if not kindness. There has been over time a notable and sustained improvement—Brody and Bo Goodnight (in *Blue Smoke*, 2005) are better men than any of their predecessors except Declan Fitzgerald—and a good deal more giving and hazarding than was ever found in Romance before Roberts took the genre by the scruff of its neck, but never yet Wimsey's absolute banishment of 'possess' in its imperative sexual mood of making women property.[3] In this light the creation in 1995 of J. D. Robb, and through her Eve Dallas and the empire-building Roarke, must have been an explosive liberation for Roberts from the generic imperatives of female objectification and male discourtesy with which she was struggling. The Romance territory she knew intimately and could manipulate almost at will would still provide topoi and tropes, but with a decision to reach and continue past Eve's marriage to Roarke the limits (if not demands) of Romance were struck down, and the issue of control could step from implicit grammar to explicit plot. Not simply modern but future people in a zapping e-world (itself an interesting narrative liberation), Eve and Roarke cannot in their natures as big-city cop and major-league businessman be as courteous or virtuous as Peter and Harriet (though Roarke's wealth, connoisseurship, and butler owe something to Wimsey's), but they can and do match one another in habitual mastery of the imperative, and so cancel out. This too, for all the boosted action and noisy soundtrack of Eve's world,

---

1 Sayers, *Busman's Honeymoon*, pp. 343–4 (Ch. XVII)

2 See Reginald Hill, *Arms and the Women: An Elliad* (2000).

3 Fascinatingly, though, in yet another mode, mythic fantasy, Roberts produced a perfect parable, 'Winter Rose' (2001, collected in *A Little Fate*, 2004). A princess in a castle deep in snowy forests is trapped in a permanent winterland by a curse. The wounded knight whom battle-fatigue allows to stray in must be allowed to leave, full willing, for the curse to be broken, whereon he can return. On a small canvas the balance of emotion, destiny, and paradox is beautifully handled, giving an emotional but algebraic clarity to desire and control lost to be won; poor Dido was never so wise.

can only be a "repose of very delicate balance", and Robb/erts's discovery and sustentation of it are little miracles of generic engineering.

Ever since *Naked in Death* and *Glory in Death* (both 1995) Robb's novels have appeared (with one minor bump) at a steady two per year, developing around Eve and Roarke a lively, amusing cast from many walks of life. Roarke's butler Summerset (initially a stiff-necked shade of Wimsey's Bunter) is a constant presence, as is Galahad the cat, but Eve's police colleagues and friends necessarily dominate—chief among them former mentor and E-Division boss Captain Ryan Feeney, E-Detective Ian McNab, psychological profiler Dr Charlotte Mira, and brassy Commander Whitney—while others widen focus and interest. Ex-grifter turned pregnant pop-sensation Mavis Freestone, Eve's best friend, with her fashion-designer mate Leonardo add several worlds to Eve's obsessive concern with murder. So do the 'Free-Ager' eco-sensibilities of rurally educated trainee turned partner Delia Peabody (romantically paired with McNab), and the sharp, eroticised ambitions of favoured TV reporter Nadine Furst—all acquired and established as friends through involvement in the whirlwind events of the first three novels. Latterly Roarke's rediscovered Irish family have added another world again, but even 22 novels down the line the constant clash of Eve's and Roarke's wills is a primary topos in almost every case.

The driving iteration is made narratively possible through an astonishingly slow passage of time. 23 ½ novels and three novellas (each dealing with at least one solved case), written over 12 years, cover only two and some years of narrative time. The first three books lead over a few months from an official interrogatory meeting to Eve's and Roarke's marriage, but 20 more have seen only two wedding anniversaries. Such Shandean slowness—and *c*.2,300 pages per calendar year is altogether bad for your worships' eyes—disallows any simple understanding of how Robb fuses Romance with Crime. Increments of the criminal solution and progress in the romantic relationship are causally connected throughout, and the singular terminal union of Romance becomes Roarke's rock-solid support within marriage for Eve's liberation from memorial and present demons under the emotional burden of working homicide—extreme but quotidian stresses that ground the melodramatic charge habitual to Romance and always a potential danger in Crime.

What makes this temporal strategy work is the construction of Eve's psyche. Without giving away too many details, whose impact in reading is considerable, she was as a child serially raped and grossly physically abused by her father. The name Dallas testifies only to the city where she was found shivering in an alleyway with a broken arm and profound traumatic amnesia, and taken into the care system, aged eight and altogether lacking name or identity. The bones of her story emerge in the first three novels via repressed memories Eve recovers, as elements of cases prompt irruptions of self-knowledge, and as her developing, intensely sexual relationship with Roarke forces her to confront her emotions as an abuse survivor. Her recovered memory project has been incrementally sustained throughout the series, through memory-flashes, detection, and above all harrowing and evolving dreams she regularly has of her father as fully restored to malignant agency, infantilising her to abuse her again. The overall psychology Robb gives Eve, policewomanship as her defence against traumatic and premature experience, owes something to Clarice Starling in Thomas Harris's massively influential *The Silence of the Lambs* (1988) but sustains the notion with original power. The psychology of a victim's haunted, partial recovery loops around to make the time-frame credible, as the rate at which Eve solves major cases does not (though it supplies a functional exhaustion), and the series as a whole demands a respected place among the post-1984 cluster of genre novels responding to abuse.[1]

The clash of Eve's and Roarke's imperatives, initially framed as her duty and need to investigate him as a suspect and his compelling sexual and emotional desire for her (Crime going to the woman, Romance to the man), typically centres on (i) her health, of which she is grossly negligent in the grip of a case, (ii) involvement of his property or commerce in crime, and most importantly (iii) the insinuating gap between personal knowledge of or trust in something, good enough for him, and the proof she not only needs officially but (given her history) relies on emotionally. Reinforced by her profession, colleagues as substitute family, and the internalised, morally imperative claims of the abused dead on whose behalf she labours, Eve could never simply give in to Roarke's demands—but the acid resonance of the first case with her repressed memories, his sensitivity to them (having also suffered gross physical abuse in childhood), and above all a political dimension to the case's events and identities, that he can handle with financial resources she and the police lack, make his help an investigative bargain neither conscience nor self-preservation can refuse.

Sex had in any case very understandably never been high on her adult agenda—

---

1   See, for example, Andrew Vachss's Burke novels, following *Flood* (1985); Robert Campbell's *In La-La Land We Trust* (1986) and sequels; Walter Mosley's Easy Rawlins novels, following *Devil in a Blue Dress* (1990); Robert B. Parker's *Double Deuce* (1992); Anna Salter's Michael Stone novels, following *Shiny Water* (1997); Stephen Dobyns, *The Church of Dead Girls* (1997); Andrew Taylor's *The Four Last Things* (1997) and sequels; Reginald Hill, *Of Beulah Height* and *Singing the Sadness* (both 1998); and Toni Cade Bambara, *Those Bones Are Not My Child* (1999).

but *that* Roarke can change (just as Wimsey discreetly awakened Harriet Vane after marriage). The racy sex scenes twice or thrice per novel, explicit but not over-anatomical, must be acknowledged as a smart commercial move while mainstream fiction absorbed the video and computer revolutions in pornography,[1] but they are also a persistent locus of mutual surrender to union that anchors Eve *and* Roarke in the competitive worlds they individually inhabit, and redeems the memories of isolation in their heads. Like Roarke's fairy-tale house, granting miraculous space and freedom in mid-Manhattan, sex is a replenishing oasis and refuge, and a critical offset for the often specifically sexual violence of the case-plots. The promise of Jane Austen's and all subsequent Romance, that loving, mutually monogamous–and-monoandrous sex is worth a lifetime more than all its rivals, is fulfilled and deeply valorised by the exemplary civic (police, entrepreneurial) lives it is shown to sustain, while the profound, private but frankly narrated joy of intense physical and emotional union sustains both partners against the terrible strains murder and careless officialdom impose. The mutual extremity of sexual release can also absorb and reconcile *some* imperative tensions, but this is a function of Eve's and Roarke's relative youth—"Harriet watched [Peter's] inner conflict sympathetically. If both of them had been ten years younger, the situation would have resolved itself in a row, tears and reconciling embraces".[2] If Robb's time-frame ever accelerates, or she is spared to see Eve reach her 40s (at her present rate another 80 or so novels), these sexual dynamics may have to change. Meanwhile they serve an important and far from gratuitous purpose, much as the famously explicit Julie Christie–Donald Sutherland scene does in Nicolas Roeg's terrifying film of Daphne Du Maurier's *Don't Look Now* (1973).

Naked in Death, for all its mass-market form and sensibilities a *very* good novel, also shows beautifully why, if belletristic prose is desirable to critics, intelligent plotting is vital to readers. It opens the series with Eve in the grip of a nightmare, scant hours after killing a man who had in thrall to a synthetic drug called Zeus (*de facto* some kind of PCP) hacked to bloody pieces his four-year-old daughter and was bent on doing as much for her. Imperatives abound, from the child's murder and the pa-

---

1   Explicitly adult Romance series like Black Lace also began in the mid-1990s. Their advice to prospective writers includes fascinating data about just what their readers do and don't want, and the line Robb/erts treads, while leaving no doubt about whose mouth or hands are where, follows it in avoiding too explicitly anatomical diction. She is less explicit than Black Lace, but writes in a way that would before the 1980s have been taboo in almost all conversation, and certainly too explicit for Romance publishers, whose sensibilities tended more to very soft-focus and suggestive ellipses.

2   Sayers, *Busman's Honeymoon*, p. 216 (Ch. X); Peter is at that stage 45, and Harriet 30-something; Roarke is also 30-something and Eve 30 when their series began.

thology of drug addiction to Eve's safety and duty. There is also Eve's involuntary self-imposition of the dream, partly Freudian 'day-residue' but already, through the little girl's resonance with Eve's own experiences of violence ("Such a small girl to have had so much blood in her"[1]), freighted with something closer to what Frank Herbert called *adab*, the 'demanding memory that comes of itself'.[2] Additionally, in 2057 police officers who use maximum force must (as Eve's awareness of duty and fear of the process let readers know) undergo 'Testing'—not only a full medical and neurological exam., stripping and probing to assure the public that no civil servant's flaw led to an avoidable death, but imposed Virtual Reality simulations of random street threats *and* a reconstruction of the fatal shooting drawn directly, in bloody detail, from the officer's own memories. For Eve that means reliving not only the event but the insult of repressed memories it agitated, while having again to repress anything but 'proper' and rational response if imperatives of public accountability are not to see her suspended, and allow murder to stroke politics while a murderer goes free. Delayed by the necessities of the new case, and then abruptly imposed through political pressure when her investigation threatens the guilty, Eve's mandatory Testing, and relationship with chief tester Dr Mira, are wonderfully structured to maintain a sharp focus on volition while the plot tensely proceeds. Like all officers (and anyone with a heart), Eve considers Testing a form of "brain rape",[3] but it is her own acute vulnerabilities, insurgent traumata, and need for an emotional and intellectual equal that make it so much more costly than she can readily sustain.

Through the opening, passing-but-never-forgotten murder of the child, and the all too real implications by 1995 of any abuse case, political reverberations also grow steadily. Motive, means, and opportunity in 2057 all connect via familial to national politics, as do Eve's motive, means and opportunity of imperative arrest, which also propagate through the convenience of Roarke's financial resources and consequent connections. One cannot say the imperial, epic dimensions of classical romance are restored, but the modern Rome is purged of a significant evil while Dido goes home with Aeneas, twenty-first century shuttles making much possible; and unlike the Wimseys as the Roarkes may be in almost everything that matters, not one of the quartet will ever put personal indulgence before another's or the state's true need. What seem at first the dullest and snobbiest clichés, like Wimsey's wealth and May-

---

1   J. D. Robb, *Naked in Death* (1995; London: Hodder & Stoughton, 1996 [New English Library]), pp. 1–2, alluding to Shakespeare, *Macbeth*, 5.1.36–8 (Lady Macbeth sleepwalking).

2   See Frank Herbert, *Dune* (1965; London: NEL, 1968), p. 488.

3   Robb, *Naked in Death*, p. 132.

fair clubmanship, prove instead the guarantors of civilised virtue, without which no personal union of intelligent individuals, however sexually passionate, has anywhere to go. Free in 2057 to indict whatever politician she cared to invent, Robb makes a visceral detestation for a certain kind of morally null maleness plain while exploring its place in the hierarchy and satisfyingly bringing it to a Capitol come-uppance—a kind of satire at which Roberts had sometimes hinted (celebrity gone wrong, say, in *Public Secrets*, 1990, and *Genuine Lies*, 1991) but never truly delivered, and which a 'hero' like Nathan Delaney in *Sanctuary* utterly negates. Even before the love between Eve and Roarke matured into marriage—and "It was Roarke's doing, of course. He's caught her at a weak moment. Both of them bleeding and bruised and lucky to be alive. When a man is clever enough and knows his quarry well enough to choose such a time and place to propose marriage, well, a woman was a goner."[1]—the relationship had a civic resonance that belied cliché, and promised an ethical writerly concern at traditional odds with the open commerce of the series.

Yet none of it could work without Roarke, who for all his fallen-angel Romance-hero beauty and corresponding imperialism knows from the first and almost without stumble the difference between sending the ball back into one's opponent's court, however firmly, and crassly impatient vaultings of the net. He will invade Eve's living-space, which as landlord he already owns, and infringe her personal space, but not without watching carefully for her response. Violently self-made, entrepreneurially ruthless, and dazzlingly wealthy as he is, it is precisely Eve's matching violence and determination, but indifference to his wealth and reputation, that attract him; and even at his most predatory and aroused he doesn't only know how to wait, but connects patience with genuine respect. After reconciliation following their first real dispute as lovers, and the first night he spends in her apartment, he challenges and holds her:

> "Eve." Roarke set his coffee down, laid his hands on her shoulders. "Why don't you want me to know you're pleased I'm staying?"
>
> "Your alibi holds. It's none of my business if you—" She broke off when he turned her to face him. He was angry. She could see it in his eyes and prepared for the argument to come. She hadn't prepared for the kiss, the way his mouth closed firmly over hers, the way her heart rolled over slow and dreamy in her chest.
>
> So she let herself be held, let her head nestle in the curve of his shoulder. "I don't

1   J. D. Robb, *Immortal in Death* (1996; London: Hodder & Stoughton, 1997 [New English Library]), p. 2.

know how to handle this," she murmured. "I don't have any precedent here. I need rules, Roarke. Solid rules."

"I'm not a case you need to solve."

"I don't know what you are. But I know this is going too fast. It shouldn't have even started. I shouldn't have been able to get started with you."

He drew her back so that he could study her face. "Why?"

"It's complicated. I have to get dressed. I have to get to work."

"Give me something." His fingers tightened on her shoulders. "I don't know what you are, either."

"I'm a cop," she blurted out. "That's all I am. I'm thirty years old and I've only been close to two people in my entire life. And even with them, it's easy to hold back."

"Hold back what?"

"Letting it matter too much. If it matters too much, it can grind you down until you're nothing. I've been nothing. I can't be nothing ever again."

"Who hurt you?"

"I don't know." But she did. She did. "I don't remember, and I don't want to remember. I've been a victim, and once you have, you need to do whatever it takes not to be one again. That's all I was before I got into the academy. A victim, with other people pushing the buttons, making the decisions, pushing me one way, pulling me another."

"Is that what you think I'm doing?"

"That's what's happening."

There were questions he needed to ask. Questions, he could see by her face, that needed to wait. Perhaps it was time he took a risk.[1]

However Roarke's hands may tighten, Eve complies because she gives herself permission to do so, subtly stressed by repetition ("let herself be held, let her head nestle"), and Roarke's awareness of his own imperatives ("questions he needed to ask") is immediately matched and mated ("that needed to wait"). Once or twice in later books he does briefly stumble into an imperative hissy fit, but so does Eve, and both in general and in sustained detail one can (bothering his origins) call Roarke the perfect gentleman. He is no more deprived of masculine pride and proper control by his courtesy and love than Wimsey, and surprisingly like His Lordship fills a clichéd outline with considerable variety. The only problem is how he can be authorially related to a destructive fool like Nathan Delaney—but in a sense Robb answers that on

1   Robb, *Naked in Death*, pp. 222–3.

Roberts's behalf, for Roarke has in fact a far *greater* deadliness and former criminality than Nathan; he simply comes equipped with a conscience as well as a brain and penis, and controls all three as unfailingly as Nathan lets one rip, turns another off, and spastically suspends the third.

The issues of control and compulsion are severely re-tested and examined in the fourth novel, *Rapture in Death* (1996)—the first after the marriage ceremony that (*inter alia*) legally debars rape as a possibility between Eve and Roarke. A minor villain with a mind-bending device based on the brain-scanning technologies of Testing equipment manages both to implant in Roarke a burning, immediate lust and to inhibit his sexual control. The result is shocking and dryly painful for Eve, and summons in Roarke the street-identity of his Dublin childhood and its ambient Gaelic, so that in penetrating her he repeatedly mutters *liomsa*, 'mine', as he heard his father do when drunk. But it is he who with immediate self-loathing calls what he has just done rape, and Eve who must, desperately and against the odds, persuade him that his shocked emotional withdrawal will be far more damaging to her than an act to which she did not consent but did not experience emotionally as any form of the repeated paternal rape she suffered as a child.[1] I had and retain some doubt that at that stage in her recovered memory project Eve could quite have managed things as she remarkably does, but my qualms don't matter because the issue is front and centre of the plot, and no-one is in doubt as to the judgements that *might* be rendered. There have also been moments where the tricky triangle of Eve, Roarke, and the NYPSD has resulted in simultaneous infringements of Eve's personal and official integrity (and so her identity) that she would (I think) resent more decisively and bitterly; in this and other lights the lurking issue of her promotion to Captain (subject to political, not meritocratic delay) poses an interesting conundrum. But the marriage, the series, and the emotional maturation of Eve and Roarke together have all held fast, and embody the achieved balance towards which Roberts's Romances have steadily moved in an asymptotic curve, approaching without ever reaching.[2]

Nor has the series for all its slow calendar pace at any time threatened stasis. Al-

---

1   See J. D. Robb, *Rapture in Death* (1996; London: Hodder & Stoughton, 1997 [New English Library]), pp. 202–07.

2   Readers seem to agree: according to "on-line fan poll" data given (without methodology) in *The Official Nora Roberts Companion*, pp. 438, 441, 448,452, Eve & Roarke are runaway winners as "Favorite Heroine" and "Favorite Hero" with 34% and 37% respectively; Eve's nearest rival is Maggie Concannon (*Born in Fire*) with 15%, Roarke's is Luke Callahan (*Honest Illusions*) with 8%; and together they cruise "Favorite Couple" with 54%. To me astoundingly, 9% declare Kyle in *Sanctuary* to be their "Favorite Villain", but Nathan is rightly no-one's favourite anything.

lowing *Naked in Death* as a standout opener and the first three novels, leading to the marriage, as of particular structural quality, Robb's first 15 novels might fairly be called very consistent, in their middling lengths as in their high generic quality, but in the last few years (coincident with Putnam's switch to hardback first editions and aggressive tranching of the market[1]) greater length and complexities of plot have been put at the service of greater quality. Both *Divided in Death* (2004) and *Visions in Death* (2004) are superior: the former includes an extremely striking and hard-edged satire on the then very new US Department of Homeland Security as well as a portrait of false marriage; the latter features a memorable serial killer and finesses with riveting skill a fusion of the existing mix with a registered and licensed psychic Eve must take seriously. *Survivor in Death* (2005) extended the portraits of marriage through a family slaughter with one young survivor-witness whom Eve must shelter and protect, and saw Mavis Freestone's protracted pregnancy intrude ever more bulgingly through her demands that Eve and Roarke be her backup birthing-coaches—a particularly happy and funny challenge. And *Origin in Death* (2005) broke the mould in a different way by finding a topically resonant theme that for the first time brought Robb's SF elements into genuine centrality.

In tracing Robb/erts's fusions of Romance and Crime I have neglected Robb's SF, because in an odd way, while necessary, it has not been important. SF and Romance have their own direct interface,[2] but the tag-line on the cover of *Naked in Death* was "In the 21st Century murder is still the same", and so it has proven: methods have changed, not least with the 'gun ban' and the dreadful Urban Wars of the early twenty-first, but good old-fashioned blunt instruments still do the job, and motives are perennial. Traffic soars aerially as well as clogging streets (Eve revealingly chose her original apartment "because it was in a heavy ground and air pattern"[3]), and e-communications and surveillance have become basic adjuncts to forensic science and canvassing witness, but saving the hum of gadgetry and computers events have not been particularly futuristic—and gadgetry is often convenient, whipped up by Roarke's industrial Research Divisions when a particular capacity is needed. Even the street drugs of Eve's day ('Zeus', 'Zoner') clearly correspond to current ones (PCP, marijuana), though there are 'improved' date-rape and other sexually coercive or disinhibitory synthetics (notably 'Rabbit', after ingesting which any woman

---

1   There have also been 'trade paper' issues—the hardback-sized paperbound format.
2   See, for example, Catharine Asaro, ed., *Irresistible Forces* (2004), a collection of novellas (including the excellent 'Winterfair' by Lois McMaster Bujold) that explicitly fuse SF and Romance.
3   Robb, *Naked in Death*, p. 2.

will cheerfully allow herself to be gang-banged unconscious in the street—Rohypnol cubed plus *datura*). All in all, if it would be unjust to dismiss the setting in the 2050s, it is fair to say that its important structural aspects—specifically Feeney and the E-Division, generally the ubiquity of full audio-visual surveillance and the sketch of urban collapse explaining the gun ban and legalisation of prostitution—were laid down in *Naked in Death* and while walked on ever since had not been extended.

Not quite for the first time but certainly in the most detail, *Origin in Death* plots its way back towards those Urban Wars via a secret, terrible project that grew from the terrorist deaths of two women and a foetus. Human cloning is only a mild extrapolation from current science but the necessary support technologies including exo-wombs are well thought through, pushing timescale, and as a private operation with technologies that are known to be possible, but are illegal and officially undeveloped, a 25–40 year span before the narrative present and after the Urban Wars is needed for the cloning project. Much sharper senses of futurity and alienation are thereby generated, and put to good use while the possible purposes of cloning oneself and others, overwhelmingly women, are systematically exposed. Without revealing a name, Eve is eventually faced with a murderer whom for the first time she does not wish to punish—three identical people, collectively accepting guilt, of whom forensics and logic can say only that one is guilty of an act all three plotted. And once there were five:

> "Where are the other two?"
> "One died at six months. We were not able to sustain. The other . . ."
> They paused, linked hands. "We learned the other lived for five years. We lived five years. But we weren't strong enough, and our intellect wasn't developing according to the required levels. He killed us. He injected us as you might a terminally ill pet. We went to sleep, and never woke. And so, we're three."[1]

Nor is this, are these, the only clone victims. There are hundreds, grown to order, nurtured, raised, groomed, trained, and sold; *geishas*, corporate and professional wives, spies and assassins, or standing for office; all, most crudely, becunted slaves.

Small wonder then, that the clone production-line plays right into those dreams of Eve's in which her own dreadful and extended experience as a powerless puppet valued only for its sexual service and monetary value to another is endlessly reworked. Late in the case, dreadfully tired, Eve waits to meet Nadine Furst in a 'privacy room' at the 'Down and Dirty', a sex club whose owner Crack owes her a favour or three:

---

1   J. D. Robb, *Origin in Death* (New York: Putnam, 2005), pp. 258–9.

She looked at the bed, and a long, liquid longing rose up in her. She'd have given up food for the next forty-eight hours for twenty minutes horizontal. Rather than risk it, she went to the menu screen and ordered a pot of coffee, two cups.

It would be hideous. Soy products and chemicals married together to, inexplicably, resemble rancid tar. But there'd be enough caffeine juiced through it to keep her awake.

She sat, tried to focus her mind on the business in hand while she waited. Her eyes drooped, her head nodded. She felt the dream crawling into her, a monster with sharp, slick claws that snatched and bit at her mind.

A white room, blazing white. Dozens upon dozens of glass coffins. She was in all of them, the child she'd been, bloody and bruised from the last beating, weeping and pleading as she tried to fight her way out.

And he stood there, the man who'd made her, grinning.

Made to order, he said, and laughed. Laughed. *One doesn't work right, you just throw it away and try the next. Never going to be done with you, little girl. Never going to be finished.*

She jolted out, fumbled for her weapon. And saw the pots and cups on the table, with the menu slot still closing.[1]

The piercing resonance is not only between what readers know Eve to have suffered as a child and recently discovered as an investigator, but of the known causes of her abuse—of which awareness is deeply rooted in the reading present and its unending, vile news of child abuse—with the possibilities of new genetech being bent to abusive service, which all can imagine. The terrible dream-vision, like all that Eve endures, is rooted both in the Romance pattern of female suffering and the Crime pattern of investigative haunting, but here all serve neither Romance's recovery and fulfilment nor Crime's suburban history and professional analyses, but instead make horribly real a dystopic warning of evil growth and unending revenance—which is righteous SF, however truly fused with the other genres.

Memory in Death and *Born in Death* (both 2006) haven't yet gone back up that SF road, but have brought Eve to eponymous godpaternity of both Mavis's and Leonardo's baby, Bella Eve Freestone, and another newborn, Quentin Dallas Applebee, whom Eve rescued as a foetus from kidnap inside his mother and subsequent sale for profit. Humbled and elated, rightly proud and (as usual) utterly exhausted from defending the powerless and redeeming the dead, Eve has also in a new way to confront the terrifying love her valour wins her, and her enormous heart sustains. Late in 2006

1   Robb, *Origin in Death*, p. 275.

a third novella in the series, 'Haunted in Death', also made it clear that Robb has sardonically clocked the eventual turn of her calendar from December 2059 to January 2060 with distinct attention to motifs of the 1960s that Roberts has previously deployed, but never Robb, which also promises fun. And so the series continues: as I write, on 9th January 2007, a message posted by Nora Roberts at Amazon.com five days ago promises (after plugging the movies of her books about to be premiered on Lifetime TV) that:

> Between movies, if you're looking for a book, *Innocent In Death*, published by Putnam, hits the stands in February. Eve Dallas has a murder to solve, and an unexpected marital bump to navigate. It's an uneasy combination, and one that strains both Eve's and Roarke's emotional resources.[1]

An "uneasy combination" with an "unexpected marital bump to navigate"? Go on with you, Nora (or J.D.), what could they possibly be? By the time anyone can read this they will also be able to read the real answer, but that's the beauty of serial reading. My own hope is pregnancy[2]—it has to happen sooner or later, and Eve's biological clock is ticking along—but (remembering Mr Shandy again) who knows? The point is that with Eve and Roarke it's far more than usually worthwhile finding out what it is that does happen next, and how these bright shiners cope, as they surely will, with that strain on their impressive resources.

Quite a lot, then, can rewardingly be made of Lieutenant Eve Dallas, as she has commanded her Homicide shift for the NYPSD from the late 2050s into the dawn of a new decade. Robb's twenty-fourth novel will appear next month as a finely printed and bound Putnam hardback, and in whatever measure it will compound Romance, Crime, and SF, fusing them all as mysteriously yet intelligibly as sodium and chlorine make common salt, essential to our metabolisms and vital to our palates but also, pressed into a wound, capable of causing an agony that arrests the heart. Handsome Roarke will profitably exercise and control his imperative moods, Eve will cauterise an evil at personal cost, someone will be saved, several someones lost, and

---

1   http://www.amazon.com/Midnight-Death-Paperback-J-Robb/dp/0425208818/sr=8-4/ qid=1168320448/ref=pd_bbs_sr_4/104-4415710-9275961?ie=UTF8&s=books, accessed 7.1.2007 at 00:33 EST.

2   *The Official Nora Roberts Companion* rather slyly remarks that "Although many readers (especially those from the romance camp) clamour for the transition of Eve into a mother, Nora has reportedly said she will never do this" (p. 292).

marriage will yet again be shown to be, as Dr Johnson once averred, 'a noble daring'; and for the best human not the most ossified Christian reasons.

One thing mediaeval romances and modern Romances have squarely in common is their repeated dismissal as mere 'escapism'. The love-stories and fabulous beasts or other predicaments of the Arthurian romances were, the critics for years assured us, at best amusing *divertissements*, matters of no real account written only to entertain, as women might embroider trifles more to pass the time than for the product. A tale might to be sure contain some things of value and interest, but those could not include the love-bits or the obvious heroic animal fantasies; and a modern Romance, often with little but love and clichés of sexual fantasy to recommend it, stands almost no chance of being critically valorised. Yet I doubt Chaucer—pointedly writing in a vernacular that most of his enemies would have dismissed as a Romance language and a barbarism—made the question of rule and sovereignty within marriage the central issue of 'The Wife of Bath's Tale' and several more of his *Canterbury Tales* because he thought it merely escapist, and the Wife herself would surely have some raucous, common-sensical things to say to the more abstracted scholars and reflex patriarchs (as she did to their disapproving ancestors among the Canterbury-bound pilgrims). Nor has Robb/erts been roughening and strengthening her hands in Romance and Crime identities alike merely because she and her readers dream of happy endings: Roberts may still serve solace with sugar, as Romance requires, but the matters for which solace is needed are also present, and the business of relationships, of living in the moment with one's partners and peers however one may dream of founding Rome, is not for most readers an escape, or even an irrelevance.

The politics of romance and Romance, that is, are not only matters of history but also matters of simple living and domesticity, and reading such tales need not be escapes from anything. Matters of survival, day by day and year to year, are by most measures far more real than the divinest dream of future Roman glory, and matters of the heart no less real in the living than matters of food and drink, or of rule and identity. Modern Romances plainly remain in a literary vernacular, scorned for abjuring the 'Latin' of 'proper literature', and may of course be trifling—but that is exactly what many did and a few still do say of those *Canterbury Tales* (all in Chaucer's chatty and combatively English verse) that wilfully take the low road and still come up smiling. The inspiring criticism of Colin Burrow and Francis Ingledew, together re-opening classical, mediaeval, and Renaissance romances simultaneously to the comedy of survival and to epic political understandings, also opens modern Romances to our own intimate as well as public politics, as lovers, readers, and citizens—and the connections are all two-way, so that one may both apprehend in Sir Gawain's or Roarke's domesticities the imperative shadows of male identity enamoured of history and nation, and hear in Eve's absolute refusal of Dido's and other female fates the Wife of Bath's impressed and laughing approval.

Looking at his daughter Lavinia, whose tongue was cut out and whose hands cut off by rapists whose most intimate abuse he will not yet allow himself to recognise, Shakespeare's Titus Andronicus (who cut off one of his own hands to try to save two of his sons, falsely accused of murder, but had it sent back by return with their heads) gives her some memorable and seriously imaginative advice about possible methods of suicide:

> **Andronicus** So, so, now sit, and look you eat no more
> Than will preserve just so much strength in us
> As will revenge these bitter woes of ours.
> Marcus unknit that sorrow-wreathen knot:
> Thy Niece and I (poor Creatures) want our hands
> And cannot passionate our tenfold grief,
> With folded Arms. This poor right hand of mine
> Is left to tyrannise upon my breast.
> Who when my heart all mad with misery,
> Beats in this hollow prison of my flesh,
> Then thus I thump it down.
> Thou Map of woe, that thus dost talk in signs,
> When thy poor heart beats with outrageous beating,
> Thou canst not strike it thus to make it still?
> Wound it with sighing girl, kill it with groans:
> Or get some little knife between thy teeth,
> And just against thy heart make thou a hole,
> That all the tears that thy poor eyes let fall
> May run into that sink, and soaking in,
> Drown the lamenting fool, in Sea salt tears.1

Amazing as they are, it isn't only Titus's astonishing imagery and imagination of defiant powerlessness reclaiming suicidal agency; nor even Shakespeare's staggering boldness in punning so repeatedly on the hands his speaker and auditor (but not audience) lack; but a little history and context that make poor Lavinia relevant. *Titus*

---

1 *Titus Andronicus* 3.2.3–22.

Andronicus (*c*.1593–4) is historically a very odd play, and unlike Shakespeare's other Roman plays occupies no specific recorded historical moment. *Julius Caesar* (*c*.1599) and its sequel *Antony and Cleopatra* (*c*.1607–08) trace republic into triumvirate and then imperium, while *Coriolanus* (*c*.1608–09) looks firmly to the early republic, but *Titus* starts with Roman victory over the Goths sometime during the Caesars' heyday and ends with a Gothic invasion of Rome, invoking 476 CE; while *Lavinia* ('purity') is a name from centuries before the founding of the city, the once-promised bride of Turnus, a Rutuli warrior Aeneas slew to claim his place and Latinian woman on what the poets and historians therefore call the 'Lavinian shore' of Italy. A part of his con-solation prize for abandoning Dido, Lavinia in Virgil (but not Shakespeare) bore him Silvius ('Woodland'), father of the kings of Alba Longa,[1] while in Shakespeare (but not Virgil) she is reduced by male predation to helpless patience. At the last Titus, invoking the example of "rash Virginius" who slew his daughter "with his own right hand, / Because she was enforc'd, stain'd, and deflowr'd" (5.3.38–40), kills Lavinia, supplying with his remaining hand the agency he presumes she would exercise if she could. Lavinia, that is, is thrice over what Eve might be—the victim of crippling abuse, of her father, and of the Romance defeat by epic masculinity that makes a woman's happiness and life the price of progress. Revere Shakespeare's analysis as one ought, it is Eve Dallas for whom Lavinia's supporters should now be cheering.

---

1   The bithplace of Romulus and Remus, and so the 'mother-city' of Rome; its site is now occupied by Castel Gandolfo, the palace that serves as the papal summer residence.

4. Of Modern Dragons

Antiquity, Modernity, and the Descendants of Smaug

> nobody can explain a dragon.
> —Ursula Le Guin[1]

> Nowhere does a dragon come in so precisely where he should.
> —J. R. R. Tolkien[2]

One would think, amid all the facets of dragons and annals of dragonlore, that their antiquity at least might be counted on; that however variant in size, morality, and disposition, dragons are, as Diana Wynne Jones advises, "always very old", both in person and in whatever they may represent as symbols.[3] After all, the founding dragon twice over of the Northern European line is the "eald ūhtsceaða" ('old night-scather') of *Beowulf*, and even for that long-dead Prince of the Geats in his Dark-Age glory, the dragon was a relict:

Hordwynne fond
eald ūhtsceaða   opene standan,
sē ðe byrnende   biorgas sēceð,
nacod niðdraca,   nihtes flēogeð
fyre befangen;   hyne foldbūend
(swiðe ondræ)da(ð). Hē gesēcean sceall
(ho)r(d on) hrūsan,   þær hē hæðen gold
warað wintrum frōd: ne byð him wihte ðy sēl.
  Swā se ðēodsceaða   þrēo hund wintra
hēold on hrūsan   hordærna sum
ēacencræftig,   oð ðæt hyne ān ābealch
mon on mōde:[4]

Then an old harrower of the dark
happened to find the hoard open,
the burning one who hunts out barrows,
the slick-skinned dragon, threatening the night sky
with streamers of fire. People on the farms
are in dread of him. He is driven to hunt out
hoards underground, to guard heathen gold
through age-long vigils, though to little avail.
For three centuries, this scourge of the people
had stood guard on that stoutly protected
underground treasury, until the intruder
unleashed its fury:[5]

1   Ursula Le Guin, *Tales from Earthsea* (New York: Harcourt, 2001), p. xv.

2   J. R. R. Tolkien, *The Monsters and the Critics and Other Essays* (ed. Christopher Tolkien, London: George Allen & Unwin, 1983), p. 31.

3   Diana Wynne Jones, *The Tough Guide to Fantasyland* (1996; rev. ed. New York: Firebird, 2006), p. 53.

4   Fr. Klaeber, ed., *Beowulf and The Fight at Finnsburg* (1922; 3rd ed., Lexington, MA: D. C. Heath & Co., 1950), ll. 2270–81. I cannot reproduce the macrons that should modify some letters y and ash (æ). The letter eth (ð, Ð) is sounded as voiced 'th', thorn (Þ, þ) as unvoiced 'th'.

5   Seamus Heaney, *Beowulf* (London: Faber, 1999), p. 72. The reparagraphing is Heaney's.

Old before its centuries of vigil and sleep in the barrow, curled about the cups and hauberks of a vanished lord and his liegemen, the nameless worm slain by Beowulf only at the cost of his own life is the primary exemplum combining hoarded gold, fiery breath, and ancient malice awoken to invade the contemporary world. And though the poet plainly didn't think it unique, merely one of its troublesome Old English and Norse kind, this dragon is now much the oldest such exemplum.

It isn't the only dragon in *Beowulf*, because the one other substantial Norse dragon of whom there are detailed accounts, Fáfnir, the dragon of the Völsungs usually slain by Sigurðr but here by 'Sigemund', is pointedly mentioned by a bard (at ll. 875 ff.)—but Fáfnir was that most peculiar of things, a weredragon, once a dwarf (or man), hence his definite history and dying exchange with his killer (in the Norse and Icelandic sources, as in Wagner) about the curse of Andvari, to whom his hoard once belonged. Fáfnir does as a dragon have fire, scales, and hoard but also a hu-

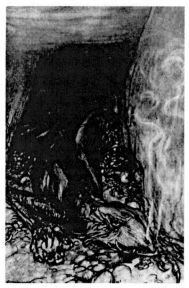

Arthur Rackham, Fáfnir

man voice, intelligence, and purpose, as his eye and immanent hand suggest in Arthur Rackham's illustration of *Siegfried*. Such qualities are alien to the "eald ūhtsceaða", and it, not Fáfnir, informed almost all later Northern European dragons. St George, for example, a third-century military martyr under Diocletian, began dragon-killing only in the twelfth century, and while his fabled heroism mixes Christian devil-slaying with prowess at the lance, the dragon is re-cognisably Beowulfian. Arabic sources cognate with *The Book of One Thousand and One Nights* (first collected from *c*.1000 CE) are probably responsible for substituting eaten virgins and repeated propitiation for hoarded gold and singular vengeance, but the fiery reptilian form, predation on the people, dumbness, animality, and malevolent antiquity of the dragon are constant.

These murderous, voiceless worms fly from *Beowulf* to the English Renaissance, through the Arthurian cycles and into the fourteenth-century *Mabinogion* and *The Voiage and Travayle of Syr John Maundeville, Knight*; on to the fifteenth and sixteenth centuries, with spots in Mallory's *Le Morte d'Arthur* and Spenser's *The Faerie Queene*. They can be seen as late as the 1660s, with a valedictory show in Athanasius Kircher's *Mundus subterraneus*, but thereafter they dwindle and disappear, as softly and silently vanishing away as any boojum. One can still find a variety of stray, mostly decorative Chinese *Tien-lung* (celestials) or *Shen-lung* (water- and cloud-dwellers), who start to appear as European trade with the Orient picks up[1]; a proportion of religious tracts and sermons continue to invoke the symbolic hell-dragons of the Christian Revelation; and there are such strange symbolisms as William Blake's; but otherwise, search as one may, with *Beowulf* all but unknown Enlightenment and Romantic dragons prove very thin on the ground. Some maps might still have been hopefully marked 'Here Be Dragons', but that 'Here' was by definition somewhere unexplored and far away, and so in decreasing supply as the European colonial empires steadily expanded. By the later nineteenth century, however, philologists and archaeologists, animated by a new sense of comparative religious thought, were becoming interested in ancient Babylonian, Sumerian, and Egyptian dragons, primarily water-dwellers quite lacking the specific constellation of tropes found in *Beowulf*. The British Museum powerfully joined in with displays of imperial classical loot (and dinosaur skeletons, once interpreted as dragon bones), and, with *Beowulf* itself beginning to return to serious philological attention, northern literary dragons began again to quicken.[2]

The two earliest creatures that are now remembered are very different, and establish distinct draconic lines of descent. In Andrew Lang's *Prince Prigio* (1889) the dragon is more-or-less a Beowulfian firedrake, certainly a beast to fear and (within the limits of context and style) take seriously; this is the line of interest here. Kenneth Grahame's 'The Reluctant Dragon' (in *Dream Days*, 1898), on the other hand, is a happily ironised vision of an elderly St George and pacifist dragon who stage a mock-battle to satisfy the bloodthirsty local villagers before settling down in harmony; the story subtly anticipates some aspects of *The Wind in the Willows* (1908), and begins to do for dragons what William Stieg's gloriously post-Modernist *Shrek!* (1990, filmed 2001) does for ogres.[3] There are also Edith Nesbit's various dragon stories for *The Strand Magazine*, collected in *The Book of Dragons* (1901), where the dragons may be truly dangerous but have some British-Museumly and Grahame-ish inflections.

---

1 *Ti-lung*, controlling rivers and springs, and *Fu-ts'ang-lung*, guarding underground hoards, are less likely to stray overseas.

2 Such histories as there are—G. Elliot Smith, *The Evolution of the Dragon* (1919), Ernest Ingersoll, *Dragons and Dragon Lore* (1928)—are largely concerned with ancient dragons and do not venture beyond St George. On the twentieth century see Anne McCaffrey, *A Diversity of Dragons* (1997), and Pamela Blanpied's mockumentary *Dragons* (1980); Susan Hepler's '"Once They All Believed in Dragons"' has some useful references but makes careless errors in plot summaries.

3 Both Grahame and Stieg inform Tamora Pierce's excellent dragon story 'Plain Magic' (1996).

Partly in print, but far more through the strange 1941 Disney animation of his story, Grahame began a line of affable, child-friendly dragons who are overtly anthropomorphic in personality and capacities, including speech, while lacking pretty much all traditional draconic characteristics unless as ironic refractions. Yet strange as it may seem, draconic destructiveness, fire, and antique malice were not so willingly foregone, and the renascent firedrakes are far more powerful than the descendants of Grahame's friendly dragon. Some would chart the fierce line of draconic descent through the various fantasies of Edward Plunkett, 18th Baron Dunsany, particularly *The King of Elfland's Daughter* (1924), and/or Eric R. Eddison's military fantasy *The Worm Ouroboros* (1922): but if Dunsany is of general generic importance, he did a great deal more for unicorns than for dragons; and while Eddison's title promisingly

combines a northern 'worm' with Greek 'ouroboros' ('tail-biter'), his tale draws most on Norse myths of the World-Serpent Jörmungandr as a metaphor for cyclical warfare, not in fiery draconic reality.[1] More telling than both, in many ways, is Nesbit's later story 'The Last of the Dragons', in *Five of Us, and Madeline* (1925), in which the dragon lurches towards the comic-ironic Grahame variety yet lacks wit and anticipates the worst of Walt Disney's sentimentality before summarily becoming, in the last line and by its own request, "the first aeroplane"—but that mechanical connection must wait.

Ouroboros, from Theodoros Pelecanos, *Synosius* (1478)

Jörmungandr or any dragon as tail-swallower offers an interesting image, and in retrospect Eddison may be seen as an early prophet of 1939, knowing the settlements of 1918–19 could not hold and 'prophesying war'. Moreover, while he lacks dragons he could write rather good pastiche-antique prose, for which Ursula Le Guin sang his praises in her marvellous essay 'From Elfland to Poughkeepsie' (1973).[2] It had also, and rather earlier, caught the ear of J. R. R. Tolkien—by no means uncritically, but nevertheless[3]—and Tolkien, *inter alia* Rawlinson & Bosworth Professor of Anglo-Saxon at Oxford 1925–45, was a notable critic of *Beowulf* and particularly that "eald ūhtsceaða", which had a central place in his seminal 1936 British Academy Lecture, '*Beowulf*: The Monsters and the Critics'. There Tolkien elegantly and persuasively

1   Additionally, Eddison's novel only became widely known after its republication in the late 1960s.
2   Collected in *The Language of the Night* (1979, rev. ed. 1989).
3   See *The Letters of J. R. R. Tolkien* (1980), esp. # 199, p. 258.

argued that far from being pagan blemishes the monsters in general and dragon in particular were central to all the poem sought to be—but rehabilitating dragons is a tricky business, and Tolkien found himself following his erudite lecture with *The Hobbit* (1937), wherein poor Bilbo Baggins, in the process of getting *There and Back Again*, found himself face-to-face with Smaug the Golden; and *that* is a very different proposition altogether.

The scale of Tolkien's Middle Earth is far greater than that of Beowulf's Geatland, and Smaug a correspondingly larger and more ambitious dragon, with a mountain for its barrow and the accumulated mining and trading riches of a Dwarf kingdom to supply its hoard—but the stamp of *Beowulf* and the "eald ūhtsceaða" are overt in Smaug's desire to own heaped gold and heirlooms, dwelling with them in underground silence through many lives of men, and in its disturbance by a thief who steals from its hoard a golden cup.[1] Its thrilling death—betrayed by Bilbo and a clever thrush, and mortally pierced in a soft spot by Bard the Bowman's black arrow—is as much St George as *Beowulf*, but other late mediaeval or Arabic accretions (virgins, steeds, lances) are stripped away, and the uncontrollable rage Smaug unleashes on the lake-town of Esgaroth is wholly *Beowulf*'s "nacod niðdraca, nihtes flēogeð / fyre befangen", "the slick-skinned dragon, threatening the night sky / with streamers of fire" (as Tolkien's drawing of the 'Death of Smaug' shows[2]). While far more dramatic than the barrow-bound sword-fight in *Beowulf*, Smaug's airborne passions of revenge and death are unproblematic (though his flaming destruction of Esgaroth makes one wonder about its closeness in time to the German aerial bombing of Guernica[3]). But the other famous image Tolkien provided, and the scene it memorably illustrated, Smaug in conversation with Bilbo, is electrified dynamite—for the episode centrally requires that Smaug speak, and so presents the entirely tricky questions of draconic interests and language. The nameless worm of *Beowulf* and Fáfnir are fused in reverse—not following the path of the *Völsunga Saga* or *Nibelungenlied*, where human Fáfnir acquires draconic form and habit, but shaping a new way forward, whereby

1 Smaug descended on the Lonely Mountain in 2770 Third Age, and was slain 171 years later in 2941; see *The Lord of the Rings* (2nd ed., in 1 vol., 1965/66; hereafter *LotR*), III.369–70.

2 The Tolkien Estate does not permit reproduction of his art in e-books. The image is available in Hammon & Scull, *J. R. R. Tolkien* (1995), and at:
   ▣ http://tolkiengateway.net/wiki/Image:J.R.R._Tolkien_-_Death_of_Smaug.jpg

3 Tolkien completed the typescript of The Hobbit by 3 October 1936, when he sent it to Allen & Unwin (*Letters*, p. 14), but made substantial revisions in proof in March 1937; Guernica was bombed on 26 April; Picasso's famous painting was first exhibited in July, at the Spanish Pavilion at the Paris International Exposition; and *The Hobbit* was published on 21 September.

the full-grown and ancient worm acquires its own capacities of mind and a voice to go with its malice, or benevolence. And if Smaug himself is by now long dead, old bones among burned timbers, the draconic consequences of his acquisition of a voice are still unfolding.

Unsurprisingly, Tolkien first created dragons within his legendarium almost at the very beginning, in 'The Fall of Gondolin',[1] drafted in 1916–17, but draconic nature changed a great deal through his various early narratives. These birth-pangs will demand some scrutiny before the end, but what matters for now is that in the evolving time-line that would eventually lead to Bilbo's and Frodo's adventures in *The Hobbit* and *The Lord of the Rings*, three full ages of the world and more than 6,000 years later than Gondolin's glory and fall, Tolkien's dragons acquired, like their progenitor in *Beowulf*, immense antiquity.

Altogether, four dragons of Middle Earth were eventually named and chronicled: in the First Age, Glaurung, Father of Dragons, and Ancalagon the Black, and in the Third Age, Scatha the Worm and Smaug the Golden.[2] The wingless but fire-breathing and very definitely talking Glaurung was bred by Morgoth (Tolkien's originary Lucifer, of whom Sauron was a servant), just as the nameless and speechless flying steeds of the Nazgûl were later bred by Sauron[3]—but neither could truly create life, only warp existing stock. Orcs, as readers of *The Lord of the Rings* learn from Treebeard, were thus made by Morgoth in mockery of Elves, as Trolls of Ents[4]; with

1   In *The Book of Lost Tales, Part II* (1984), volume 2 of *The History of Middle Earth* (12 vols, 1983–96; hereafter *HME 1–12*). Tolkien named at least one dragon before his legendarium coalesced: John Garth, in *Tolkien and the Great War*, notes the creation by 1915 of "*Fentor*, lord of dragons, [who] was slain by *Ingilmo* or by the hero *Turambar*, who had a mighty sword called *Sangahyando*, or 'cleaver of throngs' (and who is compared to Sigurðr of Norse myth)" (p. 127). 'Fentor' became 'Glorund' in 'Turambar and the Foalókë' (written by 1919, in *HME 2*), then 'Glorung' and eventually 'Glaurung' in what became *The Silmarillion* (1977).

2   *LotR* I.70 (Ancalagon), III.346 (Scatha). Glaurung and Ancalagon are named and detailed in *The Silmarillion*, and there are various references to dragons and drakes in *HME*; see also *The Children of Húrin*. Gandalf mentions others living in the far wastelands of Middle Earth, but these are unnamed and play no part.

3   *Nazgûl* named in the Black Speech the nine once-human ringwraiths, *nazg* meaning 'ring'; their rings were forged in the second millennium of the Second Age, and the Nazgûl first seen *c*.2551 (*LotR* III.364)—but their flying steeds were unknown before 3020 Third Age, during the War of the Ring. "A creature of an older world maybe it was, whose kind, lingering in forgotten mountains cold beneath the Moon, outstayed their day, and in hideous eyrie bred this last untimely brood, apt to evil. And the Dark Lord took it, and nursed it with fell meats, until it grew beyond the measure of all other things that fly; and he gave it to his servant to be his steed." (*LotR* III.115).

4   *LotR* II.89, III. 409; cf. "demons and dragons and monsters, and Orcs, that are mockeries of the

the arrival of the Eagles and simultaneous flight of the Nazgûl at the Battle of the Black Gate[1] it seems clear that the fell flying beasts similarly mock the noble birds, and are a kind of ghastly sub-dragon—but what reptilian stock Morgoth used for Glaurung (slain within the First Age by the Elf-Lord Túrin[2]) is unknown. Ancalagon the Black, the first flying and fire-breathing dragon, was bred by Morgoth from stock presumably including Glaurung's, and slain by Eärendil the Mariner at the Breaking of Thangorodrim, when Morgoth fell, ending the First Age; its precipitous, dying fall broke Morgoth's triple-peaked citadel and drove him out to his destruction. The Third-Age dragons seem a similar pair,[3] but Scatha the Worm (perhaps, like Glaurung, wingless) was slain by Fram, an ancestor of Eorl of Rohan, and Smaug by Bard, who still could not save Esgaroth. The catastrophe of Smaug's fall and their First-Age origins notwithstanding, both were lesser beings than Glaurung or Ancalagon, as their mortal rather than High-Elven slayers attest—yet however diminished they still carry, and in Smaug's case bring into *The Hobbit*, the peculiar antiquity of connection with the First Age.[4]

In *The Lord of the Rings* the burden of that im/memorial age is far more central but distributed between Bombadil, Treebeard, various Elves (notably Elrond & Galadriel as ringbearers), and the unseen Sauron, all far older than any Man, Dwarf, or Hobbit. Elrond's speech in council draws on personal memories that stretch back to the great Elven city-kingdoms of the First Age, before Thangorodrim was built or broken, but it is his first-hand knowledge of the ending of the Second Age, when Gil-Galad died and Sauron fell but the One Ring survived, that matters more.[5] And, absent dragons, the burden of malevolent antiquity is dumbly manifest in the most monstrous creations that *are* physically present—the fiery "Balrog of Morgoth" who

creatures of Ilúvatar" (*HME 5*, p. 26).

1   *LotR* III.169, 226. The eagles may also invoke John of Patmos.

2   There is an image of Glorund (later Glauring), in Hammond & Scull, *J. R. R. Tolkien* (1995), p. 51.

3   In both early and late *Silmarillion* materials it is said that in the "Terrible or Last Battle" ending the First Age "Morgoth himself makes a last sally with all his dragons; but they are destroyed, all save two which escape, by the sons of the Valar" (*HME 4*, p. 44; cf. *HME 11*, p. 346). These must be Smaug and Scatha, who were somehow able to breed, though never truly to reproduce.

4   See *The Hobbit* (1937; Boston: Houghton Mifflin, 1966), p. 238 (ch. XII): "'I laid low the warriors of old and their like is not in the world today. Then I was but young and tender. Now I am old and strong, strong, strong, Thief in the Shadows!'"

5   As one measure, consider that in Peter Jackson's film trilogy the fall of Sauron is included in the prologue to the first film, but at no point is First Age material invoked, and the whole anagogic relation of Aragorn & Arwen (Third Age) to Beren & Luthien (First Age) is omitted despite the increased importance given to the love of Aragorn & Arwen as a primary motive.

drags Gandalf into the Morian abyss, and Shelob the Great, "last child of Ungoliant to trouble the unhappy world".[1] These extraordinary beings, as the mentions of Morgoth and his spider-ally Ungoliant attest, are as much relics as Sauron himself, and the peculiar effects they produce in their antique greatness of evil require First-Age opposition. For the Balrog it is Gandalf, "servant of the Secret Fire, wielder of the flame of Anor",[2] made incarnate precisely to fight primordial evils beyond the power of Men and Elves, and for Shelob the light of Eärendil's star, captured by Galadriel in the glass she gave Frodo and probing Shelob's wounds with an agony that sends her scuttling back into the darkness under the mountain-fences of Mordor. Smaug's death in *The Hobbit*, as the last of its kind in the West, logically kept Morgoth's dragons and their get out of *The Lord of the Rings* save in passing memory of Ancalagon and Scatha, but it proved one of Tolkien's very few cop-outs all the same, for Smaug would not have been as inarticulate as the Balrog or Ungoliant's bloated daughter.

The dialogue Bilbo and Smaug share in *The Hobbit*, amusing and instrumental in the plot, is irrelevant here in detail, for the simple, blazing point is that *any* conversation with a true (as opposed to were-) dragon requires draconic language and content—inconceivable for the "eald ūhtsceaða", who utters only flame and knows only keeping, losing, and destruction. From the moment Smaug responds with ironic and deadly calm to the intruder he senses but cannot see—"Well, thief! I smell you and I feel your air. I hear your breath. Come along! Help yourself again, there is plenty and to spare!"[3]—he becomes an interlocutor with special access to antiquity; potentially, at least, a bard. It is as if one of those reassembled dinosaur skeletons were to abandon its mute testimony to the distant pre-Human past in favour of speaking nicely to an historian—as Bilbo after his fashion later becomes, of himself and Hobbitkind, through the *Red Book of Westmarch* (a name modelled on the *Llyfr Coch Hergest*, 'Red Book of Hergest', one source of the *Mabinogion*[4]). Had Bilbo only known what to ask, Smaug (if willing) could have spoken of much otherwise long forgotten: the Arkenstone, the *mithril* coat given to Bilbo, and the other treasures of his hoard were individually ancient relics, and the coat became in *The Lord of the Rings* a metonym of Durin and the Dwarf Kingdom of Khazad-Dûm in their glory,

---

1   *LotR* I. 371 ; III.332.

2   *LotR* I.344. The incarnate Gandalf came to Middle Earth only *c.*1000 Third Age (*LotR* III.365), but like all *Istari* had in his true nature as a lesser Valar seen all ages.

3   *The Hobbit*, p. 234 (ch. XII). Tolkien's illustration 'Conversation with Smaug' is reproduced in Hammon & Scull, *J. R. R. Tolkien* (1995), and at:
    ▣ http://tolkiengateway.net/wiki/Image:J.R.R._Tolkien_-_Conversation_with_Smaug.jpg

4   The other is the *Llyfr Gwyn Rhydderch*, 'White Book of Rhydderch'.

reaching back, as Smaug itself does, to the First Age.[1] The conversation it and *Elrond* might have had—or Gandalf; even (though one shudders at the thought) Saruman, or Sauron—would be as far beyond Men's understanding as the memorial deliberation of angels over the Fall.

All this Tolkien for whatever reasons (and the possibilities make a very interesting list) foreswore for his Balrogs and spiders. But dragons will out, and the comedic possibilities of draconic intelligence and speech, suppressed within the legendarium since *The Hobbit*, forcibly resurfaced outside it with the cheerfully wicked and somewhat Grahame-ish (or even Disney-form) dragon Chrysophylax Dives in *Farmer Giles of Ham* (1949). Moreover, while *The Lord of the Rings* began its ascendancy and the front-end of his legendarium became (until Harry Potter) the greatest shared fantasy of modern times, Tolkien himself dived back into the depths of the First Age and what would eventually become *The Silmarillion* (1977), reworking the materials now available in *The History of Middle Earth* (1983–96)—wherein the true dragons could again talk, though their special antiquity was largely negated in First-Age settings. These things remained largely private until after his death, but Tolkien's avuncular narrative style in *The Hobbit* had produced around Smaug's conversation some interesting (if alarming) advice for the dracological community. Bilbo, readers are reassured when Smaug first speaks, is not wholly "unlearned in dragon-lore",[2] and a slightly different version of the riddling talk that served him so well with Gollum is happily:

> the way to talk to dragons, if you don't want to reveal your proper name (which is wise), and don't want to infuriate them by a flat refusal (which is also very wise). No dragon can resist the fascination of riddling talk and of wasting time trying to understand it.

More dangerously, however:

> Whenever Smaug's roving eye, seeking for [Bilbo] in the shadows, flashed across him, he trembled, and an unaccountable desire seized hold of him to rush out and reveal himself and tell all the truth to Smaug. In fact he was in grievous danger of coming under the dragon-spell.[3]

---

1   Khazad-Dûm (Moria) was founded by Durin in the First Age, grew and endured throughout the 3441 years of the Second, and fell to the Balrog in 1980–1 Third Age (*LotR* III.352–3). As *mithril* was mined nowhere else, the coat given to Bilbo in 2941 Third Age must then have been at least one thousand years old, and might have been five thousand or more.

2   'Dragon-lore' is not Tolkien's coinage, for Ingersoll used in it 1928, but this instance is probably the source of most later usage; *OED2* does not appear to record the term.

3   All three quotations are from *The Hobbit*, pp. 234, 235, 236 (all Ch. XII).

In immediate narrative context all is well, but readers who would reconcile *The Hobbit* with *The Lord of the Rings* have a problem. The notion of Bilbo having some 'dragon-lore' might be allowed, given his acquaintance with Gandalf, but judicious observations about tactics imply a habit of conversation, or at least extended experience, and nothing about Ancalagon or Scatha recorded in *The Lord of the Rings* suggests they would have helped, or were remotely of this kind—so it is tempting to think there must be an inconsistency, and perhaps there is.

Yet despite the avuncular tone of *The Hobbit*, easily read as legitimating casual inventions of detail, some of these draconic ideas do come from the deeps of Tolkien's legendarium. The particular danger of a dragon's gaze (common enough with gorgons, basilisks and the like) was established in 'Turambar and the Foalókë' (*c.*1919) as the "foul magic" of the dragon Glorund (later Glaurung) whereby, terribly for the Elves, Túrin's "will died, and he could not stir of his own purpose, yet might he see and hear". The same worm spoke tauntingly to Túrin at some length, and had (or pretended to) gifts of prophecy, while First-Age Men believed that "whosoever might taste the heart of a dragon would know all tongues of Gods or Men, of birds or beasts, and his ears would catch whispers of the Valar or of Melko such as never had he heard before"[1]—a fairly pure chunk of the *Völsunga Saga*, where this effect of tasting Fáfnir's blood and/or roasted dragon-heart on Sigurðr's understanding of birds is critical. With various other materials that originate in the earliest surviving tales, and his own long consideration of *Beowulf* and its two very different dragons, Tolkien did by 1937 have dragon-lore for Bilbo to draw on, a sub-stratum of his legendarium that had matured for nearly two decades and in doing so fused a body-form and behaviours from *Beowulf* with an original quality of speech. And although their passage went largely unrecorded even in the dense volumes of *The History of Middle Earth*, while Tolkien transformed his 'lost tales' of Túrin and Gondolin into the high myths of Bilbo's much later millennium his dragons too were drawn through epic extensions of time, absorbing that Old English hyper-recession beyond even the lost realms represented by their hoards, to emerge with Smaug as thoroughly dangerous interlocutors, far beyond Fáfnir and to all intents and purposes practitioners of the same linguistic magic as Tolkien, knowing very well 'what's in a name'.

The reason for avoiding revelation of one's name, after all, whether to dragons or mages, is that such knowledge grants power, and almost the first thing serious students of Tolkien discover is his philological engines of composition, granting (like Adam) a name, and then (unlike anyone before him) working out what it meant and

---

1 All three quotations are from *HME2*, p. 86. 'Melko' is an older name of Morgoth.

where in which (imaginary) language it had come from, after which the story thereby discovered merely needed to be told. Study of Tolkien's brief stint in the early 1920s on the first edition of the *Oxford English Dictionary* deepens the picture, for he treated the real words whose etymologies and definitions he researched and composed (nice Germanic 'w's for the most part) in exactly that way.[1] In this creative mode Tolkien's most profound (not always most reverential, but always most responsive) successor has been Ursula K. Le Guin, and the four dragons of her *Earthsea* trilogy (1968–72) and subsequently sestet (1968–2001)—marvellously named Yevaud, Orm Embar, Kalessin, and Orm Irian—renegotiate antiquity precisely through their relation with a language of naming which is also a language of making and magic. Le Guin has also reconciled in a very different way the shades of Fáfnir and the nameless worm, drawing weredragons into a far more interesting and original light than Tolkien, who seems never to have been very interested in Fáfnir, or even C. S. Lewis, who was, as the shape-shifting moral education of Eustace Scrubb in *The Voyage of the* Dawn Treader (1952) shows.

Earthsea must therefore be the next stop, and several very interesting writers have already followed Le Guin's feminist lead. Joanne Bertin's incomplete trilogy beginning with *The Last Dragonlord* (1998) & *Dragon and Phoenix* (1999),[2] for example, or Elizabeth Kerner's trilogy *The Tale of Lanen Kaelar* (1997–2005),[3] both deserve serious thought, not least about the various military and romantic ends to which weredragonhood is being put. But there have been since Le Guin a perfectly extraordinary number of dragons in general to try and keep track of, in considering others of whom a very different argument than this one might be constructed. Amid the proliferating diversity of individual imaginations it does, however, seem clear that one other great draconic line sprang in parallel from Smaug, so that if Le Guin's are the weredragons and linguistic witnesses of antiquity, these others, whose midwife was Anne McCaffrey, are armoured beasts of burden and threateners with fire.

McCaffrey's *Dragonflight* (1968), a far-future chronicle of the planet Pern published in the same year as *A Wizard of Earthsea*, was what is in SF called a 'fix-up', a novel assembled from previously published short stories or novellas, and two of those had already attracted serious attention—'Dragonrider' won the 1968 Nebula Award for Best Novella, and 'Weyr Search' the corresponding Hugo Award. The

---

1   See Peter Gilliver, Jeremy Marshall, & Edmund Wiener, *The Ring of Words: Tolkien and the Oxford English Dictionary* (Oxford: Oxford University Press, 2006).

2   A third volume, *Bard's Oath*, has been promised ever since; there is also one earlier short story.

3   *Song in the Silence* (1997), *The Lesser Kindred* (2001), & *Redeeming the Lost* (2005).

whole Pernese legendarium then went off like a slow-motion but unstoppable bomb, and nearly 40 years later, after 16 solo novels in the series, two collections of short stories, and various guides and other epiphenomena, as well as two further series novels in collaboration with her son, Todd McCaffrey, the Dragonriders of Pern® franchise is being taken over by Todd, whose first solo series novel *Dragonsblood* appeared in 2005 as the twentieth instalment.[1] Telepathically bonded to individual humans from hatching to death, the Pernese dragons have thought and wit, but it's more horse-sense and cat-dignity than culture and they are not individually ancient at all—though the displaced antiquity breaks out in the most interesting way. But what most matters about them is their companionship of humans and necessity as a militarised force to Pernese survival, which grounds their value more deeply in body, the physical attributes of flight, fiery breath, and armoured hide, than in speech or knowledge. And like Le Guin, McCaffrey too has been richly followed, count-ing among her most recent and interesting legatees the late Vietnam veteran Chris Bunch, whose *Dragonmaster* trilogy[2] (2002–04) refights World War One with drag-ons in the place of von Richthofen and the Royal Flying Corps, and the amusing Naomi Novik, whose *Temeraire* trilogy[3] (2006) re-runs Hornblower's Revolutionary and Napoleonic Wars but with air-force dragons as well as sea-force frigates (and well enough to suggest some very interesting relations between the two). The best-known current dragon, Saphira in Christopher Paolini's *Eragon* (2002, filmed 2006) and *Eldest* (2005), is also in her companionship and military value very much a Mc-Caffrey dragon, though Paolini's fantasy world in general owes far more to Tolkien's Middle Earth, and Eragon's wanderings around it point back through McCaffrey not to Tolkien's evil dragons or their later monstrous substitutes, but to Gandalf's special relationship with Shadowfax (the great white stallion who is Lord of the Mearas).

Pernese dragons therefore must also be looked to, after Earthsea's, and that makes already for a very full agenda, but as the post-Tolkien dragon-makers I haven't mentioned outnumber those I have twenty-to-one at least,[4] there are still a hopeless number of omissions. Yet if I seriously regret some of those, it should equally be said that there are among the dragon hordes tedious and sadly devolved beasts with remarkably little to recommend them. Plainly enough, a dull author makes for a dull

---

1   During the same period McCaffrey has published at least 59 other solo or collaborative novels.

2   *Storm of Wings* (2002), *Knighthood of the Dragon* (2003), & *The Last Battle* (2004).

3   *His Majesty's Dragon*, *Throne of Jade*, and *Black Powder War* (all 2006); more are promised.

4   McCaffrey, *A Diversity of Dragons*, pp. 94–6, lists at least 91 authors of 145+ books, the vast majority post-1968—and that was in 1996, so Bertin, Kerner, Bunch, Novik, Paolini and their 13 books are missing, as well as J. K. Rowling, Irene Radford, Tamora Pierce, Peter F. Hamilton ...

dragon, but the pitfalls of the worst may also be hazards for the best and most imagi-native; Joanne Bertin carefully explained one part of the problem when she remarked in 2002:

> While I liked reading about dragons myself, I'd never considered when I wrote the book if publishers were looking for more dragon books. I just wrote the story I had to write. Once again I lucked out; dragons were (still are) popular, and a race of weredragons was considered a new angle.[1]

A *new* angle, after Fáfnir, C. S. Lewis, and Le Guin's *Tehanu* (1990), which steals the wind even from "*race* of weredragons"? And the endorsement of 'popularity'? But note "was considered"—not by Ms Bertin, who knows her dragon-lore rather better than some. And what else, *mutatis mutandis*, can be expected in the quotid-ian commerce of any overworked sub-genre? But it is not simply vulgarisation and devalued commodification as fads and trends that have engulfed dragonkind in their great modern resurgence and diaspora, for if with Le Guin and McCaffrey the drag-ons began to embrace modernity in ways neither Beowulf nor his "eald ūhtsceaða" could begin to understand, and that Tolkien had subsumed or rejected, it has led them in a great ouroborine circle, and not always to a dizzying fate.

Yevaud, Orm Embar, and Kalessin were in one sense the major dynamic that transformed Le Guin's original trilogy—*A Wizard of Earthsea* (1968), *The Tombs of Atuan* (1971), & *The Farthest Shore* (1972)—into a sestet-cycle, for the concerns of the three later books—*Tehanu: The Last Book of Earthsea* (1990) and the diptych of *Tales from Earthsea* & *The Other Wind* (both 2001)—arose largely from her continuing investigation of the place and meaning of dragons within her own legendarium. In another sense the three dragons of the initial trilogy are one kind of thing, creatures recognisably engaged with Tolkien and, through him, with *Beowulf*, while Orm Irian in the later books is of another kind, reflecting different authorial priorities (if not interests) and constellating herself with other weredragons as much as with her older Le Guinian relations. As Le Guin has retrospectively adjusted and relimned her creations, notably in her published 1992 lecture *Revisioning Earthsea* and the summary essay included in *Tales from Earthsea*, her new forms of dragon-hood have overwritten her earlier, but to understand how the dragons evolved one must see them as they began.

---

1   http://www.demensionszine.com/stories/0302i1.html, accessed on 7 Feb. 2007.

The first glimpse of Earthsea was in part specifically draconic, in the short story 'The Rule of Names', one of two set in the Earthsea archipelago to appear in *Fantastic* magazine in 1964; both were collected in *The Wind's Twelve Quarters* (1975). Like its companion-piece 'The Word of Unbinding', which anticipated the culminating problem of 'unmaking' in the first trilogy, 'The Rule of Names' established a basic law of magic—that the use of a being's true name will banish illusion and not only reveal their true shape but bind them in it. True name and reality are one—and the grasping revenger Blackbeard thinks to use that, for he believes he knows the true name of a wizard who took a hoard from a dragon that had ransacked the island of Pendor, and he has tracked that name to the island of Sattins where the wizard is hiding as (thank-you, Frodo) one Mr Underhill. When Blackbeard in rude round terms calls fat, little Mr Underhill out to a duel, a swift flicker of illusion-fights begins, but then:

> Where the cataract had been there hovered a dragon. Black wings darkened all the hill, steel claws reached groping, and from the dark, scaly, gaping lips fire and steam shot out.
>
> Beneath the monstrous creature stood Blackbeard, laughing.
>
> 'Take any shape you please, little Mr Underhill!' he taunted. 'I can match you. But the game grows tiresome. I want to look upon my treasure, upon Inalkil. Now, big dragon, little wizard, take your true shape. I command you by the power of your true name—Yevaud!'
>
> Birt could not move at all, not even to blink. He cowered, staring whether he would or not. He saw the black dragon hang there in the air above Blackbeard. He saw the fire lick like many tongues from the scaly mouth, the steam jet from the red nostrils. He saw Blackbeard's face grow white, white as chalk, and the beard-fringed lips trembling.
>
> 'Your name is Yevaud!'
>
> 'Yes,' said a great, husky, hissing voice. 'My truename is Yevaud, and my true shape is this shape.'
>
> 'But the dragon was killed—they found dragon-bones on Udrath Island—'
>
> 'That was another dragon,' said the dragon, and then stooped like a hawk, talons outstretched.[1]

Quite why or when Yevaud was hiding as a plump village wizard on Sattins is unclear, and as Le Guin remarked introducing the two Earthsea stories in *The Wind's*

1 Ursula Le Guin, 'The Rule of Names', in *The Wind's Twelve Quarters* (1975; in 2 vols, London: Panther, 1978), I.92.

Twelve Quarters:

> *readers familiar with the trilogy will notice that trolls became extinct in Earthsea at some point, and that the history of the dragon Yevaud is somewhat obscure. (He must have been on Sattins Island some decades or centuries* before *Ged found him, and bound him, on the Isle of Pendor.) But this is only to be expected of dragons, who do not submit to the uni-directional, causal requirements of history, being myths, and neither timebinding nor timebound.[1]*

Quite right too—but not for the last time Le Guin was too harsh on herself, for the critical things about Yevaud's later and greater encounter with the Archmage-to-be, Ged, are all present and correct—draconic intelligence, very dry conversation, and ulterior knowledge of the truths to which human wizards pretend. 'The Rule of Names' borrows more than Mr Underhill's name from Tolkien, but simultaneously repays the debt: Blackbeard's fate is the ending in Smaug's maw that Bilbo (and Thorin Oakenshield, with all his dwarves) might have expected save for Bilbo's chance possession of the Ring, and the danger of talking to dragons with their profound qualities as interlocutors, germinating here from Tolkien's unwatered seeds, became a central quality of Earthsea.

Ged's binding of Yevaud—a binding that is of course by oath, not with cords or chains—comes in 'The Dragon of Pendor', Chapter 5 (of 10) in *A Wizard of Earthsea*, and one might in the first place note Le Guin's pulling-back from the dragon as finale. Use as a narrative *terminum* has been from *Beowulf* onwards very bad for dragon mortality, but *A Wizard of Earthsea* is fundamentally a *doppelgänger* story of the secret self,[2] like Robert Louis Stevenson's famous *The Strange Case of Dr Jekyll and Mr Hyde*, at the end of which the hero must confront the other that is him- or herself—so Ged's medial encounter with Yevaud is only a stepping-stone, a test from which both man and dragon can emerge alive. Another great change comes with Yevaud's parenthood, and the ease with which Ged can slay the dragonets who first fly against him, by approaching on a boat and binding young wings tight with the right spell, bringing them down into the sea as arrow-straight as burning wartime aeroplanes—a massacre that earns him more of Yevaud's respect and conversation than of grieving hatred, worm's-blood running, it seems, with reptilian cold rather than mammalian heat and emotion. Yet another developmental path flashes open in

---

1 Le Guin, *The Wind's Twelve Quarters*, I.74.

2 *Doppelgänger* literally means 'double-goer', and in science also refers to the refracted mirage of the self that is sometimes created in sunlit mountain-air when walking through or just above the cloud-tops.

Ged's use of true change into dragon-form, a possibility of his mage's art, as a weapon at need—or potentially a means of deeper communication, the only reflection in *A Wizard of Earthsea* of Yevaud's capacity for were-humanity in 'The Rule of Names'. But for all these riches it is Ged's conversation with Yevaud that truly matters, and what is said about the language of that conversation:

> 'Eight sons I had, little wizard,' said the great dry voice of the dragon. 'Five died, one dies: enough. You will not win my hoard by killing them.'
>
> 'I do not want your hoard.'
>
> The yellow smoke hissed from the dragon's nostrils: that was his laughter.
>
> 'Would you not like to come ashore and look at it, little wizard? It is worth looking at.'
>
> 'No, dragon.' The kinship of dragons is with wind and fire, and they do not fight willingly over the sea. That had been Ged's advantage so far and he kept it; but the strip of sea-water between him and the great grey talons did not seem much of an advantage, any more.
>
> It was hard not to look into the green, watching eyes.
>
> 'You are a very young wizard,' the dragon said. 'I did not know men came so young into their power.' He spoke, as did Ged, in the Old Speech, for that is the tongue of dragons still. Although the use of the Old Speech binds a man to truth, this is not so with dragons. It is their own language, and they can lie in it, twisting the true words to false ends, catching the unwary hearer in a maze of mirror-words each of which reflects the truth and none of which leads anywhere. So Ged had been warned often, and when the dragon spoke he listened with an untrustful ear, all his doubts ready. But the words seemed plain and clear: 'Is it to ask my help that you have come here, little wizard?'
>
> 'No, dragon.'
>
> 'Yet I could help you. You will need help soon, against that which hunts you in the dark.'
>
> Ged stood dumb.[1]

The skill of Le Guin's plotting pays off handsomely, for the reader knows that Ged is indeed hunted, by a taloned blot of shadow that climbed through the rift he made between worlds when (as Marlowe's Faustus with the shade of Helen of Troy) he summoned in apprentice pride and showmanship the true ghost of the Lady Elfarran. Even this early in the trilogy an interesting issue of gender is also thereby opened, for mages must (like Catholic priests) be male and celibate, while Elfarran was famed

---

1   Ursula Le Guin, *A Wizard of Earthsea* (1968; Harmondsworth: Puffin, 1971), pp. 103–04 (Ch. 5).

for her female beauty. But Ged's real problem is that to master the shadow-beast he loosed into the sunlit world he must learn its name, while as a pure, formless negativity it has and can have none—or so Ged believes until Yevaud offers to tell him that name. This offer Ged must refuse, for he has but one real weapon, his knowledge of Yevaud's name, and the bargain he must strike with it is for Yevaud's oath never to fly east against the settled islands of the Archipelago. Foregoing the temptation of self-interested cowardice to claim the dragon's help for himself alone is an important part of Ged's recovery from the proud and terrible moment that loosed the shadow, and shows a strength of character that compels Yevaud's respect—but dragonly powers and knowledge remain mysterious. If one grants that Yevaud *could* have told Ged the shadow-beast's name, the minimal explanation is that, without leaving Pendor, he was magically aware of the damage done by the spell Ged had cast to summon Elfarran, and so knew of the shadow-beast's existence and freedom; and that he also knew enough (as no living mage did) to understand that where a *doppelgänger* is concerned, the true name/s must be identical. Yevaud, that is, could have told Ged the shadow-beast's name without ever knowing it himself, by saying 'Its name is your own'—but must still have had an analytical and sensory magical awareness, or capacity of direct perception, on an astonishing and near-transcendent scale. And the only explanation offered is that special relationship of dragons to the language of the making, that Segoy spoke when in the depths of time and chaos he raised the islands from the sea and gave all things their beings and their names.

Ged obtains Yevaud's oath on his own and his surviving sons' behalf foreswearing predation on the Archipelago, and Le Guin, by having a dragon in medial place, is free to put Ged's meeting with the shadow in last place, bringing her novel to its proper generic end and leaving dragons and their ways of speech to fructify. Not one is seen or heard in *The Tombs of Atuan*—but they enter the discussion when Tenar, who has from early childhood been Arha, the Eaten One, a nameless priestess of the Old Powers, and has only regained memory of her given name by Ged's grace and art magic, asks him scornfully of what she has never seen, and gets more answer than she bargained for:

> She wanted no more talk of Erreth-Akbe, sensing a danger in the subject. 'He was a dragonlord, they say. And you say you're one. Tell me, what is a dragonlord?'
>
> Her tone was always jeering, his answers direct and plain, as if he took her questions in good faith.

'One whom the dragons will speak with,' he said, 'that is a dragonlord, or at least that is the centre of the matter. It's not a trick of mastering the dragons, as most people think. Dragons have no masters. The question is always the same, with a dragon: will he talk to you or will he eat you? If you can count upon his doing the former, and not doing the latter, why then you're a dragonlord.'

'Dragons can speak?'

'Surely! In the Eldest Tongue, the language we men learn so hard and use so brokenly, to make our spells of magic and of patterning. No man knows all that language, or a tenth of it. He has not time to learn it. But dragons live a thousand years . . . They are worth talking to, as you might guess.'

'Are there dragons here in Atuan?'

'Not for many centuries, I think, nor in Karego-At. But in your northernmost island, Hur-at-Hur, they say there are still large dragons in the mountains. In the Inner Lands they all keep now to the farthest west, the remote West Reach, islands where no men live and few men come. If they grow hungry, they raid the lands to their east; but that is seldom. I have seen the island where they come to dance together. They fly on their great wings in spirals, in and out, higher and higher over the western sea, like a storming of yellow leaves in autumn.' Full of the vision, his eyes gazed through the black paintings on the walls, through the walls and the earth and the darkness, seeing the open sea stretch unbroken to the sunset, the golden dragons on the golden wind.[1]

When exactly Ged sailed the "remote West Reach" to the islands marked on maps of Earthsea as 'the Dragons' Run' and saw them dancing on the wind is uncertain, like much of his personal history between books, but the idea of dancing on the wind would prove important. Meantime, of greater importance is the humble definition of a dragonlord, not as a master but as a supplicant suffered to live and, of necessity in Earthsea, a mage—not just because of their magical power but because to exercise that power they must know the Old Speech, the only tongue in which dragons will (and perhaps can) converse. The time-signature of draconic antiquity is independently present through Ged's guess at a lifespan stretching to a millennium, a figure that with Kalessin had later to be extended, but even this is tied directly to linguistic competence.

Allegory is (supposedly) no longer a popular mode of writing or reading, but it isn't always easy to ignore either in strongly Catholic Tolkien (where Gandalf does, after all, fall into a tremendously deep pit, wrestle for three days with a fiery monster, and subsequently appear in shining white) or his successors. Though she has been

---

1   Ursula Le Guin, *The Tombs of Atuan* (1971; Harmondsworth: Puffin, 1974), pp. 92–3 (Ch. 7).

a Taoist herself from the age of 14, the sexlessness in Earthsea of Le Guin's exclusively male mages, trading secular romance for the sacred life of power, also plainly invites comparison with the Catholic priesthood, and resonance deepens with mages' exclusive use in magic of the Old Speech, much as Latin was used in the liturgy of the mass—an issue extensively debated and eventually reformed during the Second Vatican Council of 1962–5, while Earthsea was first coalescing in Le Guin's mind. But Yevaud and the great dragon-dancers on the wind whom Ged reports fit as well into this theology as they would have into the chambers of the Vatican II debates, for if the mages' Old Speech that they "use so brokenly, to make [their] spells of magic and of patterning", is analagous with priestly Latin, what then of the fluent dragons whose native tongue it is? Yevaud, maybe, could with Procrustean effort be made a devil, in its nature as old as any angel, but in Ged's vision of windborne draconic glory there is no room for name-callings and demonisations. And while the troubling allegories of priesthood, dogma, and pride continue to roil about the story, the excessive meaning of the dragons remains a puzzle as the novel moves on with Ged's and Tenar's escape from Atuan, the restoration of the ring of Erreth-Akbe, and with it the healing of the Lost Rune of Peace.

The first trilogy's resolution in *The Farthest Shore* is among the great feats of modern imagination, and matters for far more than its two dragons—but one has a central, tragic, and most honourable place. Magic is somehow draining from the world, taking with it language and reason, culture and wealth, and Ged, now Archmage and accompanied by a young prince, Arren of Enlad, quests for the source of the wrong. Attack and maritime disaster eventually lead the pair to succour with the raft-people of the furthest South Reach, and there on Midsummer morning Orm Embar finds them:

> as the eastern rim of the sea grew white, there came from the north flying a great bird: so high up that its wings caught the sunlight that had not yet shone upon the world yet, and beat in strokes of gold upon the air. [...] The mage looked up, startled. Then his face became fierce and exulting, and he shouted out aloud [...]
>
> And like a golden plummet dropped, with wings held high outstretched, vast and thundering on the air, with talons which might seize an ox as if it were a mouse, with a curl of steamy flame streaming from long nostrils, the dragon, stooped like a falcon on the rocking raft. [...]
>
> [...] Ninety feet, maybe, was he from tip to tip of his vast membranous wings, that shone in the new sunlight like gold-shot smoke, and the length of his body was no less, but lean, arched like a greyhound, clawed like a lizard, and snake-scaled.

Along the narrow spine went a row of jagged darts, like rose-thorns in shape, but at the hump of the back three feet in height, and so diminishing that the last at the tail-tip was no longer than the blade of a little knife. These thorns were grey, and the scales of the dragon were iron-grey, but there was a glitter of gold in them. His eyes were green and slitted.

[...] The voice was soft and hissing, almost like a cat's when he cries out softly in rage, but huge, and there was a terrible music in it. Whoever heard that voice stopped still, and listened.

The mage answered briefly, and again the dragon spoke, poising above him on slight-shifting wings: even, thought Arren, like a dragonfly poised on the air.

Then the mage answered one word, '*Memeas,*' I will come; and he lifted up his staff of yew-wood. The dragon's jaws opened and a coil of smoke escaped them in a long arabesque. The gold wings clapped like thunder, making a great wind that smelled of burning : and he wheeled and flew hugely to the north.[1]

The richness of imagery develops, in the spiked dinosaur-spine, details of voice, and renewed beauty and sunlit grace within the terror of the form, but this time it is a prelude and increment of tragedy. When Ged and Arren reach the Dragon's Run and see the dragons dancing on the wind, they dance in dumb rage, their voices taken from them by the draining ill of the world, and after a while, as Orm Embar helps them search for the living form of the evil's cause, the once-human but now vilely deathless wizard Cob, he too is made speechless. Yet he can still fly, and guide Ged, and in the battle with Cob can save Ged by sacrificing his own body and life—a draconic nobility made all the more piercing by the un-human age, wisdom, and strength that must be lost to right an ill wholly of human making.

Nor can this be the end, for Cob has a dead as well as a living body, and the 'farthest shore' to which Ged and Arren must travel is that of death, not merely by crossing and re-crossing (as mages with yet more priestly resonance may) the boundary wall that all pass, but by entering that bourne from which no traveller returns and crossing it to a farther strand, beyond the Mountains of Pain. In healing the breach that Cob has made in the fabrics of life and death Ged expends all his power, but Arren carries him on (as Sam carries Frodo up Mount Doom), returning them to the beach where their cold bodies and Orm Embar's carcass lie—and there, waiting for them, is Kalessin, the Eldest, at first doing nothing save stand watch:

But as [Arren] bent to lift Ged up, the dragon put out a great mailed foot, al-

1   Ursula Le Guin, *The Farthest Shore* (1972; Harmondsworth: Puffin, 1974), pp. 143–4 (Ch. 9).

most touching him. The talons of that foot were four, with a spur behind such as a cock's foot has, but these were spurs of steel, and as long as scythe-blades.

'*Sobriost*,' said the dragon, like a January wind through frozen reeds.

'Let my lord be. He has saved us all, and doing so has spent his strength, and maybe his life with it. Let him be !'

So Arren spoke, fiercely and with command. He had been overawed and frightened too much, he had been filled up with fear, and had got sick of it and would not have it any more. He was angry with the dragon for its brute strength and size, its unjust advantage. He had seen death, he had tasted death, and no threat had power over him.

The old dragon Kalessin looked at him from one long, awful, golden eye. There were ages beyond ages in the depths of that eye; the morning of the world was deep in it. Though Arren did not look into it, he knew that it looked upon him with profound and mild hilarity.

'*Arw sobriost*,' said the dragon, and its rusty nostrils widened so that the banked and stifled fire deep within glittered.

Arren had his arm under Ged's shoulders, having been in the act of lifting him when Kalessin's movement stopped him, and now he felt Ged's head turn a little, and heard his voice: 'It means, mount here.'

For a while Arren did not move.[1]

Arren is struck into dumb immobility, as Ged was speaking to Yevaud, but this time by a true offer of service rather than a threat posing as such an offer. Kalessin seems to know all that has passed, and that Ged with Orm Embar's and Arren's help has saved dragons as well as mages and everyone else; so his "profound and mild hilarity", so different from the yellow smoke that hissed as laughter from Yevaud's nostrils, may not only be at Arren's selfless impertinence. Bearing him and Ged to Roke, where no dragon has ever come, Kalessin also speaks for those with ears to hear, "I have brought the young king to his kingdom, and the old man to his home",[2] confirming Arren as *agni Lebannen*, king Lebannen (his true name) in the language that for humans allows no lie. Yet when Ged asks, Kalessin also bears him from Roke to his birth-island of Gont, the most magnificent ride into retirement there has ever been.

And there, for nearly twenty years, Earthsea rested. But if Ged really did retire from magery, his power permanently spent in his heroic deed, he continued as a man, and Kalessin as Eldest had no such option, potently worming its way forward into *Te-*

---

1   Le Guin, *The Farthest Shore*, pp. 209–10 (Ch. 13).

2   Le Guin, *The Farthest Shore*, p. 212 (Ch. 13).

hanu and *Earthsea Revisioned*. That useful word 'revisioned', a coinage by the great feminist poet and essayist Adrienne Rich[1] (an exact contemporary of Le Guin's), provided the title under which Le Guin's pivotal 1992 lecture on rethinking her creation was published, and makes it sound like a self-contained critique—but the piece was originally delivered as 'Children, Women, Men and Dragons' and should be read with two of Le Guin's earlier essays. One is the intriguingly titled 'Why are Americans Afraid of Dragons?' (1974), which supplies the blunt answer "They are afraid of dragons, because they are afraid of freedom",[2] and the other is the blandly titled 'Bryn Mawr Commencement Address' (1986)—actually an explosive and wonderful speech, much cited, in which Le Guin elaborated beautifully on gendered dialects of language, the 'father tongue' of social power and the 'mother tongue' in which stories are told.[3] Le Guin said openly in *Earthsea Revisioned* that "From 1972 on I knew there should be a fourth book of Earthsea, but it was sixteen years before I could write it"—so the revisioning should not be thought a specific event but a process drawing over those 16 years on everything that came to hand. Le Guin ended the lecture, for example, with an odd and powerful detail about the difficulty of writing this particular novel:

> The book insisted that it be written outdoors, in the sunlight and the open air. When autumn came and it wasn't done, still it would be written out of doors, so I sat in a coat and scarf, and the rain dripped off the verandah roof, and I flew.

The flying is partly the trance of creative imagination and the business of dragons, but it is also femininity and the grasp of speech:

> Well, then, if art, if language itself doesn't belong to women, women can only borrow it or steal it. *Le vol:* flighty, women are. Thieves, fly-by-nights. Off on their broomsticks.[4]

The animating thematic pun on French *voler* (meaning both 'to fly' and 'to steal') is from another great feminist thinker, Hélène Cixous in *Le Rire de la Méduse* (1975), an essay that is specifically cited in the 'Bryn Mawr Commencement Address'. Cixous was not thinking of dragons, but Le Guin would have seen at once that the pun

1   See 'When We Dead Awaken: Writing as Revision', in Adrienne Rich, *On Lies, Secrets, and Silence: Selected Prose, 1966–78* (New York: Norton: 1979).
2   Le Guin, *The Language of the Night*, p. 40.
3   Collected in *Dancing at the Edge of the World: Thoughts on Words, Women, Places* (New York: Grove, 1989).
4   Ursula Le Guin, *Earthsea Revisioned* (Cambridge, MA: Children's Literature New England, & Cambridge: Green Bay Publications, 1993), pp. 11–12, 26, 7.

points as much to draconic flight and hoarding as to the lyrical uses Cixous makes of it, and its presence in *Earthsea Revisioned* suggests clearly the sense in which *Tehanu* and the later volumes of the Earthsea sestet are far more late blooms of the greater feminism of the 1960s and earlier 1970s than reflections of any later political correctness.[1]

Some critics and reviewers who misunderstand this have been needlessly brusque in pointing to sexist faults, but Le Guin herself is wisely unapologetic about the earlier trilogy—"I like my books. Within the limits of my freedom I was free; I wrote well; and subversion need not be self-aware to be effective."[2] The daughter of anthropologist Alfred and writer Theodora Kroeber, now best remembered for contact with the remnants of the Yana Indians and Theodora's late children's novel *Ishi, Last of his Tribe* (1964), Le Guin grew up steeped not only in mythology but in critical and comparative thinking about all legendaria; she also has a Columbia MA in Mediaeval and Renaissance romance literature, and (as artists will) knew what she was doing more deeply than she realised. A gendered awareness of the *Earthsea* trilogy is certainly needed, above all for the mutual exclusion of male magery and sex, echoing the Catholic dogma of celibate priesthood, and Le Guin could (just in time for *Tehanu*) have found much of that problem newly and memorably dissected by Uta Ranke-Heinemann, another close contemporary, in *Eunuchen für das Himmelreich* (*Eunuchs for the Kingdom of Heaven*, 1988).[3] But the foundations of Le Guin's self-critique were already present at the very beginning of Earthsea, in Yevaud's brief and anomalous were-humanity, and the great drive of the later books, worked through flight and theft and the simple magics of kindness and sex, is the positive identification of women and dragons.

The complex details of *Tehanu* don't especially matter, and pursuit of them would (via the severe facial burns and crippled hand the eponymous little girl suffers) risk a major diversion away from dragons and into an overlapping but distinct set of post-war literary protagonists with fire-flayed faces.[4] One point should be noted for

---

1 If that greater feminism came a liitle later to Le Guin than others, one need only consider that she married in 1953 and by 1963 had three young children.

2 Le Guin, *Earthsea Revisioned*, p. 7.

3 Uta Ranke-Heinemann, *Eunuchen für das Himmelreich: Katholische Kirche und Sexualität* (Hamburg: Campe Verlag, 1988; trans. Peter Heinegg, as *Eunuchs for the Kingdom of Heaven: Women, Sexuality, and the Catholic Church*, New York: Doubleday, 1990). Ranke-Heinemann was born in 1927, Le Guin in 1929.

4 This unhappy group includes, most notably, Steerpike in Mervyn Peake's first two *Gormenghast* novels, and Ronald Merrick in Paul Scott's *Raj Quartet*.

future reference, that this burned girl probably derives in some measure from Nick Ut's infamous 1972 photograph of nine-year-old Kim Phuc fleeing a napalm attack by US planes. What matters more (at least initially) is that early in the novel, when (continuing directly from *The Farthest Shore*) Kalessin brings an unconscious Ged home to Gont, Tenar (who once was Arha, the Eaten One, and like Arren has gone beyond simple fear) is there to welcome them both:

> [Tenar] watched the slow beat of the wings, far out and high in the dazzling air. Then she got to her feet, retreating a little from the cliff's edge, and stood motionless, her heart going hard and her breath caught in her throat, watching the sinuous iron-dark body borne by long, webbed wings as red as fire, the outreaching claws, the coils of smoke fading behind it in the air.
>
> Straight to Gont it flew, straight to the Overfell, straight to her. She saw the glitter of rust-black scales and the gleam of the long eye. She saw the red tongue that was a tongue of flame. The stink of burning filled the wind, as with a hissing roar the dragon, turning to land on the shelf of rock, breathed out a sigh of fire.
>
> Its feet clashed on the rock. The thorny tail, writhing, rattled, and the wings, scarlet where the sun shone through them, stormed and rustled as they folded down to the mailed flanks. The head turned slowly. The dragon looked at the woman who stood there within reach of its scythe-blade talons. The woman looked at the dragon. She felt the heat of its body.
>
> She had been told that men must not look into a dragon's eyes, but that was nothing to her. It gazed straight at her from yellow eyes under armoured carapaces wide-set above the narrow nose and flaring, fuming nostrils. And her small, soft face and dark eyes gazed straight at it.
>
> Neither of them spoke.
>
> The dragon turned its head aside a little so that she was not destroyed when it did speak, or perhaps it laughed—a great "Hah!" of orange flame.[1]

Once, when a dragon spoke, "Ged stood dumb", and "For a while Arren did not move"—but if "Neither of [Kalessin and Tenar] spoke" both can and shortly will, exchanging names as equals. And at the end of the novel it is the burned and all-but-speechless child Therru, whose true name is Tehanu, who can call Kalessin back to protect Ged and Tenar, and punish (as Blackbeard was punished) the corrupt mages who have tormented and would murder the elderly couple; so once they are safe:

---

1   Ursula Le Guin, *Tehanu: The Last Book of Earthsea* (London: Gollancz, 1990), pp. 44–5 (Ch. 4).

Looking at Tenar, Kalessin spoke, in the huge voice like a broom of metal dragged across a gong: "*Aro Tehanu?*"

"The child," Tenar said—"Therru!" She got to her feet to run, to seek her child. She saw her coming along the ledge of rock between the mountain and the sea, toward the dragon.

"Don't run, Therru!" she cried, but the child had seen her and was running, running straight to her. They clung to each other.

The dragon turned its enormous, rust-dark head to watch them with both eyes. The nostril pits, big as kettles, were bright with fire, and wisps of smoke curled from them. The heat of the dragon's body beat through the cold sea wind.

"Tehanu," the dragon said.

The child turned to look at it.

"Kalessin," she said.[1]

'Suffer the little children to come unto me.' As Kalessin flew, so Tehanu ran, straight to Tenar, who could look a dragon in the eye; and in speaking to Tehanu Kalessin's words, always hitherto in the italics of the Old Speech, lose their typographical distinction. The antiquity remains, and in that Old Speech Kalessin, as 'Eldest', is named by Tehanu as 'Segoy', the first and primal maker, but the lessening of alienation, as a dragon speaks a child's name in greeting, is a sign of the fundamental kinship between burned girl and burning dragon that Le Guin forges. Implicit in the conversation that follows is the startling knowledge that Tehanu could achieve a full transformation, becoming a dragon, but forebears, that she may stay with Ged and Tenar while they need her, and with humanity a while. At the very end of *The Other Wind* she is at last set free to fly and dance with Kalessin on the wind, healed of her burns and lameness in the natal draconic identity to which they ironically correspond, but the rest of the story that grew from *Tehanu* into the most recent works of the sestet is not Tehanu's or Kalessin's, but Orm Irian's.

Introduced as a girl, simply Irian, in 'Dragonfly' (a novella, continuous with *The Other Wind*, that ends *Tales from Earthsea* as what Le Guin called a "dragon bridge" between the books[2]), this fruition of Le Guin's long dance with were-dragonhood embodies a founding legend of Earthsea that her revisioning revealed. In the beginning, it seems, dragons were as humans were, and all were one, but over time the kinds polarised, and came to the *verw nadan*, or *Vedurnan*, the Division, when what became men chose having and learning, the hoarding of scholarship and commerce,

---

1   Le Guin, *Tehanu*, pp. 216–17 (Ch. 14).

2   Le Guin, *Tales from Earthsea*, p. xiii (Foreword).

urban living and the bound kinships of earth and water; and what became dragons chose being and knowing, so that (as for poor Eliot among the Elizabethans) 'the dragon and the speech of the dragon were one' in the free kinships of fire and air. After the *verw nadan* the division grew ever more absolute, polarising the two speaking kinds of beast in their tongues (an analogue of the biblical Babel) and scattering them to opposite points of the compass (an analogue of the biblical Fall, and of diaspora)—but always there have been some among each kind whose true identity is of the other kind: latent weredragons and 'werehumans'.[1] And when at the end of 'Dragonfly' Irian comes finally to the sacred Knoll of Roke Island, where Kalessin once landed Ged and Arren and all things must be wholly themselves, she is at last fully manifest:

> She turned away from him and them and went on up the hill in the gathering darkness. As she went further from them they saw her, all of them, the great gold-mailed flanks, the spiked, coiling tail, the talons, the breath that was bright fire. On the crest of the knoll she paused a while, her long head turning to look slowly round the isle of Roke, gazing longest at the Grove, only a blur of darkness in darkness now. Then with a rattle like the shaking of sheets of brass the wide, vaned wings opened and the dragon sprang up into the air, circled Roke Knoll once, and flew.
>
> A curl of fire, a wisp of smoke drifted down through the dark air.[2]

So Irian departs to seek her other, draconic name from the bloodkin who will know it, but as Orm Irian she returns (as she had promised she would, at need) from and in *The Other Wind*:

> "*Medeu*," ['Sister'] Tehanu whispered, coming up beside Lebannen, her gaze unwavering on the dragon. The great creature's head swung round again and the immense amber eye in a socket of shining, wrinkled scales gazed back, unblinking.
>
> The dragon spoke.
>
> Onyx, understanding, murmured to the king what it said and what Tehanu replied. "Kalessin's daughter, my sister," it said. "You do not fly."
>
> "I cannot change, sister," Tehanu said.

---

1   The baldest summary is in the section on 'Dragons' in 'A Description of Earthsea', an appendix in *Tales from Earthsea*, pp. 269–71, but Le Guin simply assembles what is revealed in her tales.

2   Ursula Le Guin, *Tales from Earthsea* (New York: Harcourt, 2001), pp. 264–5 ('Dragonfly', § IV).

"Shall I?"

"For a while, if you will."

Then those on the terrace and in the windows of the towers saw the strangest thing they might ever see however long they lived in a world of sorceries and wonders. They saw the dragon, the huge creature whose scaled belly and thorny tail dragged and stretched half across the breadth of the terrace, and whose red-horned head reared up twice the height of the king—they saw it lower that big head, and tremble so that its wings rattled like cymbals, and not smoke but a mist breathed out of its deep nostrils, clouding its shape, so that it became cloudy like thin fog or worn glass; and then it was gone. The midday sun beat down on the scored, scarred, white pavement. There was no dragon. There was a woman. She stood some ten paces from Tehanu and the king. She stood where the heart of the dragon might have been.

She was young, tall, and strongly built, dark, dark-haired, wearing a farm woman's shift and trousers, barefoot. She stood motionless, as if bewildered. She looked down at her body. She lifted up her hand and looked at it. "The little thing!" she said, in the common speech, and she laughed. She looked at Tehanu. "It's like putting on the shoes I wore when I was five," she said.[1]

Thus Orm Irian, no less than a woman but no less than a dragon either, speaking in the tongue all know from the place of a dragon's heart. In these remarkable passages Le Guin assembles a vision of were-dragonhood linking flight, health, and womanhood that is far beyond anything ever dreamed of greedy Fáfnir. A number of writers (including Bertin and Kerner) gratefully owe her for it, but by working on the highest possible levels of fiction, verisimilar, allegorical, and fantastical, Le Guin accrues meaning more intensely than any rival or emergent successor.

What is so impressive isn't only that Orm Irian's amused and practical awareness of the adult human form as a vestment of her childhood echoes all the way back to Yevaud's relief at being able to shuck the confining form of Mr Underhill; nor even the beautiful, metallic consistencies and subtle play of variations in the iron, steel, and brass of the dragons' descriptions, Le Guin with apparent ease juggling six-in-hand the polarities of mammal/reptile, female/male, and human/dragon to sometimes bewildering yet never incoherent effect. What counts is rather the places each of these strengths (and others) finds in every successive escalation of meaning and reference, testifying that revisioning Earthsea was as much a matter of turning the existing narratives in different lights to see what else was there, a process of revelation

---

1   Ursula Le Guin, *The Other Wind* (New York: Harcourt, 2001), pp. 147–8 (Ch. 3).

and unfolding, as any kind of correction. The Dry Land of Death that Ged and Arren had to cross in *The Farthest Shore* is itself revealed in *The Other Wind* as no part of a natural order but a willed human creation, an unchanging, mage-made eternity, barren and desolate not simply as death *per se* but as a Christian and Western conception of singular life, a linear withdrawal trying to preserve individual identity from rebirth and the (re-)cycling of planetary life. Yet if this is high philosophy and theology, it is no less true that the stone wall Earthsea's mages once built between death and life comes tumbling down to release the craving spirits of the dead just as precipitously as the Berlin Wall fell to East German hands and voices in 1989; and amid both philosophical and political complexities the turbulent, allegorical priest-mages in their celibacy are openly drawn into a resolution that is truly re-solution, unmaking division and restoring the balances of gender and magic. As a fictional project spanning the last four decades of the twentieth century Le Guin's Earthsea sestet embodies the weighted understanding of Simone de Beauvoir and the premier feminist thinkers of the 1960s–70s; draws on Cixous with a similarly joyous response to language, and parallels the ahistoricist linguistic projects of Derrida and the Deconstructionists; remains politically aware throughout; and engages deeply with her parents' seminal work in Amerindian anthropology, particularly the primeval dream-time when animals and people were one. That concept tellingly informs the novella 'Buffalo gals, Won't You Come Out Tonight'?[1] (1987), which anticipated *Tehanu*—yet Le Guin's extended fantasy is also proudly and argumentatively a child of Tolkien (on whose prose style and structural techniques she has written brilliantly[2]), and with 'Mr Underhill' in 'The Rule of Names' she openly salutes Smaug as the great ancestor of her own splendid dragons. Moreover, she has while doing *all* of these things, and many more besides, *still* won multiple awards, not least for a prose that has grown ever more limpid and beautiful as its author ages, while also selling by the shelf-load.

For adults one might want to construe Le Guin's largest position as countering for children, on feminism's behalf, Freud's unfortunate and unhappy identification of female sexuality as a dark continent, properly labelled in its remote unknowability 'Here be dragons'; and/or as refuting, on women's behalf, the reductive and dogmatic feminist separatisms of the later 1980s and early 1990s. These and other critical positions on her work have begun to be offered,[3] while for children, the writer's

---

1   In *Buffalo Gals and Other Animal Presences* (1988).
2   See 'Rhythmic Pattern in *The Lord of the Rings*' (2001), in *The Wave in the Mind* (2004).
3   See Wayne, *Redfining Moral Education* (1995), Reginald *et al.*, eds, *Zephyr and Boreas* (1997), White, *Dancing with Dragons* (1998), & Rochelle, *Communities of the Heart* (2001).

base, who start off rather wiser than most end up, Le Guin's work valuably tells, more simply, memorably, densely, and far-reachingly than non-fiction can manage, the story of why men, American or otherwise, should be respectful but not afraid of dragons, and why all men who fear women should rather fear themselves. Perhaps, as Le Guin says in *Tales from Earthsea*, "nobody can explain a dragon", but as a social commentator and engineer, a child of the couple who more-or-less founded activist archaeology and 'salvage ethnology', the wife of a professional historian,[1] and a female citizen and author profoundly committed to the public as well as her private weal, she took the immense gift of Smaug's speech in *The Hobbit*, published when she was eight, and wrought of it the great descendant-linguists of Smaug that Tolkien had denied his marvellous and terrible creation. And for all the revisioning of the earlier in the later books, the only real, ouroborine irony is that to reach her (present) ending Le Guin had to go back to were-dragonhood, the one major thing she had discarded from Yevaud's first and still unexpected appearance as Mr Underhill (bringing all Earthsea and a living chunk of Tolkien with him) in 'The Rule of Names'.

Pern was from the very first a culture in an extremely specific state, though when Anne McCaffrey's chronicles of the planet started in 1968 no living Pernese yet knew it. It was in origin a far-future colony-world of Earth, a (supposed) planet of the star Rukbat (or Alpha Sagittarius[2]), only about 170 light years away but off the beaten interstellar track, and settled at a relatively low and peaceful level of agrarian and craft technology (though with medical and other comforts retained). The settlers were humans sick to death of prolonged ultra-high-tech. planetary-colonialist and religious warfare, and included two great leaders, one civil and one military, as well as a fully trained 'Eridani' geneticist with genome-reading and gene-splicing equipment to help the new culture bio-engineer its impact on native ecosystems. In almost every way the planet seemed ideal—humans, cattle, and horses could take to its land, and dolphins to its seas, without fear of any large predator; what the survey team had missed was the erratic orbit of a wandering planetoid in the system, the 'Red Star', that only came into conjunction with Pern every 200 years. And when it did again, eight years after the colonists first landed, a primitive but profoundly hostile

---

1   Le Guin married in 1953 Charles A. Le Guin, a fellow Fulbright scholar, whose publications include *Roland de la Platière: A Public Servant in the Eighteenth Century* (1966).

2   Alpha Sagittarius is well-known to astronomers because it lies directly between Earth and the galactic centre, where it is believed a supermassive black hole exists.

deep-space life-form that rode it in from the system's Oort Cloud[1] sought to bridge the gap to the more hospitable planet, arriving in Pern's atmosphere as a hissing silver rain that mindlessly devoured everything organic it touched; of man, woman, child, or beast caught by it all that remained were belt- and harness-buckles, zippers, and metal ornaments. In the first terrible onset of 'Thread' (and the extensive loss of equipment, including radio-contact with the orbiting colony ships, to an unpredicted volcanic eruption and massive ashfall) Pernese contact with the home worlds and outer galaxy was severed, and the colonists left isolated to devise their own defences against a desperate and lethal menace that would sweep like banded thunderstorms about the planet for 50 years in every 250.

The answer, of course, was dragons—and there was as originary stock a small native life-form that the colonists had already nicknamed dragonets (or fire-lizards) for the legendary beasts they resembled. The fire-lizards had evolved as their own defences against Thread a number of interesting characteristics—telepathic and em-pathic communication, teleportation via *Between* (a null space where Thread cracks and dies),[2] and an adapted second stomach wherein, after chewing a phosphine-bear-ing sandstone, they can manufacture a fiery breath able to sear falling or burrowing Thread. Lacking any alternative plan of defence, the millennia-old wisdom of 'Eri-dani' bioscience was turned to breeding from the fire-lizards full-size dragons that men and women could ride to sear whole falls of Thread in the air, protecting trees and crops—and the project succeeded magnificently, producing dragons of sufficient and increasing size who were also mentally enhanced, and at hatching could be tel-epathically 'Impressed' into a joyful, life-long bond with an individual rider. But by the time enough dragon-generations had passed for a full corps of dragonriders to emerge, allowing human life and culture to struggle back from the brink, the last of the inherited technology and the knowledges that went with it were gone. In the nature of a colonising group those with specific advanced skills were always few in number, and in abrupt isolation and diminution, with all hands to all pumps simply to survive, genetic engineering skills or knowledge, for example, could no more be taught for posterity than the equipment needed for gene-sequencing could be rebuilt; besides, as a pastoralist refuge from a high-tech society knowledge of simpler tradi-tions and techniques was in any case widespread. Before the first Pass of the Red

---

1   A vast spherical 'cloud' of small asteroids and comets orbiting a sun, proposed in 1950 by Dutch astronomer Jan Hendrik Oort (1900–92); in the Solar System the orbits of Oort Cloud objects are thought to range from *c.*0.3 to 1 light year in radius.

2   Paranormal ability is an obsession of McCaffrey's, featuring centrally in many of her other series.

Star ended, 58 'turns' (Pernese years) After Landing (AL), even electricity and with it most data-storage technology save quills, ink, and hide were lost—but the desperate first-generation leaders had foreseen what must happen, providing as well as they could a charter to cling to, and before long what existed on Pern was a high mediaeval feudal world with three primary institutions. The Lords Holder were aristocrats owning estates descending from the early settlement-grants; the Guilds and their Craftmasters were a necessary solution to the imposed necessities of trade regulation and skill-preservation in an economy regularly reduced to subsistence level; and the Weyrleaders (commanding the Weyrs, communities of dragons and their riders) were a pre-eminent military force, constantly conducting and/or maintaining the planetary defence against Thread, but also resembling churchmen or a government in that they were of necessity supported in their barren mountain homes by tithing of the lowland holders and craftsmen whose fields and resources they protected.

Neither the idea of a devolved colony-world nor this triadic political structure were original, and McCaffrey probably owed the latter in significant measure to Frank Herbert's *Dune* (1965), where the legs of the political tripod are the Imperial House (a military hegemony), Landsraat (an aristocratic assembly), and Spacing Guild (controlling interstellar trade).[1] The distinctive thing about Pern, however, besides its dragons, was that *all* of this history was only revealed in the books very slowly and long after the event.[2] The first novel, *Dragonflight* (1968), dropped itself and all readers deeply *in medias res*, for it is set way down the timeline, at the start of the Ninth Pass of the Red Star, around 2,500 years AL; there has, moreover, just been a 'long interval', a Pass that didn't happen, so Thread hasn't fallen for almost 450 years, and almost everyone has forgotten that it will return, as utterly destructive as ever. The Weyrs and dragonriders, meanwhile, have in the absence of their *raison d'etre* fallen both into chronic disarray, sustained (much like the castle-functionaries in Mervyn Peake's hidebound Gormenghast[3]) only by dry and incomprehensible tradition encoded as immutable ritual, and into acute social disfavour, seen as parasites

---

1   Herbert might be considered oddly missing from my narrative here, for the massive sandworms of *Dune* are clearly of the dragon family both in form and function, including a strong temporal association via the geriatric spice Melange and the 'Water of Death' they can make that induces prophecy—but if controllable as beasts of burden and at need as weapons, much like McCaffrey's dragons, they do not speak at all, and the bardic as well as prophetic dimensions of time are locked to Herbert's human protagonists.

2   For convenient overviews see Karen Lynn Fonstad, *The Atlas of Pern* (1984) & Jody Lynn Nye, with Anne McCaffrey, *The Dragonlover's Guide to Pern* (1989; 2/e 1997).

3   See *Titus Groan* (1946) and *Gormenghast* (1950); *Titus Alone* (1959) is distinct.

on an economy to which they contribute nothing. Even knowledge of the wild fire-lizards and their status as draconic ancestors and cousins has been lost, and they have become all but mythic creatures, evading sight and capture as readily as they evade Thread, and thought of something as we now think of pixies or elves. Additionally, and terribly, five of the six weyrs, that should be filled with dragons to protect all Pern when Thread comes, stand empty, the whereabouts of their occupants so long unknown that even the question has been forgotten. But as the Red Star again begins to loom in the morning and evening sky, pulsing ever more brightly and filling hearts with unease, the last dragon queen in the last and isolated Weyr at Benden clutches for the last time, laying a queen egg, so a new queen-rider must be found—and that is where McCaffrey began, with a 'bronze' dragonrider, F'lar, whose dragon (with more than a hint of Mnemosyne, the Greek goddess of memory and mother of the Muses) is Mnementh, finding a female candidate for Impression called Lessa in a 'Search' that has the hallmarks of *droit de seigneur* and other such feudal customs.

It is the density of the world-history and social structures implicit as backstory in *Dragonflight* that made it the roaring success it became, and they are so great that in one sense all subsequent chronicles of Pern—more than 20 novels, chapbooks, or collections to date, counting the works with and by Todd McCaffrey—have been ways of taking that first, extraordinary novel apart and piecing it all back together. McCaffrey is clearly not a writer of Tolkien's meticulous and over-determined persuasion, crafting and polishing all to perfection before revealing a tiny portion; instead, starting (I would guess) with a question about why one might *need* (and therefore bio-engineer) dragons, she pulled together and fused blazing ideas and visions that only revealed their inviting oddities and seeming inconsistencies as they cooled, with long hindsight. She was also by 1970 a divorced mother of three moving continents from the USA to Ireland, so money was expedient while writing-time was pressurised, and for a decade thereafter her output (while still remarkable) was lower in volume than it has ever been since.[1] Moreover, as McCaffrey in all her SF draws quite heavily on Romance (a genre she also writes) as a fundamental plot-determinant (which contributes to some rather formulaic writing in later Pern volumes), she frames almost all the novels as character-driven, and the plots are thus more likely to zig or zag with personal destinies than pursue any direct historical course through the legendarium. In consequence, while the series has been richly sustained by the diversity of the

---

1   For biographical data see Todd McCaffrey, *Dragonholder* (1999), Mary Brizzi, *Anne McCaffrey* (1986), Robin Roberts, *Anne McCaffrey* (1996), and the long 'Autobiographical Feature' at:
    ▣ http://www.answers.com/topic/anne-inez-mccaffrey ..

historical, geographical, and cultural niches that new plot-ideas can occupy (from the forgotten Terran dolphins of the Pernese oceans to the unhappy possibilities after such massive genetic engineering of cross-species infections against which dragons can have no natural defence), that has also meant that the timeline has been filled-in piecemeal and hopscotch-wise.

Matters initially went forward during the Ninth Pass in *Dragonquest* (1971), but jinked back and sideways in the first two volumes of a children's trilogy, *Dragonsong* (1976) and *Dragonsinger* (1977), before picking up the main sequence again with *The White Dragon* (1978). The last of the children's trilogy was *Dragondrums* (1979), which complements *The White Dragon*, but thereafter the exploration moved back to earlier Passes of the Red Star—the Sixth (in the 1540s AL) in *Moreta: Dragonlady of Pern* (1983) & *Nerilka's Story* (1986), and the First (beginning in 8 AL) in *Dragonsdawn* (1988), each of which deepened and rounded the overall picture, but extended the Ninth-Pass narrative not one step. McCaffrey returned to the Ninth Pass with a vengeance in *The Renegades of Pern* (1989), and in an immediate sequel, *All the Weyrs of Pern* (1991), created what has proven an overall terminum: of eight subsequent novels only *The Skies of Pern* (2001) attempts any significant further progress, all others being orchestrations of the Ninth-Pass story or additional distant backstory rather than extensions.[1] The children's trilogy (especially the first two novels) are superb books in their own right, but they have, with the other interlopers (and some odd groupings in omnibus editions, as well as variant titles and multiple imprints), served to obscure the narrative that amid all the diversity drives relentlessly through the Ninth-Pass novels—and at the heart of that action is the draconic relation with antiquity that McCaffrey seemed to have displaced, but could never wholly exclude and had in the end to embrace in a most unexpected fashion.

Pernese dragons cannot in their nature be ancient, nor have memories stretching back to Pern's antiquity (the eight years between Landing and First Fall), for they did not then exist. They can, moreover, in general readily be seen as reversing *all* the Beowulfian tropes while preserving the winged and fiery reptilian form—protection not predation of the community, companionship not antagonism with the military hero, new-hatched innocence and valiant service rather than aged cruelty, and so on. It is given both that riders and their dragons are telepathically bonded and that

---

1 *The Dolphins of Pern* (1994) *The Masterharper of Pern* (1998), and the novella 'Runner of Pern' (1998), collected in *A Gift of Dragons* (2002), are Ninth-Pass orchestrations, though *Dolphins* does push obliquely past the end of *All the Weyrs of Pern*; *The Chronicles of Pern* (1993) is set in the First Pass, *Dragonseye* (1996) in the Second, and *Dragon's Kin* (2003), *Dragon's Fire* (2006), and *Dragonsblood* (2005) just before the Third.

knowledge of the colony's foundation and technological heritage is lost, so neither man nor dragon can bear such knowledge, and in any case whatever the dragons' natural lifespan the nature of their absolute bond with their riders, achieved at hatching and enduring unto death, means that if a rider dies, a dragon will suicide by going *Between*; a dragonless ex-rider may equally wither, or at best survive as a half-man, a shadow of loss and grief. The dragons do have one odd link with language, for they hatch knowing it—as they also know their own names, each unique but all ending in *–th*, and testifying to some deeper but otherwise inarticulate awareness—but relatively little is made of it, and McCaffrey, despite her Radcliffe degree in Slavonic Languages, is not (as Tolkien was and Le Guin is) a linguistic thinker. As the riders' lifelong companions, pseudo-magical in their telepathic bonding and teleportation but profoundly real in their bulk and aggressive capacities, her dragons have all the grandeur one would expect, and the acknowledged dragon-leaders, F'lar's Mnementh and Lessa's Ramoth, are the largest ever hatched; but both, and almost all lesser Pernese dragons, are generally far closer in personality to cats and horses (to both of which McCaffrey is openly devoted) than they are to a Smaug or Yevaud. Like Le Guin's dragons the Pernese beasts have a gender connection, both in their own hierarchy (the fertile, golden queens are flown by male bronzes, while infertile female greens are flown by male browns and blues), and in the compulsive effects of their mating flights both on the riders bonded to them and on other humans who happen to be within their telepathic broadcast range—but while there is a powerful feminism in the roles of Weyrwomen, especially Lessa, and in Menolly's triumphs as a harper in the children's trilogy, the social and sexual revolutions are on Pern necessarily subordinate to and intertwined with the problem of Thread.

Much of McCaffrey's interest in SF was underlyingly political (like Herbert's, and distinctly from the slightly younger Le Guin's), founded in her childhood during the 1930s and young adult experience during the Second World War, and a major part of *Dragonflight* (and the whole Pern series) might be described as the politics of overcoming complacent conservatism. In one reading the dragons might be for Pern an anticipation of Ronald Reagan's 1980s 'Strategic Defence Initiative' or 'missile-shield', and critical objections to McCaffrey are likely to turn in some way on the social conservatism of her Pernese society under threat being supposed to endorse a Cold-War US conservatism repressing social change in the name of anti-communism. This has its truth, but in many ways F'lar's situation as the Red Star nears its Ninth Pass is more like the populist version of Winston Churchill struggling during the later 1930s to warn the British government and people of the threat Hitler posed. Come

1939–40 and the *Blitzkrieg*, however, and Britain had the Channel as a moat, while on Ninth-Pass Pern, when Thread *does* begin to fall and all are suddenly once again fervent believers in dragonkind, there is still the sheer impossibility of protecting the settled areas (greatly extended during the 'long interval') with less than one-sixth of the trained dragon-and-rider pairs necessary to do so. For all F'lar's efforts with what resources he has, strongly reminiscent of Royal Air Force heroics during the Battle of Britain in 1940–1, or of those few US pilots who managed to get airborne at Pearl Harbor, with alien death literally raining from the skies there is no more time—so McCaffrey had to make some, and the fun really began.

After Einstein, and given draconic teleportation, it is less of a stretch than it might seem for dragons to be able to travel to a *when* as well as a *where*, and McCaffrey handles Lessa's accidental discovery of this ability in Ramoth beautifully. Both she and F'lar immediately grasp one possible salvation through time-travel by sending groups of young riders and dragons back in time to mature and reproduce, that they may be ready as fully trained adults to fight the next Threadfall, due in only a few days in the present. This tactic buys a little breathing-space, and 72 extra dragons with grown riders, but no more, for the effects of being in two places at once are seriously debilitating on riders (though not, apparently, dragons), and there is still an unanswerable shortfall in the numbers needed.

Enter stage-centre the mystery of the five deserted Weyrs and their missing occupants. The whole, deeply atmospheric problem of the lost past is another great attraction of Pern that resonates throughout *Dragonflight*, and those initially in the cultural and political firing-line are the Harpers, whose guild is responsible for teaching traditional ballads and mnemonic songs, and for news-gathering and dissemination. Extolling dragons and musically presenting the rules for keeping world and home Thread-free, as well as acting to arbitrate and inform, Harpers have as much as dragons and dragonriders fallen into disfavour during the 'long interval', and are ready under their guild-leader, the MasterHarper of Pern, Robinton, to be F'lar's and Lessa's most important allies. Well into adulthood and married life McCaffrey had serious ambitions as a classical singer and is highly trained, so she knows her musicianship, and Robinton (based on Frederic H. Robinson of the Lancaster Opera Society, a close friend of McCaffrey's from the 1950s[1]) is one of her great creations; so too is Menolly, eventually a Master Harper herself, in *Dragonsong* and all subsequent Ninth-Pass novels, while Pern's Harper Hall is in general a warm and memorable place. The teaching-songs it has preserved provide chapter-epigraphs that (again

---

1 Todd McCaffrey, *Dragonholder*, p. 36, and see the dedication of *Dragondrums*.

as in Herbert's *Dune*, but with a balladic touch more reminiscent of Tolkien) open long vistas on the narrative and offer advice:

> Drummer, beat, and piper, blow,
> Harper, strike, and soldier, go.
> Free the flame and sear the grasses
> Till the dawning Red Star passes.
>
> ***
>
> Honour those the dragons heed,
> In thought and favor, word and deed.
> Worlds are lost or worlds are saved
> From those dangers dragon-braved.
>
> Dragonman, avoid excess;
> Greed will bring the Weyr distress;
> To the ancient Laws adhere,
> Prospers thus the Dragonweyr.
>
> ***
>
> Lord of the Hold, your charge is sure
> In thick walls, metal doors, and no verdure.[1]

Within the narrative these songs have done their job just well enough down the years for a core of alert and thoughtful people to be able to step forward as needed; yet some of the most troubling songs have in harpers' self-preservation not been taught as they should have been. One of these is recalled at a critical moment by Robinton, who sings to F'lar and Lessa a disturbing song with a plaintive tune full of discords and unexpected minor keys:

> Gone away, gone ahead,
> Echoes roll unansweréd.
> Empty, open, dusty, dead,
> Why have all the Weyrfolk fled?
>
> Where have dragons gone together?
> Leaving Weyrs to wind and weather?
> Setting herdbeasts free of tether?
> Gone, our safeguards, gone, but whither?
>
> Have they flown to some new Weyr

---

1   Anne McCaffrey, *Dragonflight* (1968; London: Corgi, 1970), pp. 9, 28, 46.

Where cruel Threads some others fear?
Are they worlds away from here?
Why, oh why, the empty Weyr? [1]

This haunting riddle song, so far as the living Pernese can discover, is the only record of the Weyrs' disappearance, shortly after the Eighth Pass ended in 2058 AL, but from its slender clues Lessa determines the answer: "Gone away, gone *ahead*"—to the time when they are needed, now. Someone, therefore, must let them know *when* they are needed, and from a great tapestry of the right age showing verisimilar detail of lost buildings and decorations Lessa draws a sufficient reference to travel *Between* with Ramoth to that *when*, a mighty time-leap that almost kills them both. Thus Weyrwoman and golden queen terrifyingly vanish from Pern's present to deliver the summons, but return (in smaller and less debilitating increments, using star-maps as time-guides) three days later with more than 1,800 human and as many draconic ancestors in tow.

A perfect instance of what Tolkien dubbed in fairy-tales the *eucatastrophe*, a "joyous 'turn' [...] a sudden and miraculous grace: never to be counted on to recur",[2] this extraordinary finale gilds the triumph of *Dragonflight* by massively intensifying the emotive epic resonance that the known fragments of Pernese history and military use of dragons have already added to the motif of their fiery and reptilian form. Lessa's and Ramoth's journey through time is as tremendous as any life-risking, life-saving leap into the unknown can be, and truly has a world at stake; the appearance over Telgar Hold, as Thread bears towards it, of thousands of dragons flaming the skies clean is a tremendous deliverance for the world to which readers have been so richly introduced. But as the echoes die away there is the fate of the 'Oldtimers' themselves to consider, selflessly coming forward after one lifetime fighting Thread to begin another, and subsequently finding neither the society produced by the 'long interval', nor the change in their own social status inevitably created by the absence of dragons in dominant numbers during their heroic leap over 400 years, in the least to their liking. This is in its own right a theme worthy of epic treatment (which it gets from Robinton and other composers in ballads of 'Lessa's Ride'), but also for F'lar and the Lords Holder a serious problem, so much so that the various issues caused by the Oldtimers' adaptation (or failure to adapt) to 'modernity', and their necessarily grateful (if exasperated) political accommodation as ultra-conservatives, form a good part of *Dragonquest*, *The White Dragon*, and *Dragondrums*. For dracologists McCaf-

---

1 McCaffrey, *Dragonflight*, p. 207.
2 Tolkien, 'On Fairy-Stories', in *The Monsters and the Critics*, p. 153.

frey's need for time-travel in a novel (and series) all about dragons is intrinsically intriguing, and the scale of the disturbances the Oldtimers cause offers ever more grist to the mill—but just as dragons go where they will, so it seems they do not care to be deprived of their antiquity, and the other half of the Ninth-Pass plots as far as *Dragondrums* involves a struggle to re-unite what should not have been sundered.

Pern has two principal continents, the inhabited, temperate North and the uninhabited, tropical South, abandoned after the First Fall of Thread and the volcanic eruption, and never resettled.[1] Before the arrival of the Oldtimers F'lar sent those young dragons and riders who went back ten years to mature to the South, so that they should not be too close to themselves while (literally) being in two places at once, and the southern Weyr has been retained as a pleasant place of convalescence for Thread-scored riders and dragons. While recuperating from a knife-wound inflicted by an Oldtimer, Flar's half-brother and deputy F'nor, who rides brown Canth, takes the chance to drowse on the warm southern beaches:

> Canth then irrigated himself so thoroughly with sand that F'nor was half-minded to send him back to rinse, but Canth protested, the sand felt so good and warm against his hide. F'nor relented and, when the dragon had finally made his wallow, couched himself on a convenient curl of tail. The sun soon lulled them into drowsy inertia.
>
> *F'nor*, Canth's gentle summons penetrated the brown rider's delicious somnolence, *do not move*.
>
> That was sufficient to dispel drowsy complacence, yet the dragon's tone was amused, not alarmed.
>
> *Open one eye carefully*, the dragon advised.
>
> Resentful but obedient, F'nor opened one eye. It was all he could do to remain limp. Returning his gaze was a golden dragon, small enough to perch on his bare forearm. The tiny eyes, like winking green-fired jewels, regarded him with wary curiosity. Suddenly the miniature wings, no bigger than the span of F'nor's fingers, unfurled into gilt transparencies, aglitter in the sunlight.
>
> "Don't go," F'nor said, instinctively using a mere mental whisper. Was he dreaming? He couldn't believe his eyes.
>
> *Don't go, little one*, Canth added with equal delicacy. *We are of the same blood.*[2]

Canth doesn't know how he knows of his cousinhood with the fire-lizard, but he

1   The fullest map is in *The Skies of Pern*; Karen Fonstad's *Atlas of Pern* (1980) was completed before the southern continent had been much explored.
2   Anne McCaffrey, *Dragonquest* (1971; London: Sphere, 1974), pp. 80–1 (Ch. 4).

is of course quite right: the tiny dragonet is of the species from which the dragons were genetically engineered, and F'nor's fortuitous meeting with this newly hatched queen, whom he Impresses by feeding her, signals the abrupt rediscovery by human- and dragonkind of this originary species. At almost the same Pernese time, though entirely independently, Menolly in *Dragonsong* saves a hatching fire-lizard clutch from Threadfall, and finds herself the next morning with no less than nine Impressed fire-lizards—a glorious fair that very productively accompanies her to the Harper Hall in *Dragonsinger*. For the politically hard-pressed F'lar the discovery of impressionable fire-lizards is a boon, for Impressing one can give a Holder or Craftmaster a taste of the emotional bond dragonriders enjoy, which eases the tensions stoked by the Oldtimers. The fire-lizards can also serve a practical as well as an emotional turn: for those with whom they bond they will serve as messengers and defenders, spotting snakes and vermin for farmers, or bad air for miners, as readily and contentedly as they learn to sing with Menolly or accompany F'nor on dragonback. A human partner's wish may not exactly be a command, and fire-lizards have all the mischievous and endearing qualities to which companion-animals are prone, but a partner's need or serious interest is almost always respected. And like the Oldtimers, the worst of whom are exiled to the southern continent at the end of *Dragonquest*, the fire-lizards have in their own mysterious way a temporal agenda, which it took yet another, intermediary form of dragon to translate.

For reasons best known to herself the great SF pioneer Andre Norton (herself the author of *Dragon Magic*, 1972, and a longstanding fan of both telepathy and exotic creatures) responded to *Dragonflight* by telling McCaffrey that she "ought to have a sport dragon and that he should be white and small".[1] Both McCaffrey and her then editor, Betty Ballantine, liked the notion, and a contract for *The White Dragon* was signed as early as the summer of 1970, but while the rider, Lord Jaxom of Ruatha, already existed as a baby in *Dragonflight*, and was allowed to Impress white Ruth in *Dragonquest* (and again, from another angle, in *Dragonsong*), the story proved very slow to shape itself. One major strand emerged in a chapbook, *A time when, being a tale of young Lord Jaxom, his white dragon, Ruth, and various fire-lizards* (1975), published as a commission and tribute by the New England Science Fiction Association when McCaffrey was the guest of honour at their Boskone Convention. In the chapbook's 75 pages Jaxom and Ruth recover a queen egg, laid by Ramoth and stolen by the exiled Oldtimers, a plot that depends on three crucial factors—that Ruth always knows exactly *when* he is, and has extremely acute perceptions of his own

---

1   Todd McCaffrey, *Dragonholder*, p. 55.

and other dragons' time-travel; that fire-lizards are strongly attracted to the small white dragon wherever he goes, sleeping on him when he sleeps; and that as a result, what they feel and dream, he feels and dreams, and through their linkage so too does Jaxom. All three ideas would prove essential, but in *A time when ...* they were deployed only over a short time-span, the fire-lizards 'remembering' and broadcasting dreams of Ruth and Jaxom returning the stolen egg before they have set out to do so, and so prompting their timely (and politically critical) adventure; around this action, the larger plot of *The White Dragon* remained stalled. Some of McCaffrey's difficulties may have been conceptual, but she was also side-tracked by young Menolly and the rich invention of the first two volumes in the Harper Hall trilogy. Todd McCaffrey has additionally suggested that accumulating by 1976 sufficient royalties from the first two Pern novels to buy 'Dragonhold', the house in County Wicklow where she still lives, was also a vital liberation, and that once she had settled in to her new home *The White Dragon* completed itself fairly smartly. In any case, the wait was well worthwhile, and "When it came out in 1978, *The White Dragon* flew high enough to become the first science fiction hardcover book to reach the *New York Times* bestseller list".[1]

All well and good—but what Todd McCaffrey leaves out is the distinct twist that finally brought the plot of *The White Dragon* home, and any clue as to where it came from, or rather, why it was at last enabled fully to emerge. Jaxom too, like F'nor before him, has to convalesce in the southern continent, after suffering a dangerous, febrile illness called 'fire-head' that can blind and kill, and imposes a long period of immobility; and as he fell ill in a remote cove, delightful to bathe in after fighting Thread (and with a stunning view of a distant volcanic peak) but without shelter, he and Ruth must stay there with others to tend them while he heals and protect them against Thread as necessary. Ruth is therefore sleeping on southern beaches, attracting wild southern fire-lizards, and broadcasting both to Jaxom and to others with Impressed fire-lizards the wild southerners' dreams—which are, as it turns out, not dreams but collective memories of striking and unusual events that are, moreover, somehow inherited down the fire-lizard generations. Unused to human presence since the first colonists fled the south, these wild fire-lizards have yet mentally preserved through a thousand or more generations accurate images of that originary human presence, and (as the southern cove is not so far away from it) of the volcanic eruption more than 2,500 years before that precipitated an evacuation. Triggered by renewed human presence, intensified by the Impressed northern fire-lizards, and fo-

1   Todd McCaffrey, *Dragonholder*, p. 107.

cused by white Ruth, these testimonies of the most distant past are finally recognised by the humans as revelatory visions, and what those visions guide is the inception of full-blown Pernese archaeology, and the rediscovery of the first human settlement, Landing.

In one sense the need for this development was purely internal. Among the information long lost is the simple geography of Pern, including the size of the southern continent, upon whose open lands many Lords Holder with large families of sons cast envious eyes; and among the discoveries at Landing, providing a climax to *The White Dragon*, are space-surveyed maps revealing a continent more than large enough for all. In another sense the issue of the ancestors had been lurking ever since McCaffrey had so creatively sundered her dragons and their riders, with all of Ninth-Pass Pern, from their engineered and colonialist origins. And what is truly striking is the way that after Lessa's tremendous plunge into the past in *Dragonflight*, and with the stakes rising from four centuries to the full Pernese sweep of two-and-a-half millennia, it is the fire-lizards and their descendant dragons who lead the temporal way, reclaiming for their kind the bardic connection with antiquity that Tolkien had made possible, and Le Guin was in parallel making real. For all her love of fantasy and romance rather than 'hard', scientifically rigorous SF, McCaffrey is always a locally coherent and largely naturalistic writer, at her very impressive best in the Pern novels of 1968–78. Oddly talented white Ruth, for example, came from a very thick-shelled egg, and Jaxom was drawn to help hatch her by his own birth at the cost of his mother's life; while Ruth is beloved of the fire-lizards precisely for his lesser size, inviting the sleeping proximity that permits his reception of their fragmentary and only very weakly broadcast dreams. But just as the leap-back to summon the Oldtimers, however needed by F'lar and Lessa, could only be made with Ramoth's ultimately mysterious teleportational and time-travelling abilities, so the greater leap back to eyewitness memories of Landing can only be made through the equally mysterious mental capacities of the fire-lizards from whom Ramoth descends, and of the sport dragon Ruth.

There, understandably enough, McCaffrey stalled again, for if the subsequent 1980s novels of Pern spreading back in time were richly implicit in the Ninth-Pass story so far told, the implications of *The White Dragon* for the Pernese present were not faced until more than a decade later. Volcanic explosion or no, the pre-First-Pass 'Ancients' (as distinct from the Eighth-Pass Oldtimers) were well-equipped citizens of a massively advanced galactic culture, able to cross interstellar distance, and the very surprise of the volcanic explosion (attributable to more sloppy work by the initial survey team that missed the Red Star) implies that a great deal of material would have had to have been abandoned. If covered in ash rather than lava—as much of the site is found to be at the end of *The White Dragon*—artefacts at Landing might have been very largely preserved, as at Pompeii; and sudden volcanic blasts may also be very particularly channelled, to destroy or oddly spare, as with the Mount Saint Helens eruption in 1980 (that produced, just like the Landing eruption on Pern, a 'two-faced' mountain with one side of a cone blown open). The great question for McCaffrey, therefore, was what to let her dragons, dragonriders, holders and crafts-men all turned obsessive archaeologists find, and eventually (after the three novels set back down the timeline) she bit the bullet to end *The Renegades of Pern* (1989) (mostly another Ninth-Pass orchestration) before settling properly to the problem in *All the Weyrs of Pern* (1991):

> The Aivas felt its sensors responding to a renewal of power from the solar panels on the roof above it. The wind must have become strong enough to blow the clog-ging dust and volcanic ash away from the panels. There had been enough of these incidents over the past twenty-five hundred and twenty-five turns so that Aivas had been able to maintain function, even if only at a very low maintenance level.
>
> Running through the main operating circuits, Aivas found no malfunctions. Ex-terior optics were still obstructed but, once again, the Aivas was aware of some activity in its vicinity.
>
> Was it possible that humans had returned to the Landing facility?
>
> It had not yet completed its priority assignment: to discover a means to destroy the organism that had been termed 'Thread' by the Captains. It had received no significant input to allow it to complete that task but the priority had not been cancelled.
>
> Perhaps, with the return of humans, that assignment could be completed to their satisfaction.[1]

Perhaps, indeed. An 'Aivas' is an 'Artificial Intelligence Voice Address System', and this one, as a primary new-colony resource, has not only a mainframe data-bank with massively extensive files for all fields of cultural reference and technology, and built-in capacities of printing and self-division between multiple independent work-stations, but also a talking interface that if possessing only a minimal personality is thoroughly programmed (beyond guarded deference and obedience) with awareness of human psychology, sociology, and politics. Fortunately it has in addition very good linguistics and semantics programmes, and is able to short-circuit the language

1   Anne McCaffrey, *All the Weyrs of Pern* (London & New York: Bantam, 1991), p. [7] ('Prologue').

difficulties that 2,500 years of linguistic drift and evolution would otherwise inevitably cause—almost as if, like Sigurðr–Siegfried, the Aivas had tasted Fáfnir's dragonheart and come to know all tongues.

The mighty computer being, naturally enough, inside a thick-walled and highly insulated protective building, the Pernese leaders (including F'lar, Lessa, Robinton, and Jaxom) who are first summoned to encounter it have to park Mnementh, Ramoth, and Ruth outside before entering to hear the miracle of a talking, bardic wall. The most obviously powerful point for McCaffrey's serial readers, when the Aivas informs the assembled Pernese VIPs of their own history and ancestry, is that the formal opening words of its lecture (*"When Mankind first discovered the third planet of the sun Rukbat in the Sagittarian Sector of space ..."*[1]) openly invoke the scene-setting 'Introduction' in *Dragonflight* that with minor variants prefaces most of the subsequent novels ("Rukbat, in the Sagittarian Sector ..."[2])—as if the Aivas were simply McCaffrey herself, mildly disguised, playing helpful historian to her own creations. But the really interesting thing, in terms of that conversation Smaug and Bilbo might have had if Bilbo had known what to ask, the great possibility of *The Hobbit* unfulfilled by Tolkien but here delivered by McCaffrey, is that the Aivas really *has* tasted Fáfnir's heart, and not only knows all tongues but has, bizarrely yet rightly, also *turned* dragon—what should be dumb creation come alive, astonishingly enabled with linguistic mastery to talk, and revealing as it does so the lost secrets of antiquity, which here is also explicitly time-looped with modernity. The heaped treasure-hoard on which the Aivas lies curled is its knowledge, its barrow is the ash-covered administration block that houses it, and its profound purpose is to flame and sear the very existence of Thread out of Pern's and the human future.

This strange connection of dragon and computer is potent and undeniable, but to have both a talking Artificial Intelligence and telepathic dragons in a world that is still primarily feudal in structure and late-mediaeval in social organisation (if increasingly dotted with Enlightenment advances and proto-industrial technology) is to invite serious problems.[3] Though always striving to make her narratives cohere intellectually as well as emotionally, and politically a very astute plotter, McCaffrey has never been a truly 'hard' SF writer, and the logic implicit in the Aivas's own computerine (rather than draconic) nature now demanded explanations she was not well equipped to give.

1   Anne McCaffrey, *The Renegades of Pern* (1989; New York: Del Rey, 1990), p. 339 (Ch. 16).

2   McCaffrey, *Dragonflight*, p. 7 ('Introduction').

3   An interestingly comparable collision of draconic and supercomputing paradigms occurs in Peter F. Hamilton's *Fallen Dragon* (2001).

Her acknowledgements in *All the Weyrs of Pern* fulsomely thank the Warwick bio-logist and adviser on alien plausibility (or xenologist) Jack Cohen "once again for making fact out of my fiction and rationalizing the whimsies of my imagination", and one may imagine that Dr Cohen had his work cut out.[1] He, I assume, would have been responsible for making Thread not an indigenous life-form of the Red Star (as the Ninth-Pass Pernese had always supposed) but a malevolent hitch-hiker from the Oort Cloud; and for remaking the surface of the Red Star, which F'nor and Canth (at the climax of *Dragonquest*) had found searingly dangerous and deadly, into a more survivable place, by pointing out (as Aivas briskly does) that *that* was when it was heading into its tightest loop around Rukbat, and would have been maximally heated by the solar wind, with volatiles boiling off, but *this* is when it is heading away and rapidly cooling off. Cohen might also have been responsible for the use of the anti-matter engines of the three colony-ships (happily parked in geostationary orbit with enough fuel to maintain themselves on auto-pilot, and naturally enough with open channels to the Aivas installed on the planet below) to knock the Red Star just suf-ficiently out of its present orbit that it will never again pass close enough to Pern for Thread to fall. And he must have been responsible for the considerable volume of advanced genetics that goes into a second aspect of Aivas's plan to destroy Thread, a germ-warfare attack by its own disimproved symbionts that Aivas gets the dragons to deliver to the surface of the Red Star along with the anti-matter engines. But the other great problem that now needed solving, however Cohen may have helped with the celestial mechanics, is a pure McCaffrey problem the answer to which formed the novel's (and in many ways the series's) terminal eucatastrophe.

Planning *Dragonflight* a full quarter-century earlier (hence perhaps the specificity of "twenty-five hundred *and twenty-five* turns"), McCaffrey's inspired idea of the 'long interval', 450 years without Thread over the Pernese 'turns' 2058–2508 AL, made much more plausible the necessary loss of knowledge about the planetwide threat that Thread represented. Supporting it in that first plot, as a discovery among the details of the backstory when F'lar first sensed the danger from the Red Star and tried to research Pern's history, was the fact that there had been a long interval once before, between the Fourth and Fifth Passes (808–1258 AL).[2] At the time of *Drag-onflight* and for many years thereafter these long intervals did not cause anyone the

---

1   Sensibly, he seems simply to have ignored one very basic problem, that while McCaffrey has always described Rukbat as a yellow, class G star, it is in fact a blue, class B dwarf star.

2   The dates come from *The Dragonlover's Guide to Pern*, p. 66, and fix the lengths of Passes at exactly 50 years, and of Intervals at exactly 200 years; First Pass began in 8 AL.

slightest problem, and still don't for first-time readers of *Dragonflight*—but for the children of Newton, as adult readers of SF often are and the Pernese were slowly becoming in their renewed grapplings to chart the Red Star's movements even before they found the Aivas, the long intervals pose an all but insurmountable problem. The Red Star might just conceivably (in traversing the Oort Cloud and outer margins of the Rukbat system) get clouted by a large enough asteroid to miss Pern once, but it would then be gone for good and all, and the sad fact is that in a properly Newtonian universe not all the king's horses and all the king's men can account for its having a sufficiently wobbly orbit that a trailing cloud of Oort matter could miss Pern twice but hit it nine times in eleven orbits.

Then again, the only dragons in Newton's mostly Enlightenment world were alchemical or biblical metaphors, and McCaffrey's dragons, being time-travellers, must in any case be thoroughly Einsteinian—so the answer, of course, is (as it ever was) time, and the elegant solution reverses the usual time-paradox into a pleasing guarantee. There have been long intervals, so something must have caused them; that something cannot be variable physical proximity, so it must be a cause that affects Thread directly, and hence a biological vector; but the technology to create such a vector was not accessible on Pern between First Fall and the rediscovery of Aivas, yet must have been deployed twice during that time. Time-travel is the only possible answer, and so, with the guidance of Ruth's acute time-sense, and the use of the astrogation computers aboard the orbiting colony ships to generate precise historical star-patterns that provide Ruth with a sufficient reference to pass to other dragons, massed waves of dragons with space-suited riders and enormous gloves insulating their claws grasp the huge girder frameworks of the anti-matter engines detached from each colony ship and deposit them at strategic points on the Red Star—one of them now, in mid-Ninth Pass; one of them at the end of the Eighth Pass, before the second long interval; and one of them at the end of the Fourth Pass, before the first long interval. Three staggered blows over seven orbits may or may not be a better way than one big one to knock a trespassing planetoid out of orbit, but the bio-weaponry Aivas has smaller wings of dragon seed onto the Red Star's surface do, just about, explain those long intervals, the idea being that Thread was sufficiently reduced or impaired after each biological attack that it took more than 250 years to recover in sufficient numbers to use its deep-space phase and cross to Pern. But the trouble is, who really cares anyway?

One blow of three simultaneous explosions (as most Pernese believe) or three separated by centuries and orbits (as readers know), it is or they are enough to ensure that the Red Star can never return. The menace of Thread will finally be ended just before the year 2558 After Landing, when the Ninth Pass will end slightly 'early' as the Red Star's orbit changes, and the dragonriders as well as the dragons will finally be set free from their generations upon generations of epic, abandoned struggle, as the living Pernese heroes (whom readers might themselves by this stage have been following for 23 years) will be able at last to pursue more productive lives and studies. The Aivas building at Landing has become a global university, improving life for all on Pern, and if there are some violently activist few who reject all that comes from the Aivas as modern 'abominations' that destroy tradition (a theme that develops strongly both in *All the Weyrs of Pern* and the only novel to push beyond it chronologically, *The Skies of Pern*), there is no chance of their gaining power or managing more than vandalism. The Aivas (and McCaffrey) was wise enough to ensure that some part of its disbursed (yet thereby undiminished) hoard of knowledge benefitted every craft and station in life, delivering improved cotter-pins for cart-wheels as well as improved fabrics, insulation, clean plastics technology and the like. So all is rosy, and one can begrudge no-one on Pern their hard-won peace.

It is all elegant and logical enough, but not, in a strange sense, very satisfying. As a twelve-year-old in 1976 I didn't care two hoots in reading *Dragonflight* about the Newtonian mechanics of the 'long interval', any more than McCaffrey had in writing the novel, and while I became aware of the problem not very many years later it still didn't worry me much. What mattered were the dragons and the politics of the given world, as well as the skilful romance plots McCaffrey almost always weaves. But if I tend now in re-reading to pass fairly rapidly over the pages of *All the Weyrs of Pern* that deal with the Aivas's swiftly concocted programme of genetic education and engineering for some bright and improbably successful students (and McCaffrey admits in her 'Acknowledgements', on her own and Jack Cohen's behalf, that technological lead-times are absurdly compressed as a convenience[1]), I remain fascinated by and very grateful for the pages that openly confront dragons with advanced technology, and advanced technology with dragons. Unusually for cover-art, Steve Weston's splendid illustration for the first edition's dust-jacket shows with fine precision a specific moment in the novel, when white Ruth and a golden fire-lizard queen called Farli manage to teleport themselves to the bridge of the *Yokohama*, one of the

---

1   "The author and Jack Cohen are fully aware that some of the procedures, and the development of new manufacturing techniques suggested in these pages would take many more months, years, to produce and effect than is here suggested. However, there are certain licences that an author, and her adviser, may take to produce a novel. Then, too, the Pernese had AIVAS to help them, didn't they?" McCaffrey, *All the Weyrs of Pern*, p. [6] ('Acknowledgements')

colony-ships, so that Farli can turn on the life-support systems.[1] Within the narrative both the astonishment and the humour of dragons in freefall are richly present, without lessening the explorers' bravery that Ruth and Farli show, and the novel as a whole is full of delightful touches despite occasional explanatory longeurs from the Aivas. But (as often in McCaffrey, at least where Pern is concerned) the humour and the epic bravery are only half the mix, and must contend with another proper attachment of the long draconic past, elegy that refuses to be tragedy—an epic mode dominant in *The Lord of the Rings* and already sealed, maybe, when Beowulf was nobly slain in the fullness of his years and deliverance of his people from the nameless worm he slew.

MasterHarper Robinton's health had before the discovery of the Aivas been in question for some time, and a severe heart-attack during *The White Dragon* brought him more or less permanently to the recuperative south. A new dwelling, Cove Hold, was built for him in the cove where Jaxom was convalescing as a tribute by all the Pernese to a man who had, with F'lar and Lessa, saved them when the Ninth Pass began. Robinton's special qualities had also been vouchsafed since *Dragonquest* by Mnementh's occasional willingness to speak telepathically to him, and since *Dragonsinger* by his Impressed bronze fire-lizard, Zair. In the crisis of his heart-attack these stakes were abruptly (and to the surprise of even F'lar and Lessa) raised, for Mnementh and Ramoth telepathically linked to Robinton to keep him alive (by refusing to let him surrender to 'sleep')—another bardic association for the dragons. With the discovery of Landing, and the development of the site as both a university and the hub of the Aivas's plan to destroy Thread, the problem of Robinton's restlessness in enforced retirement was solved, and he, representing the Crafts (with a retired Oldtimer, D'ram, and Jaxom's sometime guardian, Lord Lytol, representing the Lords Holder and the Weyrs), became an independent triumvir of a space held in trust for all Pern. But man is mortal, and a kidnapping attempt by abominators of the Aivas, though foiled, leaves him sickened—in body and heart from the after-effects of being overdosed with fellis-juice (a Pernese sleeping draught), in mind by the punishment his captured assailants must undergo, and in spirit by the willing violence and warped ideology revealed in the reactionary political motives of his kidnappers.

It is not, then, unduly surprising that at the end of *All the Weyrs of Pern*, with the Red Star safely deflected to its and Thread's destruction, Robinton should peacefully die in the Aivas room, his great mission accomplished. Nor, for all its strange

---

1   The image (and all the UK covers) can be seen at :
    ▣ http://home.houston.rr.com/pbolchover/covers/uk.html

echoes of ancient funerary sacrifices of a dead ruler's animal and human chattels, is it unpredictable that, as fire-lizards will, bronze Zair should loyally follow him into death—and not as a dragon would, by going *Between*, but simply on the expiring breath, to leave behind with Robinton's a tiny corpse "grey with death, curled against his [master's] neck".[1] But theirs are not the only losses that free Pern must sustain, for the Aivas too, wise beyond the way of most machines (if oddly like Arnold Schwarzenegger as the T-800 at the end of *Terminator 2: Judgement Day*, released only in July 1991 after the proofs of *All the Weyrs of Pern* must have gone to press), chooses to suicide with Robinton. Its data-banks remain passively available through the reconstructed work-stations, but the intelligent and vocal responder, the Aivas as such, is gone. Its motives remain to be guessed, but it leaves on-screen a blinking and for most readers familiar message, "And a time to every purpose under the heaven"—the source being, as the Aivas tells Robinton in his last moments, "the greatest book ever written by Mankind".[2]

McCaffrey describes herself as a Presbyterian, but Pern has always been stringently free of organised religion. Wisdom and wisdom literature, however, has fed the planet in many ways, and the presence on Pern of Ecclesiastes is in itself no more surprising than the Aivas's choice of the King James Version in speaking to Robinton. Jaxom seems two pages later to imply that the Aivas idiosyncratically revised the KJV's prepositions in its posted suicide-note (he quotes it as having said "a time *for* [rather than *to*] every purpose"[3]), but he was very upset, having only just learned of all three deaths, and this seems more likely to be a slip of McCaffrey's pen than any kind of ultra-subtle authorial pointer. Nor is there much mileage in the fact that the name 'Zair' also comes from the KJV, being a place in Edom named in 2 Kings 8:21 ("So Joram went over to Zair, and all the chariots with him"), and the whole Christian connection is awkward to take seriously where Zair and the Aivas are concerned because of the various long-standing doctrinal condemnations of suicide. Besides the sheer oddity of a scripturally-minded and peacefully self-terminating computer, the very opposite of mad HAL in *2001: A Space Odyssey*, what readers are left with, therefore, is sympathetic suicide as the ultimate seal of the Aivas's strange were-dragonhood. In joining deaths with MasterHarper Robinton and fire-lizard Zair, who represent the forces that rediscovered it and have led the project that made possible the fulfilment of its *very* longstanding "priority assignment" to destroy Thread,

1 McCaffrey, *All the Weyrs of Pern*, p. 491 (Ch. 20).
2 McCaffrey, *All the Weyrs of Pern*, pp. 488–9 (Ch. 20).
3 McCaffrey, *All the Weyrs of Pern*, p. 491 (Ch. 20).

the Aivas both behaves as the great dragons have, sometimes deeply affectingly, throughout the entire series, suiciding when their riders die, and yet resunders itself and its special, bardic access to antiquity from the new purposes of partnered dragon-and-human-kind. The Aivas, that is, refuses to continue forwards in time with F'lar, Lessa, Jaxom and the living Pernese, including the dragons, and its final assertion of dragonhood through suicide returns it to the Pernese past and leaves them all to their pursuit of Thread-free modernity. And the way it suicides (if in fact it has done that, and not simply returned to the immeasurable patience of its 2,500 year wait within its administrative barrow) is simply to fall silent; as dragons, since they were gifted by Tolkien with the speech of their own kind, have always spoken as, when, and to whom they will, or not spoken, passing silent and unseen.

Yet again there is also a strong sense of the tail-swallowing Ouroboros, as there was with Le Guin's recursion to were-dragonhood, but this time on a massive scale. McCaffrey's whole protracted struggle to bring Ninth-Pass Pern from somnolence in the face of danger to full delivery from menace was a struggle to reintegrate almost everything that she had so marvellously discarded at the very beginning, when *Dragonflight* plunged *in medias res* and the colony's foundation was relegated, with its Aivas and technologies for coping, to a past so distant it had receded into myth. Nor, plainly, would *I* take any bets against the motive force being the Pernese dragons themselves, irritated beyond acceptance by their apparent choice between speech and antiquity, and determined to make amends by grasping the whole of Pern and its time-looped legendarium firmly, even unto death, in their own mighty coils.

Kalessin as Eldest had "the morning of the world" deep in its eye, and could no more have been parted from antiquity than from its bone-marrow. The Pernese dragons, however, for all their temporal gyrations never truly recover as dragons the bardic voice they lost with enforced human ignorance of Pern's epic history; thanks to which, and given their genetically predetermined military servitude, there is in their limitations of quotidian speech (rarely complex or to any human other than their own rider) an uneasy hint of reduction to beasts of burden—little more, if the idea were to be brutally extended, than flying, fire-breathing mules with fortunately sweeter temperaments.

Perhaps the saddest of the successors who owe their worlds and dragons to McCaffrey but allow the further devolution to dumb bestiality is the late Chris Bunch, a Vietnam veteran before he was an author and in his last completed works, the *Dragonmaster* trilogy (2002–04), throwing his dragons into the grimmest warfare. Knowing of the Vietnam connection it might seem that some version of jungle Landing Zones and G.I. deliverance should be suspected, driven by the metonymic sound of that war, the unmistakable thwopping of helicopter-blades strengthened and weighted at the tip to batter through vegetation—and plainly the airborne character of much American experience in Vietnam (with the vilely false politics that began it all in the Bay of Tonkin, and bombed neighbouring nations on the sly) is relevant. So too, probably and horribly, is the extensive use in that war of incendiary weapons, white phosphorus and (above all, sprayed aerially) napalm. But (especially in the middle volume, *Knighthood of the Dragon*) the trenches, the foul, dangerous mud, and the fearsome, brutal, and relentless attrition of men, dragons, and logistical capacity points squarely not to Vietnam but to the French at Verdun or General Haig at the Somme and Passchendaele as notorious exemplars of the military lunacy and recklessness characteristic of 1914–18—and the implicit narrative displacement of wars, Vietnam onto World War One, enjoins a thoughtful pause.

It is one of the larger and more interesting oddities about Tolkien that (i) his astonishing legendarium was first coherently conceived in 1916–17, while he was serving in the trenches and during the months of immediate recovery, making it no surprise that his chronicles of Middle Earth are elegiac throughout, profoundly redolent of the shattering losses World War One inflicted with its immense casualty roster; but also that (ii) his legendarium was nevertheless most influentially and perfectly expressed in a long novel written very largely during World War Two, in the dark domestic years of 1939–45 while Tolkien was trapped in England and his sons served overseas. That collision of wars within *The Lord of the Rings*, like the infamous, last charge of the Polish cavalry against German tanks in 1939, produces complex emotional effects: the landscape of Middle Earth never quite seems the same once one recognises (for example) that the Dead Marshes Sam and Frodo must cross with Gollum, wherein they see the engulfed and preserved bodies of the men, elves, and orcs slain with Gil-Galad at the ending of the Second Age, are a bleak register of Passchendaele's unholy fusion of shambles and quagmire; and this 1914–18 reference must then be triangulated with Sauron's slave-camps of sub-human orcs around Lake Nurnen, deep in south-eastern Mordor, that (like the profoundly totalitarian One Ring itself) have very little to do with the Kaiser's War and everything to do with Hitler's even nastier and more costly one. Chris Bunch's collision of wars in the *Dragonmaster* trilogy is therefore not to be taken lightly, and may reveal to a better reader something important—but that said, it seems to this reader that if one would understand Bunch's curious trilogy clearly, memoirs of 1914–18 and of Vietnam, or a novel of the Royal

Flying Corps such as Derek Robinson's superb *Goshawk Squadron* (1971), are of more relevance that anything dracological.

Far more attractive and promising (not least for a sharp renewal of humour and irony, in limited supply from Bunch) is Naomi Novik's *Temeraire* trilogy, all published in 2006 but presumably written over the preceding year or three. As a confirmed armchair sailor and (in my father's wake) a fan from childhood of C. S. Forester's Hornblower novels, with loyalties extending to his successors (especially Patrick O'Brian) as chroniclers of the British Royal Navy during the Revolutionary and Napoleonic Wars, Novik's combination of frigates and dragons is in any case for me a kind of heaven, but she deserves real respect from all both for her narrative zip and for her dragons. The protagonist-dragon Temeraire began as a fairly straightforward Pernese, in character and attributes a loyal, loving, and at need deadly companion, but he is (as it has turned out) a five-toed Chinese *Tien-lung*, a celestial who was *en route* as an egg to France by way of an inter-emperor present to Napoleon when messenger-frigate and egg alike were captured by Will Laurence's *H.M.S. Reliant*. Laurence impresses Temeraire when he hatches and must therefore depart the Navy for the Dragon Corps—but the real fun started when a mission in the second volume, *Throne of Jade*, took the pair to China, and Temeraire therefore had a chance to talk to some highly imperial native celestials about decidedly un-British ways of draconic thinking. Ever fair-minded, as British gentleman Laurence has taught him to be, Temeraire proceeds in his philosophical studies by reading a little Tom Paine and beginning to ask some deuced awkward questions both about dragon strategies in war and about politics. Poor Laurence is by now in a thoroughgoing panic for much of the time, while also scarpering from assorted enemies on all sides, and has various strange kinds of dragon magic (which Temeraire possesses as a celestial) to cope withal, so the series is bubbling very nicely and I look forward to more instalments as they arrive. But for all the enjoyments I find myself uneasy, and it is more than puritan bells or aesthetic alarm that makes me doubt my preference for Novik over Bunch. Novik's dragons too are beasts of indentured burden (the issue Temeraire and Tom Paine must take on), sacrificed by tactics and strategies that deny them voice or individual value; and Temeraire, as much as Bunch's dragons, lacks all scent of antiquity. Being given, in their sub-Pernese and military natures, to the tactical demands of the moment, and lacking any compensatory time-travelling abilities, Novik's as well as Bunch's dragons are as lacking in history or awareness of it as water. Temeraire's voice and consciousness are growing with his maturation and education, and much may happen, but if anything temporal is to be, it will again be a struggle—and the draconic difficulty is perhaps worse (for all Novik's pleasures) than one might hope, and more widespread than apparently proliferating dragon numbers would lead one to suspect.

What is at stake, ultimately, is the reduction of the draconic not to the bestial, but to the machine. Somewhere in the mists, almost fifty pages ago, I mentioned Edith Nesbit's odd, late story 'The Last of the Dragons' (1925), at the end of which the lonely titular relict, conscious of being outmoded, chooses through the king's magic to become the first aeroplane. There is in Nesbit's rather abrupt ending a brusque inanity but also an unwelcome truth, for though Andrew Lang and the first modern literary dragons came well before the realisation of powered flight, the modern connection of dragons with aircraft cannot be avoided. Smaug's destruction of Esgaroth was composed in the months before and published six months after the German demonstration, in bombing Guernica, of what the Blitz of 1940 would look like. In Le Guin there is that unhappy sense of connection between the burned child Tehanu and the burned child Kim Phuc fleeing napalm in Nick Ut's famous photograph, and those many metallic colours in dragon-scales and wings—not only iron, a natural ore and red pigment, but steel and brass, the metals of technology and munitions, airframes and first-class coachwork. McCaffrey's extended Pern series, besides its 1930s, Battle-of-Britain, dogfighting, and missile-shield connections, has coincided in the writing with a great expansion of civil air-travel, and tellingly overlaps (save for its first two years) with the age of the 'Jumbo Jet', Boeing 747s having first flown commercially in 1970. And while it has nothing very much to do with the details of Eddison or *his* Worm Ouroboros, the ouroborine seems to have haunted the dragons of modernity, even golden and thoroughly ancient Smaug, whose fiery fall over Esgaroth is also the fate of bombers or ground-attack aircraft when an ack-ack round finds the junction of fuselage and wing.

Tolkien's very first dragons, before even Glorund who became Glaurung and fathered all the other great dragons of Morgoth, came in 'The Fall of Gondolin', initially drafted in 1916–17, and whatever Tolkien's (or one's own) attachments to Anglo-Saxon antiquity and saturation in the elegiac and pastoral modes, there is no denying what these beasts resemble:

> Now the years fare by, and egged by Idril Tuor keepeth ever at his secret delving; but seeing that the leaguer of spies hath grown thinner Turgon dwelleth more at ease and in less fear. Yet these years are filled by Melko in the utmost ferment of labour, and all the thrall-folk of the Noldoli must dig unceasingly for metals while

Melko sitteth and calleth flames and smokes to come from the lower heats, nor doth he suffer any of the Noldoli to stray ever a foot from their places of bondage. Then on a time Melko assembled all his most cunning smiths and sorcerers, and of iron and flame they wrought a host of monsters such as have only at that time been seen and shall not again be till the Great End. Some were all of iron so cunningly linked that they might flow like slow rivers of metal or coil themselves around and above all obstacles before them, and these were filled in their innermost depths with the grimmest of the Orcs with scimitars and spears; others of bronze and copper were given hearts and spirits of blazing fire, and they blasted all that stood before them with the terror of their snorting or trampled whatso escaped the ardour of their breath; yet others were creatures of pure flame that writhed like ropes of molten metal, and they brought to ruin whatever fabric they came nigh, and iron and stone melted before them and became as water, and upon them rode the Balrogs in hundreds; and these were the most dire of all the monsters which Melko devised against Gondolin.[1]

During the actual assault on Gondolin these vast metallic troop-transporters and fire-throwers (ultimately responsible under Balrog direction for the city's fall) are explicitly called "those dragons of fire and those serpents of bronze and iron".[2] And John Garth's excellent study of *Tolkien and the Great War* (1993) completes the identification:

The more they differ from the dragons of mythology [...] the more these monsters resemble the tanks of the Somme. One wartime diarist noted with amusement how the newspapers compared these new armoured vehicles with 'the icthyosaurus, jabberwocks, mastodons, Leviathans, boojums, snarks, and other antediluvian and mythical monsters'. Max Ernst, who was in the German field artillery in 1916, enshrined such comparisons on canvas in his iconic surrealist painting *Celebes* (1921), an armour-plated, elephantine menace with blank, bestial eyes. *The Times* trumpeted a German report of this British invention: 'The monster approached slowly, hobbling, moving from side to side, rocking and pitching, but it came nearer. Nothing obstructed it: a supernatural force seemed to drive it onwards. Someone in the trenches cried, "The devil comes," and that word ran down the line like lightning. Suddenly tongues of fire licked out of the armoured shine of the iron caterpillar ... the English waves of infantry surged up behind the devil's chariot.' *The Times*'s own correspondent, Philip Gibbs, wrote later that the advance of tanks

1 Tolkien, *HME 2*, p. 171.
2 Tolkien, *HME 2*, p. 177.

on the Somme was 'like fairy-tales of war by H. G. Wells'.[1]

Tolkien had been at the Somme in 1916 and seen the frightful tanks first-hand, as he had also seen the dog-fighting aircraft above; and infantry, like infants (from the Latin negative *in* + *fans*, present participle of *fari*, 'to speak'), are those who have no voice but the cry of hunger or pain.

Untempered by passage through time, these first of Tolkien's dragons at Gondolin are barely the kin even of *Beowulf*'s "eald ūhtsceaða", as ancient as it was destructive, and even the battle-fodder orcs and Balrogs they carry are silenced as infantry (or in telling US parlance, 'grunts'), for only Melko, already wholly totalitarian ("nor doth he suffer any of the Noldoli to stray ever a foot from their places of bondage"), speaks in and through them. Their creation was a stage, perhaps very necessary, in Tolkien's personal and creative recovery from his appalling experiences: as he infamously observed, "By 1918 all but one of my close friends were dead",[2] and Tolkien was himself severely debilitated by trench-fever as well as psychological and emotional traumata. To write of what he had seen was to transmute it; to sink backwards in time was to escape, in some measure; and by the time Smaug the Golden flew forward again from the First Age to wreak havoc on the Lonely Mountain and converse with Bilbo Tolkien seemed to have long purged all traces of gruesome, military modernity from his dragons, save perhaps the traces of metal in their colouring (and that, in Smaug's case, came from lying on so much gold for most of two centuries, as well as a natural shade of dragon-scale). But the coil of Ouroboros was not so easily escaped, and even as the elves and wizards of Middle Earth had to give way to the new age of men, allowing the First Age and the glories they remember to fade and fall silent with them, so in Tolkien's greatest inheritors the machine-codes of modernity have increasingly mingled with draconic biology, mythology, and the flickering, magical possibility of bardic access to lost antiquity.

Ironies abound. In one view the dragons stand revealed as incarnating an impossible temporal duality, conflating antiquity with modernity, and so pulsing with the tension that at its largest level animates the perennial, perplexing question of Tolkien's identity as both a Modernist and a pastoralist Georgian poet, with all the anti-Modernism of that label. And what should one expect when a scholar steeped in philol-

---

1   Garth, *Tolkien and the Great War*, p. 221. Ernst's *Celebes* can be seen at:
    🔳 http://www.tate.org.uk/servlet/ViewWork?cgroupid=999999961&workid=4136&searchid=6477&r
    oomid=false&tabview=text&texttype=8

2   Tolkien, *LotR*, 'Foreword', p. 5.

ogy and ancient northern epics was forced to see tanks crawl for the first time onto a battlefield that became a byword for insane slaughter and ridiculous but appallingly real sacrifice? Tolkien's dragons were born to bear the horror of his experience, registering metallic modernity but both revisioned to conceal that act of registration, and in fiery destructiveness registering another historical connection with the imagination of aerial attack in the "eald ūhtsceaða" of *Beowulf*. Little wonder, then, that both Tolkien's dragons and their descendants have carried the agony of temporal conflict forward, straining (as the generational curve has logarithmically steepened and each generation finds itself more separated than the last from parents and the past) at once both to accommodate and to escape the shock of the new.

Tolkien used to be, with almost all supposedly 'sub-literary' fantasists, openly condemned by the literary academicians as a gruesome conservative, escapist and reactionary. His great faults seem to be partly his dislike both of the machine and of its Modernist fetishisation, and partly his Edwardian and Georgian (as well as strongly Catholic) sense of gender-roles, permitting an Eowyn as shield-maiden or a Galadriel as Elven queen, but otherwise confining women to a limited domesticity and, for the most part, simple absence. That condemnation as a pure and sexist nostalgic is potentially a dangerous one—think of how Rupert Brooke is scorned for pastoral sentiment and loyalism, despite dying, and Wilfred Owen or Siegfried Sassoon valorised for embracing satire and despair—but even before Peter Jackson's enormous film-adaptations of *The Fellowship of the Ring*, *The Two Towers*, and *The Return of the King* a wide range of dissenting voices were making themselves heard. In Jackson's wide wake a new criticism of Tolkien (in such volumes as Robert Eaglestone's edited collection *Reading The Lord of the Rings*) is invigoratingly showing just how complex his responses to Modernism were. Le Guin, of course (and after her Elizabeth Kerner), had already set to work precisely on the matter of gender, insisting on draconic femininity, while McCaffrey's great time-looped saga, leading to the entry of an Aivas on the battlefield against Thread, can be seen as an absolutely stunning response to Tolkien's understandable but limiting distrust of the machine. Yet still nobody can really explain exactly why it was, in all these formidable cases, dragons and no other creature who have repeatedly been able to come in so precisely where and when they should.

5. Of Aliens in Africa

Ian McDonald and the War of the Heart of Chaganess

Little green men who pick out the White House lawn as a saucer-pad and emerge saying 'Take me to your leader' are not merely clichés, but racist and sexist technocrats. To Western human thinking this tends to seem reasonable, and the fairest-minded would agree that vulnerable aliens arriving on Earth would need urgently to communicate with the US military-political leadership from a position of strength (or concealment) if they were not to find themselves summarily abducted by Special Forces out of Roswell, or simply nuked into oblivion and asked questions afterwards—but why should vastly superior alien technocrats care about human pecking-order at all? The problem isn't helped by overblown films like Roland Emmerich's *Independence Day* (1996), in which the White House becomes the first target rather than a landing zone; the US is still where all the action is, and its President's rousing pseudo-Churchillian speech about July 4th becoming the Independence Day of the whole world is so "jaw-droppingly pompous"[1] that it passes clean through humour to become genuinely offensive, like one of Donald Rumsfeld's 'jokes'. Audiences may very understandably have cheered as the White House and other famous landmarks were spectacularly blown apart, but the film's smug assumptions of US centrality to everything suffered not the slightest damage.[2]

Where exactly this malignant set of clichés first came together remains unclear, but the finger points to the pulp magazines and B-movies of the 1940s–50s, and 'Take me to your leader' was well-enough known by 1965 for Tom Lehrer to pun on it by way of satirising Hubert Humphrey in 'Whatever Became of Hubert?'[3] The early Cold War fits well as a context, but reveals a story of devolution and vulgarisation depressing for those who prefer their aliens interesting. Before the twentieth century most

---

1 ▣ http://www.bbc.co.uk/films/2000/12/18/independence_day_1996_review.shtml. The reviewer was Neil Smith.

2 A shorter version of this essay appears in my Genre Fiction Sightline on McDonald's *Chaga* (Humanities-E-Books, 2007).

3 "As someone once remarked to Schubert / 'Take me to your *lieder*'".

extra-terrestrials, typically encountered in alternative realities rather than on other planets, were mythic or divine and there was no interest in imagining 'the alien' in the modern sense, either to love or kill. Only from the 1850s–60s, with the strangely blended natural philosophical and fictive works of the popularising French astronomer and spiritualist Camille Flammarion, did ideas of the alien begin to be seriously entertained—and then as ethereal, rather philosophical beings who certainly weren't about to land on anyone's lawn.[1]

Invasion stories, correspondingly, formed a quite different strand of early SF, the 'future war novel', a sub-genre more-or-less created in *The Battle of Dorking* (1871) by soldier-novelist and polemicist George Chesney—wherein the invaders are Germans, Chesney's whole purpose being propagandistic demonstration of British military unreadiness for an European war. It made the most enormous splash, also appearing in Canada to supply the North American market and in many translations for continental European markets within two years, and if Chesney overestimated the ease with which technology could bridge the English Channel, he made good military sense further ahead of time than almost anyone else. Sensationalist as the novel surely is, the future echoes of 1914 can be heard in *The Battle of Dorking* as much as in a strikingly prophetic letter Henry James wrote to his brother William in 1877:

> I have a sort of feeling that if we are to see the *déchéance* of England it is inevitable, and will come to pass somewhat in this way. She will push further and further her non-fighting and keeping-out-of-scrapes policy, until contemptuous Europe, growing audacious with impunity, shall put upon her some supreme and unendurable affront. Then—too late—she will rise ferociously and plunge clumsily and unpreparedly into war. She will be worsted and laid on her back—and when she is laid on her back will exhibit—in her colossal wealth and pluck—an unprecedented power of resistance. But she will never really recover as a European power.[2]

The sub-genre has been wonderfully charted by I. F. Clarke (sometime code-breaker and Professor of English at Strathclyde) in *Voices Prophesying War 1763–1984* (1966, 1992),[3] and if popular novels are rarely as accurate as James, and often share Chesney's odd underestimation of the English Channel as a moat, it is clear that future-war plots featuring human (or *mundane*) invasion remained common in Brit-

---

1 See *La Pluralité des Mondes Habités* (1862) and *Récits de l'Infini* (1872; as *Stories of Infinity*, 1874).

2 Henry James to William James, December 1877, quoted in Leon Edel, *The Life of Henry James* (definitive edition, in 2 vols, Harmondsworth: Penguin, 1977 [Peregrine]), I.499.

3 Clarke also edited an anthology, *Tales of the Next Great War, 1871–1914* (1996).

ish SF until the 1940s, persisting into the Cold War. The only one still to enjoy a mass-readership is Erskine Childers's *The Riddle of the Sands* (1903, filmed 1979 & in German 1987), but they were numerous enough for P. G. Wodehouse (a decade before inventing Jeeves & Wooster) to parody them mercilessly in *The Swoop!: or How Clarence saved England: A Tale of the Great Invasion* (1909). In the US, however, famously uninvaded since 1812 (if infiltrated by millions of il/legal human aliens), the threat of invasion is neither taken seriously nor welcome in entertainments, and outside the specific contexts of the 'Yellow Peril' and 'Reds under the Beds' (the latter informing most body-snatcher movies) mundane invasion has been unimportant in genre fiction.[1] Alien invasion has mattered far more in commercial terms, but almost always at schlock B-movie or crass block-buster levels, where aliens' massive superiority, trans-galactic reach, arrant stupidity, and rapid defeat, often by a single man who 'just says no', are all readily compatible.

What makes *Independence Day* and the McCarthyite B-movies it rehashes so depressing is the enthusiastic bigotry and determined violence of the riff they play. Movies can do astonishing things to liberate and update print fiction, as Francis Ford Coppola's *Apocalypse Now* (1979) showed in transferring Joseph Conrad's *Heart of Darkness* (1899) to Vietnam, but the supposedly similar relations claimed by lickspittle reviewers for *Independence Day* and H. G. Wells's *The War of the Worlds* (1898) are a sickening travesty. Wells's novel was *the* transformer both of invasion and the alien, incomparably reworking Chesney's basic form long before the infamous Orson Welles radio-adaptation of 1938 drove New Jersey natives running from their homes in panic. Yes, Wells's invaders are Martian technocrats bent on conquest, notoriously defeated only by their fatal vulnerability to the common cold, but Wells explicitly understood that in this form the invasion story was a paradigm for the British invasion and genocidal colonisation of Tasmania, implicitly for all imperial acquisitions of territory and subjects, and in his very first chapter, 'The Eve of the War', he has his narrator bluntly tell readers so:

> And before we judge of [the Martians] too harshly, we must remember what ruthless and utter destruction our own species has wrought, not only upon animals, such as the vanished bison and dodo, but upon its own inferior races. The Tasma-

---

1   This may be changing with the present 'War on Terrorism'. The fervid imaginations of Al Qaeda or Hezbollah units loose in the lower 48 in TV shows *Sleeper Cell* and the various series of *24* are often rhetorically framed as alien and invasive, but (just like the Yellow Peril and those sneaky Reds under the nation's beds) do not constitute an invasion force in any normal sense—and unlike the Soviet Union Al Qaeda has no following tanks or million-strong standing army to move in where its scouts and spies prepare.

nians, in spite of their human likeness, were entirely swept out of existence in a war of extermination waged by European immigrants, in the space of fifty years. Are we such apostles of mercy as to complain if the Martians warred in the same spirit?[1]

As Wells's tale is told from the 'inferior' (vulnerable) point-of-view, fictionally British but Tasmanian in real-world reference, *The War of the Worlds* specifically rewrites imperial dehumanisation of 'alien' colonial subjects as invasive alien oppression of familiar human protagonists. The plot-twist about the bacterium summons imperial propagations of syphilis and other diseases as well as anticipating biological and ecological questions with which SF would become much concerned; and though no detailed Martian culture or politics are given, much is tantalisingly implicit in the technology and behaviours Wells did describe, opening the door to quasi-scientific modern disciplines of imagining functional, 3-D, intellectually coherent aliens in social numbers. The novel is thus potently political and satirical on several fronts, yet Wells's representation of aliens as monstrous, threatening, apparently superior, and secretly vulnerable also provided a paradigm in which the only correct human response was to attempt to defeat (and implicitly exterminate) them. Reduced to a base-version story of heroic resistance to an invasive alien other whose motives and culture are irrelevant save as obstacles or vulnerabilities, this is politically amenable to many applications, and through the pulps and Hollywood became the morally obese, self-glorifying, and jingoistic national soul that shows so unattractively in the fantasies of *Independence Day*.

Potent in TV SF, notably various *Star Trek* and *Deep Space Nine* series and their broad wake of imitators, but also very widely distributed on celluloid, these invade-and/or-repel scenarios may simpl(isticall)y correspond to the US invading or politically manipulating somewhere un-American overseas, and may then be either right-wing pro-US or (occasionally) left-wing anti-US propaganda; since the mid-1960s Vietnam has been a common reference, and behind it the Pacific War of 1941–5. Invasion and repulsion also provide handy frameworks for militarised space-trooper adventures, at their worst a crude redressing of shoot-'em-up westerns in which the aliens remain monstrous, doing little more than threaten, kill, bleed something other than red, and die; settings are commonly other planets far away and long ago (or long hence), and the real world supposed firmly irrelevant even though the only good alien remains a dead alien.

In and after the 1960s, however, greater optimism and liberalism become increas-

1　H. G. Wells, *The War of the Worlds* (1898; London: Pan, 1975), p. 11.

ingly evident, as SF writers for page and screen grow more interested in communicating with than killing aliens—tales of contact rather than invasion. Blockbuster films such as Steven Spielberg's *Close Encounters of the Third Kind* (1977) and *E.T. the Extra-Terrestrial* (1982) are again potent exemplars, but Hollywood studio-straitjackets and the greater intellectual density and flexibility of printed narrative makes both works cartoonish by comparison with the best books. Among earlier novels a liberal, ecological spirit makes both Robert Silverberg's *Invaders from Earth* (1958) and Ursula Le Guin's *The Word for World is Forest* (1972) particularly effective, but in some ways the most remarkable work came when the sub-genre seemed wholly exhausted, more hack than *engagé*, and draws its energy as much from conscious revisioning and metageneric play as from newly complex, multi-stranded and deep-focus plots.

In David Brin's *The Uplift War* (1987), for example, set in a very crowded cosmos and completing a remarkable trilogy,[1] humans as the assigned custodians of an ecologically ravaged planet on which only lower animal and plant life remains suffer an invasion by the Gubru, powerful avian aliens with strongly triadic thought- and speech-patterns. Human treatment of chimpanzees and gorillas, our primate cousins, and of dolphins, sapient fellow mammals, runs in contrast to the invaders' treatment of humans and all non-Gubru, while continued protection of the occupied ecosphere determines human resistance strategies—both because it's right and because it plays best on the consciences of a watching galactic audience. Or closer to home, and finding a very different yellow brick road to Kansas, there is *Footfall* (1985) by Larry Niven & Jerry Pournelle, in some ways rewriting Joseph J. Millard's *The Gods Hate Kansas* (1941), and running the aliens-invade-earth plot with a quasi-bovine species whose mentation and socio-military culture is based on the herd. These imperialist supercows cannot understand human willingness to nuke prime farmland to get them where they eat, even if it means starving as a nation and a world afterwards; engaging both with the psychopolitics of the late Cold War and with the politicised US sale, donation, or dumping of Mid-Western grain surpluses, *Footfall* appeared in the year Mikhail Gorbachev became General Secretary of the Communist Party of the USSR.

Better still, pushing SF into a new space, there is Ian McDonald's *Chaga* (1995), *Kirinya* (1998), and *Tendeléo's Story* (2000), collectively christened the 'Chaga Saga' for their three female protagonists but no more an 'Aga Saga' in intelligence

---

1   The earlier novels were *Sundiver* (1979) & *Startide Rising* (1983); an eventually very disappointing sequel-trilogy, *Brightness Reef, Infinity's Shore,* & *Heaven's Reach,* appeared in 1995–8.

and literacy than *Independence Day* is a fine redaction of Wells.[1] McDonald begins in *Chaga* with a real astronomical issue, the mysterious 'dark side' of Iapetus,[2] but accelerates away from probability as meteoric 'biological packages' of unknown origin strike the southern hemisphere of Earth, the first hitting Mount Kilimanjaro on the Tanzanian–Kenyan border, less than 3° south of the equator. Others strike South America, Australia, and Oceania, and from each package spills a wave of change, swarming nano-somethings that do not hurt animal life as such but ruthlessly scavenge hydrocarbons, overrun habitat, and begin to build a radiating wilderness of chaotically mixed quasi-crystalline, indescribable, and mimicked forms. Asked (in an extended e-mail interview in 2000–01) about his choice of Kenya as a primary setting, McDonald was refreshingly brisk *and* resonant, without once surrendering his characteristically extrapolating imagination:

> The future's coming to Kenya as much as to Kentucky; and to me, it's more interesting in Nairobi than Nashville. Africans are tough and resourceful people. The great skiffy [Sci-Fi] cliché is the UFO/White House combo: what if it's the White Mountain—Kilimanjaro—instead? The image of the unstoppable wave of transformation was nicked from [1982 *Star Trek* movie] *The Wrath of Khan*: it's the Genesis device, slowed down, and once I had that, it became a rich source of metaphors: for colonialism, new technology, globalisation, change, death. If the Chaga is colonialism, it's a unique kind that allows the people of the poor South to use and transform it to meet their needs and empower themselves: it's a symbiosis. The Chaga creates a society which needs nothing from Western Capitalism, in fact, threatens to destabilise it: here material objects are cheap and easy to make. Skills and talents become important. This is a true knowledge economy, where a repro Lexus is worth a haircut, because how many folk do you know can do a really good haircut? So we get a democracy of commodities, and nanoprogramming skills are the economic base. There'd be a lot of copyright fights but the food would be great.[3]

1　Aga is a brand of large English kitchen range invented in 1922, designed as a modern version of the heart and hearth of a household and extremely popular in certain strata of county society; 'aga sagas' is a journalistic coinage for serial novels (usually by women) that trace a female line of descent through successive mistresses of a middle-class family kitchen. The term is exemplified by Joanna Trollope's novels, though she denies mentioning the brand more than once or twice.

2　The third largest moon of Saturn, with the most inclined orbital plane and a 'two-tone' coloration—one hemisphere bright, one dark—which means it can only be seen from Earth for half its orbit. A Voyager 2 flypast in 1981 (at *c.*966,000 km/600,000 miles) revealed the bright side as cratered ice, but the dark remains a mystery even after the Cassini flypast of 2004 (123,000 km/77,000 miles); Cassini has been retasked to flypast at 1,200 km/800 miles on 10th September, 2007.

3　http://www.infinityplus.co.uk/nonfiction/intimcd.htm

Refreshing as it is to find a discussion that understands the profound relations of SF to the Cold War of philosophies and praxes of economics, there is more. The interviewer also used the unhappy term 'Third World', and McDonald's reply was equally brisk and telling:

> I'd use the expression "Third World" only in the sense that I include Northern Ireland as a Third World country: a society of two significant social groups that have been set against each other by historical engineering; a skewed economic infrastructure based on the public sector, with a highly economically significant samurai elite (the RUC[1]); a highly-politicised population with the ability to arm itself to the teeth if it's disregarded; a post-colonial process of disengagement that failed half-way through; physical marginalisation, poor infrastructure, a monied class rapidly moving upwards that is yet unable to engage fully in either Irish or UK society; the sense of cultural inferiority that forces both social groups into re-engineering of their cultural tropes ...
>
> This is getting worthy and boring. My point is, there's more dynamic for change in "Third World" societies than in the West. Where there's change, there's conflict and where there's conflict, you have story.[2]

The whole interview is lively and impressive, but living in Jamaica has sharpened my appreciation of McDonald's analysis, for *every* factor he lists can (*mutatis mutandis*) be immediately applied to the polity here, and the same holds true in many ex-colonies. 'Third World' becomes synonymous with 'post-colonial', and McDonald's understanding of Ulster as a colony is absolute—a working, analytical awareness of culture, politics, and structure as functions of imperialism, cognate with other such throughout the former reaches of the Empire. Such awareness is seen in some of the finest (post-)imperial novels, including Rudyard Kipling's *Kim* and Paul Scott's *Raj Quartet*, and connects directly to the recurrent concern of SF with restagings of the imperial encounter—an active premise of *Chaga*. As one might surmise from McDonald's name, it's also an awareness of home, for though born in Manchester to a Scottish father and Irish mother, McDonald has lived in Ulster, principally Belfast, since he was moved there at the age of 5 in 1965, and so lived through the whole of what are euphemistically called 'the Troubles', from the stirrings of riot in 1968 to the 'Good Friday' Agreement of 1998 and beyond.

It isn't so much the murderous bombings and shootings in Ulster and elsewhere

1   Royal Ulster Constabulary.
2   ◨ http://www.infinityplus.co.uk/nonfiction/intimcd.htm

that matter, though McDonald clearly knows more about carnage than anyone would ever want to, as the epiphenomena of the conflict. The gross miscarriages of justice against Irish men and women committed in 1970–5 haunted Britain for much of the 1980s–90s, as campaigns for release variously succeeded and the British government was persistently and probably correctly accused of operating a covert shoot-to-kill policy. Much of the funding for paramilitary violence on both sides came from protection rackets, pseudo-charitable contributions, and Irish Americans, while weapons and explosives came largely from or via Libya and the armed imperial services; the vicarious amorality of such supplies, whatever the attractions of paying empire or terrorists back in their own coin, is cumulatively repugnant. The Troubles left the industrial giant of Belfast moribund and Ulster as a whole grossly economically depressed, while Eire was booming, a 'Celtic Tiger' driven by EU regional funding programmes; and in a strong sense the Troubles achieved absolutely nothing else of value. From 1968–98 a total of 3,523 people died; many more were injured: but no boundary was redrawn and political reality at the end was exactly what it had been at the beginning, that Ulster will remain part of the UK unless and until a majority of its residents votes otherwise.

Such futility activates the dystopian within SF but equally informs mordant humour and a hard-eyed vision of what really matters within and about a situation. It is these that play out in *Chaga*, crucially allowing McDonald, though as much an outsider to Kenya and Africa as the alien 'biological packages' transforming it, to speak without prejudice as he finds. His protagonist, Gaby McAslan, is as Ulster a product as he is himself, but as a 'SkyNet' journalist with more ambition than ethics and libido than discrimination, she is an unsympathetic heroine whom McDonald writes from outside (gender) as well as inside (culture). Much of what Gaby does is rooted in cliché, like her central, self-serving affair with a UN scientist-administrator ironically named 'Shepard'—but she is Ulster enough to have a knowing political eye; loves Africa and Africans, trying hard to understand and present them as individuals; and in *Chaga*'s central battle with those who would rather see refugees starve by the million than allow humans to attempt union with the alien, Gaby is on the side of the African, the alien, and the angels. This might on its own be enough to make the book work, but McDonald did not risk it, and if Gaby does reprehensible things she also undergoes a terrible purgation that draws on a source more potent even than *The War of the Worlds* and serialised only a year later, in 1899—Joseph Conrad's novella *Heart of Darkness*.

It is easy to invoke Conrad as an intertext, especially after Coppola's magnificent and terrifying *Apocalypse Now* showed why it might be well worth doing so, but rewriting *Heart of Darkness* in African terms as an outsider to the continent is seriously tricky whatever your background and credentials—as V. S. Naipaul found out the hard way in *A Bend in the River* (1979), published the year Coppola's masterpiece was first released and a great deal less impressive. Introduce a real alien, however, rather than just a trespassing European *m'zungu* and all begins to change. McDonald's UK edition challenges most readers from the very first bookshop-shelf kiss with the mystery of the word *Chaga* as a name and as a title. His US publishers preferred the blander, phrasal title *Evolution's Shore*—one might trust (more in hope than expectation) for the sales-buzz of 'evolution' in a proto-Bushy and Creationist climate rather than in fear of the off-puttingly African, but nevertheless absurdly, for what (the) Chaga is and isn't forms McDonald's central theme and the mainspring of the action.

Chaga is the name bestowed by humanity—that is to say, the mass-media—on the alien life-form that spreads out concentrically from the impact-sites. The name is chosen (and in the process grammatically de-Africanised) because the tribal lands on which the 'Kilimanjaro Event' took place are actually those of the Wa-Chagga, a prosperous agriculturalist people numbering about two million. They are Bantu, speak a variety of Kirombo dialects including Kichaga,[1] and (as transliterations go) one of the Wa-Chagga is a Chaga. Largely resident on the southern and eastern slopes of Mounts Kilimanjaro and Meru, and through urban migration in Dar-es-Salaam on the Tanzanian coast, they grow Arabica coffee for cash, bananas for food, and finger millet (ragi, *Eleusine coracara*) for beer. Predominantly Christian, and early converts, they benefitted from favourable treatment under the British and have continued to receive faith-based aid since independence.

The cultural basis of Chaga society is Bantu, but there was considerable cultural fusion even before their adoption of Christianity and subsequent incorporation into the polyethnic and multicultural Kenyan polity. Elements of the basal Niger-Congo civilisations were joined and qualified by Nilo-Hamitic ideas and practices absorbed with the once-resident upland Ongamo people before the arrival of the surrounding Masai pastoralists (whose culture is cattle- and plains-based). The identity of the Wa-Chagga, historically as for McDonald, is thus intimately bound up with their long residence on Kilimanjaro—at 19,340 ft (5,898 m) the highest African and free-standing Terran mountain.

1   See ▣ http://www.languageportraits.net/chaga.html

A composite NASA LandSat image of Mount Meru and the peaks of Kilimanjaro. Vertical scale is exaggerated by a factor of two.

The remarkable multiplicity of explanations of the name Kilimanjaro,[1] including the proposed derivation McDonald cites from Swahili, 'White Mountain', and a possible Kichaga root meaning 'that cannot be conquered', attests to its fascination. The quiescent (but not extinct) stratovolcano forms a botanically, zoologically, and micro-climatically distinct massif which determines a huge patchwork of zones by shaping air- and waterflow, migration patterns etc. while displaying its power across all surrounding lands—making it a symbolically ideal location from which McDonald's unstoppable alien Chaga remorselessly advances.

Chaga is also (optimistically enough) the common name of a potent Siberian mushroom, *Innotus obliquus*, known for millennia as a medicinal herb, of long-standing importance in Chinese medicine, and now variously marketed for its curative properties. Under trial as a tumour-reducer, it is also both an anti-viral and anti-inflammatory agent. McDonald's alien Chaga shares these properties, a theme mediated through its ability to cure Gaby's dying colleague Jake Aarons, and the Siberian identity of her useful shaman-pilot friend Oksana. Much less optimistically, Chaga is reminiscent in more than sound of 'Chagas Disease', or American trypanosomiasis, named for the Brazilian physician who first described it in 1909 and a major killer in large parts of Latin America. The pathogen is a flagellate protozoan, *Trypanosoma cruzi*, transmitted by blood-sucking insects; initial symptoms may be mild, at worst feverlike and mildly debilitating, but chronic infection leads after some years of apparent remission to major damage to the nervous and digestive systems, and to the heart. Symptoms of chronic disease may include full-blown dementia and fatal malnutrition, if sufferers live long enough, as well as an often severe cardiomyopathy that usually ensures they don't. Chagas Disease can be treated, but often, still, is not caught in time, and evacuates a human host-body of health and meaning unchecked.

Taking the Wa-Chagga people to symbolise (*inter alia*) the cultural adaptability that has made them a fusion of Niger-Congo and Nilo-Hamitic genes and cultures, all

---

1   See ▣ http://www.ntz.info/gen/n01532.html

three meanings of 'Chaga' cohere as agents of change and mutability working over (very) long time-spans at a sub-cellular level. The associations with *I. obliquus* and *T. cruzi* shape themselves as variant aspects of change, curative and pathogenic, concording with human reactions to and thoughts of the alien Chaga, within which the Wa-Chagga are yet evolving—for though they fled their lands as the alien biochemistry spread, they did so only to pile up in refugee camps neither the Kenyan government nor the hastily chartered UNECT*Afrique* authority that tries to quarantine the 'zone of infection' can manage. After a while, sick in body and mind from a squalid life no-one much cares about, they decide they would as soon return to the Chaga named after them to see if embracing it offers any improvement. But the human authorities who don't want them also maintain the quarantine imposed to 'protect' them, and preferring the alien is taboo.

A choice of Nairobi over Nashville is one thing, but the alien Chaga has equally said nothing of leaders, disdaining clichéd dialogue as well as overused landing zones. It doesn't talk, wait, defer, or seem to care about anything much; it just does what it does as remorselessly as an asteroid falls, and nothing we have can stop it. As a Masai politician, Dr Daniel Oloitip, explains to Gaby in March 2008 when she first flies in to join SkyNet's Chaga-driven East African bureau:

> 'I suppose it is a kind of cancer,' he said. [...] 'The Chaga, I mean. As there are sicknesses that eat a person's life away from inside, so there are diseases of nations. It invades the land. draws strength from it, kills what it finds and duplicates only itself. While we sit here contemplating our croissants, it is growing, it is spreading. It never sleeps. Even the name you have given it is not its own, but has been taken from the people who once lived there: what else can it be, Ms McAslan, than a cancer?' [...]
>
> 'So early in the task of nation-building, too. Why, we have scarcely fifty years of history behind us and suddenly, boom!' He softly smacked heel of hand into palm. 'Surely, God is not kind to Kenya: just as the information revolution was allowing us to take our true place in the world, we find we must go hand open to the United Nations. We shall certainly not have fifty more years. What is it they are estimating? Twenty more until the country is overrun? Seventy years is not time to be a nation. Why could it not have come down in France or England, where they have too much history; or China or India, where they have so much past they do not know what to do with it. Or America, where at least they could turn being made into another planet into a theme park.'[1]

1 Ian McDonald, *Chaga* (London: Gollancz, 1995, pp. 22–3).

Especially with the wicked humour and metafictional joking it's easy to agree with likeable Dr Dan, but care is needed. Cancers, whatever else they may be, are precisely not alien but malfunctions of our own genetics and cellular chemistry; their 'invasiveness' is always a complex and layered metaphor, and here signals the fascinating, severe torque to which McDonald subjects all attempts to read the Chaga as a colonising power. Dr Dan is also (as it turns out) quite wrong to say the Chaga replicates only itself, and if readers can't yet *know* so, they can and should see that his bitter words are opinion, not fact, for neither he nor Gaby has then been into the deep Chaga to judge for themselves. Even in a relaxed, private conversation truth is perhaps not to be expected from either a journalist or a politician, and the slipperiness of sincerity in these professions (as in prose fiction) is a leitmotif and structuring principle of McDonald's action.

A great deal happens in *Chaga*, and the scenes of street-life and gang-conflict in Nairobi as it is slowly reduced, consumed, and recycled by the alien growth are remarkable. As much as the mountain comes to her, however, the main actions (as for so many tourists to Kenya) are Gaby's journeys into the Masai Mara, the Nyandarua (or Aberdares), and to the solitary mountain-massif, Kilimanjaro, going into the growing Chaga—which is where *Heart of Darkness* begins to make itself felt. Conrad's novella is never explicitly named, but its titular phrase occurs several times in narration and dialogue, initially when a German sports-tourist, Peter Werther,[1] believed killed on the summit of Kilimanjaro in the initial meteor-strike, turns up again, "a man come back from the heart of darkness"; the phrase recurs in Gaby's interview with Werther, who also pointedly says that in the Chaga he knew "Wonder and horror",[2] echoing and qualifying Kurtz's infamous last words in Conrad's tale, "The horror! The horror!" And when Gaby finally does travel into the deep Chaga, and the chapters of *Chaga* become for a while the first-person text of her video-diary rather than third-person narration, McDonald has her mention *Apocalypse Now* to remind readers both that the master-sign of the journey into an alien continent is Conrad's, and that he is himself rewriting Conrad within Africa, not simply transferring his design, as Coppola did, to a later imperialism elsewhere.

There is no great River Congo for Gaby to navigate into the heart of the Chaga, only an overrun Kenyan marsh and mountain-lake along the way, but her whole trek with SkyNet colleagues and quarantine-busting Kenyan guides through the ex-

---

1 A distant collateral descendant of Goethe's 'Young Werther', perhaps, in *Die Leiden des jungen Werthers* (1774).

2 McDonald, *Chaga*, pp. 67, 69

traordinary organic-crystal world of the Chaga is explicitly a jungle trek towards a central mystery; both the moods and many topoi of Marlow's river-journey recur. In Conrad, of course, the heart of darkness shadowing the Congolese interior and the fate of Kurtz is also the grasping industrial bulk of late Victorian London, looming behind Marlow as he tells his tale on a boat moored on the Thames. McDonald's heart of darkness is similarly doubled, twice over. In an obvious way the "Wonder and horror" Werther found are the transformative fates imposed by the Chaga on the Wa-Chagga and other post-humans who now live within it—some of them mutations that trigger immediate visceral horror, others evolutions that promise not only an adapted but a greatly improved, extended, and enriched life. Some Wa-Chagga villages have been able to accept the differently limbed and configured children they may now produce; others have begun systematic infanticide by exposure, rejecting as compulsively as autoimmune systems the alien to which they have returned and on which they can only depend. There is also an astonishing datum Gaby discovers as a 'Chaganaut' from the mutating residents, a first a strange wonder allowing her to watch a live Manchester United match on a 'television tree' (McDonald is a great fan of the beautiful game), but with a little thought the purest dynamite: that the Chaga can synthesise improved bio-equivalents of *all* the electronics it consumes—the basis (in the second 'Chaga Saga' novel, *Kirinya*) of the radically de-capitalised information economy McDonald cited in interview. But the second doubling of the Chaga's meaning, corresponding with Conrad's anterior imperial London, is clearly the UN and military-industrial hands into which Gaby falls while trying to leave the Chaga, and coming after the alien wonders and horrors of the interior this later development stands as the true heart of moral and economic darkness

Subjected not to reasonable decontamination and debriefing procedures, but to unlawful detention and repeated gynaecological examination in a birthing-chair that amounts to systematic rape and torture, Gaby is reviled and dehumanised in exactly the manner so often attributed to slavers and aliens who abduct and experiment on humans. There is a potentially powerful motive, not explicitly spelt out at this stage, in that the gynaecological investigation is aimed at understanding what the Chaga does to human reproductive biology. But can the end justify these means? And in any case what is the end? Understanding? new treatments? or just a desperate, unprincipled fight to contain and control the economic disaster that the Chaga represents for First-World industrial economies still dependent on gross exploitation of former colonies? Even read as a purgative punishment for her professional dishonesties and careless uses of sexuality, Gaby's treatment at UN hands is brutally excessive, and of course illegal—sufficiently so that her rescue and its exposure by Dr Dan, who has come to hate the UN much more than the Chaga, is a major scandal. And McDonald does not stop there, as many might, redeeming Gaby into triumphant liberty and a journalistic *succès de scandale*, but shows both in *Chaga* and *Kirinya* the damage she suffers, continuing to weigh the wrongs she has done and goes on to do against the prices she and others pay and the public benefits that may or may not accrue from her journalistic work and self-serving ethics.

McDonald's UN is also very carefully articulated, both in the UNECT*Afrique* (and UNECT*Asie*) agencies he invents and in a verisimilar picture of real agencies, with rogue as well as dedicated components, and aid, research, and military arms increasingly at policy odds. The founding balance (or in some views paralysis) of UN interests is also shown to be progressively usurped by an impatient US, at first as a *primus inter pares* throwing its superpowered weight about, then in fairly open militarised takeover of alien contact, a strategy driven jointly by corporate desperation and the chiming imperatives of polemical self-identity—that rockets' red glare that alone can demonstrate in darkness the continued flight above all of the star-spangled banner. The patriotic military glare is largely allowed to pass as a given in *Chaga*, though not in *Kirinya*. The corporate hatred of the Chaga as freely taking and freely giving is understandable in terms of greed and unbridled self-interest; it also corresponds closely with the European commercial rapacity based on contempt for Africans that Conrad so memorably skewered. But McDonald's manipulation of Conrad is also given a very specific turn, for his central example of what is most evil about the attempted interdiction of Chaga products, the true heart of his horror, is that those living in the Chaga who were once HIV+ or dying from full-blown AIDS have been cured by their contact with the alien biochemistry. Indeed, they are in some ways the favoured of the Chaga, for the virus lodged in their cells is for the alien a gateway into their genomes that makes its apparent tasks or functions of manipulating and reforming *Homo sapiens* very much easier.

McDonald's virology has a fictional extrapolation as one component—in his 2008 the strains 'HIV1' and '2' are treatable, if one is adequately funded, and 'HIV3' manageable with complex drug regimes, if one is well-funded, while 'HIV4' remains a rapid death-sentence—but this does no more than map in expanded terms the gradient that now exists, shamefully, in treatment of HIV. Infection with the virus has for nearly two decades now been a death-sentence only for the poor, incomprehensibly many of whom have been, and are, and will be, Africans. Delivering the third Diana, Princess of Wales Lecture on AIDS, in 2003—the first two having been given by

Presidents Nelson Mandela and William Jefferson Clinton—Judge Edwin Cameron, a justice of the South African Supreme Court of Appeal and still the only public official in any African country to admit to HIV+ status, argued very clearly and with great force that AIDS has become the overwhelming moral issue of our time. It isn't 'simply' that people die in such staggering numbers, nor even the millions of orphans already left behind to care for themselves and their younger siblings, but that the deaths *could* be stopped, now; only profit prevents. AIDS is no longer the unstoppable, incomprehensible death-sentence, the fatal 'scourge' of its early days in the 1980s, but a treatable condition, so our choice not to treat the Africans and other poor who die from it is a moral choice that damns us. And Judge Cameron knows whereof he speaks: at the legal commission in 1999 where he announced his HIV+ status he coined a memorable phrase—"I am not dying of AIDS. I am living with AIDS."[1]—but he also made it clear that he knew in every moment that he could exercise that vital choice only because of his privileged job, great and loving support from family and friends, and access through wealth with racial and professional privilege to medical care and the necessary anti-retroviral drugs. The lecture extended his searingly self-aware analysis to the careless First-World wealthy—which in common African terms is almost all who live there—with devastating impact.

When, therefore, McDonald locates his heart of darkness still in Africa, but in a transformative alien biochemistry, *and* (looming as grimly as London over Marlow's shoulder) in the persisting First-World denial of life-saving AIDS treatment to millions of infected Africans (as well as everybody else in need who lacks capital resources), he really does take on a mantle of Conrad, and in it the world. When he did so in 1995, moreover, before even Judge Cameron could bring himself to articulate in public what he was beginning to know in his heart, McDonald claimed a most honourable place. In the dozen years since some things have improved, but African agony and First-World amorality are little diminished. The desperately misguided flirtation of South African President Thabo Mbeki with a bizarre form of AIDS denialism, particularly in 1999–2002, proffered the West a distracting excuse for inaction, but the same period heard the then-head of USAID, Andrew Natsios, testify in all earnestness to a formal Congressional hearing that 'Africans' (apparently a homogenous as well as inferior breed of human being):

> don't know what Western time is. You have to take these [anti-retroviral] drugs a
> certain number of hours each day, or they don't work. Many people in Africa have

---

1 Edwin Cameron, *Witness to AIDS* (with contributions by Nathan Geffen, Cape Town: Tafelberg/ London & New York: I. B. Tauris, 2005), p. 63.

never seen a clock or a watch their entire lives. And if you say, one o'clock in the afternoon, they do not know what you are talking about. They know morning, they know noon, they know evening, they know the darkness at night.[1]

They know also the darkness at noon in the heads of such as Andrew Natsios, despite his exalted position in the international development community a Bush appointee and an expert neither on aid nor AIDS; an empowered bureaucrat and placeman who spoke thus of a continent where over the previous decade tens of millions of citizens, including in the urban centres a vast number of ordinary working as well as unemployed folk, had happily adopted the use of mobile phones—not to mention digital musical and other arts technology wherever they could buy, beg, or borrow it. All that really counts is profitability, and Natsios was not only demeaning himself and insulting all, but (wittingly or blindly) providing spurious cover for the pharmacological lobby (and *their* political hacks and placemen) who care more for future income than present death, and will defend patents and exorbitant niche-marketing to their own last breaths. US aid under the Bush administration has also been tied to a raft of hedging limitations about suppressions of contraceptive advice, safe sex, abortion counselling and the like, fuelled by religious dogmatism and falsely claiming great things of the Catholic and other sectarian practices of abstention in Uganda—where many Christian priests still insist that the wife of an infected man must be celibate or risk infection from her husband, no barrier method being acceptable 'to God'.

As of 2006 Natsios is serving as the US Special Envoy to Sudan with a particular brief to deal with Darfur, and the UNAIDS report of 2006 estimated sub-Saharan AIDS deaths in 2005 at 2 million, out of 2.8 million worldwide, with 24.5 million HIV+ adults—which is to say about 11% of all black Africans aged 15–49.[2] But I am comfortable today, and so, probably, are you, having done far less individually or between us than McDonald to deserve our quiet slumber. *Chaga* cannot change the world, any more than *Heart of Darkness* could stop the 'scramble for Africa' or lessen the later catastrophe of the even quicker 'scramble from Africa'—the 12 years 1958–70 that saw independence thrown willy-nilly at most of the continent as the *quondam* colonial masters ran for their lives and wallets. But McDonald could stand up to be counted, and he's standing there still.

1   Andrew Natsios to Congress, June 2001, quoted in Cameron, *Witness to AIDS*, p, 198.
2   See ▣ http://www.unaids.org/en/HIV_data/2006GlobalReport/default.asp.

One of the greater privileges of novelists is the imagination of what J. R. R. Tolkien very usefully called eucatastrophe,[1] an abrupt twist into ending, technically a catastrophe, that is not, as in most tragedy, revelatory and maleficent, but instead a benign and thoroughgoing deliverance—'then saw I that there was a way to heaven even from the gates of hell', as it were, and moreover a way for everyone. In the further future, if he returns to the series as he has sometimes indicated he will, McDonald's Chaga will slowly deliver that and more as it transforms southern-hemisphere economic production from a failed capitalist model to an overwhelming material abundance in which alien molecular technologies mean that all can have what they need or want for the asking.[2] In the nearer term McDonald also provided, in *Kirinya*, a more spectacular deliverance turning both on another great reason (besides avoiding the White House) for setting a novel of renewed evolution in the land of the Great Rift Valley, and on that mysterious dark side of Iapetus with which he started. To go there means loosing a pack of spoilers, but the image that emerges in the finale needs them all.

The point about the Great Rift Valley, where the African continent is slowly tearing apart, is of course that it was the 'cradle of humanity', and is the site of most and the most important finds of fossil hominids. Above all are 'Lucy' and 'Baby Lucy' or 'Selam', the most complete known specimens of *Australopithecus afarensis*, both found in the Ethiopian section of the Rift Valley (in 1974 and 2000 respectively). Where else then but the Great Rift Valley should we re-evolve into something new? The point about Iapetus is not only that McDonald makes its dark side dark with a Chaga infestation, but that the Chaga also takes a fancy to another of Saturn's satellites, Hyperion, which disappears for a while and reappears as one of those marvellous things that (thanks to Roz Kaveney) SF calls BDOs, or 'Big Dumb Objects'. BDOs are dumb only in not speaking at first: typically they are abandoned alien artefacts, *Marie Celeste* spaceships with strangely configured controls or long-abandoned defence-systems that house eventually communicative AIs, but McDonald's BDO is rather more active—a reshaped moon that in defiance of Newton and Einstein alike smoothly pops itself out of orbit around Saturn and heads this way. It is this gigantic approach that triggers US military paranoia, and as one growing Chaga infestation in the southern ocean is in audible but indecipherable radio-contact with the Chaga artefact in space, the needs to dominate the arriving BDO and to control the economic

---

1   See 'Of Modern Dragons', pp. 123–4 above.

2   A similar post-capitalist galactic economy is posited by Iain M. Banks in his novels of 'the Culture', beginning with *Consider Phlebas* (1987).

'threat' of emergent Chaga-based, post-capitalist, *quondam* 'Third World' nations swing into terrifying parallel: control on the ground through control in space.

The details I can leave unspoiled, but the good guys win one for the aliens and for Africa, so the BDO's self-insertion into earth orbit is very particular. McDonald's science is generally strong, and his narratives of the near-future touched with excellent detail: his 'Huntsville' and 'Miyama' 'orbital observatories', for example, add institutes to the existing Japanese National Astronomical Observatory at Mitaka and the George C. Marshall Space Flight Center in Alabama. He's also well up on NASA image-releases, including the spectacular Hubble pictures of distant nebulae, and knows his home galaxy, so that if he says Earth is so many AU from the galactic centre, and the Chaga seems to have come from the gas-clouds around Rho Ophiuchi, you may be sure it all makes good observational sense. He also provides the Chaga (once the UN research teams manage to get some samples under a decent microscope) with a viable biochemistry that while inevitably only sketched adds considerable plausibility to the alien's habits and abilities. Needing a genuinely alien alien many writers have imagined a silicon-based and hydrogen-breathing metabolism, abandoning our own carbon-and-oxygen system, but invaders-of-Earth must be able to function here, so McDonald just shifts the Chaga's cellular basis from the usual Terran allotropes of carbon, familiar to us as graphite and diamond, to the third allotrope, C-60 and its larger brethren that in deep space gas-clouds form the geodesic spheres and tubes known informally as 'Buckyballs' and more properly (after the great architect and visionary who anticipated their structure) as Buckminsterfullerenes.

All that provides a good base for the best version I know of an idea that's been around in SF for a while, and that is in theory all but possible now, but remains a sublime imagining. (1) Take a good-sized carbonaceous chondritic asteroid, with lots of carbon and water, and manoeuvre it into geostationary orbit directly over the Earth's equator. (2) Programme automated mining and processing equipment to hollow the asteroid out, separating water, carbon, and anything else useful. (3) Store all but the carbon. (4) Turn that into tubular Carbon-60 Buckminsterfullerenes, stronger in tensile strength than diamond is hard. (5) Braid the fullerenes, strand by strand, first into ropes, then cable, and then a cable of cables, a few tens of metres in diameter with a breaking strain in the trillions of tons. (6) Drop this cable carefully out of the hollowing asteroid, allowing it to droop towards earth, and when about 44,000 miles of cable have swung in a lazy catenary curve across the 22,000 miles of space and atmosphere, (7) anchor it down. For this you will need a large massif rooted deep into the planetary mantle that is right on the equator: Kilimanjaro, alas, is too far off—even at 3° south the seasonal swing would whip a cable appallingly—but Mount Kenya, the next extinct (or at least inactive) stratovolcano to the north and at 17,058 ft (5,202 m) Africa's second tallest mountain, is less than *9 minutes* south of the true equator. So lock that cable down, not into Mount Kenya's caldera itself, but into a nice big concrete and magnetised steel collar sunk into its solid lower sides—and now anyone with a spacesuit and good mountaineering skills can climb off planet with no more by way of a power-source than their legs. Fix a good cable-car system to the cable, with passenger and freight capacity, and you have truly become the new navel of the planet, to whom the scrambling companies and even armies of the First World will come cap-in-hand to plead for their own cheap slots up and out of the gravity-well. Best of all, the in-car music during the trip, which is bound to take a good few hours, is going to come from Nairobi, not Nashville.

By any standards a tremendous image, McDonald has a still deeper and better reason for it. Stretching up to bloom in space, the cable looping from Mount Kenya to the still massive asteroid, sliding with the Earth in silent orbital lockstep, is a new World Tree, a baobab of economic and national life. The name is probably from Arabic *'abū ḥibāb*, 'source of seeds', combining *'ab*, 'father, source' and *ḥibāb*, plural of *ḥabb*, 'seed'. A proud Kenyan symbol and a resource of great value and age, the baobabs of the Kenyan plains were seemingly consumed by the Chaga, falling to its inexorable advance. But if what followed was at first a chaotic zone of destruction and consumption, deeper into the Chaga the baobab's and other Terran forms are reproduced and enlarged, so that where a 'real' baobab once stood 50–60 feet high, there may after a few months or years be a Chaga baobab 500–600 feet high—or even 22,000 miles high. Growing from the symbolic mountain and national heart of a country consumed and remade by the Chaga—and rather more responsibly than it had been by its human imperialist invaders—the World Baobab Gravity Elevator is both redress and deliverance, recapitulation and stark creation, connecting an Africa scoured of disease to the stars, and making neo-Kenyans and the rainbow nations of the Chaga generally the custodians of the human gateway to the future; as they and Ethiopians already are of the best windows on our hominid past.

In the last published instalment of the Chaga Saga, the novella *Tendeléo's Story* (2000), McDonald revised things a little by revisioning some of the story through the explicitly Kenyan eyes of a young girl, Tendeléo Bi, who manages briefly to flee the Chaga to the UK but is deported back as an unwelcome and contaminated alien to be thrust into alien change. A third full novel, *Ananda*, that extends Tendeléo's insider-perspective is reportedly half-written, but has been on hold for the best part of a decade while McDonald has brought SF to other less-than-traditional settings and cultures: *River of Gods* (2004) is already *the* novel of mid-twenty-first century India, and the imminent *Brasyl* (2007) sounds as if it tries to do as much for Lusophone South America. Nor have Ireland and Ulster been neglected in his blog, though the relative calm and productivity since the Good Friday agreement have drawn the urgency of satire, if not of vision, and McDonald has not written of them directly in fiction since the excellent *Sacrifice of Fools* (1996).

Few writers in SF or any other field have had so clearly moral and ethical a career as McDonald. As much as any writer shaped by the endless broil and self-consumption of Ireland's hopes and sons—Wilde, Synge, Yeats, Joyce, and Beckett not excluded—he brings his hard-taught knowledge of the human heart in all its glories and meanness to the service of his work, and he is, no less than the great Modernists, in the process of remaking his genre of choice. Perhaps when those little green men do come along they will choose the White House lawn, or Kenya's White Mountain, as McDonald so happily imagined, but they might also care to try Whitehead, in Ulster's County Antrim, a little place on the northern shore of Belfast Lough across the water from Ballymacormick Point, where Gaby McAslan grew up and McDonald sometimes goes walking.

6. Of Organelles

Octavia E. Butler's Strange Determination

> At the present, I feel so unhopeful.
> —Octavia Butler (June 1947–Feb. 2006), Jan. 2006[1]

An organelle (you had better know at once) is a self-contained structure within an eukaryotic cell—the kind that have a nucleus and form the massive, differentiated agglomerations we call plants and animals. The most important is the nucleus itself, containing within each cell the DNA of the whole organism; there is also the mitochondrion, an oval a little more than one-billionth of a metre long that takes in proteins the cell manufactures for it and in return supplies energy. This happens in the eukaryotic cells making up your body as in those making up mine, and we would both be in a sad way without our self-recharging cellular batteries, but mitochondria also provide, strangely and imaginatively, a perspective of human evolution and heredity that once grasped is not easily forgotten.[2]

The 'double helix' structure of DNA, like a twisted rope-ladder with chemical joints in the middle of each rung, was discovered in the 1950s. Both the abbreviation and the fact of DNA's importance to heredity are now widely known, but the salient details (worked out after Watson's & Crick's famous 1953 paper in *Nature*) rather less so. Deoxyribonucleic acid evolved about 4.5 billion years ago, and its function and structure are closely bound together through the T-shaped *nucleotides* that create the double helix—Adenine, Cytosine, Thymine, & Guanine (pairing to make rungs), each fixed to a ribose base (linking to make ropes). Adenine will only pair with Thymine (and *vice versa*), Cytosine with Guanine (and *vice versa*)—so every rung is C–G/G–C or A–T/T–A, and if the helix unzips, forming two strands, each will *exactly* rebuild its missing pair and so replicate the DNA. Groups of three paired bases form a chemical unit coding for a particular amino acid, so the sequence

---

1   ▣ http://nyc.indymedia.org/en/2006/01/63925.html
2   A shorter version of this essay appears in my Genre Fiction Sightline on Butler's *Xenogenesis* trilogy (Humanities-E-Books, 2007).

of bases determines sequences of acids which (depending on sequence) form this or that protein which (depending on sequence) ... and so on, manufacturing blood, bone, nerve, muscle, flesh, fat, hair and all we are. DNA is stored in *chromosomes*, long folded strands, of which the highly evolved primate *Homo sapiens* normally has 46, in 23 pairs. Particular sections of a chromosome form a *gene*, controlling (say) eye colour; vast numbers of nucleotide-triplets encoding proteins make up each gene, and very many genes each chromosome. The Human Genome project, mapping all nucleotide sequences, has found some 50,000 genes, but also shown long stretches of DNA which do not seem to code for anything but continue to be replicated. Dismissively labelled 'junk DNA', its function (if any) is currently one of the great scientific mysteries—always an attraction to SF writers and readers alike.

The point about mitochondria is that they turned out, rather surprisingly, to have their own DNA. There isn't enough of it to contain the recipes for all that mitochondria need, so they are dependent on the cell's nuclear DNA, but it also turned out that, as an apparently incidental effect of the chemistry of fertilisation, mitochondrial DNA was passed strictly down the female line, not in the same sexually dividing-and-pairing fashion as nuclear DNA. With Y-chromosome testing this has allowed over the last two decades remarkable and definitive statements about human ancestry and historical migration by genealogists and anthropologists. In Alex Haley's *Roots: The Saga of an American Family* (1976), a huge TV hit in 1977 with a sequel in 1979, the enslaved Kunta Kinte's modern descendant is able to complete his journey back to his roots when a West African griot, a historian-bard, sings him a list of local villagers abducted nearly three centuries before and he hears his ancestor's talismanic name. Thirty years later what happens, increasingly, is that samples of a modern African American's or Caribbean citizen's DNA are compared with samples on record for various African regions and peoples, or with that of specific individuals, to confirm or deny distant cousinhood. Simi-lar work has been done all over the world[1] and for most such genealogy is the true benefit of the discovery of DNA, nuclear or mitochondrial, but for SF writer Octavia Butler the les-son was quite contrary.

Strange fruit: an overview of DNA
(Picture Credit: Michael Ströck)

Her central observation was that

1   Since 1991 genealogy has become *huge* on the Web, regularly trailing only religion and pornography as dominant site-content.

mitochondria have their own DNA because they were once a distinct species. Necessarily younger than DNA itself, they are thought to have evolved *c*.4 billion years ago, alongside eukaryotic cells, and at some juncture the two entered symbiosis, a mutually beneficial biological pact. Eukaryotic cells hosted mitochondria, synthesising for them proteins they needed; in return mitochondria delivered surplus energy to eukaryotic cells—and still do. Advertisements for Actimel and other active yoghurt cultures have made us aware of the 'good bacteria' we host in our guts, lactobacilli that digest dairy produce for us—a simple symbiosis. Mitochondria take mutual dependency to a far more profound level, ensconced deep within each and every one of our cells, and Butler's question was should we therefore call ourselves not 'I', an individual of one species, but 'we', a collective of many species? Put another way, are mitochondria extinct if they live only inside others' cells? Within the plot of her remarkable trilogy of *Dawn* (1987), *Adulthood Rites* (1988), & *Imago* (1989),[1] first collected as *Xenogenesis* but in 2000 re-titled *Lilith's Brood*, this most obviously matters because humanity might go the same way, absorbed, mitochondria and all, into an alien 'Oankali' genome that has already incorporated scores of species. Outside the plot there are resonances with issues of the later Cold War, recalling 'the Borg' collective in later series of *Star Trek* as well as theoretical works like Donna Haraway's *Cyborg Manifesto*[2] (1991), which cites Butler, and Gaian views insisting on the interconnection and interdependence of all species.

For any writer, especially one not scientifically trained, this would be a strikingly different take on mitochondria to come up with, implicit in genetic science but not at all what the rest of the lay world was making of the data. For an African-American female pioneer of SF it was, and is, considerably more.

Octavia Butler's father Laurice, a shoe-shiner, died while she was a baby, and she was raised by her mother and maternal grandmother, a maid, as an observant Baptist in a poor, mixed-race neighbourhood. Shy, dyslexic, and isolated by relative height in every age-group (as an adult she was over six feet), Butler began writing at age 10, in 1957, to escape loneliness and boredom. Aged 12 she saw David McDonald's pleasingly ludicrous British B-movie *Devil Girl from Mars* (1954), thought rightly that she could do better herself, and began a lifelong interest in reading, watching, and writing SF.

---

1   Plot-summaries of all three are given in an appendix.

2   Donna Haraway, "A Cyborg Manifesto: Science, Technology, and Socialist-Feminism in the Late Twentieth Century," in *Simians, Cyborgs and Women* (1991), pp.149-181; and at:
   ▣ http://www.stanford.edu/dept/HPS/Haraway/CyborgManifesto.html .

Though she graduated from Pasadena City College in 1968 and took courses at California State University and via UCLA extension programmes, the major influences on Butler's thinking (after race, gender, and religion) came from one spectacular public obsession and two workshops. The obsession was the 'Space Race', culminating in the intense excitement of Apollo 11's first manned moon-landing in July 1969, followed by Apollos 12–17 (1969–72); as the snowy TV pictures of the desolate lunar landscape streamed, amazingly, into living-rooms, seeming to realise the 'High Frontier' dream of a Human destiny in space, the quality of public interest was of a kind that those experiencing it never forgot, and those who didn't cannot easily understand. In parallel, the workshops were first, in 1969–70, the Screenwriters' Guild 'Open Door Program', designed to mentor poor Black and Latino writers, where Butler met SF great Harlan Ellison; and second, in 1970, the newly-founded Clarion SF Writers' Workshop at Michigan State, where she met Samuel R. Delany—her only major African-American precursor in SF and, after winning Nebula awards at the age of 24–5 for *Babel-17* (1966) and *The Einstein Intersection* (1967), a blazing star.

Despite some early successes through the workshops[1] Butler found it hard to establish herself, partly because overtly racial and gendered concerns in her writing went against what were perceived as SF norms, and her own gender and race made her unusual as an SF writer. Her first novel, *Patternmaster*, completed by 1974, appeared in 1976, to be followed by four further novels in the same series—*Mind of My Mind* (1977), *Survivor* (1978), *Wild Seed* (1980), & *Clay's Ark* (1984)—that were well-received by the SF fans who discovered them but otherwise made little impact. If thinner in texture and less precise in prose than her later work, the series is never less than gripping, and in its visions of alien possession as much as in its African and American topographies plainly a work of the African Diaspora, interrogating the lost history of slave-descendants and reusing the palimpsest that Atlantic slave-traders created by depriving the enslaved of their cultures.[2]

The novel that made Butler's name, especially among African-Americans, interrupted this series but extends the same concerns—yet *Kindred* (1979), which has

---

1   Her first publication, the short story 'Crossover', appeared in the 1971 Clarion anthology, when Butler was 24, and Ellison bought another, 'Child Finder', for *The Last Dangerous Vision*, an anthology that never appeared; all the stories purchased for it remain unpublished.

2   The historical extremity of the Atlantic slave trade is not widely understood outside Black communities, but should be; the people of Judah for example, entered their Babylonian bondage with their own musical instruments (Psalms 137:1–4)—hardly the conditions of the Middle Passage. See Erna Brodber, *The Continent of Black Consciousness* (2003), especially ch. 1.

now sold more than 250,000 copies and is regularly set in schools and colleges, is as regularly rejected as SF, and Butler widely quoted (in supposed confirmation) as herself calling it a 'grim fantasy'. The novel's savage plot fully justifies the adjective 'grim'—a modern African-American Californian woman in a mixed-race marriage repeatedly and involuntarily time-travels to the ante-Bellum South of her ancestors, a Black slave of free African birth and her White owner. But as time-travel of any kind is well outside the mainstream realist tradition, and every other novel Butler wrote is pure SF, it seems a foolishness to reject, via the label 'fantasy', the generic contexts on which, as much as on slave narratives, *Kindred* signifies. But the foolishness holds fast: it is still usually *Kindred* alone that is admitted to the academy and classroom, and there is an awkward gap between Butler's racial and SF identities, especially in her reception by African-American scholars and in African Diasporic studies.

An African-American woman writing ovarian (rather than seminal) SF *in the 1980s* in any case poses some awkward questions about race, gender, and genre. Surveys of SF rarely mention (if race explicitly figures at all) more than two African-American writers, Delany and Butler herself, though more recent ones may add any of Charles R. Saunders, Steven Barnes, Nalo Hopkinson, Tananarive Due, and Walter Mosley. Explaining the apparent scarcity, some critics and readers are happy to posit SF as intrinsically 'white', reasonably pointing to its largely European and North-American origins and the rarity within the genre of *explicit* treatments of human race. Much less reasonably, they then extrapolate a general disinterest in SF among people of colour, ignoring, for example, the patent problem with generic labelling—roughly speaking, that similar works by African, South American, and Euro–North American writers will tend to be sharply differentiated in sales and criticism as, respectively, 'Fabulism', 'Magic/al Realism', and 'Science Fiction', and any questions of generic overlap or multiplicity ignored. Such falsely exclusive and misleadingly regionalised tags are clearly responsible in part for the apparent scarcity of non-white SF writers, severing the fantasy elements of (say) British Indian Salman Rushdie's *Midnight's Children* (1981),[1] or Anglo-Maori Keri Hulme's *The Bone People* (1984), from their science-fictive-and-fantastical brethren—just as *Kindred* is excluded by its reception from SF contexts, and Walter Mosley's *47* (2005), praised in reviews for its fantastical take on slave history, is even now being separated from his three SF and many

---

1   Rushdie can be potently related as well to nineteenth-century Bengali SF writers like Jagadananda Roy, Jagdish Chandra Bose, and Premendra Mitra as to anything else; see Debjani Sengupta, 'Sadhanbabu's Friends: Science Fiction in Bengal from 1882–1961', at:
   ▣ http://www.sarai.net/journal/03pdf/076_082_dsengupta.pdf.

crime novels by its labelling and marketing as a young adult's or children's book.

Similarly, assertions about the number of non-white *readers* of SF are almost all speculative, and need to be taken very sceptically. There was for years a parallel presumption, that women did not read SF let alone participate in fandom (so clearly for 'geeky' young men), but research on *Star Trek* and *Doctor Who* fans reveals extensive organisation and participation by women.[1] One can with proper caution say only that there is a *perception* of SF as lacking non-white writers and readers, and look to its probable causes in SF marketing, and in the blockbuster SF films that have for 20 years dominated Hollywood production,[2] where there are patently still serious problems with bigotry. Black characters, for example, remain as rare (and when they do appear, as stereotyped) in SF as in other mainstream film genres (Westerns or Romances, say), while writers like Ursula Le Guin who have created characters of colour find that publishers impose cover-illustrations, and in the event of screen-adaptation producers enforce casting, of Whites. Butler's *Xenogenesis* suffered badly from this, the first paperback of *Dawn* absurdly showing a Marvel-cartoonish white woman, and the yellow-green cover that *Lilith's Brood* sported until 2006 also fails clearly to signal a protagonist of colour. In 'Shame',[3] an excellent essay on such bleaching in the SciFi Channel's disgracefully slapdash and irresponsible 2004 adaptation of Le Guin's first two *Earthsea* books, Pam Noles explores the difficulties with parents and self-identity such bigotry caused her as a young African-American fan of SF, and sharply indicts both the mentality and the misunderstandings it generates. Links to essays by Le Guin detailing her lack of control over the adaptation and angry dismay both at what was done and at the unbelievable arrogance and dishonesty of the director,[4] with additional responses to her and Noles's essays, are given in the Bibliography, and show how complex the situation becomes when children of colour attracted to SF (or narratives with SF trappings) become aware of the racial implications of how 'humanity' and 'aliens' are represented.

The problem is fundamental, for arguably *all* SF that encounters alien life is in

---

1   See John Tulloch & Henry Jenkins, *Science Fiction Audiences: Watching* Doctor Who *and* Star Trek (1995).

2   Most lists of 'top grossing' films now put at least 7 SF movies in their top ten.

3   ▣ http://www.infinitematrix.net/faq/essays/noles.html.

4   "I wonder if the people who made the film of *The Lord of the Rings* had ended it with Frodo putting on the Ring and ruling happily ever after, and then claimed that that was what Tolkien "intended..." would people think they'd been "very, very honest to the books"?" Director Robert Lieberman made the quoted claims about his Earthsea adaptation in *Sci Fi* magazine. See: ▣ http://www.ursulakleguin.com/Earthsea.html

some measure concerned with human race relations. By mapping *intra*-human relations onto *inter*-species relations in an SF narrative, typically fearful human reactions to whatever is different, and general or individual assumptions about our own and others' rights, are fused and interrogatively foregrounded. At the same time the vulnerability of spaceships to vacuum, of exploring parties in hostile planetary environments to alien flora and fauna, and of humankind at large to some implacable alien military threat all necessitate in the name of survival a human unity that transcends whatever racial, cultural, sexual, or religious differences might otherwise be paramount. Very many narratives of alien encounter have been written, and the aliens encountered have ranged from the primitive to incomprehensibly advanced and from hyperaggressive monstrosity to transcendent benignity, but the central encounter of human protagonists with alien antagonists makes representation of biological and mental difference the core topos, and human reactions to otherness the determining trope.

The first series of *Star Trek* offers a good example of the ramifying politics of such representation. A total of 80 episodes were transmitted in the US 1966–9, and there are, reductively, two basic (and very old) plots to one or both of which almost all episodes conform. The first is 'Us vs Them', the Federation Navy (represented by the USS *Enterprise*) versus the 'Evil Empire' of the Klingons—which represents the Cold War conflict of market capitalist and planned communist philosophies of politics and economics. The second is 'Can we trust you?' which involves a new member of the crew with distinctive costume and make-up, of whom established crew-members are suspicious but who proves valuable and loyal in a crisis—which endorses the Civil Rights movement and urges federated unity in racial and cultural diversity (or *e pluribus unum*, 'out of many, one', the motto on the Great Seal of the USA). Moreover, though usually only a bit part in terms of dialogue, the frequent screen-presence of communications officer Lieutenant Uhura (played by African-American Nichelle Nichols) was a significant step in mainstream Black representation; Asian-American actor George Takei was also a regular as physicist and helmsman Lieutenant Sulu. Uhura later shared with Captain Kirk (William Shatner) the first broadcast interracial kiss on US TV—albeit under alien compulsion, a factoid that seems ironically diagnostic. And in *Star Trek* series and films made after the collapse of the USSR in 1991 individual Klingons (once *de facto* Russians) were incorporated into the Federation, overcoming prejudices against them as 'the enemy'. Almost all are played by African-Americans (notably Michael Dorn as Lieutenant-Commander Worf), but Klingon culture, once given Soviet and Mongol warrior trappings to promote its fearsome enemy status and prideful, militarised thinking, has become distinctly Amerindian in parallel valorisation of a second internal US other. SF works in all media continue to use both basic plot-structures, often with the same, broadly centrist aims of endorsing multiculturalism while defining 'us' against 'them', but occasionally to argue (or assert) a 'need' for species (and so racial) segregation.[1]

Gender issues like Uhura's and Kirk's kiss don't intrude into discussions of SF and race by accident; the connection is intrinsic. Just as SF, in representing the 'other' and reactions to 'otherness', is all but designed to represent racial interaction, so it is a site of contested gender representation, attracting *engagé* feminist and/or queer writers and readers. It also often interrogates representations of white male heterosexuality and the patriarchal nuclear family as norms, for as aliens are racially other so they may be of variant genders, reversing or transcending human valorisations of heterosexuality as guarantor of the romantic sublime and patriarchy. The book that established SF as a locus of modern gender debate was Le Guin's *The Left Hand of Darkness* (1969), which sends a Black male human as ambassador to a race that is humanoid but unsexed. Individuals are neuter save in regular periods of *kemmer*, when they are sexually potentiated and seek mates. In each pairing one will become male, one female, but which cannot be predicted, and both revert neuter afterwards; one becoming pregnant stays female to gestate, then reverts neuter, so the same person may be both a mother and father. A variety of thought experiment, asking what the world might be with differing gender identities, *The Left Hand of Darkness* showed that a readable adventure could also be philosophically and politically serious. In parallel, from the 1960s–80s, Andre Norton, Marion Zimmer Bradley, Marge Piercy, and Joanna Russ bought other female perspectives to SF. Some feminists deplored this as a sell-out but a second wave of writers, spearheaded by Butler, took the debate beyond them, deploying gendered racial awareness to criticise hierarchies within Black and feminist as much as other human Cultures.[2]

Cinematic SF has also been important. Sigourney Weaver in the *Alien* films, Linda Hamilton in the *Terminator* films, and Milla Jovovich in the *Resident Evil* series all potently valorise women—but as Weaver shows, eventually *blending* with the

---

1   The most famous and interesting instance is in westerns rather than SF, but strongly connected— Asa Earl Carter (1925–79), a sometime Klansman and speechwriter for segregationist Alabama governor George Wallace, who later renamed himself Forrest Carter, claimed Cherokee heritage, and wrote the novels *The Rebel Outlaw Josey Wales* (1973, filmed 1976) and *The Education of Little Tree* (1976), a false autobiography. Admiration for Amerindian culture and odd insistence on segregation mark both works.

2   See Patricia Melzer, *Alien Constructions: Science Fiction and Feminist Thought* (2006).

Alien queen, such valorisations can slide into very conservative constructions of the female *as* demonic alien other. The fantastical can also revive old demonisations of women as siren-songed above and toothed below, embodying the violent and fearful ignorance of female sexuality characteristic of adolescent or emotionally arrested men. The period of these blockbuster franchises has also seen such popular pseudo-feminisms as 'girl power' that claim empowerment while buying into materialisms without questioning their patriarchy or economic values. For some feminists the militarisation of women in SF films has also been especially unwelcome, endorsing immoral values of warfare and brute force, but for others guns and future hardware are excellent and much-needed gender-levellers, and the more technologised human existence becomes, the more sexism's claims of 'natural' biological and 'revealed' religious male superiority will become patently laughable and impotent.

As female SF writers of colour, Butler, Hopkinson, and Due also raise questions about the possible conflicts of female and coloured 'otherness'. The issue has been open since Freud unhappily described female sexuality as *un continent noir* ('a black continent'), and even in the 1960s–70s the *Mouvement de Libérations des Femmes* sang a *Hymne des Femmes* (Hymn of the Women) that claimed *nous sommes le continent noir* ('we are the black continent').[1] Unsurprisingly, Black feminists (and others) have difficulty with this, and the problem is acute for any female writer of colour who wishes to represent *intra*-racial sexism or *intra*-gender racism as well as the *inter*-racial varieties of both. But SF can profitably raise the stakes through embodiments of the alien that estrange human racial or sexual characteristics. Biology, sexuality, mentation, and identity may all in SF be divorced through tropes including digitised or disembodied minds, genetic engineering, and time-travel or slippage, and the results will in some way pressure 'facts' about current human modes of gender and forms of identity. There is also the difficulty that a feminist plot driving to resolution of gender differences may erase 'racial' identity, or *vice versa*, so that SF tends (like theatre) to enact *political* difficulties in competition for time, attention, and identity generated by racial and gendered liberation movements—partly explaining the common hostility of Black critics to Black, and Feminist to female, SF writers.

The female body as the site of reproduction and object of patriarchal control can also become central to SF, as in *Xenogenesis*—an aspect stressed by its variant title, *Lilith's Brood*. Aliens have (particularly since the 1980s) tended to abduct, constrain, and biologically or mechanically penetrate human bodies of both sexes, figuring feminisation through rape. SF narratives also have a surprisingly strong interface

---

1   See ▣ http://encorefeministes.free.fr/poly.php3.

with 'recovered memories' of child abuse by (familial) adults, and humans in alien clutches may be infantilised as well as feminised.[1] High-tech examination by aliens figures patriarchal objectification of the female body (and all bodies in surgery), but other plots invert human gender, as when insect-aliens lay larvae in male bodies, impregnating them—a notorious trope of the *Alien* films and the theme of Butler's award-winning short story 'Bloodchild'. Alien bodies must also be presented, and the meanings of flesh, in any shape and function, are a continual SF theme—the obverse of the generic association with robots, technology, computing, and Artificial Intelligence.

Then again, in 1516 Sir Thomas More published the book known as *Utopia*, an invented island where all is perfect and frailty overcome. The name was a coinage in Latin from Greek, built on a vital pun: *ou-topia* is 'not-place' or nowhere, *eu-topia* 'good place'—suggesting Utopia was unreachable (as living humans were in More's very Catholic eyes unalterably Fallen from God's Grace). A satirical parable partly modelled on narratives of exploration and travel, More's idea was developed as a framework by many writers, notably Jonathan Swift in *Gulliver's Travels* (1726–7), but generated in opposition to 'unreal good places' the even more potent idea of *dystopias*, bad places that can too often be understood as very real, or warnings of what might come to be so. For emergent SF this was a ready-made invitation, and three great dystopias of the earlier twentieth century powerfully influence the genre and global culture. *We* (Russian 1920, trans. 1924) by Yevgeny Zamiatin shows in-dustrially dehumanised labour; *Brave New World* (1932) by Aldous Huxley imagines scientific rationalisation of culture and breeding; and *1984* (1949) by George Orwell famously warned that 'Big Brother is Watching You' in its vision of techno-surveil-lance and thought-control. SF also offers in the *visiting* alien a version of imperial satires like *Oroonoko* (1688) by Aphra Behn, in which a 'primitive'non-caucasian slave or colonial subject, brought to the imperial centre as an object of display and amusement, exposes barbaric failings and values in the imperium—as in any alien encounter there is the possibility of embarrassing Human emotional or political as well as technological inferiority.[2] Raw, hostile planets offer arenas for harsh justice and survivalism, so right-wing and/or religious rejections of techno-futures, with tra-ditional conservative scepticism about human goodness and reason, are found amid more utopian left-wing visions of progress. But since 1945 the dominant dystopian

---

1 See a fascinating article by Roger Luckhurst, 'The Science-Fictionalization of Trauma: Remarks on Narratives of Alien Abduction', in *Science-Fiction Studies* #74, Vol. 25.1 (March 1998): 29–52.

2 The oddest recent instance is a novel by historian E. P. Thompson, *The Sykaos Papers* (1988).

model has been post-catastrophic. Nuclear holocaust or a runaway bio-weapon were the favourite causes but asteroid impact, global warming, mass irradiation or pollution, and viral epidemics have now (via Hollywood) entered the common imaginary of species-ending disasters.

Xenogenesis takes such catastrophic destruction only as a point of departure, beginning some decades after a nuclear exchange (initially US–USSR but spiralling out) destroys most animal life and poisons the biosphere. Interested in neither the immediate politics of pushing the button nor in describing the destruction, Butler's wasted Earth is directly experienced only by the aliens who restore it biologically while allowing their organic shuttles to feed on urban debris and further human cultural erasure. As the trilogy progresses from a recreated Earth-fragment on the alien spaceship to the western Amazon basin (and those wanting an immediate overview in more detail should see the plot-summaries provided as appendices to this essay), values of organic living and human society are repeatedly interrogated and valorised. Implicitly, the world we *readers* inhabit is doomed to this future, its catastrophe yet to happen but inevitable, and Butler's view of the present often seems just that bleak: she acknowledged and fought against pessimism in her thought[1] and fiction with one major counter-trope, feeling oneself any pain one causes. That this does not guarantee *morality* is a major theme of *Xenogenesis*, where some among the aliens are subject to this condition, but it does preclude cruelty, sadism, and spite, if not ignorant injury to others. In *Parable of the Talents* (1993) and *Parable of the Sower* (1998) Butler used mutant empaths to achieve the feedback of suffering, invoking models of mutually beneficial parasitism or partnership in animals, but within both novels the reasons for natural selection against any such ability are painfully clear, and with hope so frail and fantastical in another post-catastrophic world both *Parable* novels remain, like *Xenogenesis*, potently dystopian.

These complexities of interacting race, gender, sub-genre, and philosophical attitude have no simple resolution, but there is a degree of subordinate clarity in the paradox most clearly articulated by Butler and Hopkinson—that their beloved and vital SF, a genre fantastically concerned with otherness and compulsively staging racial issues, should be so problematic for writers and readers of colour. Concern with gender and race highlights the necessity of reading SF as radical *and* conservative, advancing one agenda over another or pretending via the futuristic trappings of the genre to false radicalism. The large, tendentious case that tempts some—White SF writers sending White protagonists to meet Black aliens only to reassert White

---

1   Her notes 'About the Author' persistently describe her as "a pessimist if I'm not careful".

superiority and Black badness by killing or taming them—is also reduced: it implies that SF's compulsive re-enactment of racial supremacies and suppressions is intrinsically hostile to Black liberation, but the variant understandings of Human essence that are among Black (and especially feminist) SF's recurrent concerns shows this up as at best a heresy (a truth pushed to the point of falsehood), and more probably just another tom-fool generalisation. But there is also, specifically in *Xenogenesis*, a much more radical and dismissive analysis, playing religion against biology, and that is where those energetic mitochondria of ours will (shortly) come in.

Xenogenesis is a trilogy because its aliens, the grey, betentacled Oankali, have three sexes—equivalent male, equivalent female, and neuter, gene-manipulating *ooloi* (from the Greek for 'egg'). Oankali are also, like many insects, metamorphic: 'children' are genuinely neuter at birth, and in nonage always addressed with special neuter pronouns for the sexless immature; at metamorphosis they may become any sex. Males and females more or less match human genders and roles, but (another insect characteristic) females double in size on metamorphosis, becoming substantially larger than males and ooloi. Ooloi alone after a period as sub-adults undergo a second metamorphosis, coming to full maturity with an additional pair of arms that contain an extremely sensitive filamentary organ through which they can link directly into others' bodies and nervous systems. In mating, which must occur as a triad, the male and female may have a sensory illusion of direct contact, but in fact all contact is via the mediating ooloi, who takes gametes from both partners and combines them in a gender-specific organ, the *yashi*, within which the genetic makeup of the offspring can be examined and adjusted at a molecular level before being implanted in the female's womb-analogue to gestate.

Everything good one might possibly imagine about genetic engineering, from simple avoidance of genetic disorders and hereditary diseases to fixing specific characteristics and grafting-in desirable capacities or organs from other creatures' genomes, is for ooloi not simply a 'natural' thing to do but a compulsive *raison d'etre*. The Oankali evolved on a planet where symbiosis rather than parasitism or predation became the major evolutionary pathway. Even the massive, multi-generational arkship in which they arrived is not a built machine, but an aware, highly sapient organism capable of reproduction and engineered from the genomes of many scores of species. The entire Oankali purpose as a (compound) species is to seek out and incorporate the interestingly alien, like a Human collector's delighted acquisition of a new piece but incorporated into the material and genetic being of the collector species. Where we have zoos and libraries, Oankali have in every cell a complete record of their own and many other species' histories and capacities that every individual can from early 'childhood' read as easily and unerringly as humans breathe. Only ooloi can manipulate genes, but choices between viable evolutionary designs are by universal adult consensus, achieved through chemical bonding and the inability of individual Oankali to conceal thoughts and memories from one another's biochemical perceptions, which makes lying and physical violence inconceivable among themselves. By comparison, the self-deluding, self-harming proclivities of Human survivors, inexhaustibly keen to demonise and attack their alien saviours, are plainly dysfunctional, but the problem (besides our Human nuclear autogenocide and all-round stupidity) is that conscious control of their genome means that to avoid stagnant overcontrol Oankali evolution *requires* alien breeding partners. Their present candidates for what they see as an entirely normal and beneficial 'gene trade' are, if they can clone enough individuals from survivors and irradiated bodies to make it all viable, the surviving members of *Hom. sap.*, and despite their post-nuclear predicament the few grown-up monkeys left don't much care for the deal, preferring to become 'Resisters'.

Dawn deals with Lilith Iyapo, a young African-American widow who chooses (in so far as she has any choice) to accept Oankali help. *Adulthood Rites* deals with her son Akin, the first male Human-Oankali 'construct' (or miscegenate offspring). *Imago* deals with a later child, Jodahs, the first *ooloi* 'construct'. Each novel is divided into books whose titles provide an additional map:

Dawn	Womb	Family	Nursery	The Training Floor
Adulthood Rites	Lo	Phoenix	Chkahichdahk	Home
Imago	Metamorphosis	Exile	Imago	

The books of *Dawn* follow Lilith's rebirth in partnership with her Oankali saviours— or captors—and the need for her to rebreed humanity. Those of *Adulthood Rites* name places (for Oankali living things) that contrast Human names (Phoenix, Home) with Oankali ones (Lo, Chkahichdahk). The first and last books of *Imago* invoke insect development—an imago is an adult insect after metamorphosis, such as a butterfly that has been caterpillar and pupa (and the plural, delightfully, is 'imagines', pronounced 'im-á-gin-és')—while the middle one, 'Exile', posits a condition at odds with 'Home'. Thus the trilogy as a whole drives from foetal development to post-metamorphic adulthood, and from that which is wholly human to the genesis of a post-Human race.

Historically, Butler's tri-gendered Oankali point straight back to Le Guin's tri-gendered aliens in *The Left Hand of Darkness*. Connections with 1960s feminism blend with the influences of the Civil Rights Movement, and in this sense the ooloi are a traditional form of SF thought-experiment, but one could also see, in the ooloi replacement of actual physical male-female contact by an illusion of that contact, a resonance with the far more misanthropic feminism of the 1980s associated with Andrea Dworkin and Catherine McKinnon. In plot terms, the ooloi are necessary for the forced hybridisation of Humans and Oankali that forms the central action of the trilogy, but are nevertheless subject to an increasingly potent critique within the narrative as the *primus inter pares* of the Oankali genders, unaccountable seducers and manipulators. Finally, and despite that critique, they are throughout also authoritative 'spokesaliens' for an Oankali understanding of human beings that is savagely double-edged.

The major twist is that, able to read the human genome and memories with molecular accuracy and certainty, Oankali in general and ooloi in particular find human beings to be "beauty and horror in rare combination".[1] The horror of humankind is embodied in the nuclear war—an utterly irrational, multiply genocidal form of competition that for the Oankali was a pure expression of what we are genetically. As a male called Jdahya explains to Lilith Iyapo, the 'Human Contradiction' that Oankali find viscerally repellent and morally intolerable arises from two characteristics, and the powerful tendency of more recently evolved characteristics to be subordinate to older ones:

> Jdahya made a rustling noise that could have been a sigh, but that did not seem to come from his mouth or throat. "You are intelligent," he said. "That's the newer of the two characteristics, and the one you might have put to work to save yourselves. You are potentially one of the most intelligent species we've found, though your focus is different from ours. Still, you had a good start in the life sciences, and even genetics."
>
> "What's the second characteristic?"
>
> "You are hierarchical. That's the older and more entrenched characteristic. We saw it in your closest animal relatives and in your most distant ones. It's a terrestrial characteristic. When human intelligence served it instead of guiding it, when human intelligence did not even acknowledge it as a problem, but took pride in it or did not notice it at all . . ." The rattling sounded again. "That was like ignoring cancer. I think

---

1   Octavia E. Butler, *Lilith's Brood* (New York: Aspect, 2000), p. 153 (*Dawn*, Bk III, Ch. 6). Butler's best male critic, Roger Luckhurst, took the phrase as the title of an early article on her.

your people did not realize what a dangerous thing they were doing."

"I don't think most of us thought of it as a genetic problem. I didn't. I'm not sure I do now." Her feet had begun to hurt from walking so long on the uneven ground. She wanted to end both the walk and the conversation. The conversation made her uncomfortable. Jdahya sounded . . . almost plausible.

"Yes," he said, "intelligence does enable you to deny facts you dislike. But your denial doesn't matter. A cancer growing in someone's body will go on growing in spite of denial. And a complex combination of genes that work together to make you intelligent as well as hierarchical will still handicap you whether you acknowledge it or not."[1]

Jdahya immediately complicates things again, insisting "it isn't a gene or two" but "the result of a tangled combination of factors that only begins with genes", yet the force of the passage lies precisely in its reductivism—and that echoes the theorist who most directly informs Oankali genetic historiography and prophecy, US myrmecologist (or ant-man) turned sociologist E. O. Wilson.[2]

Wilson's major text, *Sociobiology: The New Synthesis* (1975), itself makes various complicating gestures, but its message was briskly summarised by Wilson himself in his autobiography, *Naturalist* (1994):

> Genetic determinism, the central objection raised against [my *Sociobiology*], is the bugbear of the social sciences. So what I said that can indeed be called genetic determinism needs saying here again. My argument ran essentially as follows: Human beings inherit a propensity to acquire behaviour and social structures, a propensity that is shared by enough people to be called human nature. The defining traits include division of labour between the sexes, bonding between parents and children, heightened altruism toward closest kin, incest avoidance, other forms of ethical behaviour, suspicion of strangers, tribalism, dominance orders within groups, male dominance overall, and territorial aggression over limiting resources. Although people have free will and the choice to turn in many directions, the channels of their psychological development are nevertheless—however much we might wish otherwise—cut more deeply by the genes in certain directions than in others. So while cultures vary very greatly, they inevitably converge towards these traits [...]. The important point is that heredity interacts with environment to create a gravitational pull toward a fixed mean. It gathers people in all societies into the

---

1   Butler, *Lilith's Brood*, pp. 38–9 (*Dawn*, Bk I, Ch. 5).

2   Wilson curiously reverses the path of Eugène Marais (1871–1936), author of *The Soul of the Ape* (1919, pub. 1969) and *Die Siel van die Mier* (1925; as *The Soul of the White Ant*, 1937).

narrow statistical circle that we define as human nature.[1]

In yet another of her marvellous essays, this one simply called 'On Genetic Determinism', Ursula Le Guin has shown just how sloppily phrased, patriarchally revanchist, and weasel-worded this summary is ("other forms of ethical behaviour" indeed), and she is spot on.[2] Wilson *was* sloppy, constantly pushing sharp observation into malignant heresy, and all too often extrapolating from ants to mammals to people as if there truly were no serious or relevant differences so far as genetic algebra was concerned. He does not read at all well against his most important successor, the infinitely more careful Richard Dawkins, whose trilogy of *The Selfish Gene* (1976), *The Extended Phenotype* (1982), and *The Blind Watchmaker* (1986) make the real case for what we presently can/not say about our own genetics. It seems however to have been the political bluntness and arrogant carelessness of Wilson's self-righteously (bad) case that sank most productively into Butler's mind. If subordinating tool-use and intelligence to hierarchical imperatives did not make nuclear self-immolation inevitable, it made it one possible outcome of unbridled competition—and for Oankali the various probabilities add up to a Wilsonian certainty of self-destruction backed by an accurate multi-species memory stretching over millennia.

Other things being equal, Oankali thus wouldn't touch *Homo sapiens* genetically with a bargepole, intelligence or no, and their objection cuts far below issues of gender or race; but things *aren't* equal, because humans, poor Lilith in particular, whose mother and grandmother died of the disease, have what Jdahya is pleased to call "a talent for cancer".[3] In this memorable phrase Jdahya makes necessary a clear understanding, for despite the importance in some common cancers of viral vectors, it is not an infection, and though often proximately caused by exposure to various chemicals, it is fundamentally an internal process. Some genes are active only *in utero*, while we develop—sets of instructions for making new organs, and for rapid increases in size. Once we are born these have done their job and switch off; others remain active until we reach full adult size and/or sexual maturity. Cancers are inappropriate reversions of cells to growing status, and so at some level, whatever the triggers and proximate causes may be, genetic malfunctions—which to Oankali chemical perceptions, especially ooloi ones, makes them a lesson. Studying how our malfunctioning bodies are able to turn certain locked genes back on, and especially how those like Lilith with genetic predispositions to cancer come by that inheritance,

1   E. O. Wilson, *Naturalist* (Washington: Shearwater Books, 1994), pp. 332–3.
2   Ursula Le Guin, 'Of Genetic Determinism', in *The Wave in the Mind*, pp. 152–9.
3   Butler, *Lilith's Brood*, p. 22 (*Dawn*, Bk I, Ch. 3).

Oankali ooloi learn to control such reactivation—and that means, immediately, the advent of nerve, organ, and limb regeneration, and in the construct species, with techniques refined, conscious shapeshifting, instructing one's body to grow or reabsorb features at will. This, and other 'simpler' genetic gifts of improved health, strength, and memory, Oankali will gladly give, but while they let Resisters run free, none who abandon ooloi supervision are left able to sire or conceive.

When Butler was writing the human genome project was incomplete and genetic science considerably less advanced, but her plot shows strong research and clear understanding. The project of species miscegenation is backed by discussion of auto-immune suppression derived from transplant work, and it is clear Oankali genetic abilities were designed to be plausible. Moreover, various Oankali abilities that may seem absurd have clear models among Terran marine and insect life. But Butler's most interesting biological argument turned (at last) on mitochondria, for the Oankali too have an organelle. Jdahya explains to Lilith in *Dawn* that "One of the meanings of Oankali is gene trader. Another is that organelle—the essence of ourselves, the origin of ourselves. Because of that organelle, the ooloi can perceive DNA and manipulate it precisely".[1] And at the beginning of *Imago* the construct-ooloi Jodahs, who has three Oankali and two Human parents, one of every gender, explains his ooloi parent's role:

> [My] construction itself and a single Oankali organelle was the only ooloi contribution to my existence. The organelle had divided within each of my cells as the cells divided. It had become an essential part of my body. We were what we were because of that organelle. It made us collectors and traders of life, always learning, always changing, in every way but one—that one organelle. Ooloi said we *were* that organelle—that the original Oankali had evolved through that organelle's invasion, acquisition, duplication, and symbiosis. Sometimes on worlds that had no intelligent, carbon-based life to trade with, Oankali deliberately left behind large numbers of the organelle. Abandoned, it would seek a home in the most unlikely indigenous life-forms and trigger changes—evolution in spurts. Hundreds of millions of years later, perhaps some Oankali people would wander by and find interesting trade partners waiting for them. The organelle made or found compatibility with life-forms so completely dissimilar that they were unable even to perceive one another as alive.[2]

1   Butler, *Lilith's Brood*, p. 41 (*Dawn*, Bk I, Ch. 5).
2   Butler, *Lilith's Brood*, p. 544 (*Imago*, Bk I, Ch. 4).

Not just mitochondria, then, but Shirley Conran super-mitochondria, laying claim to Oankali and now Human essence, with a vast menagerie of species in between. The genealogists (among them, after *Roots*, many of the African-American intelligentsia) were only interested in what mitochondrial DNA might say about the past, but in Butler's vision it is far more a question of what it suggests or even forecasts for the future. Despite their own massively successful symbiosis with the eukaryotic cell, clearly the model for the Oankali organelle, mitochondria have proliferated through all species without affecting—or do they *create?*—the predatory competition and insane individual triumphalism that might yet end us all in male apocalypse.

Umbrella titles, however convenient, are as often a distraction and liability as anything else, but the shift from *Xenogenesis* in the 1990s to *Lilith's Brood* since 2000 poses a surprising challenge. Like all mass-market genres SF is prone to variant titles as a tic of publishers' repackaging—one US, one UK, and one for the omnibus, or equivalent—and these rarely seem more than commercially significant, seeking a current buzzword or new cover to freshen display, pump sales, and at worst con readers into buying as new what they have already read. But where *Xenogenesis* is good Greek technospeak, *Lilith's Brood* sounds like a horror film yet plugs equally into the Old Testament and Rabbinical mythology. It isn't clear if the change was at Butler's instigation or her publisher's, but both titles must themselves be Butler's, and reward thought.

Science fiction regularly uses the prefix *xeno-*, from Greek *xenos*, 'a stranger', to denote the alien. *Xenobiology*, for example, is the study of alien anatomy, biochemistry etc., alongside *xenodiplomacy*, if one prefers one's aliens peaceful, *xenopolitics*, should one get further, *xenocide*, if all goes horribly wrong, and so on. The strongly technical and SF-specific impact of *Xenogenesis* as a coinage and title is backed up by Butler's narrative requirements of some fairly hard science as well as intensive consideration of alien thinking and morality—but *Lilith's Brood* retrospectively stresses *-genesis* in the *biblical* sense, recalling Butler's strongly Baptist childhood. An Assyrian name in Isaiah 34:14 for a blood-sucking night-monster, reduced in translation to "screech owl" (AV) or "night-jar" (RSV), Lilith is also, in rabbinical mythology, the first wife of Adam, cast out in favour of Eve for refusing to lie under him—hence the feminist magazines *Lilith* and *Spare Rib*. 'Brood', which might once have summoned broody mothers or hens (as in Luke 13:34[1]), also now carries a

---

1   "O Jerusalem, Jerusalem, which killest the prophets, and stonest them that are sent unto thee ; how often would I have gathered they children together, as a hen *doth gather* her brood under *her* wings, and ye would not!" (AV)

strong taint from horror movies of demonic lairs filled with progeny, so *Lilith's Brood* as a title activates a distinctly religious sense of the narrative. And this is *also* backed up by Butler, not only in showing religion among Human Resisters as small-minded and intolerant, full of loudly revived religious oaths that ring peculiarly hollow on an irradiated earth, but in her protagonists Lilith and Jodahs, whose name summons 'Judas' and who is clearly shown in *Imago* as both betrayer and messianic saviour.

Theology has always been important to SF, from More's *Utopia* to contemporary authors like Mary Doria Russell and Peter F. Hamilton—and rightly so, for our encounter with reasoning alien life, when it comes, will be the greatest test of religious thought there can be. If the little green men have a two-thousand-year-old legend of a crucified god, Rome will do brisk business; if, once someone has explained religion, they howl with laughter, traffic will be the other way. But in Russell's *The Sparrow* (1996) & *Children of God* (1998), where Jesuits send a mission to the alien home planet before the echoes of first contact have died, or Hamilton's extraordinary *Night's Dawn* trilogy (1996–9),[1] where the dead return *en masse* in the 27th century, religious issues are spelt out, not buried or allegorised, as they seem to be in Butler. There is, however, one clear concept that stitches together scientific *Xenogenesis* and religious *Lilith's Brood*, for it has had both religious and scientific incarnations: determinism, the opposite of free will.

In extreme religious form, Calvinist 'Predestination' holds that every human soul is marked before its existence in God's books of the saved or damned, and that *nothing* one does/n't do can alter this; hence (the perfect gloomily Scottish summary) James Hogg's wonderful gothic chiller, *The Private Memoirs and Confessions of a Justified Sinner* (1824), in which a living 'saint' figures he might as well be saved for a sheep as a lamb. Too vile in its implications for most, this contorted doctrine gave way with the Enlightenment to a supposed scientific absolute, Newton's clockwork universe in which all ticked from certain cause to inevitable effect. If one could (as God might) hold every single atom's nature and position in one's head, one could mathematically run the whole universe back or forward in time with absolute precision. Physics being what it was, only one set of things could happen at each stage, and the laws of physics were now known; only measuring and computing ability was lacking to reconstruct Adam's and Eve's most private conversations, or slip forward to see how apocalypse will start. This is the 'Newtonian determinism' that Laurence Sterne so blissfully mocked in *The Life and Opinions of Tristram Shandy, Gentleman* (1759–67), where the hero's conception was (as he reports it) affected by his father's

---

1   *The Reality Dysfunction* (1996), *The Neutronium Alchemist* (1997), & *The Naked God* (1999).

possible failure to have wound up the household clock and his mother's uncertainty at a crucial moment as to what might be chiming; the novel remains a hoot—but Einstein and quantum mechanics put permanently paid to the theory it mocks. And yet again a replacement soon sprang forth in the form of DNA, that mysterious double helix that E. O. Wilson (and all Oankali) believe absolutely controls what a species can/not be—'genetic determinism'. In the Oankali view, moreover, genetic determinism is fully as potent as Calvinist Predestination, for no matter what any one of us thinks or does, s/he is from conception to death in the wholly destructive grip of the 'Human Contradiction', doomed with all willy-nilly to extinction. In most Christian doctrine baptism cleanses babies of 'Original Sin', the mortal offence against God we are doctrinally held to inherit from Adam's and Eve's transgressions in Eden, but in *Xenogenesis* there is seemingly *nothing* but complete submission to Oankali genetic oversight that can save us.

In this light it becomes less surprising that Jodahs/Judas, as an ooloi the least human of the three principal protagonists, should arrive in *Imago* to save (among others) two Human siblings called Jesusa and Tomás. This religious climax has been carefully worked towards, through the resonances of Lilith; through the Resister church in the village called Phoenix that regenerates religious oaths, most often 'hell', which Akin (kidnapped by Resisters in *Adulthood Rites*) spreads among Resisters and Constructs alike; and through Akin's suffering as a child on his parental species' behalves. Phoenix as a name promises fiery resurrection but never multiplication—the whole point of the phoenix myth (which may or may not be invoked by Job) is that there can be only one living at a time[1]—and what rises from the settlement's ashes at the end of *Adulthood Rites* is Akin's Mars colony where unaltered Humans will be (as Oankali see it, pointlessly) allowed to try again, even to renewed self-destruction. Conversely, the hidden village of fertile Resisters that Jodahs finds and saves in *Imago* has multiplied, but in their insistent independence very wrongly, dooming their children to vile blights, compulsory incest, and a crucifyingly renewed descent into extinction as their recessive genes become dominant and foetal viability fails.

The Human Contradiction, that is, is installed by Butler very early in *Dawn* as Humankind's original genetic sin, and in that novel's last paragraphs Lilith dreams of escaping the Oankali prohibition of unsupervised human fertility:

---

1 Things seem to be different in J. K. Rowling, but while multiple phoenixes seem implicit in some remarks, only Dumbledore's pet phoenix Fawkes has actually figured in the plots. On the putative phoenix in Job 29:18 see George Sajo, 'Phoenix on the top of the palm tree' (2005), at:
　▣ http://www.studiolum.com/en/silva5.htm.

Another chance to say, "*Learn and Run!*"

She would have more information for them this time. And they would have long, healthy lives ahead of them. Perhaps they could find an answer to what the Oankali had done to them. And perhaps the Oankali were not perfect. A few fertile people might slip through and find one another. Perhaps. *Learn and Run!* If she were lost, others did not have to be. Humanity did not have to be.

She let Nikanj lead her into the dark forest and to one of the concealed dry exits.[1]

Lilith is (understandably, but nevertheless) so overwhelmed by Oankali potency that she forgets what she already knew: that a sufficient gene-pool is needed; that Humanity has already reduced itself to extinction with insane nuclear war; and that the Earth, which would but for the Oankali be no more than a sterile cinder, is still mostly uninhabitable. She lives (thanks entirely to Oankali) to see what she foolishly hoped come true and exactly what then happened to the "few fertile people" who did "slip through". Rubbing salt in the wound, only one of Lilith's Oankali-manipulated, 'compromised' and miscegenate children can anneal and rectify this new human disaster.

The very last sentence of *Dawn* also points an interesting way, for "the dark forest", literal in context, recalls the "dark wood" in which the first line of Dante's *Inferno* famously says he found himself. For Dante the shade of the Roman poet Virgil was needed as a guide through Hell and Purgatory before he escaped into Paradise, but for Lilith, despite her sense of symbolic damnation by Oankali, there is "one of the concealed dry exits"—a luxury Dante was denied. Butler's trilogy as a whole makes good sense as a Dantean *Commedia* of a hell (Lilith's in *Dawn*), purgatory (Akin's in *Adulthood Rites*), and paradise (Jodahs's in *Imago*), and much then snaps into focus. The persistent irony of Akin's and others' uses of 'Hell' as an oath, for example, makes potent sense if we are by then in purgatory, and the more obviously ironic action of Jodahs-Judas saving (Doubting) Tomás and Jesusa as a trilogy-finale is tellingly framed if we are at that last stage entering paradise.

Clearly enough Butler had a quarrel with as well as an allegiance to the religion of her childhood.[2] The scientific and religious determinisms of the trilogy might therefore best be seen as both at odds *and* intertwined, overlapping to reinforce or cancel one another. At the beginning, on the Oankali ship with Lilith in desperate shock,

---

1   Butler, *Lilith's Brood*, p. 248 (*Dawn*, Bk IV, Ch. 9).

2   She called herself "a former Baptist" in the note 'About the Author' in *Bloodchild* (1/e, p. 145).

science dominates; by the end, with Jodahs as genetic messiah, a new religion—but the spiritual destiny Jodahs promises the sorry remnants of Humanity is an Oankali destiny in the stars. Its realisation will require reduction of what is left of Earth to a sterile rock, as dead and soon as cratered as the moon. Perspectives of scientific and other liberations alternate with visions of scientific and other damnations; the action tilts up hopefully throughout, but drags with a despair about human beings that is never really answered, because there are in reality no Oankali to transform us.

And this there is no getting round. Whether called *Xenogenesis* or *Lilith's Brood*, the trilogy begins with human nuclear self-annihilation through miscalculation and moral nullity, and explains it as genetically inevitable, an Original Sin as gross as a millstone round our necks. If it wasn't nuclear war it would be, oh, eco-catastrophe, say, or runaway global warming induced by our complete inability to recognise that finite resource and unchecked consumption don't compute, and that irredeemably trashing the biosphere is a bad idea. And the millstone is bound to a genetic explanation that can be neither proven nor refuted, but has a horrid plausibility precisely through its over-generalisation. Granting all Darwin suggested and others have refined in the theory of evolution, it makes cruel sense that more anciently evolved characteristics should dominate more recent ones; and plain sense that in the particular, unhappy case of *Hom. sap.* an old characteristic is hierarchical behaviour (class, sex, power games, war, status) and a new one the primate intelligence and curiosity that makes us tool-users. As one Scottish inheritor of James Hogg's gloomy outlook had put it a few years earlier:

> A geneticist fella told me we humans differ from other brutes by drinking when not thirsty, eating when not hungry, fucking all round the calendar regardless of climate and torturing and killing helpless creatures of our own kind. In plain language, we have an inborn capacity for intoxication, greed, lust, cruelty and murder: a fact which your thinking moralist will always find more significant than our ingenuity in constructing such bizarre containers of ourselves as the Polaris submarine, Sistine Chapel, and suspender-belt.[1]

So Alasdair Gray in *1982 Janine* (1984): the tone is funnier, and much angrier, but in context equally heavy with suicidal despair, while the connection with genetics is identical.

Butler's case, that is, has within its fantasy and fiction a relentless realism, and her

---

1 Alasdair Gray, *1982 Janine* (1984; Harmondsworth: Penguin, 1985), p. 184.

conclusions are bleak—but the trilogy does manage to import from religious belief, Dantean or Baptist, a movement towards redemption, however proto-apocalyptic. As much might be said of many things, but no-one before Butler in SF (or anywhere else) had in such a manner locked the drives both to death and survival into cellular chemistry. Though the Oankali organelle is plainly modelled on the mitochondrion, the effects of the two are as opposed as Oankali symbiosis and Human hierarchy:

> "Human beings fear difference." Lilith had told [Akin] once. "Oankali crave difference. Humans persecute their different ones, yet they need them to give themselves definition and status. Oankali seek difference and collect it. They need it to keep themselves from stagnation and overspecialization. If you don't understand this, you will. You'll probably find both tendencies surfacing in your own behaviour." And she had put her hand on his hair. "When you feel a conflict, try to go the Oankali way. Embrace difference."[1]

This is integration with—or rather without—a vengeance, and the trilogy's concern, for all Butler's *engagé* Blackness and feminism, is not with Lilith as an African-American woman but with her *Brood* of miscegenate, oddly gendered children—whose cells contain *both* Oankali organelle and mitochondrion, whose determinisms duke it out biochemically. It doesn't matter morally or philosophically that the Oankali organelle is a sure-fire winner in this particular contest, God being on the side of big battalions, because as soon as there is a conflict any organelle might lose, absolute determinism is cancelled.

The truly curious thing, though, is that from an African Diasporic perspective what matters is less one or other organelle than any organelle, for as a self-contained structure within all cells—necessarily symbiotic, overlooked but essential, perhaps possessed (like the mitochondrion) of its own secret, self-determining DNA—all organelles are potentially a metaphor for the African enslaved in the New World. It varies the trope of *maronage* (from the encapsulated 'maroon' cultures created by escaped slaves on Caribbean islands), and what must be determined within Akin and other miscegenate 'constructs', racial and cultural, are the choices and mechanics of their symbiosis. What must be foregone is predetermined identity, species or individual—so that far from embodying genetic determinism, let alone Wilson's revanchist slippage from genetics to culture, the organelles of *Xenogenesis* present superimposed choices between forms of ghettoisation and false purity that deform

---

1 Butler, *Lilith's Brood*, p. 329 (*Adulthood Rites*, Bk II, Ch. 4).

and destroy, and alliances of difference within a Hegelian dialectic of species.

Born in 1947, Butler came of age with Civil Rights, in large part spurred by the fallout from the world war she just missed, and she as much as anyone, more than anyone not Black, knew intimately what Haley's populist vision in *Roots* of rediscovered African historicity meant, or might mean. *Kindred* also places Butler squarely in at least one mainstream African-American tradition, and like her earliest novels in the *Patternmaster* series confronts the fearful dislocation enslavement imposed on Black history. But even there she forced her protagonist to confront awkward complexities, and in *Xenogenesis* the genealogical quest is not simply spurned but violently written off, any redemptions of African-American ancestry undermined by the all-destroying nuclear war and Oankali revelation of the 'Human Contradiction' in our most basic programming, Black, White, Brown, or Yellow. Instead, for readers of all colours, Butler offered a vision of the future, looking to the organelles not as a window on the past but as a revelation of community and potential. How truly pessimistic Butler's case is, or how it deploys pessimism as a spur, readers must decide for themselves, but that she offered an extremely determined and original critique of much contemporary thinking, Black, White, or just self-limitingly black-and-white, is not open to doubt.

Amid the shock of her sudden death in February 2006 it remains unclear whether Butler died from a stroke, causing her to fall and strike her head, or fell and struck her head, causing cranial haemorrhage. It doesn't much matter to the sense of cruelly premature loss—she was only 58—but in a mordant way the baffled post-mortem repeats the great question of her fiction about unforeseen and unavoidable self-abruptions (the genetics of ageing and arterial occlusion) and the operations of free will (with intended or accidental consequences). In the interview from which I took my unhappy epigraph,[1] given less than a month before her death, Butler remained, as ever, strangely determined to insist not on the inevitable but on choice and alterity:

Q. We're speaking at time of crisis in the country between the Iraq war and Katrina. As a writer what makes you hopeful for the future?

A. At the present, I feel so unhopeful. I recognize we will pay more attention when we have different leadership. I'm not exactly sure where that leadership will come from. But that doesn't mean I think we're all going down the toilet, I just don't see where that hope will come from.

---

1   http://nyc.indymedia.org/en/2006/01/63925.html

Appendix to Chapter 6

Xenogenesis / Lilith's Brood (1987–9): A Plot Summary

Before the trilogy begins, there is a nuclear war, beginning as an USA–USSR exchange but expanding to include all nuclear powers. The overwhelming majority of humans have died in fission fireballs, or from radiation, rioting, starvation etc. in their aftermath.

Dawn (1987)

African-American Lilith Iyapo awakens. She remembers her pre-war life and widowhood—her husband and son died in an auto accident—and knows she has woken previously to interrogations by an anonymous voice, but little else. This time her captors show themselves: the Oankali, grey humanoids with head and body tentacles. Lilith learns that when they realised the nuclear war was not a consensual species suicide they intervened to assist survivors and begin to restore the biosphere. She has been on a spaceship in suspended animation for 50 years.

She joins the family of her Oankali mentor, Jdhaya, and learns. The Oankali have three sexes, male, female, and neuter gene-manipulating ooloi, with electromagnetic and chemical perception at a molecular level: natural and compulsive genetic engineers driven to meld themselves with other species, the price of their assistance is the absorption of remnant humanity in a new race of Oankali-human hybrids. Yet they find humanity as repellent as desirable: repellent because we have an unsurvivable genetic paradox subordinating intelligence to hierarchical behaviour, a 'Human Contradiction' making us destructive of all life, including ourselves; desirable for our amazing 'talent for cancer', the ability to turn back on genes that become dormant after birth, from which the Oankali learn regeneration of lost tissue, and ultimately shape-shifting.

Lilith's task is to awaken and lead a group of human survivors, first in a nursery, then a training-floor recreating a slice of Amazonia. The Human Contradiction expresses itself potently, in racism, sexism, and patent stupidity—refusals to accept the situation, yearnings for violence. Attempted rape and eventually murder occur.

It is too dangerous for Lilith to go to Earth with her group, who would kill her as a 'traitor to humanity', but the Oankali begin to waken other groups, and release some in Amazonia—free to stay with Oankali settlers, or fend for themselves in the jungle. But only those with the Oankali will be able to breed: all reproduction will be controlled by ooloi. Lilith, still on board the spaceship, is impregnated with her first hybrid child.

Adulthood Rites (1988)

Decades have passed. Lilith is living with a Human-Oankali family in a bio-village on earth, and has had several 'construct' daughters; so too has the Oankali female in the marriage. Construct children each have five parents (one of every human and Oankali sex) but have to be close to the gestating mother's species, so human-born constructs look more human and Oankali-born ones look more Oankali—but the Oankali are metamorphic, and human-looking children become more Oankali-looking at metamorphosis, and vice-versa. All constructs are longer-lived, healthier, smarter, and stronger by far than pre-war human norms.

Lilith's son Akin is the first human-born construct male. His ooloi parent, Nikanj, has risked him, but the Oankali are wary of human-born construct males because they must embody so much of the deadly Human Contradiction. The very human-looking Akin, whose only tentacle is his tongue, is by human standards very precocious, aware in the womb and able to speak a few months after birth, but emotional experience must happen over time—and very problematically, as he is kidnapped by human bandits who sell him to a 'Resistor' village desperate for children. The Oankali collectively decide, against the wishes of Lilith and Akin's family, to leave Akin with the Resistors, so he can understand them; eventually rescued after more than a year, he does understand Resistors well, but has lost his sibling-bond, a chemical harmony he would have had with the Oankali-born sibling closest to his age.

Twenty years later this is still a problem. Obsessed with Resistors, their desperate claim of injustice and mortal genetic flaw, Akin and his should-be sibling-pair travel to the spaceship to understand their Oankali inheritance. Each gene-trade produces a three-way split among a Oankali group: here, into Dinso, who will meld with humans and stay on earth, Toaht, who will meld with humans and leave on a new spaceship, and Akjai, who act as a baseline referent and will not participate in this gene-trade, continuing in the original spaceship. Akin meets Akjai Oankali with different physical forms, and realises the grey humanoid form was adopted simply to approximate human expectations. Through an Akjai ooloi Akin manages to persuade the Oankali consensus to allow a 'Human Akjai', a Martian colony of humans with restored fertility who will be allowed to try to breed their way out of the Human Contradiction. The Oankali find this plan grossly immoral and without hope of success, but having set Akin to learn the Resistors' needs they accept his judgement.

Returning to earth to spread word of the new Martian colony among the Resistors, Akin sees that many accept his offer but some refuse. He undergoes metamorphosis among them, and ends up looking wholly Oankali. Visceral loathing of the alien, a surrender to the unthinking joy of violence even when it is known to be self-destructive, and a callousness of life and alterity all surface in fire and death. Despite the hopes of the new colony, its prospects may be bleak.

Imago (1989)

Further decades have passed. Many Human-Oankali construct males now exist, but to Nikanj's horror his and Lilith's child Jodahs becomes ooloi. The regenerative and shape-shifting powers of the new hybrid race make their ooloi potentially lethal, able to spread uncontrollable mutation through anything they touch, and the family are forced into exile to keep Jodahs in isolation. Jodahs has a hard time, but finds that with human mates to stabilise him he would be able to achieve mature and safe ooloi adulthood ; his sibling also becomes ooloi, and faces the same dilemma, that there are no available and willing humans to fulfil their need.

Travelling far afield, Jodahs finds a human brother and sister, hideously deformed by genetic disease—the product of a tiny, hidden village that found one fertile girl and back-bred mother to son to establish a breeding pool. Some children do survive, but all suffer terribly from the diseases of inbreeding. Jodahs is able to heal them, and with his sibling goes to the village, converting them with his abilities and dominating them chemically with his ability to minister to them—a messiah of revelation, liberation, and betrayal. Other construct children begin to become ooloi, and Jodahs is able in his own completeness to persuade the Oankali consensus of the new race's stable and safe maturity. He founds a bio-village absorbing the fertile village and the new ooloi, that will eventually become a ship to carry the new construct race out into the star-lanes and a galactic future of their own.

7. Of Stormwings and Valiant Women

The Tortallan World of Tamora Pierce

Very few writers for children can, in the nature of things, hope to find many adult readers. If a career runs long enough they may retain into parenthood those who read them as children, but acquisition of first-time adult readers in any number seems pretty much a pipe-dream. Even the few instances that do come to mind—Arthur Ransome in a previous generation, J. K. Rowling in this one—seem exceptions to prove the rule. Rowling is in any case multiply anomalous, and the effort of creating 'adult' Harry Potter dust-jackets, sparing grown-ups the shame of being seen to read a book with a brightly illustrated cover, maintains the problem even as it seeks to bypass it.[1]

Since realising in the summer of 1990 that I had ignored the children's sections of bookshops for too long while intriguing novels for pre-teens and adolescents were appearing, I have kept an eye open and sought recommendations. With books for the very young parents are usually reading them too, aloud, and often have views about what is worthwhile and what wastes trees. But turn to the fictions labelled '9–12', '12–15', or 'Young Adult', books that children who get the bug begin to read for themselves, and adult opinion falls sharply away. Everyone knows about Harry Potter, and quite a few (thanks to the religious fuss he caused and a hit stage-adaptation) about Philip Pullman's Lyra Belacqua,[2] but after almost two decades of finding a very considerable number of children's books that strike me as seriously worthwhile and in some cases truly excellent novels, it remains surprisingly hard to find adults who have bothered to read any of them.

Not least as trees continue to be pulped for chick- and lad-lit or Booker-shortlist flavours of the month, adult ignorance of good children's books seems a shame. I remember clearly how important to my early teens some novels were, especially when

---

1   A shorter version of this essay appears in my Genre Fiction Sightlines on Pierce's *Immortals* and *Protector of the Small* quartets (Humanities-E-Books, 2007)

2   In *Northern Lights* (1995), *The Subtle Knife* (1998), and *The Amber Spyglass* (2000), collectively called *His Dark Materials*.

unhappy and oppressed children made good, and passages in some books I first read then—Anne MacCaffrey's *Dragonsong* (1976) and *Dragonsinger: Harper of Pern* (1977) with their heroine Menolly come especially to mind[1]—can still bring a lump to my throat on re-reading now. It isn't only the density of young Menolly's world and the vividness of her sufferings and talent that summon the emotion, but the revelation through them of her determination and the possibility of winning through. *She* faced acid alien Thread, which was exciting, and met fire-lizards and dragons, who were wonderful, but she also had parents who deliberately allowed an infected cut on her palm to curb her musicality by crippling her fingers, then exaggerated her disability so she would believe herself properly incapable of playing, and discouraged her from singing lest she remind herself or others of what she had 'lost'. 'Girls can't be harpers' declares her fisherman father, who so fears social disapproval of her tuning that he prefers her needless mutilation. This was something else, slamming one's own miseries into humbling perspective, and it's a lesson good children's books go on inculcating with great skill.

The best authors I have discovered—the somewhat older Diana Wynne Jones, Ivan Southall, and Robert Westall (all of whom I missed by shifting to 'grown-up' literature rather young), with the younger Michelle Magorian, William Nicholson, Garth Nix, David Almond, & 'Lian Hearn',[2] as well as Pullman and Rowling—are *very* thought-provoking reads. Magorian's *Goodnight Mister Tom* (1981, filmed 1998) has become well-known in the UK since its TV adaptation (with the late John Thaw as Tom) for a pioneering take on the particular British trauma of abrupt evacuation to the countryside in 1939; her later books, still largely ignored, are just as good, extending her exploration of world-wartime childhood and adolescence. Nix won with *Sabriel* (1995) a firm place on my automatic hardback purchase list, and as the trilogy it began was completed with *Lirael: Daughter of the Clayr* (2001) and *Abhorsen* (2003) his international readership began to expand as it ought; a subsequent series for slightly younger readers, starting with *Mister Monday* (2003) and presently up to *Lady Friday* (2007), with *Superior Saturday* announced for 2008, seems to be confirming his new commercial status. But one writer above all, much to my surprise, seized my imagination and curiosity, and has since been leading me a fascinating, invigorating dance.

Although she had been published in the UK since the mid-1990s I first stumbled on Tamora Pierce only in 2003, when some Scholastic Press issues in the UK

1   See 'Of Modern Dragons', pp. 119–20, 122, 126.

2   A pseudonym of Australian Gillian Rubinstein; Southall and Nix are also Australian.

prompted shops to stock a range of her novels, and their display became more visible on the shelf. As luck would have it the ones I picked out first were her newer and lesser 'Circle' series. I liked *The Magic in the Weaving* well enough to whip through the two quartets, *Circle of Magic* (1997–9) and *The Circle Opens* (2000–03), in a few late May afternoons, buying the last novel of the second quartet, *Shatterglass*, in satisfying hardback—but when a world grips me an extra tenner never seems too much. I enjoyed them all, and found *The Circle Opens* a fascinating mix of craft-knowledge, pedagogy, and crime writing: but fun as it was, the earlier quartet seemed limited, freely fantastical, aimed at younger children, and a little thin in world creation, so while I looked forward to Pierce's future work, the back catalogue didn't immediately appeal.

There was also a problem with her other series novels, in that there were a lot of them—12, at that time—and no bookshop ever seemed to have them all, that a new reader might sort out where to begin. Some of Scholastic's cover-art was also unattractive to me, whatever it did for its target group, and other series writers kept me busy when 'real' literature and relentlessly real students didn't. But on a rainy afternoon in March 2004 I found a complete set of *The Immortals* (1992–6) mixing London and New York paperback editions, liked the US cover-art, and took the plunge. Fascinating elysium. Rapid visits to every bookshop in reach pieced together the volumes of the other Tortallan quartets, *Song of the Lioness* (1983–8) and *Protector of the Small* (1999–2002), and if the earlier was indeed the slightest, the world it established was still extremely interesting, and the ways it developed in the eight later books simply breathtaking. I haven't read and re-read a series with such intensity to piece together its elements for a decade, and not for any children's author since I foolishly concluded I'd left childish things behind, but reading Pierce has been an education—and we can all do with those.

Since then three further novels of Tortall have appeared—a diptych, *Trickster's Choice* & *Trickster's Queen* (2004–05), and *Terrier* (2006), the first in a trilogy called *The Provost's Dog*[1]—making 15 in all. Each of the sub-series has a distinct heroine and time-frame, but all save *The Provost's Dog* (which goes back in time about 200 years) are temporally continuous, though with some years elapsing between each, and a cast that accumulates. Alanna, the heroine of *Song of the Lioness*, is aged about 10 when it starts, and somewhere in her 20s and 30s becomes the mother of three children including Alianne, heroine of the diptych and about 18 when it ends, so together the first 14 novels cover only about 40 years; there have been deaths as well as births

---

1   Volumes 2 and 3, *Bloodhound* and *Elkhound*, have been announced for 2007–08

along the way, but the young from *Song of the Lioness* are still alive in the diptych. Then again, each sub-series is strongly self-contained, so re-appearances by figures from previous books are often no more than glimpses, and news of them is as likely to be reported in passing as to be fully narrated in a scene. Even those who often figure substantially—notably Sir Alanna, the Tortallan monarchs King Jonathan & Queen Thayet, military commander Raoul of Goldenlake, and the mage Numair Salmalín—are displaced on each re-appearance from the narrative positions they once held, re-entering as intimidatingly highborn strangers to the new heroine, so as each character ages different aspects of their personality and the impressions they make on others are added, refracting as much as extending one's sense of them.

THE FIVE TORTALL SERIES

Song of the Lioness	*The Immortals*
Alanna: The First Adventure	Wild Magic
In the Hands of the Goddess	Wolf-Speaker
The Woman who Rides like a Man	The Emperor-Mage
Lioness Rampant	The Realms of the Gods

Protector of the Small	*'the diptych'*	*The Provost's Dog*
First Test	Trickster's Choice	Terrier
Page	Trickster's Queen	[Bloodhound]
Squire		[Elkhound]
Lady Knight		

The geography and crypto-zoology[1] of the world Tortallans inhabit has similarly been dynamically expanded and developed with each sub-series, and it is as well to sort both out before turning to Pierce's remarkable heroines and what they do. There are, moreover, reasons to sort hard: the crypto-zoology is extremely rich, and the geography very unusual for fantasy, openly corresponding in rough but clear ways with real countries and cultures, yet warped into narrative convenience, much as magic can in this fictional world sometimes bend reality. The maps provided have never been bigger than a page and vary in scale, but the widest view (published in *Lioness Rampant*, 1988, and reproduced in the electronic version of this book) shows all that is needed.

---

1   Crypto-zoology is the study of unreal animals, not only in fantasy fiction. Lake-monsters like Nessie and tales of proto-humans like the Yeti or Sasquatch occur all over the world: a good crypto-zoologist can tell you that statistically some 70% of Nessie's kin prefer 'bottomless' lakes, often narrow glacial lakes of depths greater than *c.*400 ft that could not be determined without modern technology, as well as how many toes Asian Yetis and North American 'Bigfeet' are respectively likely to have.

The name 'Carthaki Empire' in relation to 'Great Inland Sea' might first give one pause, followed by northern 'Scanra', particularly given the knowledge that 'Scanrans' are large, tribal, shaman-supported, blond warriors with distinctly Germanic habits of the kind described by the Roman historian Tacitus. Juggle one's eyes a little, and what the map in effect shows is northern Africa, Europe, and central Asia, so thoroughly squished that the landmasses resemble a point during the break-up of the ancient supercontinent of Pangea, with Africa hinging away from Europe and the Mediterranean Sea still connecting through the Black Sea to what became the Indian Ocean.[1] The countries of Galla, Tusaine, Tyra, and Maren, all to the east of Tortall, are little explored in the novels (and Galla, despite its name, is not France), but beyond this buffer-zone the strange correspondences with reality resume. The eastern lands that Alanna visits in *Lioness Rampant* plainly represent northern India and the Far East, complete with the Himalayas ('The Roof of the World'); yet Sarain, though west of these analogue Hiamalayas, is an amalgam of Laos and Cambodia, complete, when Alanna goes there, with a tribal and ethnic civil war causing tens of thousands of civilian casualties.[2]

Tortall itself, a large, topographically varied country that has greatly expanded by conquest and absorption over recent centuries, is mostly a compound Western Europe, combining English, French, Spanish, and German elements into a generic late-mediaeval kingdom; its culture of feudal chivalry has an Alexandrian or Roman context but a predominantly British surface and mores. To the north, Scandinavian Scanra is mountainous and cold, maintaining with its blue-eyed and very white-skinned blond/e/s a sense of the real, but south-eastern Tortall strangely includes the lands of the dark-skinned tribal Bazhir, who are like Bedouin nomads and live in deep desert that is African or Middle Eastern. One could fairly think Tortall an amalgamated Rome, stretching from a Hadrian's Wall (the River Drell, marking the Scanran border) to the desert provinces of the Middle East and Africa (somehow brought north of the analogue-Mediterranean)—but the narrative frames of successive quartets dictate otherwise. *Song of the Lioness* and *Protector of the Small* are variants on the school series, dealing respectively with the first and second Tortallan women to become knights after a culturally imposed gap of more than a century in female training-at-arms; so the narratives require late-mediaeval military technologies and feudalism to sustain chivalric education and adventure, which forestalls any strong Roman cor-

1   See the animation at ▣ http://en.wikipedia.org/wiki/Image:Pangea_animation_03.gif.
2   Born in 1954, Pierce grew up in San Francisco 1963–9 and was at Penn State University 1972–6, so her interest in and harsh judgements of war will originally relate to Vietnam.

relations. In any case, history aside, Tortall is such a mixed-up place that it resembles the contemporary EU and USA as multicutural and polyethnic agglomerations as much as it does any particular historical empire.

Similarly, if Northern 'Africa' is occupied by Carthak, that empire despite its name is not ancient Carthage (modern Libya), homeland of Dido and Hannibal (and Rome's greatest enemy). It is also an amalgam, a version of Alexander the Great's empire or its Ptolemaic successor in Egypt, economically dependent on slavery and strongly flavoured with the notoriously piratical city-states of the later mediaeval 'Barbary Coast' (modern Algeria and Morocco), that until the early nineteenth century regularly raided southern European shipping and coasts. More distant lands reported south of Carthak include 'the grass plains of Ekellatum', which sound like the Kenyan Masai Mara or South African *veldt*, but while the Carthaki capital was visited in *The Emperor Mage* (1995) no book has yet taken readers further south to see for themselves.[1]

Where things start to get seriously complicated is out in the 'Emerald Ocean', or what should be the Atlantic, with two large archipelagos less than a week's sail from land that are certainly not the Canaries and Azores. Further north, the Yamani Isles, present on the maps from the first but fairly blank until the end of *The Immortals* and *Protector of the Small*, emerge as a full-blown version of imperial Japan, complete with language, dress, customs, philosophy, sword and steel technologies, politics, nobility, and roaming bandits who sound like masterless *samurai* (or *ronin*). Further south, the Copper Isles, also present from the first as the source of a nasty princess very troublesome to Alanna, and allies of Carthak in *The Immortals* but still fairly blank while unvisited, emerge in the diptych as an equally full-blown version of colonial Indonesia, complete with tropical climate, oppressing rulers, oppressed darker-skinned natives, language, customs, dress, technologies, double nobility, and developing nationalist insurgency. Allowing for a little compression, climate is more or less maintained in relation to nominal latitude, southern Tortall, Carthak, and the Copper Isles being (sub-)tropical, while Scanra, northern Tortall, and northern Galla have snowbound mountain winters; but quite what either archipelago is doing where it is, Pangean mix or no, is not easily figured out.

The distinctness of the quartets and diptych help (or perhaps hinder) by keeping the various referential dimensions self-contained. Despite the general influence of J. R. R. Tolkien's massively coherent *The Lord of the Rings*, which Pierce first read

---

1   The Tortall short story 'Student of Ostriches' is set in a land resembling the Masai Mara.

aged 12, in 1966,[1] she does not make a fetish of detail, so readers needn't either. But the Tortall books are linked, their world constant and casts overlapping, so some mutual assimilation is inevitable: *Protector of the Small* actively explores heroine Keladry's memories of a Yamani childhood, and a clash of Euro-Asian values comes to Tortall via Prince Roald's marriage to Princess Shinkokami. Events with Alianne in the Copper Islands remained more discrete, and what impact they may have has been postponed by the move back in time with *Terrier*, but the diptych is (save a brief beginning) set in the Isles, and like the third volume of *The Immortals* worked in reverse, taking a Tortallan into a non-European culture. A hasty reader might think, and the politically correct among school librarians worry, that in general Tortall is uncomfortably more deserving and kinder than its neighbours. Scanrans, poor, disorderly, and reliant on brigandage, full-blown invasion, or migration south, are thoroughly unscrupulous; Carthakis (commandeered by the unbalanced Emperor Mage Ozorne, but recovering under Emperor Kaddar) are inveterate raiders, invaders, and slavers whom the Gods recently punished; and the Copper Isles, before nice, white Alianne liberated them, were the source only of a sadistic royal and a pirate fleet. Countries other than European Tortall are generally mistrusted, and the further East, racked by endemic wars, is mostly a source of refugees. Political correctness aside, isn't this a little disturbing? or even racist?

But these *are* hasty worries, as the plots persistently show, and mixing things up so much, historically and geographically, *mobilises* issues; it does not individually *endorse* particular histories in some reactionary fashion. Princess Josiane, the sadistic royal, is a Rittavon, a dynasty with the worst possible bloodline and habits—and she is not a 'Raka' native of the Copper Isles, but one of the 'Luarin' mainlanders who colonised them in 174–81 Human Era (H.E.) and over three centuries have gone to appalling dictatorial and colonialist seed.[2] Alianne, moreover, does not patronisingly liberate anyone except herself, having been sold into Island slavery through the connivance of a Raka god who wants her peculiar talents at the service of His upcoming nationalist rebellion. The same kinds of twists in evolving perspective, carefully structured, are present at even the grandest scale: Tortall's European feudal and chivalric culture, for example, imposes a rigid social system and cultural prohibitions that are given oppressive reality, but the whole idea has been their systematic modification by women. Alanna in *Song of the Lioness* challenges the patriarchy of

---

1 Tolkien was recommended by a smart seventh-grade teacher in the year of *LotR*'s one-volume US publication, and had immediate influence; see Donna Dailey, *Tamora Pierce* (2006), pp. 36–8.

2 *Song of the Lioness* begins in about 425 H.E., and the diptych is set in 462–3 H.E..

knighthood and monarchy, and Daine in *The Immortals* fights exploitation and abuse of animals. Daine is also, like Keladry in *Protector of the Small*, a reluctant killer enraged by slavery, war, and the politics that drive them. Keladry is also a sterling, sometimes satirical protector of children and refugees with an increasingly acute class-consciousness, while Alianne in the diptych helps a people and a nation liberate themselves from abusive and impious foreign rule. Most recently, Rebaka (Beka) Cooper in *The Provost's Dog*, whose concerns transpose the chivalric code via intense urban poverty to policing on behalf of the exploited, has through her experience as a slum-child a crackling awareness of the bigotries and class-weighted injustices against which she can pit her life, body and soul, but which she cannot ever hope to eradicate.

Pierce, that is, while very evidently committed to gender and social equality in law and custom, is also a realist and moralist who recognises differences that make people, beliefs, laws, customs, and individual behaviours unequal in many ways and degrees. Her contemporary feminism is properly far more interested in blending realism and imagination than observing political correctness, and the stories and nations she creates offer a wide range of liberations for all to consider. Nor has she forgotten her own beginnings as a reader:

> Fantasy is also important to a group that I deeply hope is small: those whose lives are so grim that they cling to everything that takes them completely away for *any* length of time. I speak of readers like I was, from families that are now called dysfunctional. While the act of reading transported me out of reality for the time it took me to read, nothing carried over into my thoughts and dreams until I discovered fantasy. I visited Tolkien's Mordor often for years, not because I *liked* what went on there, but because on the dead horizon, and then throughout the sky overhead, I could see the interplay and the lasting power of light and hope. It got me through.[1]

Real oppressions of whatever kind can be brutal in their effects, and Pierce, for all her delight in fantasy, is deeply committed to changing conditions and perceptions that enable them. If the suffering of her folk is sometimes brutally real, that is but verisimilitude. Taking a different tack, however, one could also argue that her successive quartets also clearly show Pierce reading and criticising herself in a very interest-

---

1   Tamora Pierce, 'Fantasy: Why Kids Read It, Why Kids Need It' (1993), in Sheila Egoff *et al.*, eds, *Only Connect: Readings on Children's Literature* (1969; 3rd ed., Toronto, New York, & Oxford: Oxford University Press, 1996), pp. 182–3.

ing and productive manner—and to follow that self-critique requires the complex, magical crypto-zoology and theology that have become distinguishing features of the Tortallan world.

In these days of Harry Potter magic and magical training seem a commonplace of children's and young adult books, but are less so than you might think. There have of course always been stories with curses, enchantments and the like, but the highly organised magical education systems in Rowling, Pierce, and others are much more recent. In Tolkien's *The Lord of the Rings* (largely written in 1939–45 and first published as a trilogy in 1954–5) the wizards Gandalf and Saruman are incarnate *valar* (quasi-angels) rather than magical men; their power, like that of Tolkien's doomed Elves, is singular, passing, and will not come again. Rowling and Pierce are quite different, for in their worlds, though not everyone has magical ability or talent, many humans do and are yet nor more nor less than human.

Once one has added such naturally occurring magical ability to a fictional world with social and historical depth, one must ask about the training of mage-children. The pioneer was (as so often) Ursula Le Guin in the *Earthsea* trilogy (1968–72), where the Gontish mage-boy Ged is first apprenticed to the best local talent, then sent to the School of Wizardry on Roke Island. What he learns there is what Alanna the Lioness learns, and the 'Black Robe' mage Numair Salmalín teaches Daine in *The Immortals*, that to use magic affects the balance of the world[1] and the greater part of a mage's skill is self-control. Pierce's magical–scientific university in Carthak owes something to the School on Roke, but mixes magic and science in a different way—an interesting trick she also pulls off superbly with specifically forensic magic and science in her second 'Circle' quartet, *The Circle Opens* (2000–03), and is further developing in *The Provost's Dog*.

Pierce has also been careful not to allow magic to become a prop of the wrong kind. In *Song of the Lioness* it was set at odds with chivalric knighthood as physical endeavour. In *The Immortals* it was necessarily central because of Daine's semi-divine identity and 'wild magic', but Keladry in *Protector of the Small* hasn't a magical bone in her body, and the limited magics that Alianne has in the diptych, and Beka in *Terrier*, help their particular work but are a source of real problems and embarrassments as well as occasional solutions. Most of the celebrated children's books to feature magic are actually quite moral about it in this way, 'bad' children who do not learn wisdom tending swiftly to nasty ends (as happens to a teenager in *The Woman*

1   See Pierce's Tortall short stories 'Elder Brother' and 'The Hidden Girl' for a prime example.

IMMORTALS

basilisks   Lizards with grey beaded hide and pouches, who walk upright. Great travellers and linguists, able to turn things to stone (which they eat).

centaurs   Given to archery, they live in herds herdmasters can cull.

chaos-dwellers   Beings of Uusoae, who can take any form.

coldfangs   Large, poisonous lizards around whom ice blooms. They act as guards or trackers of thieves through all Realms.

darkings   Small black blobs, created by Ozorne (as a stormwing) from his blood and magic to act as his spies, and later rebelling against him.

dragons   Winged lizards, with scaly, jewel-coloured, and powerful bodies, limbs, and tails who grow to a hundred foot or more, and are mages.

giants   Their bones are used to make the 'killing devices' and they fight the Tortallans in person, apparently for the fun of it.

griffins   A combination of giant lion and eagle, clawed, beaked, feathered and winged but sinuously powerful on the ground. No-one can lie around a griffin.

hurroks   'Horse-hawks'—flying, fanged and clawed carnivorous horses who reek of stale hay and rotting meat and are angry with everything.

the Kraken   A truly massive but urbane super-squid.

kudarung   The Raka word for winged horses. Of all sizes, beautiful and benevolent, they are the symbol of Raka royalty and legitimacy.

ogres   Some ogres are no more than brutish mercenary killers up to 12 feet tall—but others prefer farming; they are blue-skinned and -blooded..

spidrens   Spiders with human heads and steel fangs, violent, predatory, and always malign. Best hunted at night, when their webs glow.

stormwings   Flying creatures with human heads and torsos, razor-feathered steel wings, legs, and claws. They drink human fear and flock at battlefields.

tauroses   Bull-headed rapists: only male ones exist, attacking human women on sight and trying to rape them to death.

the Three Sorrows   Slaughter, a hyena, Starvation, a mangy dog, and Malady, a rat, vast but invisible to mortal sight.

tree-sprites   Harmless little dryads, from Greek mythology.

unicorns   One-horned horses; there are vegetarian and flesh-eating kinds, the latter's saliva being a deadly poison.

water-sprites   Harmless little naiads, from Greek mythology.

winged apes   Pierce's invention—the most limited Immortals, able to create magic fog and wield weapons as well as fly.

DEITIES

the Badger   The First Male badger, Daine's protector on behalf of Weiryn.

the Black God   The God of Death, ruler of the Peaceful Realm; reputed kind as he refuses none. The Graveyard Hag, his daughter, has sway in Carthak.

Broad Foot   The First Male duckmole, or duck-billed platypus.

the Cat   When in the Divine Realms, a constellation; when incarnate in the mortal realm the constellation disappears. Alanna's Faithful in Song of the Lioness and Beka's Pounce in Terrier.

the Crooked God   The nameless patron deity of thieves.

Father Universe   The absolute male principle, co-creator of all.

Gainel, Master of Dream   A tall man with infinitely deep eyes, who alone stands with one foot in Chaos and may visit the mortal realm only in dreams.

the Graveyard Hag   A one-eyed hag who gambles, jokes, and avenges. Her sacred animals are rats and spotted hyenas.

the Great Mother Goddess   The chief goddess, triple-aspected but usually in her martial prime, close to stern, chaste huntress deities like Diana.

the Green Lady   Daine's mother Sarra, transformed after being killed by raiders into a local Goddess of childbirth and matters of the heart.

the Horse Lords   K'miri gods of storm and fire, invoked as inoffensive oaths by the important K'miri refugees in Tortall.

Kidunka the World Snake   A mighty serpent, lord of the Banjiku tribes (whom he left under a terrible misapprehension for a very long time, as slaves).

Kyprioth   A joker, like Norse Loki or Amerindian Crow. His sacred animals are crows, and he has a nasty temper as well as innate charm and odd dress-sense.

Mithros the Sun Lord   The chief god, a powerful dark-skinned man in early middle age usually dressed like a senior Roman army officer; primarily a male god of warfare, weapons, & pride. Plainly a version of Mithras.

Mother Flame   The absolute female principle, co-creator of all.

Uusoae, Queen of Chaos   That against which gods and some men strive; others follow their mortal-half that is chaos. She appears as everything at once, mutating in hideous combinations, and her appetite is insatiable. In some ways an allegory of entropy.

Weiryn of the Hunt   Daine's father, a vigorous, antlered man with green lights in his skin who resembles Herne the Hunter.

who Rides Like a Man). In Daine's case a similar control is applied by her initial ignorance and distrust of her magical powers, and by the time she develops them fully her care and control have been repeatedly tested. Additionally, once in her power her duties are overwhelmingly dictated by necessities of war, and the poor girl has few enough chances for irresponsibility anyway—not that she'd take one. A trope distinguishing 'wild magic' such as Daine has from 'the Gift', the tamer, more trainable magic that humans usually have, is also important. Varieties of wild magic used by the Bazhir and an Eastern people called the Doi feature in *Song of the Lioness*, but as more-or-less tamed human tools, not the animal-centred and divinely inherited wildness Daine learns to trust and control. As no-one else can emulate her, and she lacks the Gift, another important limit to the nature of her magic is set in place, and much thereby forestalled.[1]

Despite Alanna's god-touched career, Daine's semi-divinity, and the nature of magic, this is all fundamentally dealing with human politics, institutions, and abilities. But like Rowling, only very much more so, Pierce has wholly magical animals, Immortals, as well as an eclectic pantheon of interfering deities. The god/desse/s were present from the beginning, but the Immortals (distinguished from gods by being killable but sharing with the animal gods silver claws) weren't, for (as it turned out) they had all been banished to the Divine Realms by powerful mages centuries before, beginning the 'Human Era' of Tortall's calendar. The barrier-spells, however, were rediscovered in *c*.450 H.E. by the Emperor Mage Ozorne of Carthak: the action of *The Immortals* primarily concerns the war he began with those powers—Immortals wreaking almost as much havoc simply by appearing somewhere as by actually doing anything—and after the war they remain an enlivening feature of all countries. Given their numbers and variety, summary lists of Immortals and deities are for readers' convenience given on the following pages, and show plainly that though Pierce customises creatures beautifully, most are not her inventions. Among the Immortals basilisks, centaurs, dragons, griffins, and ogres, for instance, are 'real' in the sense of being very widespread and often detailed crypto-zoological beasts, while the anomalous 'Three Sorrows'—Slaughter, a hyena, Starvation, a dog, and Malady, a rat, visitations whom the gods at times release into the world, vast and invisible to mortal sight—are clearly adapted from Christian sermonising. More allegories than beasts (though real enough that a duck-billed platypus god called Broad Foot can

---

1   In her 'Circle' books Pierce creates a distinction between 'academic' and 'ambient' magic, one working out from human power, the other drawing on the power in natural things, that reworks and develops the distinction in the Tortallan books between 'the Gift' and Wild Magics.

meta/physically fight Malady with his poison-spurs), the 'Three Sorrows' are a version of the 'Four Horsemen of the Apocalypse' described in chapter 6 of Revelation. The horsemen are given power "to kill with sword, and with hunger, and with death, and with the beasts of the earth" (KJV, 6:8), but this is often brought down to 'war, starvation, and malady'—exactly Pierce's trio (though her choice of the hyena as an emblematic animal is idiosyncratic). But other Immortals are original creations, and the best of them truly striking: coldfangs, hurroks, and tauroses are all memorably nasty (and tauroses pitiable), but the two that truly linger in memory to demand thought are spidrens and stormwings, as part-human part-animals properly called 'grotesques'.[1]

One might first note that there is among Pierce's Immortals in general both a pattern of nice and nasty variants, so that hurroks (slurring 'horse-hawk') are distorted *kudarung* (winged horses like the Greek semi-divinity Pegasus), and a sensitivity to grotesquerie—for the hurroks horribly blend vegetarian and carnivore, as opposed to (say) the harmonious blending in griffins of lion and eagle, both noble predators. Her unicorns similarly come in nice vegetarian and skin-crawling carnivorous varieties, the latter having horribly poisonous saliva. The nice and nasty variants probably go back as a pattern to *The Lord of the Rings*, where Tolkien similarly mixed up 'real' myths (elves, dwarves, trolls) with his own inventions (orcs, hobbits), and made the bad ones distorted versions of the good; as he explains, evil mocks and perverts good because it cannot create for itself.[2] But the major grotesques are Pierce's own, and within the narratives of *The Immortals* both spidrens and stormwings are repeatedly distinguished by their human parts, not least because they can speak for themselves and so lack the special relationship wholly animal Immortals have with Daine in her role as an interspecies translator.

The two part-human grotesques also become increasingly distinct from one another, and though they cannot form a nice–nasty pair as such begin oddly to push in that direction. Nothing good is ever said of spidrens, giant spiders with human heads and steel teeth, and throughout *The Immortals* and *Protector of the Small* the only valid response is killing them before they kill you. They too (like the giant spiders in the woods outside Rowling's Hogwarts) might despite their original grotesquerie be traced back to Tolkien, whose ancient and evil spider-like Shelob catches Frodo

---

1   'Grotesque' is from Italian *grottesco*, 'of a cave', but the original 'caves' were specifically buried Roman rooms that had mosaics and other images mixing human and animal forms. See Neil Rhodes, *Elizabethan Grotesque* (1980).

2   See 'Of Modern Dragons', pp. 92–3.

in the Pass of Cirith Ungol, and who has other horrible spider-offspring of Ungoliant in *The Hobbit* and throughout his legendarium. But stormwings—who have human bodies and heads with steel wings and claws, and are filthy beyond belief in person and habits—have no obvious antecedent other than (in a general bird-human way) the Greek Harpies, from which they are in critical ways quite distinct; and if the stormwings' behaviour is unspeakably vile, the need to come to terms with *all* that they represent is a major theme in *The Immortals* and the later volumes of *Protector of the Small*. A stormwing hero emerges, as well as two stormwing monarchs with dry wit, and in many ways the stormwing narrative that plays out is a tragedy. It's also a marvellous and very interesting conundrum, because stormwings are, besides being vile, in origin and driving purpose utterly *moral*, and as such become centrally caught up not simply as dangers to the heroines, but as self-aware agents of their education.

This pedagogic role is variously shared with the assorted interfering deities to whom mortals and Immortals alike are to differing degrees subject. The US remains a strongly and overtly Christian country in a way no longer true of most European nations, and Pierce stands out as a US Children's writer partly because her fictional worlds are both so plainly *not* Christian and in many ways actively *un*-Christian. She is certainly not alone in writing so, but the best fantasy narratives to deal with religious issues and challenge the reductivity of monotheistic dogma (such as Lois McMaster Bujold's *The Curse of Chalion*, 2000, and its sequels[1]), though popular with older teenagers and drawing in stronger younger readers, are not written for or marketed to children or young adults as such.[2] Nor are the kind of SF books, like Mary Doria Russell's *The Sparrow* (1996) and *Children of God* (1998), that take the theological challenge of alien life seriously—besides which, Pierce is as unusual in her deities as in her grotesques and other Immortals.

The basic model for any world that has a parallel, real heaven inhabited by multiple god/desse/s who interfere in human affairs remains Homer's *Iliad*. Most events in that foundational epic (and romance) happen because god/desse/s get up to no good, favouring one human or nation over another and generally stirring the pot. Even in versions of the story that blame Helen of Troy's great beauty for 'launching a thou-

---

1   Bujold, *Paladin of Souls* (2003) and *The Hallowed Hunt* (2005); her current series *The Sharing Knife*, started with *Beguilement* (2006), also treats of religious matters.

2   Pierce herself rightly notes, however, that "Fantasy, even more than other genres, has a large crossover audience, with Y[oung] A[dult]s raiding the adult shelves once they deplete their part of the store or library, and adults slipping into the youth sections". (Pierce, 'Fantasy' in *Only Connect*, p. 180).

sand ships', it remains true that she was so disruptively beautiful because she was a daughter of Zeus, who raped her mother Leda in the form of a swan—so that both Helen's beauty and her consequent life, rooted in and propagating violence, are the god's brutal and brutalising handiwork (or cobwork). Pierce's gods are usually rather more restrained and constrained than Homer's, but share temperaments, while her pantheon comes from all over the world and out of her own head, representing many different kinds of god/desse/s and ways of thinking about who and what They might be. Quasi-Greek and -Roman gods are more or less in charge, but quasi-Asian and -animist gods are also present and liable to act independently. A broad mythic cosmography underlies it all—creation by a paired fe/male principle, Father Universe and Mother Flame; a division into three Realms, Mortal, Divine, and Peaceful (where the dead go), plus the distinct Dragonlands. But there are also (in a major departure from classical and Western religious traditions) First Male and Female animal god/desse/s of each species—and in some cases, such as Old White and Night Black, the First Wolf and Wolfen[1] who figure in *Wolf-Speaker*, a First Pack as well—as well as First Plants and at least two First Bridges of various kinds (but these last are all confined to the Divine Realms, and how they influence mortals has never been explored). Additionally, one child of Universe and Flame was Chaos, and its queen, the unpronounceable Uusoae, who controls half of everything, will eventually overthrow all in disorder (as in scientific theories of the 'Big Crunch', ending the universe). Mortal men and women are in their natures half-chaos; Immortals and gods are free of chaos, and the divine-mortal mix in Daine's blood can be a serious problem in travelling between the Realms, but is also her gateway to interspecies diplomacy.

In a general sense one can see that Pierce's theological structures serve the political and ethical causes she believes in, which are, broadly speaking, feminism and animal rights. The temples of the Great Mother Goddess in Tortall (and to a lesser degree their equivalents in the thinner 'Circle' world) are refuges and courts for battered women, and with the consent of the state maintain private armies who seize and punish those who hurt women. Children may or may not be similarly protected, but the issue is often raised. The First Animals also object to and where they can help to prevent human cruelty to their kinds: they accept predation by hunting and slaughter for food, but rightly loathe sadism—a quality very rare in the animal kingdom other than among human beings. They also repeatedly stand for ecological sensitivity, so that all humans and animals—or as they tellingly call themselves, 'the People'—may

---

1 'Wolfen' was the old term for a female wolf; cf. 'foxen', whence the modern 'vixen'. Though archaic, it seems preferable to 'First Bitch', however scientifically correct that might be.

thrive together in harmony amid natural wealth. And individual creatures, especially birds often regarded as pests (starlings, crows, pigeons), are variously shown to be interesting in themselves and the servants of a particular god. It's no surprise, then, to identify Pierce (b. 1954) as at heart a good 1960s–70s feminist, nor to learn from her website that she is a great animal- and bird-lover, keeping many and feeding very many more.[1]

The fact remains that *everyone* in Tortall is wholly religious—their assorted deities show themselves in dreams, visions, and reality often enough that no-one has the slightest doubt of their collective and individual reality—but *no-one* is Christian (or anything else monotheistic). To be God-touched like Alanna the Lioness is a burden, and few so touched have ever been happy; Daine endures but hates her divine burden in Carthak, when the Graveyard Hag temporarily delegates certain of her punitive powers and urges; and Alianne uses Kyprioth's attentions as best she can when needs must, but takes out the small change in haunted dreams and unhappy days. God/esse/s can (D.G.) be fooled if one is a fast enough thinker with a glib enough tongue to lie only by omission; they also both make mistakes (the dinosaurs all died in one) and like Homer's Greek deities are prone to hissy fits and sheer meanness that They justify as character-building for puny mortals. It's thus no surprise either that among the Tortallan population there is a tough-minded attitude to religion, giving it a central place and nervous respect mixed with commonsense aversion. Humans thoroughly respect god/esse/s if they know what's good for them, but would rather They kept away, thanks all the same. Nor do many of Tortall's religious find any difficulty in being pious while approving slavery, capital punishment, acute social snobbery, and gross exploitation of people and the environment. It's also all often rather *funny*, and the special humour of *The Immortals* is divinely capped at its end, when the chief dragon, Diamondflame (openly distrusting Mithros the Sun Lord to return Daine safely to the Mortal Realm), says briskly "—*Come, Gods annoy me.—*" and the Graveyard Hag snaps back "As dragons annoy us", before cheerfully winking at Daine.[2] The exchange may learnedly be read as Pierce's take on the *dracomachy*, "the technical term among dracologists for combat between the god and the dragon", and as Anne McCaffrey observes "Having one is virtually the law in this business"[3]—but it is also in its nature (and even more so in its delightful particularity) an irreverence that cuts deeply against Christian models of unquestioning piety and obedience to the father.

---

1   See ▣ http://www.tamora-pierce.com/index.html.
2   Tamora Pierce, *The Realms of the Gods* (New York: Random House, 1998), pp. 269–70 (Ch. 10).
3   Anne McCaffrey, *A Diversity of Dragons*, p. 14.

Adults who worry that reading Harry Potter books endangers the reader's soul, or believe a singular God will punish those who do so, will thus also worry about or believe the same of reading Pierce; but frankly, shame on them all. Nothing very much can usually be done about these beliefs, by definition irrational (as all faith proudly is, and must be), and rarely open to argument anyway. But there is a very clear and strong case that all Pierce's novels are strongly moral. Her morality is not the same as any particular religious morality, but it is clear, vivid, and righteous, and the values of female strength and independence, ethical treatment of animals, and ecological sustainability, as well as her constant stress on human possession of Free Will and the consequences of each choice, are for very many people, religious and otherwise, of the utmost tangible *and* spiritual importance. No-one guided by perception and reason (as distinct from dogma, faith, or revelation) could sensibly argue that Pierce is anything but a very good author for children (and plenty of adults I can think of) both to read and to take firmly to heart. And as with Ursula Le Guin's overlapping self-revision of Earthsea as her feminist and theological perspectives developed with age,[1] Pierce's self-criticism and revisioning in successive quartets are in their very dynamism and flexibility potent rebukes to the fossil certainties of fundamentalism, in religion as elsewhere.

Most writers for children, however committed as teachers and feminists, would think their job well done if they had written and published a successful quartet of young adult novels about the first woman for over a century to become a knight. Pierce went on to consider in turn the first person (and woman) ever to be a Wild-mage, the *second* woman to become a knight, the first woman in three centuries to become spymaster of the Copper Isles, and most recently a woman who isn't first anything, just an honest, talented 'Puppy' determined to become a good 'Dog', a Provost's Guardswoman in Tortall's proto-police force. Similarly, if Alanna the Lion-ess, Daine the Wildmage, Lady Knight Keladry of Mindelan, Alianne Cooper, and Trainee Guardswoman Rebakah Cooper are plainly similar heroines, strong women followed from early age to adulthood, professional success, and sexual maturity, they are also, despite the rich fantasy creations that surround them, steadily and pointedly becoming more everyday folk.

Alanna is both of noble birth and 'God-touched', a chosen vessel of the Great Mother Goddess. Her striking purple eyes and powerful magecraft prove it, as do her emblematic success in training as a knight, divine cat-companion Faithful (also

1   See 'Of Modern Dragons', pp. 108–15.

purple-eyed), and amazing feats of heroism. Daine seems a step *up*, for she is undoubtedly semi-divine, the daughter of Weiryn of the Hunt (and as her mother Sarra becomes, after being murdered by bandits, a minor goddess, the Green Lady, sort of divine on both sides)—but for most of *The Immortals* Daine doesn't know of her paternity or her mother's post-mortem fate, and is far more deeply scared of and humble about her own powers and possibilities than Alanna. Keladry is much more normal and has no magical talent at all: though highly trained and unusual, she makes it through determination, bruising hard work, innate kindness, and an unwillingness to let bullying go unchecked. Alanna's daughter Alianne has 'the Sight' and a God to call on, but Kyprioth the Jester causes her as much grief as He gives opportunities, and the joys she wins are her own. Alianne's distant paternal ancestor Beka Cooper is in most ways most normal of all, lacking even Keladry's advantages of minor nobility and relative wealth, though she is also extremely determined (hence *Terrier*)—but like Alanna she has the companionship and help of a purple-eyed cat, this time called Pounce but plainly the same happily interfering divine feline, as well as the helpful ability (for a policewoman) to hear ghosts. These complicate the curve, but cannot disguise it, for, most unlike Alanna, Beka was born and for her first eight years raised in an inner-city slum, the 'Cesspool' of the Tortallan capital Corus, to which she has returned to work; Pounce, however divine, is as geared to Beka's urban police life and needs as Faithful was to Alanna's romantic and questing ones; and the contrast outlines the self-critique Pierce has pursued.

In *Song of the Lioness*, published when Pierce was aged 29–34 but deriving from a novel she had completed by 1976,[1] when she was 22, noble Alanna is bursting with female pride and indignation at being absurdly and horribly undervalued in a sexist world. Righteously aided by the Goddess and the amusing Faithful, she shows us all just what a girl, and a Lioness, can do. But how many of us have the advantages of a school for knights, a divine cat, and a friendly goddess? To be fair, Alanna does have problems with boyfriends, as a woman wearing armour and notoriously trained to kill may, even if very sexy—which Alanna isn't, though very striking with her purple eyes and armour. But the real problem isn't lust-riddled spinsterhood, it's choosing between (i) Prince Jonathan of Conté, heir to the Tortallan throne and her

---

1   It sounds an interesting process. The novel was for adults, but Pierce mentally bowdlerised chunks of it to create stories while working as a housemother; later a friend and agent suggested turning the one adult novel into four young adult ones, and a career was born. For biographical accounts see Donna Dailey, *Tamora Pierce* (2006) and the bio-pages at Pierce's excellent website, ▣ http://www.tamora-pierce.com/.

Knight-Master as a squire, with whom she loses her virginity (no-one the wiser), and (ii) George Cooper, Tortall's 'Rogue' or King of Thieves—again, not exactly every woman's problem. The most realistic thing about it all, romantically and pedagogically speaking, is that in the end Jonathan (as King Jonathan IV of Tortall) has to marry for political reasons, and his Queen, Thayet, is a woman Alanna rescued in the East, and goes on liking even when she doesn't want to. Thayet is also a royal beauty, a natural diplomat, and a born leader, and Alanna is too honest not to realise that she would herself make Jonathan a terrible queen and be a liability both for him and for the Tortall she is sworn to defend.

So—after thinking it through while writing *The Immortals*, published when she was aged 38–42 and more concerned with animal rights than feminism, Pierce returned to the subject of female knighthood, and in *Protector of the Small* wrote aged 45–8 a quartet of extremely impressive novels. Without magic or a goddess (though with a faithful mongrel dog, Jump, of sterling character and dubious morals), Keladry of Mindelan—Kel to her friends—has to rely on herself, time and again, to combat chauvinistic prejudice and finds that she can safely do so: she *can* do it. To make Kel's courage and general pyschology of character more plausible Pierce gave her a very particular early childhood: her parents were ambassadors from Tortall to the Yamani Isles, and early in their residence her mother was able to save two sacred swords by holding off some pirate-raiders until the imperial guard came. As part of the Emperor's thanks Kel's parents moved into his palace, and under palace routine she trained with other children under experts in combat disciplines and self-defence—standard for Yamani ladies of rank. The different culture shifts the light: noblewomen may be trained (like Tortallan knights) to kill others, and more disturbingly to kill themselves, but they are still pawns of men from birth, and of their mothers-in-law after marriage.

Kel's Yamani physical stamina and stoicism prove vital in surviving the criminal bullying to which she is subjected by some of her peers in page-training while adults largely turn blind eyes to the problems. She is also given older brothers who have trained as knights and can advise her, and all the Mindelan siblings have a background explaining their determinations: their father only a second-generation noble, whose standing depends on his success in securing a Yamani treaty, a diplomatic coup secured in turn by the marriage of King Jonathan's son and heir Prince Roald to the Yamani Princess Shinkokami—whom Kel unwittingly befriended in the imperial palace when Shinkokami's parents were temporarily in disgrace, and other, more knowing children shunned her in case the disgrace rubbed off. Liking Shinkokami personally,

Kel (and her brothers) also believe both in their parents' diplomatic work and in the greater motives of cultural tolerance and international alliance that prompted King Jonathan and Queen Thayet to send the mission. They sweat to train as knights and to uphold the Tortallan monarchy because they believe in Jonathan and Thayet as reformers and peacemakers, though Jonathan himself sometimes disappoints Kel (as he did Alanna) in his compromises, especially about female equality.

The same background interestingly explains the force of Kel's class-consciousness, of necessity suppressed by protocol during her Yamani childhood but rapidly developing with maturity in sexist, snobbish Tortall. To the 'old nobility', her father's recent title simply marks him out as a 'Johnny-come-lately' gatecrasher of their 'natural' (i.e. older and more familiar) ranks and privileges. Antiquated laws on Tortall's books support a horrible *status quo* in which nobles may fight to the death over (supposed) insults, while if the victim is a commoner, and especially a servant, anything short of murder is punishable at most by a fine. Masters legally take servants' independent earnings at a cruel rate, and beating is common. So too are domestic violence, harassment, sexual assaults, and rape, although the temples of the Great Mother Goddess act as sanctuaries and justicers for battered women, with their privately maintained squads of hard women armed with sickles who can be sent to mete out justice. The monarchy and magistrates of Tortall accept these squads, but (perhaps because they exist) do not themselves do what they ought to protect women. Money is shown as a major consideration in corrupting justice, paired with social snobbery sometimes amounting to violent bigotry, and often revealing habituations to abuse.

Despite all this, the bases of *Protector of the Small* and *Song of the Lioness* are in many ways similar—Alanna and Kel are, after all, undergoing the same training in the same school—but the later quartet develops much more unpredictably. Both quartets send brave, maturing heroines on a quest of great significance, but where Alanna in *Song of the Lioness* went to a distinct sub-culture, the desert Bazhir, to prove herself away from home-ground, then won the fabled Dominion Jewel from a Himalayan mountain-spirit who tested her with icy cold and in armed combat, Kel in *Protector of the Small* faces a challenge that is different in every way. Her Knight-Master as a squire is Raoul of Goldenlake, himself a great hero called 'the Giantkiller' for the obvious (and in Tortall literally true) reason, but also a thoroughly professional Knight-Commander of the King's Own, the brigade-strength business-end of the standing Tortallan army. And when Kel thinks the problems in military logistics that Raoul is setting her as homework irrelevant to any possible future, he memorably sets her (and readers) straight:

> "At our level, there are four kinds of warrior," [Raoul] told Kel. He raised a fist
> and held up one large finger. "Heroes, like Alanna the Lioness. Warriors who find
> dark places and fight in them alone. This wonderful, but we live in the real world.
> There aren't many places without *any* hope or light."
>
> He raised a second finger. "We have knights—plain, everyday knights, like your
> brothers. They patrol their borders and protect their tenants, or they go into trou-
> bled areas at the king's command and sort them out. They fight in battles, usually
> against other knights. A hero will work like an everyday knight for a time—it's
> expected. And any knight has to be clever enough to manage alone."
>
> Kel nodded.
>
> "We have soldiers," Raoul continued, raising a third finger. "Those are warriors,
> including knights, who manage so long as they're told what to do. These are more
> common than lone knights, thank Mithros, and you'll find them in charge of com-
> panies in the army, under the eye of a general. Without people who can take orders,
> we'd be in real trouble.
>
> "Commanders." He raised his little finger. "Good ones, people with a knack
> for it, like, say, the queen, or Buri, or young Dom, they're as rare as heroes. Com-
> manders have an eye not just for what they do, but for what those around them
> do. Commanders size up people's strengths and weaknesses. They know where
> someone will shine and where they will collapse. Other warriors will obey a true
> commander because they can tell that the commander knows what he—or she—is
> doing." Raoul picked up a quill and toyed with it. "You've shown flashes of being
> a commander. I've seen it. So has Qasim, your friend Neal, even Wyldon, though
> it would be like pulling teeth to get him to admit it. My job is to see if you will
> do more than flash, with the right training. The realm needs commanders. Tortall
> is big. We have too many still untamed pockets, too cursed many hidey-holes for
> rogues, and plenty of hungry enemies to nibble at our borders and our seafaring
> trade. If you have what it takes, the crown will use you."[1]

This has many merits, beyond clear prose and good analysis. Raoul is a kind teacher
who thinks to build up Kel's confidence. "At *our* level", he says, casually including
her with himself, the giant-killing Knight-Commander of the King's Own, and extends to her not a promise (maybe to be kept, maybe forgotten, as so many to children
are) but a solid and ponderable civil truth: "The realm needs commanders. [...] If you
have what it takes, the crown will use you."

1   Tamora Pierce, *Squire* (London: Scholastic, 2001), pp. 116–18 (Ch. 6).

The training Kel gets with Raoul, riding with the King's Own to every corner of Tortall to fight mortal and immortal enemies and help with disaster-relief after raids and an earthquake, is a superior apprenticeship in command, and her talent does a great deal more than flash. Even the stubbornly chauvinistic training-master Wyldon had seen enough in her over his four years in charge to have to rethink from a strictly military point-of-view some of his most cherished routines—a self-similar iteration at a mid-plot level of Pierce's self-revising concerns. But in her last year as a squire, on the northern border with Scanra in a summer plagued by hit-and-run raids, a new factor enters the war and the Tortallan world. Clanking like the dreadful tanks first seen at the Battle of the Somme in 1916, the Scanran 'killing devices' are made from iron-clad giants' bones and equipped with double-jointed arms spiked at every extremity and fingered with long, lethal knives. Worst of all, as Kel (commanding a small squad after their sergeant is wounded) discovers in managing to kill a device, by hog-tying it into momentary immobility and smashing open its armoured head-dome, what powers the awful things is a trapped child's ghost, dissipating with release but not without a last tearfully uncomprehending and aubible 'Mama?' And children, Kel slowly realises as soldiers and a shaken Raoul stare at the dead monster, are somewhere dying wholesale and to order so that a mercenary mage can with his special 'death magic' re-imprison each small ghost in the head-dome of a 'device'.

Killing this peculiarly disgusting mage, whose name turns out to be Blayce the Gallan,[1] becomes Kel's quest after her graduation, an obligation opportunistically laid on her by the 'Chamber of the Ordeal' of knighthood—a sort of minor God (or very old and unbreakably strong bit of sessile architectural magic) that oversees the chivalric quality of squire-candidates by hammering psychically at their flaws to see what people are made of, and has become disapprovingly aware of Blayce's death magic, a hubris. Military need, however, puts Kel in command of a refugee camp supposedly out of harm's way behind the front lines, guarding 300 adults and 200 children without a chance to follow her quest. But after a Scanran strike force abducts all the refugees, enslaving adults and marking the children (their real target) for the attentions of Blayce, Kel and a motley band of the friends she has made ignore orders and strike out in a commando raid deep behind enemy lines to burn the evil out, killing Blayce and rescuing most of the refugees as well as various others. Through all

1   The name Blayce summons the priest-magician Blaise, Merlin's master in the surviving fragments of Robert de Boron's Arthurian poem *Merlin* and the traditions descending from it, but the connection seems more a general thickening of the narrative soup than a specific allusion carrying a particular point.

the exciting trappings of knighthood and a very good war story, the unexpected but glaring truth is that the mage, Blayce, is a serial child-abuser, a paedophile as well as a killer. He pampers and dresses-up the abducted children until the time is 'right' to kill them, and if details of his sexual perversion are never made explicit, his irresponsibility, cruelty, use of torture, summary executions, and desecration of both adults' and childrens' corpses are all spelt out. Perched in his remote Scanran castle, sending squads of mercenary soldiers to scour the countryside and raid refugee-camps for children to 'process' into killing devices, Blayce is like the child-stealing monsters of northern legend, nicors such as Grendel, or the Danish–German Erlking, made famous by Goethe's great poem and reworked for the Nazi evil of the mid-twentieth century in Michel Tournier's magnificent *Le Roi des Aulnes* (1970). He is also recognisably a modern child molester and serial killer whom Kel literally cuts off at the knees, and then at the neck. Rescuing some 200 living children from his vile chambers, and exterminating his evil with sword and fire like the villagers in *Frankenstein* movies, Kel is a one-woman Society for the Protection of Children, a crusader like Esther Rantzen, who founded the charity Childline in 1980s Britain, or the parents in the US who campaigned throughout the 1990s for 'Emily's Law'. She may also be a Tortallan Lady Knight who must command a refugee camp, but the forceful truth of her campaign to hunt and kill the disgusting Blayce is a very different kind of fantasy.

Despite a general dearth of good criticism of both children's and fantasy literature, it is fascinatingly clear that their generic fusion has always been evolving, thanks largely to Sheila A. Egoff's *Worlds Within: Children's Fantasy from the Middle Ages to Today* (1988). The more recent, accelerating development of children's fantasy is partly charted in Susan Lehr's collection *Battling Dragons: Issues and Controversy in Children's Literature* (1995) and Michael Cart's monographic *From Romance to Realism: 50 Years of Growth and Change in Young Adult Literature* (1996), as well as successive editions of Egoff's popular critical anthology *Only Connect: Readings on Children's Literature* (1969, 1980, 1996), and C. W. Sullivan III's more specialised *Young Adult Science Fiction* (1999). More analytical work has also started: Roberta Trites has offered a social and psychoanalytical perspective of various books in *Disturbing the Universe: Power and Repression in Adolescent Literature* (2000), and Joanne Brown & Nancy St. Clair a more literary-critical but overlapping one focused sharply on recent work (including *Song of the Lioness*) in *Declarations of Independence: Empowered Girls in Young Adult Literature, 1990–2001* (2002). But while all help in one or another way to provide context, and Trites in making power rather than sexuality central takes a long step in his direction, none have anything much to say that bears directly on the sheer achievement in a children's novel of Blayce and his intensity of evil.

At least one children's writer had tackled serial killing before, but not without protest. There was a terrific though inchoate fuss in 1993 when *Stone Cold* by Robert Swindells won the Carnegie Medal for Children's Literature. Written when there were many young people living rough on London's streets (because rules about social benefit and living at home had been changed for 16–18-year-olds), *Stone Cold* tells of a young runaway who has to live rough through a winter, and becomes a witness to a serial killer preying on homeless folk no-one but other vagrants will miss. It's a good, honourable book, and deserved its award, but also a bleak, cheerless tale.[1] Pierce by dressing her far worse serial abuser and killer as a mage and his 'killing devices' makes a very tough issue enjoyably available to a larger and younger audience. She also pushes everything further to connect the male child-killer with warfare, for Blayce's production-line sacrifice of 'peasant' or 'enemy' children, vile in itself, is also driven by the endless need to slaughter soldiers in useless royal and political wars of national self-aggrandisement—a position made startlingly clear through the point-of-view given to Kel by her charges, the refugees driven forth and children orphaned by war. Children are thus made doubly central throughout the quartet as victims *and* avengers (Kel is only about 19 at its end): while adults either hideously prey on children or faff about doing nothing, Kel and her friends act, sometimes blindly but often and ultimately with vital success.[2] And for all the excitements of an old formula adapted to excellent purpose, reality is flesh-solid, from Kel's 'monthlies' and the sexual bigotries men fling at her, to the stench when a belly-cut with a long weapon finds bowel and the way body-parts look when the devices' knife-hands stop flailing.

It helps that there are a lot of sources and models, all miraculously balanced. Just as the disparate gods of Pierce's pantheon all rub along, so fantasy novel and school story, quest and romance, crime tale, buildungsroman, and re-enacted legend all fuse into a single, multi-faceted plot. The Erlking and Frankenstein resonances (whether or not one notices them at the time) help to balance the modern serial-killer and paedophile side of Blayce, while that modern side stops the older mythic elements

---

1   There is also Fernando Vallejo's *La Virgen de los Sicarios* (1994, filmed 2000), translated as *Our Lady of the Assassins*, about teenage killers-for-hire and pederasty in Medellin, Columbia, one of the centres of the cocaine trade, but while *about* children it is not really *for* children.

2   The same trope occurs in *Shatterglass* (2003, *The Circle Opens* 4), which features a more typical serial killer among the *prathmuni* (Hindu 'untouchable or *harijan* equivalents) of a tropical city.

from being too fusty or cute. Knightly derring-do and romance must repeatedly give pragmatic way, as in accepting the wartime necessity of a refugee-camp, and therefore a commander of it, whom the "realm needs" to do that job even if Kel sometimes feels it in her heart as a sorry and patronising let-down after all her efforts in training. In parallel, even if Kel breaks military discipline to mount her rescue mission, the mission is itself as disciplined as its outcome is remarkable, and Kel (with all her surviving friends) does not hesitate to return to the Tortallan lines and whatever music may await. Similar waves of imaginative agency and realistic patience equally tied to imperatives of public service and protection animate the diptych and *The Provost's Dog*, and might as a very clever way of both grounding and pedagogically exploiting the fantastical be followed into those sub-series. But the other reason that Pierce was able to make such an outrageous and vile character as Blayce the Gallan work so astonishingly well was a running issue that Kel as protagonist inherited from Daine in *The Immortals*, and had to fight through all over again for herself—the matter of stormwings, stranger than any serial killer could ever be and altogether the oddest things in Pierce's writing.

Stormwings were created to have depths, and Pierce is clever in how she reveals them. As much as Daine, her clever pony Cloud, and her mage-master (and eventually beloved) Numair, stormwings form the story of *The Immortals*, from early in *Wild Magic* to the end of *The Realms of the Gods*. But unlike those heroic people (and pony), unswervingly heroes for our support and empathy from their first appearances, stormwings change, and make readers change too.

The first stormwings Daine (and readers) ever see are also the first Immortals she has ever seen. The 'Human Era' in Tortallan dates means 'Human-only Era', and began when an alliance of mages (never described in detail) managed to banish all Immortals to the Divine Realms. Although for the great god Gainel, Master of Dream, this was a sorry blow, leaving human imaginations to wither and human dreams impoverished in day-residues, the gods collectively let this pass, and when Alanna was born in *c*.420 H.E. no basilisk, ogre, spidren, or stormwing had been seen for that many years, inevitably retreating into half-understood legend and incomprehensible place-names. So when, only a few months after the murder of all her family by raiders, and her own subsequent degeneration into wolf-behaviour as a means of survival, Daine finds her trail menaced by flying horrors divorced from mortal creation she can sense only visceral wrongness:

Shrieks, metallic and shrill, tore the air. Eight giant things—they looked like birds at first—chased the hawk out of the cover of the trees. Immense wings beat the air that reached the women and ponies, filling their noses with a stink so foul it made Daine retch. The ponies screamed in panic.

Daine tried to soothe them, though she wanted to scream too. These were *monsters*. No animal combined a human head and chest with a bird's legs and wings. Sunlight bounded off talons and feathers that shone like steel. She counted five males, three females: one female wore a crown of black glass.[1]

Everything counts to damn the stormwings. Beyond the shock of their grotesquerie and stench, the hawk they chase is Numair, shape-shifted, and they are serving the Emperor Mage Ozorne of Carthak, who has rediscovered the spells used to banish the Immortals, and is letting them back with careful placement to disrupt and weaken the nations he would absorb into his empire. This glass-crowned queen, Zaneh Bitterclaws, is also an especially nasty piece of work even by stormwing standards, whose lasting enmity for Daine as an archer who leaves her eye as arrow-ruined as Harold's in 1066, and in this first encounter brings down seven of her flock, is a running theme of *Wild Magic*. Bitterclaws dies at the last, in the novel's finale, but the fact of stormwings remains, and they are never absent from Daine's thoughts for long.

Stormwings can be slain by one another, by mages, by a good archer, or by large enough animals that catch them on the ground, but while their razor-edged steel feathers are beautiful and natural in form, they equally threaten death by chopping and rapid dissection (anticipating and framing in advance the whirring knife-hands of Blayce's profoundly unnatural 'killing devices'). So far, so good, however nasty, but there is another key behaviour and attribute that Daine's travelling companion and employer Onua remembers from old legends immediately after their first encounter with Bitterclaws and her flock:

"What *were* those things? Do you know?"

"I've heard tales, but—they aren't supposed to exist, not here. They're called Stormwings." [Daine] heard awe and fear in Onua's voice.

"What are Stormwings?"

"The Eaters. [...] But they're *legends*. No one's seen them for three, four centuries. They lived on battlefields, desecrating bodies—eating them, fouling them, scattering the pieces."[2]

1   Tamora Pierce, *Wild Magic* (New York: Random House, 1997), pp. 26–7 (Ch. 2).
2   Pierce, *Wild Magic*, p. 31 (Ch. 2).

Smearing the corpses of a battlefield with dung and urine, completing the dismemberments of war, and playing with the results isn't traditional fare in *any* literature—save,
very lately and limitedly, representations of serial killers like Denis Nilsen and Jef-
frey Dahmer who liked to pose body-parts or play with whole fresh corpses. That the
razor-feathered wings anticipate the killing devices' knife-hands is subtly confirmed,
for though stormwings are in no way themselves serial killers, they are bound to war
as the greatest of all serial killers, and the context within which the killing devices
are conceived.

Stormwings flocking to battlefields to fulfil their nature is reported, and seen by
Daine (but not detailed for readers) in the climactic fight of *Wild Magic*, so when in
Wolf-Speaker she again sees the steel-winged Immortals renewed loathing is understandable. They are also still working for Ozorne by helping terrorise the northern
Tortallan fief of Dunlath, so there is righteous enmity as well as personal detestation. Daine's hatred, however, meets unexpected opposition, both Numair and Cloud
forcefully reminding her that even stormwings are what they were made to be, while
growing experience of other Immortals (including spidrens, hurroks, a disoriented
dragon, that dragon's orphaned kit whom Daine adopts, and a kindly basilisk called
Tkaa) progressively gives Daine better contexts in which to consider and understand
stormwing qualities. And a necessary prompt comes, tellingly, from a still *younger*
girl, the ten-year-old, orphaned Maura of Dunlath, who flees her castle-home because she knows her ruling half-sister Yolane and brother-in-law Belden are commit-
ting high treason. Finding her with stormwings circling close above, Daine assumes
Maura is in danger and rides in fast only to have Maura block her shot:

> Stormwings were landing on the ground in front of them. Three moved out of
> Daine's sight. Turning, she saw them settle on the road behind her, cutting off any
> escape. Coldly she levelled her weapon at the nearest Stormwing, a male who
> wore a collection of bones braided into his long blond hair.
>
> He stared back at her, contempt in his eyes, then looked back at the younger girl.
> "Tell her we mean you no harm, Lady Maura."
>
> "You're on speaking terms with *them?*" Daine asked.
>
> Maura shrugged. "They visit Yolane and Belden a lot. He is Lord Rikash."[1]

An awkward three-way conversation follows:

> "Let us talk of this away from prying ears," Rikash said, an eye on Daine.

1   Tamora Pierce, *Wolf-Speaker* (London: Scolastic, 1999), pp. 160–1 (Ch. 6).

"We can speak of it now. Daine can't tell anyone. She's stuck here, too."

"Quiet!" ordered the Stormwing. "You're a *child*. You do not understand what is taking place, and you must not speak of matters you cannot comprehend."

Her sense of humour overpowering her hatred of Stormwings. Obviously he liked Maura, or he would have bullied rather than debated with her. She also could see debate was useless. Maura had the bit between her teeth, and would not obey orders. "Go on," she urged the fuming immortal. "Shut her up. I never thought to see you stinkers baulked by anyone, let alone a ten-year-old."

Rikash turned red under his dirt, and a few of his own flock cackled. "It is hard for us to bear young," he said, a hint of gritted teeth in his voice. "That being the case, we value others' young, particularly when they are neglected. Affection has led me to indulge Lady Maura more than is wise."[1]

This is a virtue neither Daine nor younger readers in this world where reading is so often a refuge can ignore, and childcare is the stormwings' most important motif after their battlefield behaviours. Spidrens, by contrast, like the young of other species, whether children or kittens, only for their tender taste, and when spidren nests are exterminated with 'blazebalm', Tortall's very own napalm, the spidren young must also be killed (events Kel has to face in *First Test*). Implicitly, therefore, spidrens bear multiple young with ease, and part of their terror (as with the spiders in Tolkien's Mirkwood) is their ability to multiply and infest. Contrariwise, while details are never given, the stormwing birthing process is revealed (here and elsewhere) as exceptionally hard; few great steel eggs are laid, still fewer hatch, and stormwing numbers, despite their immortality, have declined (not least thanks to Daine's bow). Their care for others' young, first voiced here by Rikash, is shown in the rest of *The Immortals*, runs intermittently through *Protector of the Small*, peaking in the last volume, and flowers again in *Trickster's Queen*, where stormwings rescue some street-children caught in a spreading riot. Bitterclaws was plainly evil in her arrant hostility, but if Rikash stinks from doing the things stormwings do, he is nevertheless shown to be a cultured thinker richly capable of kindness, as well as a soldier under orders. Though neither trusts the other an inch, when he and Daine face off towards the end of *Wolf-Speaker* (just as she did with Bitterclaws to end *Wild Magic*), neither's heart is in violence and a long stand-off begins.

A second pivot for Daine's evolving attitudes is provided in *The Emperor Mage*. Travelling to Carthak Daine again meets Rikash, and his flock-monarch, King Jok-

---

1   Pierce, *Wolf-Speaker*, pp. 163–4 (Ch. 6)

hun Foulreek—but she also finds the previous monarchs of this flock, Barzha Razorwing and her consort Hebakh, in Ozorne's private menagerie of Immortals. Rikash and other stormwings had thought her killed by Foulreek in combat, when in fact he had plotted with Ozorne to betray Razorwing and Hebakh to captivity as the price of a stormwing alliance. These captive royals are impressive creatures, as dignified in appalling circumstance as Bitterclaws was a screeching menace when free, and they have things to say that strike home as only home truths can. The plot winds to a conclusion in which Ozorne escapes Daine only by *becoming* a stormwing (the mechanics don't matter here, but are well accounted for), at which point his human spells fail and Barzha is free. As Rikash sets off in pursuit of her and the fleeing Ozorne, he is able to give Daine some very good news about Numair, whom she had believed dead, and the balance of her feelings shifts again in a slowly mellowing acceptance of all living things for what they are.

Her journey of virtue is completed in *The Realms of the Gods*—the Divine Realm being also a place of Immortals. Trapped there awhile, Daine finds that Rikash, whose poetic surname is Moonsword, has made himself known to her divine parents, Weiryn and Sarra, as well as her mentor the Badger. Finding herself dining with one great, two minor, and three animal gods, as well as the mage she is beginning to discover she loves and a stormwing, Daine passes far beyond the feelings she felt as she first saw Bitterclaws. The rest of the novel plays out the mutual debts between Daine and Razorwing, who with Rikash and her flock help Daine's and Numair's quest by carrying them across the 'Sea of Sand', a purgatorial place the gods sometimes use to cleanse heroes by taking them there until their "mortal impurities have been seared away".[1] And in her carrying sling, as the night-hours of the flight pass, Daine has another chance to talk to Rikash, letting the last key datum fall into place:

> "I heard somewhere that immortals are born in dreams. or our dreams give them shape—something like that. Now, I can see folk dreaming winged horses and unicorns. Even dreaming that a winged horse or unicorn would go bad makes sense. Haven't we all thought something's a joy, only to find that it's evil inside. But—forgive my saying it; no offense intended—how could *anyone* dream a stormwing?"
>
> His smile was cruel. "Ages ago, a traveler in the mortal realms went from place to place and found only the leavings of war—the starving, the abandoned, the dead. It was the work of armies, fighting over ground they soon lost again. That traveler sickened of waste—of death. She wished for a creature that was so

---

1   Pierce, *The Realms of the Gods*, p. 150 (Ch. 6).

repulsive, living on war's aftermath, that even *humans* would think twice before battle. That creature would defile what mortal killers left, so that humans couldn't lie about how glorious a soldier's death is. *She* dreamed the first Stormwing."[1]

It shouldn't take the insistent feminine pronoun Rikash applies to the traveller for readers to recognise an authorial wellspring here, for who but Pierce herself dreamed stormwings up? Given her childhood immersion in *The Lord of the Rings* one source (beyond the Harpie armature) may lie in Wormtongue's denunciation of "Gandalf Stormcrow" as one of the "pickers of bones, meddlers in other men's sorrows, carrion-fowl that grow fat on war".[2] But there are more than fantasy connections, and that "work of armies, fighting over ground they soon lost again" resonates with the European Thirty Years' War of 1618–48 that provided the setting for Bertold Brecht's great play *Mutter Courage und ihre Kinder* (1939/41), a staple of anti-war activism in which Mother Courage herself, battening commercially on war while her children die to keep it going, desperately needs the lesson stormwings teach.

Brecht is a very interesting connection in himself, a great pedagogue as well as a great theatre-maker whom Pierce might have discovered as early as her San Francisco years in childhood, but the stormwings' moral is also and directly the message of Wilfred Owen's very widely anthologised and taught World War One poem of trench experience, '*Dulce et Decorum Est*'—perhaps the greatest anti-war anthem of the twentieth century. Walking behind a dying man after a chlorine-gas attack, unable to look away or block his ears, Owen called modern warfare and perennial recruitment as he saw them, and as they were:

> If in some smothering dreams you too could pace
> Behind the wagon that we flung him in,
> And watch the white eyes writhing in his face,
> His hanging face, like a devil's sick of sin ;
> If you could hear, at every jolt, the blood
> Come gargling from the froth-corrupted lungs,
> Obscene as cancer, bitter as the cud
> Of vile, incurable sores on innocent tongues,—
> My friend, you would not tell with such high zest
> To children ardent for some desperate glory,

---

1   Pierce, *The Realms of the Gods*, p. 182 (Ch. 7).
2   Tolkien, *The Lord of the Rings*, II.117 (*The Two Towers*, Bk 1, Ch. 6).

> The old Lie: Dulce et decorum est
> Pro patria mori.[1]

The "old Lie" is from the *Odes* of the Roman poet Horace: 'it's sweet and proper to die for your fatherland' (III.ii.13). Bishops, heroes, politicians, and family have told it down the ages, one way and another, to make a loss of husband or son seem less bitter. Then again, tell that, as they say, to the marines, and you wouldn't like the answer. And what the connection reveals is that stormwings on the battlefield have much the same effect as machine-guns, barbed-wire, tanks, and poison-gas—or magical killing devices—in declaring 'honourable' combat long dead.

Through stormwings' moral purpose Pierce built the foundation necessary to conclude her quartet with tragedy as well as romantic resolution, and did so with brisk power. Ozorne as stormwing having proved as tricky as Ozorne the Emperor Mage, he has forged a grand alliance of enemies against Tortall, and a secret alliance with Uusoae, Queen of Chaos. He has also suborned a majority of stormwings to his side, using them (deeply unnaturally for stormwings) as merely one more kind of killer. Only Razorwing, Rikash and 60-odd others remain loyal to stormwings' moral purpose—preventing war, not waging it—and they must in the end fight their own more mercenary kind over that purpose, a stormwing civil war in which, inevitably, yet more perish. As the tensions rise before the final battle, Daine finds an unexpected companionship:

> Leaning on the rail, [Daine] squinted at the shore. She wanted to get *moving*.
> "Fretting about your stork-man?" Rikash inquired, lighting on the rail beside her. He dug steel talons into the wood. "He'll be fine. Mages always are."
> "I'd feel better if I could be there to look after him."
> "Then stay."
> "I can't," Daine replied, shaking her head. "I don't want Kitten there without me when the big noise starts. In the Dragonlands, I saw—she's just a baby still. She ought to be in a safe place. Since she isn't, I need to be with her, as much as I can."
> "You're breaking my heart," drawled the immortal.
> "Got a bit of sand in your crop?" she demanded irritably. "A swallow or two of oil should wash it right out the end that does your thinking for you."
> To her surprise he laughed. Around them, she saw gold-skinned Yamanis and

1 *The Collected Poems of Wilfred Owen* (ed. C. Day Lewis, London: Chatto & Windus, 1963), p. 55. See also: http://www.bl.uk/onlinegallery/themes/englishlit/wildredowen.html

Tortallans make the Sign against evil. "I deserved that. Don't mind me."[1]

This time 'Kitten', the dragonet in Daine's care, is the orphaned youngster in the case, as Maura of Dunlath was in *Wolf-Speaker*, but everything else has changed completely. The camaraderie of Daine and Rikash now scares others, for whom stormwings were never as purely evil as they once seemed to Daine, but who don't share jokes with them either, let alone elicit what amounts to an apology.

The inevitable last movement, of course, as Pierce is no Hollywood gooey-ender, is that Rikash dies in the battle, assailing a Chaos-dweller loosed by Ozorne that threatens Raoul of Goldenlake and takes three Immortals and the Badger god to kill:

> *"Rikash—no!"* someone cried in a voice that cracked as it rose. *"No! No! NOOOOO!"* It was her voice. If she screamed loud enough, long enough, he would live. She hadn't realized that he meant something to her. She hadn't known he was her friend.[2]

The phrasing echoes almost the first lesson the Badger taught Daine way back in *Wild Magic*—*"If you* look *hard and long, you can find us. If you* listen *hard and long, you can hear any of us, call any of us, that you want."*[3]—and the wheel has come full circle. The mature Daine as confident Wildmage can do almost anything, looking, listening, and becoming, but she cannot recall Rikash from the dead, and she mourns him, as Razorwing and Hebakh do. Daine can and does intercede with the gods on the surviving stormwings' behalf, and readers learn at the very end of *Trickster's Queen* that her second child by Numair, after daughter Sarralyn, is "baby Rikash".[4] But the stormwing himself is gone to the Peaceful Realm, and what baby Rikash commemorates is not so much an Immortal's valiant death as the lesson he taught in life about care of and for the young, and the valiant life of the growing woman who learned it.

Then again, just how complex an achievement Lord Rikash Moonsword is, as stormwing and tragic casualty of war, is suggested by the fact that his apotheosis at once embodies full defence of stormwings' purpose (he is backing his rightful

---

1   Pierce, *The Realms of the Gods*, pp. 216–17 (Ch. 9).
2   Pierce, *The Realms of the Gods*, p. 242 (Ch. 9).
3   Pierce, *Wild Magic*, p. 24 (Ch. 2).
4   Tamora Pierce, *Trickster's Queen* (New York: Random House, 2004), p. 242.

flock-monarch and Tortall's King Jonathan as a ruler who does not start wars) and yet undoes it by restoring heroic death to the battlefield. The tutelary classical poet may not quite be Horace, but Juvenal's *Quis custodiet ipsos custodes?*, 'who watches the watchmen?', is pertinent enough, for who will defile this stormwing body and dishonour its sacrifice? Not all fighting, however ultimately vain and needless, can be avoided, and sacrifice will be revered by those it saves and those who mourn. The whole conundrum also spills forward into *Protector of the Small*, and in one sense Blayce the Gallan and his vile killing devices were necessary in the later quartet *because* of the revelations in *The Immortals* about stormwings' moral purpose. If Kel as much as the younger Daine starts with a visceral loathing of the flying Immortals, and believes that the stormwings' denial of chivalric violence goes against her own deepest calling and purpose, she too must learn tolerance; and where Daine has her wide experience of other Immortals and friendship with Rikash to teach her, Kel has the counter-example of Blayce and his devices to make her rethink her standards of condemnation. Pierce, moreover, makes very good use of the powerful accumulation of paradox created by including such creations as stormwings in a quartet whose heroine longs and trains fiercely to be a chivalric knight, and the considerable discipline of imagination required pays off handsomely as Kel must come to terms with stormwing truths more graphically than the pitch of *The Immortals* to slightly younger readers allowed.

That said, and remembering Pierce's awareness of "Y[oung] A[dult]s raiding the adult shelves once they deplete their part of the store or library, and adults slipping into the youth sections",[1] one interesting sign of her quality as a writer is how uncertain her 'reading age' has become. Prompted by publishers' cover-art, booksellers tend to put *Song of the Lioness* and *The Immortals* in the 9–12 or 12–15 brackets, with *Protector of the Small*, the diptych, and *Terrier* in 12–15 or 15+. The sense of a younger target-group for *The Immortals* and a somewhat older one for *Protector of the Small* is not silly, and partly reflects the ways in which Daine's adventures are as fantastical as Daine herself, with an antlered-god father and a murdered mother who becomes a goddess, while Kel's are more graphically rooted in experiences far closer to the worst of the nightly news bulletins, if with infinitely superior and braver political analysis. But both quartets, being about growing-up and superbly constructed, lead, push, and pull their younger readers over such boundaries without ever sacrificing adult interest, and the plain truth is that all of Pierce's books are novels from which no-one who is or wants to be grown-up should be debarred. If she takes her

1   See p. 200, n.2 above.

readers, young or old, deep into very serious territory indeed, she does so with great skill, great boldness, and considerable finesse, and for her stinking or slicing steel nightmares as well as her wondrous and valiant women, readers and their parents can give heartfelt thanks.

Zoology aside, one reason *The Immortals* brought me up so short and left me so thoughtful, after Rikash Moonsword had done his worst, was an earlier scene in *The Realms of the Gods* that even as I was first reading it I knew would challenge critical description and scholarly accounting. Once upon a time I did a fair amount of work on late-mediaeval and Renaissance allegory, a subject of serious complexity, that I have always been glad to have done but find myself sighing about internally when it becomes necessary, once again, to try to explain to a student certain Platonic first principles.[1] Fortunately, all that matters here is a simple and very old distinction, between *read* and *written* allegory, that Pierce managed to blow all to smash in half-a-dozen pages.

For *read* allegory the obvious example is parables. A sower goes out to sow with mixed results, which happens all the time—but the reader knows better, and by the sower understands the preacher, by the seed the Word, and by the stony ground and thorns whatever they think most inimical to evangelical success. This mode *of reading* (which is *not* necessary to write a story about partial crop failure) is primarily religious and at least as old as the biblical Song of Songs (or Song of Solomon), whose seductive flagons and sensual apples have always been highly embarrassing to austerely-minded and repressed Christians. Consequently it is thought best to explain them as an allegory of Christ's marriage to his church having nothing whatever to do with sex, or even flagons and apples.

Written allegory, however, is quite another kettle of fish, and begins only with the *Psychomachia* by the Hispanic Roman Prudentius, written in the fourth century CE. The title, Prudentius's coinage from Greek, literally means 'soul-fight' or 'mind-fight', and is traditionally translated as 'The Battle for Mansoul'. In this improbable but hugely influential tale the personified Vices and Virtues fight for an Everyman's soul—more or less 'Enter left, Lust. Enter right, Chastity. They fight', and so on. In consequence any number of entirely horrid philosophical and logical complications happen instantaneously, with more in train as written allegory lives up to its rule-of-thumb definition as 'narrative metaphor'. Just how horrid these complications are

---

1   Specifically the 'Third Man' rule, which says that universals cannot be self-instantiating—i.e. the one thing that, say, 'redness' cannot be is red.

is most economically suggested by Faithful's pained confession, in Bunyan's *The Pilgrim's Progress*, that:

> I met with Shame, but of all the men that I met with on my pilgrimage, he, I think, bears the wrong name [...] he objected against religion itself; he said it was a pitiful, low, sneaking business [...] Yea, he put me so to it, that my blood came up in my face, even this Shame fetched it up[1]

Wrongly-named indeed, for if Shame is the thing itself, why is Faithful the one to blush? There is an explanation at least as complicated as the problem that begins with Plato's 'third man rule', but fortunately its details don't matter (you breathe again). What does is simply that having caused pretty much all written allegory grief but not despair from its inception in Prudentius on, the problem became overwhelming sometime between Spenser's *The Faerie Queene* (1590, 1596) and Bunyan's *The Pilgrim's Progress* (1678, 1682), with the result (so say the histories) that written allegory thereafter more-or-less died.

Though critics and many authors are reluctant to admit it, most serious readers know, if you push them a little, that written allegory is actually still more-or-less alive, albeit not always very well. It tweaks most strongly in names, as it should, and cannot easily be dismissed either when insistent (as with, say, Sepulchrave Groan in Mervyn Peake's *Titus Groan* and *Gormenghast*) or when insinuating (as with Humbert Humbert in Vladimir Nabokov's *Lolita*, a "double rumble" its author especially admired as "very nasty, very suggestive", "hateful" and "kingly"[2]). But in SF and fantasy written allegory isn't a nominal tweak of any kind, and readily becomes a truly hazardous beast: whole planets and ecosystems can be made to personify complex ideas, as they do to enormous profit in Sherri S. Tepper's strange novel *Grass*, but once you admit a didactic correspondence with metaphysics into such a creation awkwardness begins to compound alarmingly. Say, for example, that Rowling's spectacularly unpleasant Lord Voldemort *is* ... what, exactly? Pure Evil? Racism Incarnate? Lucifer in modern togs? Whichever, what then of his boyhood as Tom Marvolo Riddle, or his school rivalry with the hairy Hagrid (who *is* ...?)—and so on, right out of the window.

Pierce, however, rushes right in where scared angels scatter. In *The Realms of*

---

1   John Bunyan, *The Pilgrim's Progress from This World, to That which Is to come: Delivered under the Similitude of a Dream Wherein is Discovered, The manner of his setting out, His Dangerous Journey; And safe Arrival at the Desired Countrey* (1678; ed. Roger Shattuck, Harmondsworth: Penguin, 1965), pp. 107–08.

2   Vladimir Nabokov, *Strong Opinions* (London: Weidenfeld and Nicholson, 1974), p, 26. The interview (with Alvin Toffler) originally appeared in *Playboy* in January 1964.

the Gods, Daine and Numair have been scooped by Daine's parents into the Divine Realms. There the great god Gainel, Master of Dream, with whom she once had supper, comes to her in a sequence of sleeping visions, first as Rattail, a wolf she once knew and loved, then as himself, and shows her true but dream-metaphoric images of the gods fighting ceaselessly against the wiles of Uusoae, and (He fears) losing. On a certain night, as they travel the Divine Realms, the dream-space Gainel creates for Daine expands to include Numair, physically with Daine in the Divine Realms but also asleep and dreaming. The two can speak to and hear one another, as well as Gainel, and are shown a chess-board on which black pieces representing Uusoae and the forces allied to Chaos, including 'real' characters like Ozorne and representative figures (a spidren, a winged ape), fight a white set consisting of King Jonathan, Queen Thayet, others Daine and Numair know, and two rooks that look like and plainly represent themselves. At Gainel's commands they watch themselves and their friends lose and die, then fight again and win, delivering the strategy they follow in the remainder of the Immortals' War that Ozorne has unleashed.

In reading nothing is difficult for a moment, but let critics beware! There are at least three removes involved, dream-simulacra of Daine and Numair seeing chess-pieces emblematising themselves while mentally in a divine space and physically a divine place. Moreover, in that divine place food explodes in mortal mouths because (as Queenclaw, goddess of house cats has explained when Daine eats less breakfast than her mother thinks right) "In the Divine Realms, you eat the essence of things, not the shadow".[1] 'Essence' tells us beyond doubt that Father Plato (involved in all written allegory) is indeed about, and when (just before the chess-game dream-vision strategic conference) the animal gods Badger and Broad Foot (who has an Australian accent appropriate to a duck-billed platypus, divine or otherwise) force a vision (nevermind how) of stormwing Ozorne creating his darkings (nevermind what) in a shadowy cave, alarm-bells start ringing loud. Plato's famous cave is well-connected to his implicit rules about written allegory, and setting mad, magical, and metamorphosed ex-emperors loose in it is no kind of child's play—but because this *is* child's play the problems are themselves baffled. In an adult SF novel the nature of the stakes demanded from readers would almost certainly ensure either complete narrative disaster or a triumph in which coming to terms with the allegorical plays a central part (which is what Tepper pulled off in *Grass*); they could *not* simply be ignored. But in *The Immortals*, as so often in Pierce, it all slides right along, and what ought to trouble her and her readers—'ought' because full-blown allegory of any kind commonly

---

1   Pierce, *The Realms of the Gods*, p. 39 (Ch. 2).

induces in the novel something very like autoimmune rejection and is as commonly fatal—simply doesn't.

It isn't that children's writing is somehow exempt. The best children's books are so precisely because they most fully transcend whatever didacticism and education they contain; try selling children one that's heavy-handed, let alone fully allegorical, and they'll give it (in my experience) *very* short shrift. *The Pilgrim's Progress*, last of its line, alone among overt written allegories survived with mass popularity into the twentieth century, but has declined greatly in readership since—perhaps, Pierce makes me wonder, because she and other fantasy writers, especially those working for older children, have taken up a surprising amount of the slack. It's both fun and a perfectly serious question for philosophers to wonder what Plato would have made of stormwings, ethically and ontologically, and the conclusion might well be that (despite everything) they are (like Pierce's culture of origin) too Christian for him to have understood. *Quelle blague!*

What is clear is that the coherence, density, and richness of Pierce's strangely realistic and highly ethical fantasy plotting makes for novels to which many lights and considerations can be brought, and all will gain a response. Less celebrated than Rowling, she deserves a wide audience of all ages, delivering at a faster pace novels just as inventive and moral, and in some ways easier to read. Perhaps it says something about me that the young protagonists who have most gripped my allegiance, from Anne McCaffrey's would-be harper Menolly to Pierce's would-be guardswoman Beka Cooper, have been girls; or perhaps it says something about the valiant women who created them.

Bibliography

Works by the primary subject/s of each essay come first, followed by secondary and incidental sources; and series come before non-series books. Series mentioned in maintext are given complete, but with non-series novels only those mentioned or a representative selection. Chaucer, Shakespeare, and the King James Bible are omitted from Other Sources and Books Mentioned .

1. Of Serial Readers

C. S. Forester (1899-1966)
The Happy Return (London: Michael Joseph, 1937)
A Ship of the Line (London: Michael Joseph, 1938)
Flying Colours (London: Michael Joseph, 1939)
The Commodore (London: Michael Joseph, 1945; as *Commodore Hornblower*, with an additional chapter, New York: Bantam, 1965)
Lord Hornblower (London: Michael Joseph, 1948)
Mr Midshipman Hornblower(London: Michael Joseph, 1950)
Lieutenant Hornblower (London: Michael Joseph, 1952)
Hornblower and the 'Atropos' (London: Michael Joseph, 1953)
Hornblower in the West Indies (London: Michael Joseph, 1958)
Hornblower and the Hotspur (London: Michael Joseph, 1962)
The Hornblower Companion (London: Michael Joseph, 1964)
Hornblower and the Crisis (London: Michael Joseph, 1967)

▣ http://www.csforester.org/

Reginald Hill (b. 1936)
A Clubbable Woman (London: Collins, 1970)
An Advancement of Learning (London: Collins, 1971)
Ruling Passion (London: Collins, 1973)
An April Shroud (London: Collins, 1975)
A Pinch of Snuff (London: Collins1978)
Pascoe's Ghost and Other Brief Chronicles of Crime (London: Collins, 1979)

A Killing Kindness (London: Collins, 1980)

Deadheads (London: Collins, 1983)

Exit Lines (London: Collins, 1984)

Child's Play: a tragi-comedy in three acts of violence with a prologue and an epilogue (London: Collins, & New York: Macmillan, 1987)

Under World (London: Collins, & New York: Scribner, 1988)

Bones and Silence (London: Collins, & New York: Delacorte Press, 1990)   CWA Gold Dagger, 1990.

One Small Step (London: Collins, 1990)

Recalled to Life (London: Collins, & New York: Delacorte Press, 1992).

Asking for the Moon (London: HarperCollins, 1994)   Collects 'Pascoe's Ghost' (1979), 'Dalziel's Ghost' (1979), 'One Small Step' (1990), & 'The Last National Serviceman' (1994).

Pictures of Perfection: A Dalziel and Pascoe novel in five volumes (London: HarperCollins, & New York: Delacorte Press, 1994)

The Wood Beyond (London: HarperCollins, & New York: Delacorte Press, 1996).

On Beulah Height (London: HarperCollins, & New York: Bantam, 1998)   Barry Award, Best Novel, 1999.

Arms and the Women: an Elliad (London: HarperCollins, & New York: Delacorte, 2000)

Dialogues of the Dead: or Paronomania! ~~an aged worm for wept royals a warm doge for top lawyers~~ *a word game for two players* (London: HarperCollins, 2001; New York: Delacorte, 2002)

Death's Jest-Book (London: HarperCollins, 2002; as *Death's Jest Book*, New York: HarperCollins, 2003)

Good Morning, Midnight (London & New York: HarperCollins, 2004)

The Death of Dalziel (London & New York: HarperCollins, 2007)

'Where the Snow Lay Dinted', in Martin Edwards, ed., *Northern Blood 2: A Second Collection of Northern Crime Writing* (Newcastle upon Tyne: Flambard, 1995), pp. 79–93   An earlier version appeared as 'In the Steps of the King', in the Mail on Sunday (London), 26/12/1993.

'A Candle for Christmas', in *Ellery Queen's Mystery Magazine* (January 2000), pp. 4–29   Macavity Award, Best Short Story, 2001.

'A Gift for Father Christmas', in three parts in the *Daily Express* (London), 24/12/2002, Features p. 33; 26/12/2002, Features p. 37; 27/12/2002, News p. 29

'Brass Monkey', in *Ellery Queen Mystery Magazine* (January 2003), pp. 38–54

'The Game of Dog', in Martin Edwards, ed., *Mysterious Pleasures: A Celebration of the Crime Writers' Association's 50th Anniversary* (London: Little, Brown, 2003), pp. 181–96

'Fool of Myself', in Simon Brett, ed., *The Detection Collection* (London: Orion, 2005), pp. 169–83   Only Dalziel appears; the book celebrates 75 years of the Detection Club.

No Man's Land (London: Collins, & New York: St Martin's Press, 1985)

There Are No Ghosts in the Soviet Union and Other Stories (London: Collins, 1987; as *There Are No Ghosts in the Soviet Union: A Novella and Five Stories*, New York: Avon Books, 1989)

The Stranger House (London & New York: HarperCollins, 2005)

Thomas Harris (b. 1940)

Red Dragon (New York: Putnam, 1981)

The Silence of the Lambs (New York: St Martin's Press, 1988)   Anthony and Bram Stoker Awards, Best Novel, 1989.

Hannibal (New York: Delacorte, 1999)

Hannibal Rising (New York: Delacorte, 2006)

http://www.randomhouse.com/features/thomasharris/

'Bill James' (b. 1929)

You'd Better Believe It (London: Constable, 1985)

The Lolita Man (London: Constable, 1986)

Halo Parade (London: Constable, 1987)

Protection (London: Constable, 1988)

Come Clean (London: Constable, 1989)

Take (London: Macmillan, 1990)

Astride a Grave (London: Macmillan, 1991)

Club (London: Macmillan, 1991)

Gospel (London: Macmillan, 1992)

Roses, Roses (London: Macmillan, 1993)

In Good Hands (London: Macmillan, 1994)

The Detective is Dead (London: Macmillan, 1995)

Top Banana (London: Macmillan, 1996)

Panicking Ralph (London: Macmillan, 1997)

Lovely Mover (London: Macmillan, 1998)

Eton Crop (London: Macmillan, 1999)

Kill Me (London: Macmillan, 2000)
Pay Days (London: Constable, 2001)
Naked at the Window (London: Constable, 2002)
The Girl with the Long Back (London: Constable, 2003)
Easy Streets (London: Constable, 2004)
Wolves of Memory (London: Constable, 2005)
Girls (London: Constable, 2006)

Patrick O'Brian (1914–2000)
Master and Commander (Philadelphia: Lippincott, 1969; London: Collins, 1970)
Post Captain (Philadelphia: Lippincott, & London: Collins, 1972)
H.M.S. Surprise (Philadelphia: Lippincott, & London: Collins, 1973)
The Mauritius Command (London: Collins, 1977; New York: Stein & Day, 1978)
Desolation Island (London: Collins, 1978; New York: Stein & Day, 1979)
The Fortune of War (London: Collins, 1979; New York: Norton, 1991)
The Surgeon's Mate (London: Collins, 1980; New York: Norton, 1992)
The Ionian Mission (London: Collins, 1981; New York: Norton, 1992)
Treason's Harbour (London: Collins, 1983; New York: Norton, 1992)
The Far Side of the World (London: Collins, 1984; New York: Norton, 1992)
The Reverse of the Medal (London: Collins, 1986; New York: Norton, 1992)
The Letter of Marque (London: Collins, 1988; New York: Norton, 1991)
The Thirteen-Gun Salute (London: Collins, 1989; New York: Norton, 1991)
The Nutmeg of Consolation (London: Collins, & New York: Norton, 1991)
Clarissa Oakes (London: HarperCollins, 1992; as *The Truelove*, New York: Norton, 1992)
The Wine-Dark Sea (London: HarperCollins & New York: Norton, 1993)
The Commodore (London: HarperCollins, 1994; New York: Norton, 1995)
The Yellow Admiral (New York: Norton, 1996; London: HarperCollins, 1997)
The Hundred Days (London: HarperCollins & New York: Norton, 1998)
Blue at the Mizzen (London: HarperCollins, & New York: Norton, 1999)
The Final Unfinished Voyage of Jack Aubrey (London: HarperCollins, 2004; with the additional title *21*, New York: Norton, 2004)

▣ http://www2.wwnorton.com/pob/pobhome.htm

Anthony Powell (1905–2000)

A Question of Upbringing (London: Heinemann, 1951)
A Buyer's Market (London: Heinemann, 1952)
The Acceptance World (London: Heinemann, 1955)
At Lady Molly's (London: Heinemann, 1957)
Casanova's Chinese Restaurant (London: Heinemann, 1960)
The Kindly Ones (London: Heinemann, 1962)
The Valley of Bones (London: Heinemann, 1964)
The Soldier's Art (London: Heinemann, 1966)
The Military Philosophers (London: Heinemann, 1968)
Books Do Furnish a Room (London: Heinemann, 1971)
Temporary Kings (London: Heinemann, 1973)
Hearing Secret Harmonies (London: Heinemann, 1975)

http://www.anthonypowell.org.uk/indexnf.htm

J. K. Rowling (b. 1965)

Harry Potter and the Philosopher's Stone (London: Bloomsbury, 1997)   Nestlé Smarties Gold Award, 9–11 category, 1997.
Harry Potter and the Chamber of Secrets (London: Bloomsbury, 1998)   Nestlé Smarties Gold Award, 9–11 category, 1998.
Harry Potter and the Prisoner of Azkaban (London: Bloomsbury, 1999)   Nestlé Smarties Gold Award, 9–11 category, & Whitbread Children's Book of the Year, 1999.
Harry Potter and the Goblet of Fire (London: Bloomsbury, 2000)   Blue Peter Book Award, 2000; Hugo Award, Best Novel 2001.
Harry Potter and the Order of the Phoenix (London: Bloomsbury, 2003)
Harry Potter and the Half-Blood Prince (London: Bloomsbury, 2005)
Harry Potter and the Deathly Hallows (London: Bloomsbury, 2007)

http://www.jkrowling.com/

Other sources and books mentioned

Airth, Rennie, *River of Darkness* (London: Macmillan, 1999)
Auden, W. H., 'The Guilty Vicarage', in *The Dyer's Hand and other essays* (London: Faber & Faber, 1963)
Burn, Gordon, '*...somebody's husband, somebody's son.*': *The Story of Peter Sutcliffe* (London: Pan, 1984)

Granger, John, ed., *Who Killed Albus Dumbledore: What* Really *Happened in Harry Potter and the Half-Blood Prince? Six expert Harry Potter detectives examine the evidence* (Wayne, PA: Zossima Press, 2006)

Hammett, Dashiell, *Red Harvest* (New York: Knopf, 1929)

Hawkins, Harriet, 'Thank you, Dr Lecter', in *The Modern Review* (Autumn 1991): 30–1

James, P. D., *Innocent Blood* (London: Faber & Faber, 1981)

— *A Taste for Death* (London: Faber & Faber, 1986)   Macavity Award, Best Novel, 1987.

Kellerman, Faye, *Straight into Darkness* (New York & Boston: Warner, 2005)

Kohout, Pavel, *Hvězdná hodina vrahů* (Prague: Mladá Fronta, 1995; as *The Widow Killer*, trans. Neil Bermel, New York: St Martin's Press, 1998)

Knox, Father Ronald, 'Introduction' in Ronald Knox & H. Harrington, eds, *Best Detective Stories of the Year 1928* (London: Faber & Faber, 1929)

Lennard, John, 'Reginald Hill', in Jay Parini, ed., *British Writers Supplement IX*, (New York & London: Charles Scribner's Sons, 2004), pp. 109–26

Moore, Alan, & Campbell, Eddie, *From Hell, being a melodrama in sixteen parts* (Paddington, Australia: Eddie Campbell Comics, 1999)

Morrison, Blake, *The Ballad of the Yorkshire Ripper and other poems* (London: Chatto, 1987)

Peace, David, *Nineteen Seventy Four* (London: Serpent's Tail, 1999)

— *Nineteen Seventy Seven* (London: Serpent's Tail, 2000)

— *Nineteen Eighty* (London: Serpent's Tail, 2001)

— *Nineteen Eighty Three* (London: Serpent's Tail, 2002).

Pullman, Philip, *The Amber Spyglass* (London: Scholastic, 2000)

Robinson, Peter, *Aftermath* (New York: Morrow, 2001)

Ruskin, John, *"Unto this last": Four Essays on the First Principles of Political Economy* (London: Smith, Elder, 1862)

Symons, Julian, *Bloody Murder: From the Detective Story to the Crime Novel: A History* (London: Faber & Faber, 1972; as *Mortal Consequences*, New York: Harper, 1972; with revisions, Harmondsworth: Penguin, 1974; 4th ed., London: Pan, 1994)

Todd, Richard, *Consuming Fictions: The Booker Prize and Fiction in Britain Today* (London: Bloomsbury, 1996)

Tucker, James, *The Novels of Anthony Powell* (London: Macmillan, 2006; New York: Columbia University Press, 1976)

Watson, Colin, *Snobbery with Violence: English Crime Stories and Their Audience* (London: Eyre & Spottiswoode, 1971)

Whited, Lana A., ed., *The Ivory Tower and Harry Potter: Perspectives on a Literary Phenomenon* (Columbia: University of Missouri Press, 2002; with a new epilogue, 2004)

2. Of Purgatory and Yorkshire

Dorothy L. Sayers (1893–1957)

Whose Body? (London: Gollancz, 1923).

Clouds of Witness (London: Gollancz, 1926)

Unnatural Death (London: Gollancz, 1927)

Lord Peter Views the Body (London: Gollancz, 1928)

The Unpleasantness at the Bellona Club (London: Gollancz, 1928)

Strong Poison (London: Gollancz, 1930)

Five Red Herrings (London: Gollancz, 1931)

Have His Carcase (London: Gollancz, 1932)

Hangman's Holiday (London: Gollancz, 1933)

Murder Must Advertise (London: Gollancz, 1933)

The Nine Tailors (London: Gollancz, 1934)

Gaudy Night (London: Gollancz, 1935)

Busman's Honeymoon: A Love Story with Detective Interruptions (London: Gollancz, 1937)

In the Teeth of the Evidence (London: Gollancz, 1939)

Lord Peter: The Complete Lord Peter Wimsey Stories (New York: Harper & Row, 1972)

'The Omnibus of Crime', in Dorothy L. Sayers, ed., *Great Short Stories of Detection, Mystery & Horror* (London: Victor Gollancz, 1928)

'Emile Gaboriau 1835–1873: The Detective Novelist's Dilemma', in *The Times Literary Supplement*, 2 November 1935.

The Man Born to be King: a play-cycle on the life of our Lord and Saviour Jesus Christ, Written for Broadcasting (London: Gollancz, 1943)

Unpopular Opinions (London: Gollancz, 1946)

Are Women Human? Astute and Witty Essays on the Role of Women in Society (Grand Rapids, MI: Eerdmans, 1971)

Sayers on Holmes: Essays and Fiction on Sherlock Holmes (introduction by Alzina Stone Dale, Altadena, CA: Mythopoeic Press, 2001)

Les Origines du Roman Policier: A Wartime Wireless Talk to the French: The Original French Text with an English Translation (ed. and trans. Suzanne Bray, Hurstpierpoint: Dorothy L. Sayers Society, 2003).

The Comedy of Dante Alighieri the Florentine, translated by Dorothy L. Sayers
Cantica 1: Hell (Harmondsworth: Penguin, 1949 [Penguin Classics])
Cantica 2: Purgatory (Harmondsworth: Penguin, 1955 [Penguin Classics])
Cantica 3: Paradise (Harmondsworth: Penguin, 1962 [Penguin Classics])   The last 14 cantos were completed by Barbara Reynolds.

The Dante Papers of Dorothy L. Sayers
Vol. 1: Introductory Papers on Dante: The Poet Alive In His Writings (London: Methuen, 1954)
Vol. 2: Further Papers on Dante: His Heirs and His Ancestors (London: Methuen, 1957)
Vol. 3: The Poetry of Search and the Poetry of Statement and Other Posthumous Essays on Literature, Religion and Language (London: Gollancz, 1963)

The Letters of Dorothy L. Sayers, chosen and edited by Barbara Reynolds
Vol. 1: 1899–1936: The Making of a Detective Novelist (London: Hodder & Stoughton, 1996)
Vol. 2: 1937–1943: From Novelist to Playwright (Hurstpierpoint & Swavesey: The Dorothy L. Sayers Society & Carole Green Publishing, 1998)
Vol. 3: 1944–1950: A Noble Daring (Hurstpierpoint & Swavesey: The Dorothy L. Sayers Society & Carole Green Publishing, 2000)
Vol. 4: 1951–1957: In the Midst of Life (Hurstpierpoint & Swavesey: The Dorothy L. Sayers Society & Carole Green Publishing, 2002)
Vol. 5: Child and Woman of her Time: A Supplement to the Letters of Dorothy L. Sayers (Hurstpierpoint & Swavesey: The Dorothy L. Sayers Society & Carole Green Publishing, 2002)

with Muriel St. Clare Byrne (1895–1983)
Busman's Honeymoon: A Detective Comedy in Three Acts (London: Gollancz, 1937; with *Love All*, ed. Alzina Stone Dale, Kent, OH: Kent State University Press, 1984)

with Jill Paton Walsh (b. 1937)

Thrones, Dominations (London: Hodder & Stoughton, 1998)

A Presumption of Death (London: Hodder & Stoughton, 2002)

Barbara Reynolds (b. 1914)

Dorothy L. Sayers: Her Life and Soul (London: Hodder & Stoughton, 1993; rev. eds 1998, 2002)

The Passionate Intellect: Dorothy L. Sayers' Encounter with Dante (Kent, OH, & London: Kent State University Press, 1989)

Reginald Hill

See also under 'Of Serial Readers'.

A Fairly Dangerous Thing (London: Collins, 1972)

A Very Good Hater (London: Collins, 1974)

Urn Burial (by 'Patrick Ruell', London: Hutchinson, 1975; as *Beyond the Bone*, Sutton & New York: Severn House, 2000)

Another Death in Venice (London: Collins, 1976)

'The Educator: The Case of the Screaming Spires', in Dilys Winn, ed., *Murder Ink: The Mystery Reader's Companion* (New York: Workman, 1977), pp. 470–2

'Desmond Bagley', 'H. R. F. Keating', & 'Michael Kenyon', in Klein, Kathleen Gregory, Pederson, Jay P., & Benbow-Pfalzgraf, Taryn, eds, *St James Guide to Crime & Mystery Writers* (1ˢᵗ ed., 1978; 4ᵗʰ ed., Farmington Hills, MI: Gale Group, 1996)

'Holmes: The Hamlet of Crime Fiction', in H. R. F. Keating, ed., *Crime Writers* (London: British Broadcasting Corporation, 1978), pp. 20–41

'A Pre-History: Crime Fiction Before the 19ᵗʰ Century', in H. R. F. Keating, ed., *Whodunit? A Guide to Crime, Suspense and Spy Fiction* (London: Windward, & New York: Van Nostrand Reinhold, 1982), pp. 20–5

'A Little Talent, Lots of Practice', in *The Writer* (Boston), November 1985

'Looking for a Programme', in Robin Winks, ed., *Colloquium on Crime: Eleven Famous Crime Writers Offer Intriguing Insights Into How and Why They Write as They Do* (New York: Scribners, 1986), pp. 149–66

'Serial Rites', in *The Writer* (Boston), December 1988

'The Plot's The Thing!', in *The Writer* (Boston), November 1995

'Foreword', in Michael Kenyon, *The Whole Hog* (1967; London: Black Dagger Crime, 1996), pp. 1-2

'Introduction', in Hillary Waugh, *Last Seen Wearing ...* (1952; London: Pan, 1999), pp. vii-x

'The uneventful life and quiet times of Reginald Hill', in *Reginald Hill: Your FREE guide to the works of Britain's finest crime writer* (London: HarperCollins, 2000), pp. 5–7.

'Message from the Author', at ▣ http://www.randomhouse.com/features/reghill

'Lord Byron (1788–1824)', at ▣ http://www.twbooks.co.uk/cwa/hillonbyron.html

Other sources and books mentioned

Allingham, Margery, *The Tiger in the Smoke* (London: Chatto & Windus, 1952)

Browne, Sir Thomas, *Hydriotaphia, Urne-Buriall, or, A Discourse of the Sepulchrall Urnes lately found in Norfolk* (with *The Garden of Cyrus, or The Quincunciall, Lozenge, or Network Plantations of the Ancients, Artificially, Naturally, Mystically Considered* (London: for Henry Brome, 1658)

Clarke, Stephan P., ed., *The Lord Peter Wimsey Companion* (1985; 2/e, Hurstpierpoint: The Dorothy L. Sayers Society, 2002)

Dickens, Charles, *A Tale of Two Cities* (London: Chapman & Hall, 1859)

Eliot, T. S., *Murder in the Cathedral: A Play in Verse* (London: Faber & Faber, 1935)

Freeling, Nicolas, 'Dorothy L. Sayers', in *Criminal Convictions: Errant Essays on Perpetrators of Literary License* (London: Peter Owen, 1994)

Heilbrun, Carolyn G., 'Sayers, Lord Peter, and Harriet Vane at Oxford', in *Hamlet's Mother and other Women: Feminist Essays on Literature* (New York: Columbia University Press, 1990)

Keating, H. R. F., 'Dorothy L. Sayers', in Susan Malling & Barbara Peters, ed., *AZ Murder Goes ... Classic* (Scottsdale, AZ: Poison Pen, 1997; rev. ed. 1998)

McGregor, Robert Kuhn, with Ethan Lewis, *Conundrums for the Long Week-End: England, Dorothy L. Sayers, and Lord Peter Wimsey* (Kent, OH, & London: Kent State University Press, 2000)

Woolf, Virginia, *The Waves* (London: Leonard & Virginia Woolf at the Hogarth Press, 1931)

3. Of Pseudonyms and Sentiment

Nora Roberts (b. 1950)   A selection only.
First Impressions (New York: Silhouette, 1984)
Storm Warning (New York: Silhouette, 1984)
Risky Business (New York: Silhouette, 1986)
Sacred Sins (New York: Bantam, 1987)
Brazen Virtue (New York: Bantam, 1988)   Rita Golden Medallion, Best Suspense, 1989.
Sweet Revenge (New York: Bantam, 1989)
Public Secrets (New York: Bantam, 1990)
Genuine Lies (New York: Bantam, 1991)
Divine Evil (New York: Bantam, 1992)   Rita Award, Best Romantic Suspense, 1993.
Carnal Innocence (New York: Bantam, 1992)
Honest Illusions (New York: Putnam, 1992)
Private Scandals (New York: Putnam, 1993)   Rita Award, Best Contemporary Single Title, 1994.
Hidden Riches (New York: Putnam, 1994)   Rita Award, Best Romantic Suspense, 1995.
Born in Fire (New York: Jove, 1994)
True Betrayals (New York: Putnam, 1995)
Born in Ice (New York: Jove, 1995)   Rita Award, Best Contemporary Single Title, 1996.
Montana Sky (New York: Putnam, 1996)
Born in Shame (New York: Jove, 1996)
Sanctuary (New York: Putnam, 1997)
Homeport (New York: Putnam, 1998)
River's End (New York: Putnam, 1999)
Carolina Moon (New York: Putnam, 2000)   Rita Award, Best Romantic Suspense, 2001.
Midnight Bayou (New York: Putnam, 2001)
A Little Fate (New York: Jove, 2004)   Collects the fantasy stories 'The Witching Hour' (2003), 'Winter Rose' (2001), and 'A World Apart' (2002).
Blue Smoke (New York: Putnam, 2005)
Angels Fall (New York: Putnam, 2006)

with 'J. D. Robb'
Remember When (New York: Putnam, 2003)   Rita Award, Best Romantic Suspense, 2004.

'J. D. Robb' ('b. 1995')
Naked in Death (New York: Berkley, 1995)
Glory in Death (New York: Berkley, 1995)
Immortal in Death (New York: Berkley, 1996)
Rapture in Death (New York: Berkley, 1996)
Ceremony in Death (New York: Berkley, 1997)
Vengeance in Death (New York: Berkley, 1997)
Holiday in Death (New York: Berkley, 1998)
Conspiracy in Death (New York: Berkley, 1999)
Loyalty in Death (New York: Berkley, 1999)
Witness in Death (New York: Berkley, 2000)
Judgment in Death (New York: Berkley, 2000)
Betrayal in Death (New York: Berkley, 2001)
Seduction in Death (New York: Berkley, 2001)
Reunion in Death (New York: Berkley, 2002)
Purity in Death (New York: Berkley, 2002)
Portrait in Death (New York: Berkley, 2003)
Imitation in Death (New York: Berkley, 2003)
Divided in Death (New York: Berkley, 2004)
Visions in Death (New York: Putnam, 2004)
Survivor in Death (New York: Putnam, 2005)
Origin in Death (New York: Putnam, 2005)
Memory in Death (New York: Putnam, 2006)
Born in Death (New York: Putnam, 2006)
Innocence in Death (New York: Putnam, 2007)

'Midnight in Death', in J. D. Robb, Susan Plunkett, Dee Holmes, & Claire Cross,
   Silent Night: Stories of Romance and Suspense (New York: Jove, 1998)
'Interlude in Death', in J. D. Robb, Laurell K. Hamilton, Susan Krinard, & Maggie
   Shayne, *Out of This World* (New York: Jove, 2001)
'Haunted in Death', in J. D. Robb, Mary Blayney, Ruth Ryan Langan, & Mary Kay
   McComas, *Bump in the Night* (New York: Jove, 2006)

▣ http://www.noraroberts.com/

Winston Graham (1912–2003)

Ross Poldark: A Novel of Cornwall, 1783–1787 (London: Werner Laurie, 1945)

Demelza: A Novel of Cornwall, 1788–1790 (London & Melbourne: Ward, Lock & Co.,1946)

Jeremy Poldark: A Novel of Cornwall, 1790–1791 (London & Melbourne: Ward, Lock & Co.,1950)

Warleggan: A Novel of Cornwall, 1792–1793 (London & Melbourne: Ward, Lock & Co.,1953)

▣ http://www.poldark.org.uk/

Catherine Cookson (1906–98)

The Mallen Streak (London: Heinemann, 1973)

The Mallen Girl (London: Heinemann, 1973)

The Mallen Litter (variant title, *The Mallen Lot*, London: Heinemann, 1974) omnibus edition, as *The Mallen Novels* (London: Heinemann, 1979)

Dorothy L. Sayers
See under 'Of Yorkshire and Purgatory'.

Other sources and books mentioned

Asaro, Catherine, ed., *Irresistible Forces* (New York: New American Library, 2004)   Contains novellas by Jo Beverley, Lois McMaster Bujold, and others fusing SF & Romance.

Bambara, Toni Cade, *Those Bones Are Not My Child* (New York: Pantheon, 1999)

Burrow, Colin, *Epic Romance: Homer to Milton* (Oxford: Clarendon Press, 1993)

Campbell, Robert, *In La-La Land We Trust* (New York: Mysterious Press,1986)

Dobyns, Stephen, *The Church of Dead Girls* (New York: Metropolitan, 1997)

Dryden, John, *The Works of Virgil: containing his Pastorals, Georgics, and Æneis. Translated into English Verse* (London: Jacob Tonson, 1697)

Herbert, Frank, *Dune* (Philadelphia: Chilton Books, 1965)   Nebula Award, Best Novel, 1965; Hugo Award, Best Novel 1966.

Hill, Reginald, *On Beulah Height* (London: HarperCollins, 1998)

— *Singing the Sadness* (London: HarperCollins, 1998)

Ingledew, Francis, *'Sir Gawain and the Green Knight' and the Order of the Garter* (Notre Dame: University of Notre Dame Press, 2006)

Little, Denise, & Hayden, Laura, eds, *The Official Nora Roberts Companion* (New York: Berkley, 2003)

Mosley, Walter, *Devil in a Blue Dress* (New York: Norton, 1990)

Parker, Robert B., *Double Deuce* (New York: Putnam, 1992)

Salter, Anna, *Shiny Water* (New York: Pocket, 1997)

St Clair, William, *The Reading Nation in the Romantic Period* (Cambridge: Cambridge University Press, 2004)

Smiley, Jane, *A Thousand Acres* (New York: Knopf, 1991)   Pulitzer Prize for Fiction, 1992.

Taylor, Andrew, *The Four Last Things* (London: HarperCollins, 1997)

— *The Judgement of Strangers* (London: HarperCollins, 1998)

— *The Office of the Dead* (London: HarperCollins, 2000)

Vachss, Andrew, *Flood* (New York: D. I. Fine, 1985)

4. Of Modern Dragons

J. R. R. Tolkien (1892–1973)

The Hobbit (London: George Allen & Unwin, 1937)

The Fellowship of the Ring (London: George Allen & Unwin, 1954)

The Two Towers (London: George Allen & Unwin, 1955)

The Return of the King (London: George Allen & Unwin, 1955)
   omnibus edition, as *The Lord of the Rings* (Boston & New York: Houghton Mifflin, 1966, & London: George Allen & Unwin, 1967)

The Silmarillion (London: George Allen & Unwin, 1977)   Gandalf & Ditmar Awards, 1978.

Unfinished Tales of Númenor and Middle Earth (ed. Christopher Tolkien, London: George Allen & Unwin, 1980)   Mythopoeic Fantasy Award, Best Book, 1981.

The History of Middle-Earth (ed. Christopher Tolkien)

Vol. 1: The Book of Lost Tales, Part 1 (Boston & New York: Houghton Mifflin, 1983)

Vol. 2: The Book of Lost Tales, Part 2 (Boston & New York: Houghton Mifflin, 1984)

Vol. 3: The Lays of Beleriand (Boston & New York: Houghton Mifflin, 1985)

Vol. 4: The Shaping of Middle Earth (Boston & New York: Houghton Mifflin, 1986)

Vol. 5: The Lost Road and Other Writings (Boston & New York: Houghton Mifflin, 1987)

Vol. 6: The Return of the Shadow: The History of The Lord of the Rings, *Part 1* (Boston & New York: Houghton Mifflin, 1988)

Vol. 7: The Treason of Isengard: The History of The Lord of the Rings, *Part 2* (Boston & New York: Houghton Mifflin, 1989)

Vol. 8: The War of the Ring: The History of The Lord of the Rings, *Part 3* (Boston & New York: Houghton Mifflin, 1990)

Vol. 9: Sauron Defeated: The History of The Lord of the Rings, *Part 4* (Boston & New York: Houghton Mifflin, 1992)

Vol. 10: Morgoth's Ring: The Later Silmarillion, Part 1 (Boston & New York: Houghton Mifflin, 1993)

Vol. 11: The War of the Jewels: The Later Silmarillion, Part 2 (Boston & New York: Houghton Mifflin, 1994)

Vol. 12: The Peoples of Middle Earth (Boston & New York: Houghton Mifflin, 1996)

Farmer Giles of Ham (London: George Allen & Unwin, 1949)

Sir Gawain and the Green Knight, Pearl, and Sir Orfeo, translated by J. R. R. Tolkien (ed. Christopher Tolkien, London: George Allen & Unwin, 1975)

Pictures by J. R. R. Tolkien (ed. Christopher Tolkien, London: George Allen & Unwin, 1979)

The Letters of J. R. R. Tolkien (ed. Christopher Tolkien and Humphrey Carpenter, London: George Allen & Unwin, 1980; with expanded index, Boston & New York: Houghton Mifflin, 2000)

The Monsters and the Critics and Other Essays (ed. Christopher Tolkien, London: George Allen & Unwin, 1983)

J. R. R. Tolkien: Artist and Illustrator (edited with commentary and essays by Wayne G. Hammond & Christina Scull, Boston & New York: Houghton Mifflin, 1995)

with Christopher Tolkien (b. 1924)

The Children of Húrin (Boston & New York: Houghton Mifflin, 2007)

回 http://www.tolkienestate.com/
回 http://www.tolkiensociety.org/

Ursula Le Guin (b. 1929)

A Wizard of Earthsea (Berkeley, CA: Parnassus Press, 1968)   Boston Globe–Horn Book Award, 1969; Lewis Carroll Shelf Award, 1979.

The Tombs of Atuan (New York: Atheneum, 1971)   Newbery Silver Medal, 1972.

The Farthest Shore (New York: Atheneum, 1972)   National Book Award, 1972.
   omnibus edition, as *Earthsea* (London: Gollancz, 1977); as *The Earthsea Trilogy* (Harmondsworth: Penguin, 1979)

Tehanu: The Last Book of Earthsea (New York: Atheneum, 1990)   Nebula Award, Best Novel, 1990.
   omnibus edition, as *The Earthsea Quartet* (Harmondsworth: Penguin, 1993)

Tales from Earthsea (New York: Harcourt, 2001)   Endeavour Award, 2002; two of the stories, 'The Finder' & 'The Bones of the Earth', won Locus Readers Awards, 2002.

The Other Wind (New York: Harcourt, 2001)   World Fantasy Award, Best Novel, 2002.

'The Word of Unbinding' (1964) & 'The Rule of Names' (1964), in *The Wind's Twelve Quarters* (New York: Harper & Row, 1975)

Earthsea Revisioned (Cambridge, MA: Children's Literature New England, & Cambridge: Green Bay Publications, 1993)

The Left Hand of Darkness (New York: Walker, 1969)   Nebula Award, Best Novel, 1969; Hugo & Ditmar Awards, Best Novel 1970; James Tiptree Jr Retrospective Award, 1996.

The Word for World is Forest (New York: Berkley, 1972)   Hugo Award, Best Novella, 1973.

Buffalo Gals and Other Animal Presences (Santa Barbara, CA: Capra Press, 1987)   The title-novella, Buffalo Gals, Won t You Come Out Tonight won the Hugo Award for Best Novelette and World Fantasy Award for Best Novella, 1988.

Language of the Night: Essays on Fantasy and Science Fiction (ed. Susan Wood, 1979; rev. ed. Ursula Le Guin, London: Women's Press, 1989/New York: Harper-Collins, 1992)

Dancing at the Edge of the World: Thoughts on Words, Women, Places (New York: Grove Press, 1989)

The Wave in the Mind: Talks and Essays on the Writer, the Reader, and the Imagination (Boston: Shambhala, 2004)

'Earthsea Miniseries: (Talking about why I couldn't talk about the miniseries before it was shown)', at:
   🔲 http://ursulakleguin.com/MiniEarthsea.html

'Earthsea Miniseries: A Reply to Some Statements Made by the Film-Makers of the Earthsea Miniseries Before it was Shown', at:

▣ http://ursulakleguin.com/Earthsea.html

'To the People who Wrote Me about the SciFi Channel Miniseries', at:

    ▣ http://ursulakleguin.com/Earthsea-Thankyou.html

'Frankenstein's Earthsea', in *Locus* (January 2005), and at:

    ▣ http://locusmag.com/2005/Issues/01LeGuin.html

'A Whitewashed Earthsea: How the SciFi Channel Wrecked my Books', at:

    ▣ http://www.slate.com/id/2111107/

Joanne Bertin (b. 1953)

The Last Dragonlord (New York: Tor, 1998)

Dragon and Phoenix (New York: Tor, 1999)

'Dragonlord's Justice' in Byron Preiss, John Betancourt, & Keith R. A. DeCandido, eds, *The Ultimate Dragon* (New York: Dell, 1995)

▣ http://www.demensionszine.com/stories/0302i1.html

Elizabeth Kerner (b. 1958)

Song in the Silence: The Tale of Lanen Kaelar (New York: Tor, 1997; abridged edition, New York: Starscape, 2003)

The Lesser Kindred (New York: Tor, 2001)

Redeeming the Lost (New York: Tor, 2005)

▣ http://elizabethkerner.com/

Anne McCaffrey (b. 1926)

Dragonflight (New York: Walker, 1969)   Two shorter pieces from which Dragonflight was fixed-up won awards in 1968, 'Dragonrider' the Nebula, & 'Weyr Search' the Hugo for Best Novella.

Dragonquest (New York: Ballantine, 1971)

A time when, being a tale of young Lord Jaxom, his white dragon, Ruth, and various fire-lizards (Framingham, MA: New England Science Fiction Association Press, 1975)   This novella was incorporated into The White Dragon.

Dragonsong (New York: Atheneum, 1976)   Children's Book Showcase & American Library Association Awards, 1976; Horn Book Fanfare Citation 1977.

Dragonsinger: Harper of Pern (New York: Atheneum, 1977)   American Library Association Award.

The White Dragon (New York: Ballantine, 1978)   Gandalf, Ditmar, & Streza Awards, 1979.

Dragondrums (New York: Atheneum, 1979)   Balrog Best Novel Award.

Moreta: Dragonlady of Pern (New York: Ballantine, 1983)

Nerilka's Story: A Pern Adventure (New York: Ballantine, 1986)

Dragonsdawn (New York: Ballantine, 1988)

The Renegades of Pern (New York: Ballantine, 1989)

All the Weyrs of Pern (New York: Ballantine, 1991)

The Dolphins' Bell (Newark, NJ: Wildside Press, 1993)   This novella illustrated by Pat Morrissey was incorporated into The Chronicles of Pern, and links to The Dolphins of Pern.

The Chronicles of Pern: First Fall (New York: Ballantine, 1993)   Gathers five stories: 'The P.E.R.N. Survey', 'The Dolphins' Bell', 'The Ford of Red Hanrahan', 'The Second Weyr', and 'Rescue Run'.

The Dolphins of Pern (New York: Ballantine, 1994)

Dragonseye (variant titles, *Red Star Rising: The Second Chronicles of Pern* & *Red Star Rising: More Chronicles of Pern*, New York: Ballantine, 1996)

The Masterharper of Pern (New York: Ballantine, 1998)

The Skies of Pern (New York: Del Rey, 2001)

A Gift of Dragons: Illustrated Stories (New York: Ballantine, 2002)   Collects the stories 'The Smallest Dragon Boy' (1973), 'The Girl who Heard Dragons' (1994), and 'Runner of Pern' (1998), with one new one, Ever the Twain (2002).

Omnibus editions: *The Dragonriders of Pern* (*Dragonflight*, *Dragonquest*, *The White Dragon*) (New York: Del Rey, 1988)

The Harper Hall of Pern (*Dragonsong*, *Dragonsinger*, *Dragondrums*) (New York: Doubleday, 1979)

On Dragonwings (*Moreta*, *Dragonsdawn*, *Dragonseye*) (New York: Del Rey, 2003)

'Beyond Between' (1999), in Robert Silverberg, ed., *Legends II: New Short Novels by the Masters of Modern Fantasy* (New York: Tor, 2003)

'Retrospection', in Denise DuPont, ed., *Women of Vision* (New York: St Martin's Press, 1988)

'Autobiographical Feature' at ▣ http://www.answers.com/topic/anne-inez-mccaffrey

▣ http://www.annemccaffrey.net/index.php

with Todd McCaffrey (b. 1956)
Dragon's Kin (New York: Ballantine, 2003)
Dragon's Fire (New York: Ballantine, 2006)

with Jody Lynn Nye (b. 1957)
The Dragonlover's Guide to Pern (1989; 2/e, New York: Ballantine, 1997)

with Richard Woods (b. 1941) & John Howe (b. 1957)
A Diversity of Dragons (New York: HarperPrism, 1997)
Todd McCaffrey
Dragonholder: The Life and Dreams (So Far) of Anne McCaffrey by her son (New York: Ballantine, 1999)
Dragonsblood (New York: Ballantine, 2005)

◉ http://toddmccaffrey.org/todd/

Chris Bunch (1943–2005)
Storm of Wings (London: Orbit, 2002)
Knighthood of the Dragon (London: Orbit, 2003)
The Last Battle (London: Orbit, 2004)

Naomi Novik (b. 1973)
His Majesty's Dragon (variant title, *Temeraire*, New York: Del Rey, 2006)
Throne of Jade (New York: Del Rey, 2006)
Black Powder War (New York: Del Rey, 2006)
    omnibus edition as *Temeraire: In the Service of the King* (Mechanicsburg, PA: Science Fiction Book Club, 2006)

◉ http://www.temeraire.org/

Christopher Paolini (b. 1983)
Eragon (Paradise Valley: Paolini International, 2002; New York: Knopf, 2003)
Eldest (New York: Knopf, 2005)

◉ http://www.alagaesia.com/

Other sources and books mentioned

Beowulf & The Fight at Finnsburg (ed. Fr. Klaeber, 1922; 3rd ed., Lexington, MA: D. C. Heath & Co., 1950)

Blanpied, Pamela Wharton, *Dragons: A Guide to the Modern Infestation* (New York: Warner, 1980; as *Dragons: The Modern Infestation*, Woodbridge: Boydell Press, 1996)

Brizzi, Mary T., *Anne McCaffrey* (Mercer Island, WA: Starmont House, 1986 [Starmont House Reader's Guides])

Cixous, Hélène, *Le Rire de la Méduse*, in *L'Arc* 61 (June 1975): 39–54; as *The Laugh of the Medusa*, trans. Keith and Paula Cohen, in *Signs* 1.4 (Summer 1976): 875–93.

Dunsany, Edward Plunkett, Lord, *The King of Elfland's Daughter* (London & New York: Putnam, 1924)   回 http://www.dunsany.net/18th.htm

Eaglestone, Robert, ed., *Reading The Lord of the Rings: New Writings on Tolkien's Trilogy* (London: Continuum, 2005)

Eddison, Eric R., *The Worm Ouroboros* (London: Jonathan Cape, 1922)

Fonstad, Karen Wynn, *The Atlas of Pern* (New York: Ballantine, 1984)

Garth, John, *Tolkien and the Great War* (London: HarperCollins, 2003)

Gilliver, Peter, Marshall, Jeremy, & Wiener, Edmund, *The Ring of Words: Tolkien and the Oxford English Dictionary* (Oxford: Oxford University Press, 2006)

Grahame, Kenneth, 'The Reluctant Dragon', in *Dream Days* (New York & London: John Lane, 1898)

— *The Wind in the Willows* (London: Methuen, 1908)

Green, Roger Lancelyn, ed., *The Hamish Hamilton Book of Dragons: Dragons in Ancient and Modern Times* (London: Hamish Hamilton, 1970; as *A Cavalcade of Dragons*, New York: Henry Z. Walck, Inc., 1970; as *A Book of Dragons*, Harmondsworth: Puffin, 1974)

Hamilton, Peter F., *Fallen Dragon* (London: Macmillan, 2001)

Heaney, Seamus, *Beowulf* (London: Faber & Faber, 1999)   Whitbread Book of the Year, 1999.

Hepler, Susan, '"Once They All Believed in Dragons"', in Susan Lehr, ed., *Battling Dragons: Issues and Controversy in Children's Literature* (Portsmouth, NH: Heinemann, 1995), pp. 220–32

Ingersoll, Ernest, *Dragons and Dragon Lore* (New York: Payson & Clarke Ltd, 1928)

Jones, Diana Wynne, *The Tough Guide to Fantasyland* (London: Vista, 1996; revised and updated ed., New York: Firebird, 2006)

Kircher, Athanasius, *Mundus subterraneus, in XII. libros digestus, quo divinum sub-terrestris mundi opificium ... universæ denique naturæ majestas et divitiæ summa rerum varietate exponuntur, etc.* (in 2 vols, Amsterdam, 1665)

Kroeber, Theodora, *Ishi, Last of his Tribe* (Berkeley: Parnassus Press, 1964)

Lang, Andrew, *Prince Prigio* (Bristol: J. W. Arrowsmith/London: Simpkin, Marshall & Co., 1889)

Le Guin, Charles A., *Roland de la Platière: A Public Servant in the Eighteenth Century* (Philadelphia: American Philosophical Society, 1966)

Lewis, C. S., *The Voyage of the* Dawn Treader*: A Story for Children* (London: Geoffrey Bles, 1952)

The Mabinogion, in the *Llyfr Coch Hergest* ('Red Book of Hergest'), Jesus College Oxford MS 111, dated *c.*1382–1410, and the *Llyfr Gwyn Rhydderch* ('White Book of Rhydderch'), National Library of Wales MS Peniarth 4, dated to the mid-fourteenth century; see also 🔲 http://www.llgc.org.uk/drych/drych_s082.htm

Mallory, Thomas, *Le Morte d'Arthur* (Westminster: William Caxton, 1485)

Nesbit, Edith, *The Book of Dragons* (London & New York: Harper Brothers, 1901)

— 'The Last of the Dragons', in *Five of Us, and Madeline* (London: T. Fisher Unwin, 1925)

Norton, Andre, *Dragon Magic* (New York: Ace, 1972)

Peake, Mervyn, *Titus Groan* (London: Eyre & Spottiswoode, 1946)

— *Gormenghast* (London: Eyre & Spottiswoode, 1950)

— *Titus Alone* (London: Eyre & Spottiswoode, 1959)

Pierce, Tamora, 'Plain Magic', in Douglas Hill, ed., *Planetfall* (Oxford & London: Oxford University Press, 1996)   See also under 'Of Stormwings and Valiant Women'.

Ranke-Heinemann, Uta, *Eunuchen für das Himmelreich: Katholische Kirche und Sexualität* (Hamburg: Campe Verlag, 1988; trans. Peter Heinegg, as *Eunuchs for the Kingdom of Heaven: Women, Sexuality, and the Catholic Church*, New York: Doubleday, 1990)

Reginald, Robert, & Slusser, George, eds, *Zephyr and Boreas: Winds of Change in the Fictions of Ursula K. Le Guin* (San Bernadino, CA: Borgo Press, 1997)

Rich, Adrienne, *On Lies, Secrets, and Silence: Selected Prose, 1966–78* (New York: Norton: 1979)

Roberts, Robin, *Anne McCaffrey: A Critical Companion* (Westport, CT, & London: Greenwood Press, 1996 [Critical Companions to Popular Contemporary Writers])

Robinson, Derek, *Goshawk Squadron* (London: Heinemann, 1971)

Rochelle, Warren G., *Communities of the Heart: The Rhetoric of Myth in the Fiction of Ursula K. Le Guin* (Liverpool: Liverpool University Press, 2001)

Smith, G. Elliot, *The Evolution of the Dragon* (Manchester: Manchester University Press, 1919)

Spenser, Edmund, *The Faerie Queene: Disposed into Twelve Books fashioning XII Moral Vertues* (London: William Ponsonby, 1590, 1596)

Stevenson, Robert Louis, *The Strange Case of Dr Jekyll and Mr Hyde* (London: Longmans, Green, 1886)

Stieg, William, *Shrek!* (New York: Sunburst, 1990)

The Voiage and Travayle of Syr Iohn Maundeville, Knight (manuscript copies from 1357, published Westminster: Wynkyn de Worde, 1499)

Wayne, Kathryn Ross, *Redefining Moral Education: Life, Le Guin, and Language* (Lanham, MD: Austin & Winfield, 1995)

White, Donna R., *Dancing with Dragons: Ursula K. Le Guin and the Critics* (Ontario: Camden House, 1998 [Literary Criticism in Perspective])

5. Of Aliens in Africa

Ian McDonald (b. 1960)

Chaga (variant title, *Evolution's Shore*, London: Gollancz, 1995)

Kirinya (London: Gollancz, 1998)

Tendeléo's Story (Leeds: P S Publishing, 2000; with Peter F. Hamilton, *Watching Trees Grow*, in tête-bêche format, London: Gollancz, 2002)   Sturgeon Award 2000.

Desolation Road (New York: Bantam, 1988)

Empire Dreams (New York: Bantam, 1988)

Out on Blue Six (New York: Bantam, 1989)

King of Morning, Queen of Day (New York: Bantam, 1991)   Philip K. Dick Memorial Award 1992.

Hearts, Hands and Voices (variant title, *The Broken Land*, London: Gollancz, 1992)

Speaking in Tongues (London: Gollancz, 1992)

Kling Klang Klatch (with David Lyttelton, London: Gollancz, 1992)

Scissors Cut Paper Wrap Stone (New York: Bantam, 1994)

Necroville (variant title, *Terminal Café*, London: Gollancz, 1994)

Sacrifice of Fools (London: Gollancz, 1996)

Ares Express (London: Earthlight, 2001)

River of Gods (London: Simon & Schuster, 2004)   British Science Fiction Association
   Award, Best Novel, 2004.

Brasyl (New York: Pyr, 2007)

'The Little Goddess' (2005) at:

⊡ http://www.asimovs.com/_issue_0604_5/littlegoddess.shtml.

'Cyberabad', a blog, at ⊡ http://ianmcdonald.livejournal.com/

⊡ http://www.infinityplus.co.uk/nonfiction/intimcd.htm
⊡ http://trashotron.com/agony/columns/2004/08-23-04.htm

Ursula Le Guin

See under Of Modern Dragons .

David Brin (b. 1950)

Sundiver (New York: Bantam, 1979)

Startide Rising (New York: Bantam, 1983)   Nebula Award, Best Novel 1983; Hugo Award,
   Best Novel, 1984.

   omnibus edition, as *Earthclan* (Garden City, NY: Doubleday, 1986)

The Uplift War (New York: Bantam, 1987)   Hugo Award, Best Novel, 1988.

Brightness Reef (New York: Bantam, 1995)

Infinity's Shore (New York: Bantam, 1996)

Heaven's Reach (New York: Bantam, 1998)

⊡ http://www.davidbrin.com/

Other sources and books mentioned

Banks, Iain M., *Consider Phlebas* (London: Macmillan, 1987)

Cameron, Edwin, *Witness to AIDS* (with contributions by Nathan Geffen, Cape Town:
   Tafelberg/London & New York: I. B. Tauris, 2005)

Chesney, Lt. Col. Sir Henry T., *The Battle of Dorking: Reminiscences of a Volunteer*
   (Edinburgh & London: W. Blackwood, 1871; as *The Battle of Dorking: being an
   account of the German invasion of England: capture of London & Woolwich, &c.
   &c. &c. as told by a volunteer to his grandchildren*, Toronto: Copp, Clark, 1871)

Childers, Erskine, *Riddle of the Sands* (London: Smith, Elder, 1903; later eds add 'The' and the subtitle 'A Record of Secret Service')

Clarke, I. F., *Voices Prophesying War 1763–1984* (London: Oxford University Press, 1966; rev. ed., as *Voices Prophesying War: Future Wars, 1763–3749*, 1992)

— ed., *Tales of the Next Great War, 1871–1914: Fictions of Future Warfare and Battles* (Syracuse: Syracuse University Press, 1996)

Conrad, Joseph, *Heart of Darkness* (London & Edinburgh: W. Blackwood, Feb.-Apr. 1899; in *Youth: A Narrative, and Two Other Stories*, Edinburgh: w. Blackwood, 1902)

Edel, Leon, *The Life of Henry James* (definitive edition, in 2 vols, Harmondsworth: Penguin, 1977 [Peregrine])

Flammarion, Camille, *La Pluralité des Mondes Habités étude où l'on expose les conditions d'habitabilité des terres célestes, discutées au point de vue de l'astronomie et de la physiologie.* (Paris: Mallet-Bachelier, 1862)

— *Récits de l'Infini: Lumen, Histoire d'une Comète, Dans l'Infini* (Paris: Didier, 1872; trans S. R. Crocker as *Stories of Infinity: Lumen, History of a Comet, In Infinity*, Boston: Roberts Bros, 1873).

Goethe, Johann Wolfgang (von), *Die Leiden des jungen Werthers* (Leipzig: Wengandschen Buchhandlung, 1774; variously revised and translated, usually as *The Sorrows* [or *Suffering*] *of Young Werther*)

Kipling, Rudyard, *Kim* (London: Macmillan, 1901)

Millard, Joseph J., *The Gods Hate Kansas*, in *Startling Stories* (Chicago: Better Publications, 1941)

Naipaul, V. S., *A Bend in the River* (London: André Deutsch, 1979)

Niven, Larry, & Pournelle, Jerry, *Footfall* (New York: Ballantine, 1985)

Scott, Paul, *The Jewel in the Crown* (London: Heinemann, 1966)

— *The Day of the Scorpion* (London: Heinemann, 1968)

— *The Towers of Silence* (London: Heinemann, 1971)   Yorkshire Post Fiction Award, 1973.

— *A Division of the Spoils* (London: Heinemann, 1975)

— *Staying On* (London: Heinemann, 1977)   Booker Prize, 1977.

Silverberg, Robert, *Invaders from Earth* (New York: Ace, 1958)

Wells, H. G., *The War of the Worlds* (London: Heinemann, 1898)

Wodehouse, P. G., *The Swoop!: or How Clarence saved England: A Tale of the Great Invasion* (London: Alston Rivers, 1909)

6. Of Organelles

Octavia E. Butler (1947–2006)
Dawn (New York: Warner, 1987)
Adulthood Rites (New York: Warner, 1988)
Imago (New York: Warner, 1989)
　　boxed as *Xenogenesis*, from 1989
　　omnibus edition as *Lilith's Brood* (New York: Aspect, 2000)

Patternmaster (Garden City, NY: Doubleday, 1976)
Mind of My Mind (Garden City, NY: Doubleday, 1977)
Survivor (Garden City, NY: Doubleday, 1978)
Wild Seed (Garden City, NY: Doubleday, 1980)
Clay's Ark (New York: St Martin's, 1984)
　　omnibus edition, excluding *Survivor*, as *Seed to Harvest* (New York: Aspect, 2007)

Kindred (Garden City, NY: Doubleday, 1979)
The Evening and the Morning and the Night (Eugene, OR: Pulphouse Publications, 1991)
Parable of the Sower (New York: Four Walls Eight Windows, 1993)
Parable of the Talents (New York: Seven Stories Press, 1998)   Nebula Award, Best Novel 1999.
Fledgling (New York: Seven Stories Press, 2005)

Bloodchild and other stories (New York: Seven Stories Press, 1996, 2/e 2005)   The 1/e collects five stories ('Bloodchild' [Nebula Award, Best Novelette, 1984; Hugo Award, Best Novella, 1985], The Evening and the Morning and the Night , Near of Kin , Speech Sounds [Hugo Award, Best Short Story, 1984], and Crossover) and two essays, Positive Obsession and Furor Scribendi . The 2/e adds the stories Amnesty and The Book of Martha .

'The Book of Martha', at:
🔲 http://www.scifi.com/scifiction/originals/originals_archive/butler2/butler21.html
'Amnesty', at
🔲 http://www.scifi.com/scifiction/originals/originals_archive/butler/butler1.html

'Octavia E. Butler' in *Journeys* (Rockville, MD: Quill & Brush/PEN/Faulkner Foundation, 1996)

Samuel R. Delany (b. 1942)
Captives of the Flame (variant title, *Out of the Dead City* New York: Ace,1963)
The Towers of Toron (New York: Ace, 1964)
City of a Thousand Suns (New York: Ace, 1965)
    omnibus edition, as *The Fall of the Towers* (New York: Ace, 1970)

Tales of Nevèrÿon (New York: Bantam, 1975)
Flight from Nevèrÿon (New York: Bantam, 1978)
Nevèrÿona: or The Tale of Signs and Cities (New York: Bantam, 1983)
The Bridge of Lost Desire (variant title, *Return to Nevèrÿon*, New York: Bantam, 1987)

The Jewels of Aptor (New York: Ace, 1962)
The Ballad of Beta-2 (New York: Ace, 1965)
Babel-17 (New York: Ace, 1966)   Nebula Award, Best Novel, 1966.
The Einstein Intersection (variant title, *A Fabulous, Formless Darkness*, New York: Ace, 1966)   Nebula Award, Best Novel, 1967.
Empire Star (New York: Ace, 1966)
Aye, and Gomorrah: And Other Stories (New York: Ace, 1967)
Nova (Garden City, NY: Doubleday, 1968)
Driftglass (Garden City, NY: Doubleday, 1971)
Dhalgren (Garden City, NY: Doubleday, 1974)
Triton (variant title, *Trouble on Triton,* New York: Bantam,1976)
Distant Stars (New York: Bantam, 1981)
Stars in My Pocket Like Grains of Sand (New York: Bantam, 1984)
The Complete Nebula Award-Winning Fiction (New York: Bantam, 1986)
We, in Some Strange Power's Employ, Move on a Rigorous Line (New York: Tor, 1990)
They Fly at Ciron (New York: St Martin's, 1995)
Phallos (Whitemore Lake, MI: Bamberger, 2004)

The Jewel-Hinged Jaw : Notes on the Language of Science Fiction (Elizabethtown, NY: Dragon Press, 1977)
Starboard Wine (Hastings on Hudson, NY: Ultramarine, 1984)
The Motion of Light in Water: East Village Sex and Science Fiction Writing: 1957–1965 (New York: Arbor House, 1988)   Nebula Award, Best Non-Fiction Book, 1989.
▣ http://www2.pcc.com/staff/jay/delany/

Charles R. Saunders (b. 1946)
Imaro (New York: Daw, 1981)
The Quest for Cush (New York: Daw, 1984)
The Trail of Bohu (New York: Daw, 1985)

Steven Barnes (b. 1952)
Streetlethal (New York: Ace, 1983)
Gorgon Child (New York: Tor, 1989)
Firedance (New York: Tor, 1993)
Lion's Blood: A Novel of Slavery and Freedom in an Alternate America (New York: Mysterious Press, 2002)   Endeavour Award, 2003.
Zulu Heart (New York: Aspect, 2003)

Ride the Angry Land (New York: Ace, 1980)
The Kundalini Equation (New York: Forge, 1986)
Blood Brothers (New York: Tor, 1996)
Iron Shadows (New York: Tor, 1998)
Charisma (New York: Tor, 2002)
Great Sky Woman (New York: Ballantine, 2006)

回 http://www.lifewrite.com/

   with Larry Niven (b. 1938)
Dreampark (New York: Phantasia Press, 1981)
The Barsoom Project (New York: Ace, 1989)
The California Voodoo Game (variant title, *The Voodoo Game*, New York: Del Rey, 1992)

The Descent of Anansi (New York: Tor, 1982)
Achilles' Choice (New York: Tor, 1991)
Saturn's Race (New York: Tor, 2000)

   with Larry Niven and Jerry Pournelle (b. 1933)
The Legacy of Heorot (New York: Simon & Schuster, 1987)
The Dragons of Heorot (variant title, *Beowulf's Children*, New York: Tor, 1995)

Nalo Hopkinson (b. 1960)
Brown Girl in the Ring (New York: Aspect, 1998)
Midnight Robber (New York: Aspect, 2000)
Skin Folk (New York: Aspect, 2001
The Salt Roads (New York: Warner, 2003)
The New Moon's Arms (New York: Warner, 2007)

Whispers from the Cotton Tree Root: Caribbean Fabulist Fiction (ed. Nalo Hopkin-
    son, Montpelier, VT: Invisible Cities Press, 2000)
Mojo: Conjure Stories (ed. Nalo Hopkinson, New York: Warner, 2003)
So Long Been Dreaming: Postcolonial Science Fiction & Fantasy (ed. Nalo Hopkin-
    son & Uppinder Mehan: Vancouver: Arsenal Pulp Press, 2004)
Tesseracts Nine: New Canadian Speculative Fiction (ed. Nalo Hopkinson & Geoff
    Ryman, Calgary: Paperback Edge, 2005)

回 http://www.sff.net/people/nalo/

Tananarive Due (b. 1966)
The Between (New York: HarperCollins, 1995)
My Soul to Keep (New York: HarperCollins, 1997)
The Black Rose (Westminster, MD: One World, 2000)
The Living Blood (New York: Atria, 2001)
The Good House (New York: Atria, 2003)
Joplin's Ghost (New York: Atria, 2005)

回 http://www.tananarivedue.com/

Walter Mosley (b. 1952)
Blue Light (New York: Little, Brown, 1998)
Futureland (New York: Warner, 2001)
47 (New York: Little, Brown, 2005)
The Wave (New York: Warner, 2006)

What Next? A Memoir toward World Peace (Baltimore: Black Classic Press, 2003)
Workin' on the Chain Gang: Shaking Off the Dead Hand of History (New York: Bal-
    lantine, 2000).

Life Out of Context: Which Includes a Proposal for the Non-violent Take-over of the House of Representatives (New York: Nation Books, 2006)

'Walter Mosley' in *Journeys* (Rockville, MD: Quill & Brush/PEN/Faulkner Foundation, 1996)

回 http://www.hachettebookgroupusa.com/features/waltermosley/index.html

Ursula Le Guin
See under Of Modern Dragons .

Mary Doria Russell (b. 1950)
The Sparrow (New York: Villard Books, 1996)   James Tiptree Jr Memorial Award, Best Novel, 1997; Arthur C. Clarke & British Science Fiction Association Awards, Best Novel, 1998.
Children of God (New York: Villard Books, 1998)

回 http://users.adelphia.net/~druss44121/

Peter F. Hamilton (b. 1960)
The Reality Dysfunction (London: Macmillan, 1996)
The Neutronium Alchemist (London: Macmillan, 1997)
The Naked God (London: Macmillan, 1999)
    omnibus edition, as *The Night's Dawn Trilogy*, Des Moines, IA: Oxmoor House, 2000)
The Confederation Handbook (London: Macmillan, 2000)

回 http://www.peterfhamilton.co.uk/

Other sources and books mentioned
Behn, Aphra, *Oronooko: or, the Royal Slave. A true history.* (London: Will Canning, 1688)
Brodber, Erna, *The Continent of Black Consciousness: On the History of the African Diaspora from Slavery to the Present Day* (London: New Beacon Books, 2003)
Carter, Forrest (Asa Earl Carter), *The Rebel Outlaw Josey Wales* (Gantt, AL: Whipporwill Publishers, 1973)
— *The Education of Little Tree* (New York: Delacorte, 1976)
Dawkins, Richard, *The Selfish Gene* (Oxford: Oxford University Press, 1976)
— *The Extended Phenotype: The Gene as the Unit of Selection* (Oxford: Freeman, 1982)

— *The Blind Watchmaker* (Harlow: Longman Scientific and Technical, 1986)

Gray, Alasdair, *1982 Janine* (London: Jonathan Cape, 1984)

Haraway, Donna, 'A Cyborg Manifesto: Science, Technology, and Socialist-Feminism in the Late Twentieth Century', in *Simians, Cyborgs and Women: The Reinvention of Nature* (New York; Routledge, 1991), pp.149–81; and at:
  ▣ http://www.stanford.edu/dept/HPS/Haraway/CyborgManifesto.html

Haley, Alex, *Roots: The Saga of an American Family* (Garden City, NY: Doubleday, 1976)

Hogg, James, *The Private Memoirs and Confessions of a Justified Sinner* (London: Constable, 1824)

Hulme, Keri, *The Bone People* (Wellington: Spiral, 1984)   Booker Prize, 1985.

Huxley, Aldous, *Brave New World* (London: Chatto & Windus, 1932)

Luckhurst, Roger, 'The Science-Fictionalization of Trauma: Remarks on Narratives of Alien Abduction', in *Science-Fiction Studies* #74, Vol. 25.1 (March 1998): 29–52

Marais, Eugène, *The Soul of the Ape* (wr. 1919; Cape Town: Rousseau, 1969)

— *Die Siel van die Mier* (Pretoria: Van Scheik, 1934; trans. Winifred de Kok, as *The Soul of the White Ant*, London: Methuen,1937).

Melzer, Patricia, *Alien Constructions: Science Fiction and Feminist Thought* (Austin: University of Texas Press, 2006)

More, Sir Thomas, *De Optimo Reipublicae Statu, deque Nova Insula Utopia* (1516; as *A frutefull pleasaunt, wittie worke, of the beste state of a publique weale, and of the newe yle, called Utopia written in Latine, by the right worthie and famous Syr Thomas More knyght; and translated into Englishe by Raphe Robynson, sometime fellowe of Corpus Christi College in Oxford*, London: Richard Tottel, 1551)

Noles, Pam, 'Shame' at: ▣ http://www.infinitematrix.net/faq/essays/noles.html.

— 'The Shame of Earthsea: A Public Response To What Some Folks Are Saying About That Essay', at:
  ▣ http://andweshallmarch.typepad.com/and_we_shall_march/2006/01/the_shame_of_ea.html

Orwell, George, *1984* (London: Secker & Warburg, 1949)

Rushdie, Salman, *Midnight's Children* (London: Cape, 1981)   Booker Prize & James Tait Black Memorial Prize for Fiction, 1981.

Sajo, George, 'Phoenix on the top of the palm tree: multiple interpretations of Job 29:18', at ▣ http://www.studiolum.com/en/silva5.htm

Sengupta, Debjani, 'Sadhanbabu's Friends: Science Fiction in Bengal from 1882–

1961', at: ▣ http://www.sarai.net/journal/03pdf/076_082_dsengupta.pdf

Sterne, Lawrence, *The Life and Opinions of Tristram Shandy, Gentleman* (in 7 vols, York: Anne Ward, 1759–67)

Swift, Jonathan, *Travels into several remote nations of the world : in four parts / by Lemuel Gulliver, first a Surgeon, and then a Captain of Several Ships* (in 2 vols, London: Benjamin Motte, 1726–7).

Thompson, E. P., *The Sykaos Papers, being An Account of the Voyages of the Poet Oi Paz to the System of Strim in the Seventeenth Galaxy; of his Mission to the Planet Sykaos; of his First Cruel Captivity; of his Travels about its Surface; of the Manners and Customs of its Beastly People; of his Second Captivity; and of his Return to Oitar. To which are added many passages from the Poet's Journal, documents in Sykotic script, and other curious matters. Selected and Edited by Q, Vice-Provost of the College of Adjusters. Transmitted by Timewarp to E. P. Thompson* (London: Bloomsbury, 1988)

Tulloch, John, & Jenkins, Henry, *Science Fiction Audiences: Watching* Doctor Who *and* Star Trek (London & New York: Routledge, 1995)

Watson James D., & Crick Francis H., 'Molecular structure of Nucleic Acids', in *Nature* 171 (1953): 737–8.

Wilson, E. O., *Sociobiology: The New Synthesis* (Cambridge, MA: Belknap Press of Harvard University Press, 1975)

— *Naturalist* (Washington: Shearwater Books, 1994)

Zamiatin, Yevgeny, *My* (wr. 1920, trans. Gregory Zilboorg, as *We*, New York: Dutton, 1924)

7. Of Stormwings and Valiant Women

Tamora Pierce (b. 1954)
Alanna: The First Adventure (New York: Atheneum, 1983)
In the Hand of the Goddess (New York: Atheneum, 1984)
The Woman Who Rides Like a Man (New York: Atheneum, 1986)
Lioness Rampant (New York: Atheneum, 1988)
Wild Magic (New York: Atheneum, 1992)
Wolf-Speaker (New York: Atheneum, 1994)
The Emperor Mage (New York: Atheneum, 1995)
The Realms of the Gods (New York: Atheneum, 1996)
First Test (New York: Random House, 1999)
Page (New York: Random House, 2000)

Squire (New York: Random House, 2001)
Lady Knight (New York: Random House, 2002)
Trickster's Choice (New York: Random House, 2003)
Trickster's Queen (New York: Random House, 2004)
Beka Cooper: Terrier (New York: Random House, 2006)
'Elder Brother', in Bruce Colville, ed., *Half-Human* (New York: Scholastic, 2001)
'Student of Ostriches', in Tamora Pierce & Josepha Sherman, eds, *Young Warriors: Stories of Strength* (New York: Random House, 2005)
'Hidden Girl', in Helen J. & M. Jerry Weiss, eds, *Dreams and Visions* (New York: Tor, 2006)

Sandry's Book (variant title, *The Magic in the Weaving*, New York: Scholastic, 1997)
Tris's Book (variant title, *The Power in the Storm*, New York: Scholastic, 1998)
Daja's Book (variant title, *The Fire in the Forging*, New York: Scholastic, 1998)
Briar's Book (variant title, *The Healing in the Vine*, New York: Scholastic, 1999)
Magic Steps (New York: Scholastic, 2000)
Street Magic (New York: Scholastic, 2001)
Cold Fire (New York: Scholastic, 2002)
Shatterglass (New York: Scholastic, 2003)
The Will of the Empress (New York: Scholastic, 2005)
'Plain Magic', in (i) Douglas Hill, ed., *Planetfall* (Oxford & London: Oxford University Press, 1996), and, with a slightly variant text, (ii) *Flights of Fantasy* (Logan, IA: Perfection Learning, 1999 [Literature & Thought])   This second book is not listed on Amazon, and must be ordered directly from the publishers; confusingly, there is another *Flights of Fantasy* (New York: Tor, 1999), edited by Merecedes Lackey.
'Testing', in Helen J. & M. Jerry Weiss, eds, *Lost and Found* (New York: Tor, 2000)
'Huntress', in *Firebirds Rising: An Original Anthology of Science Fiction and Fantasy* (New York: Firebird, 2006)
'Time of Proving', in *Cricket* 34.1 (September 2006), pp. 12–18

'Fantasy: Why Kids Read It, Why Kids Need It', in Sheila Egoff *et al.*, eds, *Only Connect: Readings in Children's Literature* (1969; 3rd ed., New York: Oxford University Press, 1996)   Pierce's essay appears only in the 3rd edition.

▣ http://www.tamora-pierce.com/

J. K. Rowling
See under 'Of Serial Readers'.

Arthur Ransome (1884–1967)
Swallows and Amazons (London: Jonathan Cape, 1930)
Swallowdale (London & Toronto: Jonathan Cape, 1931)
Peter Duck (London & Toronto: Jonathan Cape, 1932)
Winter Holiday (London & Toronto: Jonathan Cape, 1933)
Coot Club (London & Toronto: Jonathan Cape, 1934)
Pigeon Post (London & Toronto: Jonathan Cape, 1936)   Carnegie Medal, 1937.
We Didn't Mean To Go To Sea (London & Toronto: Jonathan Cape, 1937)
Secret Water (London & Toronto: Jonathan Cape, 1939)
The Big Six (London & Toronto: Jonathan Cape, 1940)
Missee Lee (London: Jonathan Cape, 1941)
The Picts And The Martyrs: Or Not Welcome At All (London: Jonathan Cape, 1943)
Great Northern? (London: Jonathan Cape, 1947)
Coots in the North (London: Jonathan Cape, 1988; as *Coots in the North and other stories*, 1992)

Anne McCaffrey
See under 'Of Modern Dragons'

Philip Pullman (b. 1946)
Count Karlstein (London: Chatto & Windus, 1982)
I Was a Rat!: or The Scarlet Slippers (London: Doubleday, 1999)

The Ruby in the Smoke (Oxford: Oxford University Press, 1985)
The Shadow in the Plate (Oxford: Oxford University Press, 1986; as *The Shadow in the North*, Harmondsworth: Penguin, 1988)
The Tiger in the Well (Harmondsworth: Penguin, 1991)
The Tin Princess (Harmondsworth: Penguin, 1994)

Northern Lights (London: Scholastic, 1995; as *The Golden Compass*, New York: Knopf, 1996)   Carnegie Medal & Guardian Award, 1996.
The Subtle Knife (London: Scholastic, 1997)
The Amber Spyglass (London: Scholastic, 2000)   Whitbread Children's Book of the Year, 2001.

Lyra's Oxford (London& New York: David Fickling Books, 2003)

▣ http://www.philip-pullman.com/

Diana Wynne Jones (b. 1934)
Cart and Cwidder (London: Macmillan, 1975)
Drowned Ammet (London: Macmillan, 1977),
The Spellcoats (London: Macmillan, 1979)
The Crown of Dalemark (London: Mandarin, 1993)

Charmed Life (London: Macmillan, 1977)   Guardian Award, 1978.
The Magicians of Caprona (London: Macmillan, 1980)
Witch Week (London: Macmillan, 1982)
The Lives of Christopher Chant: The Childhood of Chrestomanci (London: Methuen
    Children's, 1988)
Mixed Magics (London: Collins, 2000)
Conrad's Fate (London: Collins, 2005)
The Pinhoe Egg (London: Collins, 2006)

Dark Lord of Derkholm (London: Gollancz, 1998)
Year of the Griffin (London: Gollancz, 2000)
Fire and Hemlock (London: Methuen, 1984)
Howl's Moving Castle (London: Methuen Children's, 1986)
A Tale of Time City (London: Methuen, 1987)
Castle in the Air (London: Methuen Children's, 1990)
A Sudden Wild Magic (New York: Morrow, 1992)
Hexwood (London: Methuen Children's, 1993)
The Merlin Conspiracy (London: Collins, 2003)

The Tough Guide to Fantasyland (London: Vista, 1996; revised and updated ed.,
    New York: Firebird, 2006)

▣ http://www.leemac.freeserve.co.uk/

Ivan Southall (b. 1921)
Hills End (Sydney: Angus & Robertson, 1962)

Ash Road (Sydney: Angus & Robertson, 1966)
To the Wild Sky (Sydney: Angus & Robertson, 1967)
Josh (Sydney: Angus & Robertson, 1971)   Carnegie Medal, 1972.
The Long Night Watch (London & Sydney: Methuen, 1983)

Robert Westall (1929–93)
The Machine-Gunners (London: Macmillan, 1975)   Carnegie Medal, 1976.
Fathom Five (London: Macmillan, 1979)
The Scarecrows (London: Chatto & Windus, 1981)   Carnegie Medal, 1982.
Futuretrack 5 (Harmondsworth: Kestrel, 1983)
The Cats of Seroster (London: Macmillan Children's, 1984)
Urn Burial (Harmondsworth: Kestrel, 1987)
Echoes of War (Harmondsworth: Kestrel, 1989)
Blitzcat (London: Macmillan Children's, 1989)   Nestlé Smarties Medal, 9–11 category,
    1989.
The Kingdom by the Sea (London: Methuen Children's, 1990)   Guardian Award, 1991.
Stormsearch (London: Blackie, 1990)
Gulf (London: Methuen Children's, 1992)
The Wheatstone Pond (Harmondsworth: Viking, 1993)
Falling into Glory (London: Methuen, 1993)
Blitz (London: Collins, 1995)
A Time of Fire (London: Pan Macmillan Children's, 1994)

Children of the Blitz: Memories of Wartime Childhood (London: Viking, 1985)

Michelle Magorian (b. 1947)
Goodnight Mister Tom (Harmondsworth: Kestrel, 1981)   Guardian Award, 1982.
Back Home (London: Viking, 1985)
A Little Love Song (London: Methuen, 1991)
In Deep Water and other stories (London: Viking, 1992)
Cuckoo in the Nest (London: Methuen Children's, 1994)
A Spoonful of Jam (London: Mammoth, 1994)
Be Yourself (London: Egmont, 2003)

▣ http://www.michellemagorian.com/

William Nicholson (b. 1948)

The Wind-Singer (London: Egmont, 2000)   Nestlé Smarties Gold Award, 9–11 category, 2000; Blue Peter Book Award, 2001.

The Slaves of the Mastery (London: Egmont, 2001)

Firesong (London: Egmont, 2002)

▣ http://www.williamnicholson.co.uk/05/index.asp

Garth Nix (b. 1963)

The Ragwitch (Sidney: Pan,.1990)
Shade's Children (New York: HarperCollins, 1997)

Sabriel (Pymble, NSW: HarperCollins, 1995)
Lirael: Daughter of the Clayr (Crow's Nest, NSW: Allen & Unwin, 2001)
Abhorsen (New York: Eos, 2003)
Across the Wall: A Tale of the Abhorsen and other stories (variant sub-title, *Tales of the Old Kingdom And Beyond*, New York: Eos, 2005)

Mister Monday (New York: Eos, 2003)
Grim Tuesday (New York: Eos, 2004)
Drowned Wednesday (New York: Eos, 2005)
Sir Thursday (New York: Eos, 2006)
The Lady Friday (New York: Eos, 2007)

▣ http://www.garthnix.co.uk/

David Almond (b. 1951)

A Kind of Heaven (North Shields: Iron Press, 1997)
Skellig (London: Hodder Children's, 1998)   Whitbread Children's Book Award, 1998; Carnegie Medal, 1999.

Kit's Wilderness (London: Hodder Children's, 1999)   Nestlé Smarties Silver Award, 9–11 category, 1999.

Heaven Eyes (London: Hodder Children's, 2000)
Counting Stars (London: Hodder Children's, 2000)
Secret Heart (London: Hodder Children's, 2001)
Where Your Wings Were (London: Hodder Children's, 2002)

Wild Girl, Wild Boy: A Play (London: Hodder Children's, 2002)

The Fire-Eaters (London: Hodder Children's, 2003)   Nestlé Smarties Gold Award, 9–11 category, & Whitbread Children s Book Award, 2003; Boston Globe–Horn Book Award, 2004.

Clay (London: Hodder Children's, 2005)

▣ http://www.davidalmond.com/

'Lian Hearn' (b. 1942)

Across the Nightingale Floor (New York: Riverhead, 2002)

Grass for His Pillow (New York: Riverhead, 2003)

Brilliance of the Moon (New York: Riverhead, 2004)

The Harsh Cry of the Heron: The Last Tale of the Otori (New York: Riverhead, 2006)

Heaven's Net is Wide: The First Tale of the Otori (New York: Riverhead, 2007)

▣ http://www.lianhearn.com/

Lois McMaster Bujold (b. 1949)

The Curse of Chalion (New York: Eos, 2000)   Mythopoeic Fantasy Award, Best Book, 2002.

Paladin of Souls (New York: Eos, 2003)   Hugo & Nebula Awards, Best Novel 2004.

The Hallowed Hunt (New York: Eos, 2005)

The Sharing Knife: Beguilement (New York: Eos, 2006)

Dreamweaver's Dilemma: A Collection of Short Stories and Essays (ed. Suford Lewis, Framingham, MA: New England Science Fiction Association Press, 1995)

▣ http://www.dendarii.com/

Mary Doria Russell
See under 'Of Organelles'

Other sources and books mentioned

Brown, Joanne, & St. Clair, Nancy, *Declarations of Independence: Empowered Girls in Young Adult Literature, 1990–2001* (Lanham, MD, & London: The Scarecrow Press, 2002 [Scarecrow Studies in Young Adult Literature, No. 7])

Brecht, Bertolt, *Mutter Courage und ihre Kinder* (wr. 1939, premiered 1942; trans. Eric Bentley, as *Mother Courage and her Children*, London: Methuen, 1962)

Bunyan, John, *The Pilgrim's Progress from This World, to That which Is to come: Delivered under the Similitude of a Dream Wherein is Discovered, The manner of his setting out, His Dangerous Journey; And safe Arrival at the Desired Countrey* (London: N. Ponder, 1678)

Cart, Michael, *From Romance to Realism: 50 Years of Growth and Change in Young Adult Literature* (New York: HarperCollins, 1996)

Dailey, Donna, *Tamora Pierce* (New York: Chelsea House, 2006 [Who Wrote That?])

Egoff, Sheila, Stubbs, G. T., & Ashley, L. F., eds, *Only Connect: Readings on Children's Literature* (Toronto & New York: Oxford University Press, 1969; 2nd ed., 1980; 3rd ed., 1996)   Each edition has distinct content, and together chart issues in criticism as well as creation. The 3rd edition was additionally edited by Wendy Sutton.

Egoff, Sheila A., *Worlds Within: Children's Fantasy from the Middle Ages to Today* (Chicago & London: American Library Association, 1988)

Horace (Quintus Horatius Flaccus), *Carminum* (in 4 books, wr. *c*.25–13 BCE, as 'Odes', trans. Niall Rudd, in *Horace: Odes and Epodes* (Cambridge, MA: Harvard University Press, 2004 [Loeb Classical Library L033N])

Lehr, Susan, ed., *Battling Dragons: Issues and Controversy in Children's Literature* (Portsmouth, NH: Heinemann, 1995)

Nabokov, Vladimir, *Lolita* (Paris: Olympia Press, 1955)

— *Strong Opinions* (London: Weidenfeld and Nicholson, 1974)

Owen, Wilfred, *Collected Poems* (ed. C. Day Lewis, London: Chatto & Windus, 1963)

Prudentius, Aurelius Clemens, *Psychomachia* (wr. *c*.380, as 'Fight for Mansoul', with 'Daily Round', 'Divinity of Christ', 'Origin of Sin', and 'Against Symmachus (1)', trans. H. J. Thomson, in *Prudentius 1* (London: Heinemann, 1949 [Loeb Classical Library L387])

Rhodes, Neil, *Elizabethan Grotesque* (London: Routledge & Kegan Paul, 1980)

Sullivan III, C. W., ed., *Young Adult Science Fiction* (Westport, CT: Greenwood Press, 1999 [Contributions to the Study of Science Fiction and Fantasy 79])

Swindells, Robert, *Stone Cold* (London: Hamish Hamilton, 1993)   Carnegie Medal, 1994.

Tepper, Sherri S., *Grass* (New York: Bantam, 1989)

Tournier, Michel, *Le Roi des Aulnes* (Paris: Gallimard, 1970; trans. Barbara Bray, as *The Erl-King*, London: Collins, 1972)   Prix Goncourt, 1970.

Trites, Roberta Seelinger, *Disturbing the Universe: Power and Repression in Adoles-*

cent Literature (Iowa City: University of Iowa Press, 2000)

Vallejo, Fernando, *La Virgen de los Sicarios* (Bogota: Alfaguara, 1994; trans. Paul Hammond, as *Our Lady of the Assassins*, London: Serpent's Tail, 2001)

Humanities-Ebooks
Genre Fiction Sightlines

studies of Crime Writing, Science Fiction
and Writing for Children

The first five titles in this series were published in Spring 2007:

Science Fiction

Octavia E Butler: Xenogenesis / Lilith's Brood
Ian McDonald: Chaga / Evolution's Shore

Crime

Reginald Hill: On Beulah's Height
Walter Mosley: Devil in a Bue Dress

For Children

Tamara Pierce: The Immortals

all Sightlines titles,
other categories in Humanities Insights,
and a wide range of Ebooks are available from:

http://www.humanities-ebooks.co.uk

Lightning Source UK Ltd.
Milton Keynes UK
UKOW021249070912

198581UK00003B/20/P